REBECCA MASCULL

The Wild Air

HODDER

First published in Great Britain in 2017 by Hodder & Stoughton
First published in paperback in 2017 by Hodder & Stoughton

An Hachette UK company

A CIP catalogue record for this title is available from the British Library

Paperback ISBN 9781473604452
eBook ISBN 9781473604421

Typeset in Plantin Light by Palimpsest Book Production Limited,
Falkirk, Stirlingshire

Printed and bound by Clays Ltd, St Ives plc

Hodder & Stoughton policy is to use papers that are natural,
renewable and recyclable products and made from wood grown in
sustainable forests. The logging and manufacturing processes are expected to
conform to the environmental regulations of the country of origin.

Hodder & Stoughton Ltd
Carmelite House
50 Victoria Embankment
London EC4Y 0DZ

www.hodder.co.uk

This story belongs to Poppy and so does my heart.

This book is dedicated to the memory of Katie Millinship.

PROLOGUE

1918

'I'm not going to die here,' she said.

Della talked aloud to herself. She did that when it was marvellous and she revelled in the complete wonder of flying, the secret joy of it. Or when it was bad. When the mist came down or the wind got up something terrible and she was fighting the weather in order to come back alive. There'd been patches of thick fog over the Channel that morning, a scrap here and there of blue-sky clarity but otherwise a freezing soup of white. The effort to stay straight and sane in that blindness was gruelling.

It was bitterly cold up there. Despite the woolly scarf covering her mouth, she could still taste the smoke. Sprits of black oil were flung back at her, not much but constant, insidious, landing inky on her goggles. But she mustn't try to wipe it yet; the oil would just smear and then she wouldn't be able to see a thing; she'd have to lift them and expose her eyes to the smut and the filth. The airflow from the propeller alone assailed her at a hundred miles per hour or more. The wind was the air turned angry. It swatted and swiped at her.

The engine was roaring, the rushing wind deafening. When she spoke to calm herself she couldn't hear the words, but just mouthing them gave comfort. She could hear them in her mind. They were the only things there. Her head was empty when she flew, as empty as the sky above. It was your body that did the flying. You have to feel it in every muscle, be a part of it, become it.

She spoke again: 'I've got the touch.'

They always said that about her, *She's got the touch.* She can feel yaw in her bones, knows where the air is coming from and how it'll lift or drop. She can step into an aeroplane and strap it on and fly. It's a kind of magic trick. After all, it's simply deflecting air. It's preposterous. Only a fool would do it, some said. There's no road to steer on like an automobile, no brake to apply, no side track to save you. It's freedom and it's fear, all at once.

'Not far now,' she told herself, as if comforting a child. 'The sea's behind us.'

The land scrolled beneath like a toy farm, glowing squares of light here and there marking life and habitation, hearth and home. It would be peaceful if it weren't for the clamour of the wind and the engine. But then, she smelt fuel. Stronger, keener. Then sputtering, then the engine stopped. Failed utterly. The horror of it froze her. Within a second, the aeroplane was pitching forwards, its power gone. Her hands gripped the stick. Terror took hold and the animal part of her mind longed for the ground to come, for the impact and the destruction, for it all to be over. The exertion necessary to fly, to concentrate, to save yourself, was exhausting. At least death would mean rest.

'Must keep the nose down. Must land,' she said, her voice high and shrill, shocking her out of her stupefaction, and she grasped the stick and eased her feet on the rudder bar to bank into position for landing. Seeing a field to the right, with its flat acres of mud beckoning to her, she pitched the nose down and hoped to heaven the undercarriage wouldn't smash into that line of poplars edging the field. As she struggled to maintain control, her machine pitched forwards, the ground hurling itself at her face, and the thought leapt into her mind that she had failed him, by crashing, by abandoning him to his fate, by dying.

I

Auntie Betty arrived in the first week of 1909, a cold, crackle-foot day when the sea was sorely vexed with the land. In the old times it would have bitten great chunks of clayey cliff from Sea Bank Road. Now the concrete seawall offered protection, a brave urban shoulder against nature built three years before and renamed the Kingsway. Della was barrelling down it on her bicycle, a cloud of icy dust hounding her wheels. Before turning into Bradford Street, she looked out across the heaving estuary hurling insults at the flat sands and saw the broad-winged gulls above bank and yaw, dive and flap, flicking their wingtips as a glance to the wind's fury. Steering her bike around the corner, she nipped across to the corner house and spotted her father seated as usual in the bay window, the wild sea reflected back at her making him appear as a ghost of a man lost beneath the waves. She raised a hand as her bicycle slowed, but he made no sign of seeing her. She hopped off as promptly as her long skirt allowed. As she wheeled her bike around the back and leaned it against the wall, she cursed her girl's clothes and wished her only brother had been born before her, so that his breeches would have been big enough to borrow. Anything close-fitting would do, to keep her clothes free from the oiled moving parts. Knickerbockers and puttees would serve. But Pop would have a stroke if he caught her disgracing herself like that: 'Ye gods!' he'd cry, and forbid it outright. For a theatre man, he was queerly old-fashioned when it came to females. She'd wanted to chop her long, fine, mousy hair, but Pop wouldn't hear of that. As it was, every day she wound it into a low knot at her neck to keep it out of the way.

She patted the handlebars of her bicycle, something she always did after dismounting, so fond of her steed she was and the freedom it gave her. She opened the side door and strode into the house to find a stout, round, wrinkly-faced woman seated imperiously at the oblong slab of the kitchen table, at the head of which stood Mam, florid-cheeked and sharp-eyed.

'I hoped you'd be back sooner to welcome Great-Aunt.'

The woman turned her narrow, dark gaze on the girl and said, 'So, this is Cordelia.'

'She won't speak to you,' said Mam. 'She hardly speaks at all.' Yet she added softly, 'But it isn't bad manners. It's just Della's way.'

'Suits me,' replied the aunt. 'It'll mean less bother when we share a room.'

'She suits me too,' smiled Mam, all annoyance about Della's tardiness evaporated. She never could be grumpy with Della for long, or any of her children; a sweet soul, Mam. 'Back in a tick.'

Her mother left the kitchen and Della heard her open Pop's study door down the hall. Words were swapped, Pop's utterances short and displeased, but the sense of it was lost on Della as her great-aunt spoke again.

'Sit down by me, young lady.' Her voice was peculiar, not local, not even like a Yorkie. Della had never heard an American speak. When Mam had said that Pa Broughton's sister was coming back home to Cleethorpes after twenty years away, this piqued her interest before she recalled that her mother's aunt would be an old woman, and to a girl of fourteen all old women are intolerable. 'I am your great-aunt, but you may call me Auntie Betty. You may not know my history and it is an interesting one. I sailed over to America with your grandfather some years back and fell for a fisherman and married him. I was a fishwife for a long while in a wild old place, much wilder than here, even on a day like this. One day, across the hard and windswept sands, I saw the great bird fly and I felt somehow it was a sign for me to fly away home. I thought of my lost youth and my home town here, but I had my life out there and put it out of mind. But my husband was a lifesaver too, you see, and one night he was out a-rescuing and perished by drowning. Then, I got lonesome and, well, I had nothing to stay for, and with some of my dead brother's money, I booked passage to England and here I am.'

Della stared and – despite this being the most interesting thing she'd heard since they said the pier was burning down six years before – she did not say a word. It was true she was taciturn, unlike her family, who talked incessantly, all over and under and inside each other's conversations, fighting for sound-space, until her poor head throbbed with it. What a relief it had been to go to school, where Miss Dimelow demanded silence from the girls, all in white aprons with white floppy ribbons in their hair. The dull-headed yet boisterous ones sat at the front, while the self-sufficient ones like herself could sit unhindered and unheeded at the back and thankfully be left well alone. Sometimes one of them was called to the front to point at the blackboard with a chalky finger, reading the words scribed in copperplate: fish, dish, wash. But that was the only speech required of her. She shuffled through her schooldays head-down, neither lagging nor excelling, average and therefore invisible. Her two much older sisters were so garrulous and vivid – Gertrude (or Gertie), beautiful and gay, and Miranda (or Midge), arch and talented – that Della stood behind them at school, sometimes noticed with a pat on the head or a brisk hug, and found no need to say a word or make a friend while the glorious elder Dobbs sisters reigned in the playground. Puck, as a brother, paid no attention to her at school. Sisters were mostly personae non

gratae for boys, certainly to older brothers and even those
two years younger like Puck. He ignored her entirely, as if
they were no relation whatever. It wasn't something she minded
or even questioned: an unwritten playground law. But he was
fond with her at home and that was enough.

Once her sisters had left, in quick succession – Midge to
stage school and Gertie to a good marriage – she became
aware that she had no friends, not one. She formed an awkward
acquaintanceship with some quiet girls, yet they were bookish
and she was never keen on books. She never knew exactly
what she was keen on, except the rare occasions when they
did something practical, modelling clay or potting up seedlings.
Her hands were mercurial, as if they had their own manual
mind. But they didn't do practical things at school very often,
and when Pop had his accident a couple of years back and
Mam said she must leave school to help at home, she welcomed
it. That was, until she realised what her mother had had to
put up with day after day, until she saw clearly what her father
had become.

She could hear him now down the passageway, his voice
raised at Mam, its tone strident and bullying.

'He doesn't want me here,' drawled Auntie Betty, winking
at Della to show she didn't give a damn whether he did or
not. 'He doesn't like it that my brother made his fortune on
the railways in America and when he died gave half of it to
your mam. That's why you have this attractive house here,
despite your pop's infirmity. He doesn't like that, being a kept
man.'

'What are you telling the girl?' said Mam, appearing noise-
lessly at the kitchen door.

'Just a tidbit of family history.' And she winked again at
Della, who couldn't help but smile. She knew nothing of this,
only that they had moved last year to this much nicer house,
with more rooms on the ground floor for Pop to get about
easily; and she knew about the sending out of the laundry,

and the hiring of a house parlourmaid for cleaning and a cook to do breakfasts and lunches, though Mam still liked to do the evening meal when she could and the servants did not live in – Pop abhorred the company of strangers nowadays. She had not questioned, as children rarely do, how they could afford it all. Before the accident (and before the money came, she now realised), Mam had made do with a woman who came every day to do the heavy work. But Mam did all the rest, for years managing four children and a husband, though Pop was often on the road touring the provinces' theatres, rarely at home, and thus a source of curiosity and wariness for the children and a man of few demands on Mam, until the accident.

The automobile had been taking Pop to the Grand Opera House in Hull for a performance in a Granville Barker play, when a van smashed into the side of the car. The van driver died in the road, gory and broken, but Pop lived, though he lost the use of his right arm and right leg for a year, and became a bed-bound giant, prone to bouts of fury and blame. He improved to the point of walking with a limp, but his right arm remained withered and thus, his acting career was over. He moved from his bed to a chair in his new study, facing out towards the sea, learning to write with his left hand and – Mam told her – penning melancholy plays about men trapped by dreary circumstance. No company would stage them, though the great and successful Midge herself touted them around London. And Pop's misery deepened. They all felt for him, they all pitied him, of course they did. Yet that angered him further. He was a bear in a cage, was reduced to his rage, had only rage left in him.

Just then, the back door crashed open and there was Puck, red-faced yet shivering, his cocoa-coloured hair sticking up wildly, clutching his air rifle in one hand and in the other a dead rabbit, which he flung on the table with a flourish. Mam clapped her hands and laughed. Thank heavens for Puck.

'And you must be Julius.'

'And you must be Great-Aunt Elizabeth. And nobody calls me Julius, except old Drummer at school. Everybody calls me Puck. It's my middle name. But Della hates her middle name because it's Titania and has a rude word in it. And so you must call me Puck, Aunt. I say, you're a bit broad in the beam. But I suppose everyone from America is fat, except the sporting types.'

'Now, now, Puck,' said Mam, taking her woollen cardigan from a chair and placing it around her son's cold shoulders.

A shout came from the study. 'Is that my boy?' Pop called, his voice high and yearning. 'Come here, you rascal!' To which call Puck leapt, shrugging off Mam's cardie to the floor, to regale his father with thundering good yarns about his exploits. A lame-dog life is of no use to me, Puck would say, and even Pop forgave him that.

'The prodigal son,' said Auntie Betty in a stage aside, laconic.

Thence Della was not required to speak again that day, as Puck did all the talking for all of them all of the way through supper, paragraphed only by staccato demands from Pop down the passage. Though they did not need the rabbit – their improved fortunes had meant Puck was no longer required to hunt small animals for food – he so enjoyed killing things, nobody had the heart to stop him. And everyone loved Mam's rabbit pie, rich with waxy potatoes and onion gravy. Pop ate alone in his study, but called in Puck to entertain him afterwards; the drug of Puck's homecoming from boarding school over Christmas had been his father's only respite from gloom since the boy had left them last September. Their new circumstances meant a good school for their only son, at last, to give him a good start in life, a chance of something better, of escape, Pop said. That idea was the only thing that brightened Pop's eye, in the dark days when Puck was gone from home and the house ached, vacant and grey without him. Nobody could make you laugh like Puck did, and nobody else could make Pop smile, nobody else at all.

Later that night, while Puck slumbered in his palatial top-floor room known as The Crow's Nest (sent to bed early with a chill), Della sat up on the quilt and blankets Mam had laid on her bedroom floor for her to sleep on. She watched her great-aunt's myriad minute ablutions before sleep. Wrapped in a woollen dressing gown and flannelette nightie, her white hair released from its hairgripped bun and trained over one shoulder in a long, thick plait, she settled herself in Della's bed that creaked in protest and made Della wish for it, though it was rather thrillingly like a bivouac, roughing it in a make-shift bed on the wooden boards. It reminded her of when she used to ask to drape a fringed blanket over the kitchen table and make a den. Mam often said no, being too busy on it all the day through, but there were golden times when she would say yes, and Della would hide there joyously. Those were the days when she shared a room with Gertie and Midge and felt keenly that she needed somewhere of her own, even if it were just the space beneath a table. Once her elder sisters had left, Mam said she was too old for such silliness and the child's-eye view from beneath the table of legs and feet and adult purpose was gone forever.

It was chilly on her bedroom floor – as everyone knows, heat rises, she thought, peering at the high ceiling – and she wrapped a blanket tight around herself as her great-aunt turned down the gas lamp to darkness. They lay in silence for a time, Della listening to the woman's deep, restful breathing keep time with the waves beyond, taking in the foreign scent of foot lotion. Then Auntie Betty spoke.

'Is there anything you wish to ask me? I must be a curious sight to you and something tells me your quiet ways are not evidence of a dull mind but quite the opposite. Speak, if you wish. I am quite without judgement.'

Nobody at home ever asked her to speak. Pop and Midge

only complained that she did not; Mam and Gertie had always accepted her quietude yet gently mourned it; and Puck didn't mind at all. He never had, as it was the perfect foil to his loudness. But now, there was a thing Della wished to say. She'd been harbouring it all day, so she said it.

'What was the great bird you saw?'

2

'Do you like bedtime stories?'

Della considered when had been the last time this magical event occurred. It could have been Gertie, years ago, before she left, married Eric, got that smart house in the Avenues in Hull complete with full complement of servants and then had those three rollicking boys Pop loved so. For boys were everything, and girls made a good marriage, or went on the stage, or helped Mam. There was no other definition of girl in Pop's mental dictionary, whereas to be a boy was an open-ended existence of highways and skyways, as free as the gulls.

'Not since I was a strutling.'

Auntie Betty laughed, a high girlish thing unsuited to her girth. 'Oh, it's years since I heard a word like that. How I've missed this place.'

Unaccustomed to conversation with anyone but Mam, Puck or herself, Della lay screwed up in a cocoon of timidity. But she wanted to know more.

'Why did you go?'

'I wanted to escape, of course. My father was very strict. Yours had nothing on him. We had to stand at the table to eat our dinner, every day of our childhood.'

'You couldn't sit down to eat? *Ever?*'

'Never, not at supper anyhow and not when we were little. So, you can see why, when my brother said he was going to the States to make his fortune on the railways I said to him, Take me with you. We were close and he was affectionate and

I was a spinster at forty years of age, a great disappointment to my father.'

Della's cheeks flushed unseen in the dark, that phrase having been applied to herself by Pop more than once, but not said by Mam, never Mam (though she feared her mother felt it). Dull brown hair, dull brown eyes, dull brown freckles. Everything about herself felt dull and brown.

'So I knew I was a burden in my home and yet I was fully old enough not to be a burden to my brother bound for the New World. And indeed, I troubled him no further than our ship itself, as I met my future husband on it. My, he was so handsome, big strong arms and that American accent, lilting and lovely. Truman Perry, his name was. I used to fly kites on Cleethorpes beach when I was a child. Well, Truman was to be my kite, lifting me up from my home and carrying me away. He was travelling back from Liverpool where his people came from. His mother was dying there and all his family and their friends had clubbed together to send him the fare for his passage, so that she could see her son for one last time. But she passed before he got there and he was returning to America full of sadness and longing. Unmarried he was and in his forties, surprised to find a well-dressed woman such as I who knew about fishing and lifeboats and the life of the sea. And by the end of the journey across the ocean, we knew that I would trouble my brother no further. That I was newly engaged and would be going with Truman to his home on the Outer Banks in North Carolina, a village of Currituck County, a desolate place at first sight, but I thought it beguiling. Miles and miles of dunes as tall as buildings. A place called Kitty Hawk.'

Della tried to picture it, trackless and storm-tossed. Just then, the wind whipped up and rattled the window frame, making a point.

'It was my home for twenty years. Strange to think on that now. When I landed there – you could only reach the place by boat, along the snaky way of sand islands named the Outer Banks – I thought to myself, I've come all this way to end up on another windy shore, yet more harsh and out-of-the-way than even my tiny childhood home. You see, the railway only came to Cleethorpes when I was about your age. And with it came the tourists and the town shrugged off its wild past and civilised itself. So going to Kitty Hawk was like a step back into my baby days, when the village was simpler, was for itself alone, and not for visitors. I liked that about Kitty Hawk. It made no excuses for itself. It just was.'

Auntie Betty paused to cough, chesty.

'Did you miss your mam?' said Della, so quiet, her aunt asked her to repeat herself.

'Oh, mine was dead, long dead. I went to escape my pa. And my prospects. A spinster's life, consisting of general nursemaid and slave to my ageing father. I just couldn't bear the thought of spending decades in that house, ageing with him and regret building up in my head like layers of dust at the thought of what could have been.'

Della shuddered; someone was walking over her grave as her mind's eye filled with the shapeless years stretching ahead, if no husband stepped into that blank space. And why would there be a husband? Plain and shy, plain and shy – that had been the litany of her father's disappointment.

'Kitty Hawk had a scattering of houses built upon the sand, not painted, not plastered, not varnished. Shingled roofs made from cedar trees. A few families, neighbourly and friendly. Farmers, sailors and fishermen, though the last only worked five months of the year and had to find other employment for the rest. Truman helped out at the life-saving station at Kill Devil Hills. In the village there was the church, school, general store, two carpenters, a physician and a preacher. The women were housekeepers, dressmakers, widows. Only about three hundred of us altogether. Humans, that is, though there were thousands of mosquitoes, bedbugs and wood ticks. Every one of them – bugs and people – born in North Carolina. I was the only immigrant.'

'You weren't lonely?'

'Not at all. I had my Truman. I'd never been loved like that before. Never been loved, I'd say. Not since my mother died and that was when I was too infantile to know her. My Truman'd put his arms around me and the whole world would fall away. He'd kiss me and . . .'

Della's eyes grew wider, waiting. She was well aware that she knew nothing of romantic love, and hadn't even read novels, which was where she supposed girls learned about such things. Nobody she knew talked this way, certainly no woman in her sixties – could Mam, in her forties now, ever think of such things? Had she ever felt that for Pop? Impossible. Auntie Betty was a different species, bringing strange tales from another world. *All Americans must be like this*, she marvelled.

'Well, that's my business. Anyhow, no children came for us. I don't know why. God's way. Truman's people were Methodists and I'd go to that church and pray and pray. But it did no good. I was barren. A great sadness to us. And I always loved children, loved to watch them and hold them, little hot parcels of love on your hip. I couldn't bear it that I was barren, so I went to the woman in the town who called herself the midwife and said I'd help her. She trained me in the ways of childbirth and when she got too old to carry on, I became the town midwife. Never had a child of my own, but spent my days and nights helping new children come into the world. I was very happy that way. Truman spent his days fishing, attending shipwrecks, catching wildfowl. Sometimes he'd work with foreigners – I mean, wealthy gentlemen from the cities who came for the hunting and angling. He'd tell me how they would drink all the time and nearly shoot each other dead in their drunkenness! That taught me, more than anything, that money and class are not the same thing, certainly not. The wage was useful but we were always glad when they went, the invaders, leaving us and our place alone. But there were two gentlemen that came who were different. Brothers from Ohio. They came because it was a lonely place, windy place, miles of flat sands. The perfect place for them and their big birds.'

Now they'd come to it. Della had fallen headlong into Auntie Betty's memories and forgotten where they'd started. Big birds, the great bird. She pictured a swan, then an egret, a heron – all local to her shore. Then a random stream of images from the school encyclopaedia – vultures, eagles. A sailor taking a shot at an albatross. What on earth was Auntie Betty talking about?

'Flying machines. That's what they brought with them. Gliders first, like great kites made for a man. No engine though and awful for steering. I told you, I flew kites as a child. I knew about kites. I made my own, improved them, got them to fly higher and brisker. My brother and I were crazy for it. So when they came, with their gliders, I told Truman how kites work, how the wind plays with them, how it moves over and under a shape, lifting and twisting it. I surprised Truman, I surprised myself. I'd forgotten how my brain used to be, in my youth, the long summer days spent chattering with Alfred – Pa Broughton to you – puttering about with our kites and perfecting them. We just had a mind to do it, the right kind of mind. But he was a boy and could use that mind, put it to good use, I mean. And so he did, apprenticed to the railways, soon an engineer. And thence to America to make his career building railway tracks and making, oh my, some money, a lot of money. I had that mind too, a mechanical mind. Could see how things worked at first glance. I fixed everything around our house. I was better at it than Truman, so he let me get on with it.'

'I fix bikes,' said Della.

'Do you now?'

'I do. Mam bought me a bike last year and I go everywhere on it. All over, up top town, through the villages.'

The bicycle had been purchased for chores, for her to fetch things for Mam. But it soon became her companion. She loved nothing more than to pedal furiously about, willing herself to go further and faster, the wind in her face and leg muscles straining. She'd go for miles sometimes, through Holton-le-Clay or Waltham, over to Tetney or even out to Grainthorpe once, up and down the coast. That's why she was late that afternoon, setting herself a speed record on Humberston Avenue.

'You fix your bicycle, you say?'

'Yes. And others too. A neighbour of ours saw me fiddling with mine one day in the street and he asked me did I know what I was doing? Yes thanks, I said. Could you fix mine then, do you think? he said, so I did. After that, a friend of his asked me and then another. I stand for a while and stare at the bike. I must seem odd. But I'm thinking, about what might be wrong, looking at all the parts and fiddling with them in my head. And I always work it out. And now I fix quite a few around here, quite a few.'

'That's the most I've heard you say all day.'

The most I've said in months, thought Della.

'Fixing things,' continued Betty, 'that's Broughton blood in you. Could turn a hand to anything, the Broughtons.'

'I never knew that,' said Della, a small voice.

'Your mam never told you about her pa? She had it too, but turned hers to music. A natural piano player she was, just took to it like a duck to water. Could play anything, by ear. Anything. Didn't she teach you? I saw the instrument in the parlour, lid down, no music on it. Don't she play no more?'

'She tried to teach me. I had no talent for it.'

'But you do for fixing, eh?'

'I didn't know that was a talent.'

'Course it is. Some people think too much with their heads. Broughtons think with their hands.'

A window opened in Della's mind, a dozen windows flung open. All this time, she'd crept through her life shamed by her uselessness. And now, to discover she had had a talent, born in her, handed down like a precious heirloom. She could be special. She could shine.

'Climb up here, on the bed, dearie. You must be cold down there. We can snuggle up like a pair of possums and talk easier.'

She clambered up and saw her aunt's kind old face in the moonlight, and wanted to throw her arms about her and thank her. But she had not lost her shyness all in one night. So she perched at the end of her own bed and wrapped herself in the fringed blanket. Sleep tight, Mam used to say when they were three girls together and shared a bed. And sleep tightly they did, elbows in backs and full of complaint. Yet in the night, when they were cold and dream-ridden, her sisters would hold her safe and warm. She realised how much she missed them, missed that.

Auntie Betty said, 'You heard of the Wright brothers? They used to fix bicycles, just like you. And then they changed the world.'

They talked long into the night, of the two Ohio brothers: Wilbur came first, stayed with the postmaster and used his wife's sewing machine to stitch linen wings; Orville came later and the two of them set up camp in a windswept hut, decked out with clinical precision; mechanical, methodical. The gliders were first, tested aloft on the great winds across the sands, one brother or the other taking his life in his hands on each bumpy ride. Then came the engine tests, to find a shape and design that would lift the extra weight, and that of a man. The real problem was not only power, but control. The chaos of flight was found in its manoeuvrability.

'Birds make it look easy,' said Della.

'But it's not. To get something aloft is the first challenge, but to keep it up there and to control it is quite another thing.

The brothers experimented for years, on and off, staying a while and then back and forth to Ohio. They had blazing rows in their hut, their voices lost in the wind, but you could hear them if you crept up close, like Truman did sometimes. Some of the other lifesavers helped them often, dragging the aeroplane across the sands, which the brothers could not have managed alone. Truman was there a few times, with other onlookers – perhaps a local businessman, or a number of boys. The women were busy in their homes. But there were a few occasions where Truman's tales got the best of me and I went out to Kill Devil Hills and watched them test their bird there; failing, crashing, trying again. There came the day when they got it right, in December of '03. I wasn't there and neither was Truman. But his friends were, the lifesavers, and they took a picture – you seen it? The first powered flight, powered by an engine and carrying a man and controlled. That's the key thing. Many have tried it, got up in the air but it's about staying there and steering the damn thing. That's what they cracked that day. Afterwards, more and more of us from the village went down there to watch them. Some said if God had meant us to fly, He'd've given us wings. And I thought to my own self, He did – and we call it the mind. Birds do make it look easy, Della, you're right – but by God, they *have* it easy. We had to *think* our way into the air.'

Della wanted to ask a hundred more questions about the mechanics of the thing – really, the engineering of it, though she was not familiar with the word. But it was late and her aunt was tired out and the questions would have to wait.

They settled down top to tail in her bed that night and just as they were drifting off to sleep, Della made time for one more question:

'Why did the big bird make you want to come home?'

'I don't know, child. There was something in me, like an unanswered question, when I saw that flyer lift up and leave the earth. I was back on my childhood beach, flying kites with

my brother, my whole life ahead of me – as if my life would
be an open vista like the blue skies above Cleethorpes – the
freedom of them. And a miniature me, my skirts dragging in
wet sand – wanting to lift up with my kite and fly away to
the rest of my life.'

Della recalled that she'd felt the same when she'd run from
school with the others to watch the pier burn down and they
stood on the sands and watched the flames lick the sky and
she wanted to rise on them like a phoenix, flap wings and fly
away. That was in 1903, the same year the Wright brothers
flew – great-aunt and great-niece watching the skies together
on opposite sides of the ocean.

'It's a mystery.' Auntie Betty's voice grew fainter, sliding
into sleep. 'Something spoke to me, said Go Home. Maybe
it was just to meet you, Della. Maybe that was it.'

And her next sound was a grunt and a snore and she was
far gone. But Della lay wide awake for hours.

3

Puck had pneumonia. The doctor came and confirmed it. Pop's distress lay thick in the house like sea fret. Mam's worries were never shared, merely borne and that done quietly. Pop could never hide a feeling and Della even heard him moaning through his study door, as if he felt the boy's pains in his own lungs and heart, which he did, in his way. His boy was kept in bed, curtains drawn tightly, not a chink of light allowed to disturb the patient.

Della missed him. They no longer played together as they once had, as she was a young woman by now and busy in the house with Mam, and Puck ranged wide and free, but their childhood closeness had formed a bond that drew him back to her after every adventure. 'Look, Della!' was his usual herald when he came skittering in from outside, mud on his cheeks or sand in his hair. He was always out getting into scrapes in ponds or caught by the tide. He was a brutal naturalist, a butterfly collector, a keeper of beetles in boxes and sticklebacks in jars. Kept them till they died and never mourned; in fact, was more fascinated by them still and dead than alive and wriggling. She never minded, always greeted his finds with quiet, intense interest and helped him press samples of weeds between heavy books or dispose of his cadavers when he had tired of them. When Puck was around six months old and sitting up, Pop took a treasured photograph in the backyard, the boy playing with his toes on a mat, with a two-year-old Della sitting to one side, legs crossed and comfy, her left hand placed protectively behind his back, defensive, proud. That's how they'd always been when they were little, Puck and Della.

The minute the doctor said Puck's condition was serious, Mam shouted for her and they packed her a bag. Auntie Betty had moved out a few days before, into her new house opposite the Dolly, known to outsiders as the Dolphin Hotel. Her brother's legacy had bought her a tidy dwelling with sea views and a long, narrow garden filled with spring bulbs. She said that she could've bought a mansion with her brother's money but, 'It'd only take more cleaning.' The plan was to send Della up the street to Betty's house, away from infection, to stay for as long as it took for the invalid to recover. Pop was not happy about this, saw its necessity but had words with Mam. Della could hear the argument and its main theme was Betty's influence. They were thick as thieves, came the accusation, and no good would come of it. Betty had been living with them for two months while she organised her affairs and everyone in the house knew Pop was sick of it. So, Della was told to see him in his room before she went.

It was an occasion to be summoned to her father's study. Pop seldom came out. He could walk quite well nowadays; he limped, yet had adequate locomotion to get about. But he chose not to. Apparently, he practised callisthenics in his room every day to keep him limber, but would avoid the outside world whenever possible. 'Far from the madding crowd,' he'd say. That's where he liked to be. She knocked sheepishly on his door and waited until his voice came, low and crouching, like a watchful cat: 'Enter.'

When she saw him, the nerves his voice occasioned would flutter and lessen. In his face she saw a kind of appeal to her there, to everyone – *Don't you pity me*, it said. *Don't you dare.* He was still a handsome man, not tall but seemed it, thick wavy chestnut hair with distinguished white sideburns, as well as large, brown, expressive eyes – ideal for the stage. He lowered his gaze, his useless hand resting in his lap and the good one stretched out along the arm of his prodigious chair. How she wanted to say, 'Hello, Pop. How's tricks?' They had more ease with each other once, though he was rarely demonstrative of his feelings for her. But now, he was a closed book, closed in on all sides in fact by heavy curtains and row upon row of volumes darkly bound. His massive roll-topped desk brooded beside him, piled with writing paraphernalia and dog-eared manuscripts. At least the view beyond was wide and liberating – the broad flat sands and the sea miles out, tame and tiny that day; and the room was toasty, heated by an anthracite-burning stove, the warmest room in the house, bar the kitchen.

'Della, I understand you're to go to your mother's aunt while Puck is sick.'

She nodded.

'Speak up, dear. You won't get anywhere in life without a voice.'

'Yes, Pop.'

'Now then, that woman – Betty Broughton – well, she's . . . What was that? What are you saying?'

'Betty Perry,' she said, meek but clear. 'She married a man called Perry.'

'Nobody likes a pedant, Della.' A hard stare. 'Anyhow, whatever she calls herself – and whatever fondness your mother may harbour for her – the fact is she was the Broughton disgrace for years, marrying that common fisherman she'd only just met on a ship! Her arrival is not auspicious and yet I have put up with it on your mother's account. In this difficult time of Puck's illness, I suppose you must go somewhere to escape contagion, yet near enough to be of use, and so her house it must be. But I wish you to know I do not approve of that woman and you must remember at all times that she is not a person to model yourself after, Della. Not the right sort at all.'

'Yes, Pop.' She offered him a little smile. She always tried to, whenever she was permitted to see him, as if to say, *It's all right, old chap.*

But he had already looked away and by doing so, dismissed her.

In the hall, she put on her coat and hat, grabbed her carpet bag to escape, and Mam came, gave her a hug and held on tight, her bag crushed between them. Della pulled away first. *For the first time in a long time,* she thought.

She said, 'I'll be all right, Mam.'

And Mam said, 'I know,' and straightened Della's shirt collar. 'Help Betty with her house, will you? It's a mess. I'll send a box with your things later.' She watched her mother turn and climb the stairs to Puck's room, effortful and tired. With a twitch of guilt, she turned and verily bolted to her bike, stuffing her bag into the basket and whizzing off up the Kingsway to her great-aunt's house, which when she arrived she squinted at, blinded, as the low March sun was mirrored in the windows like golden, square eyes.

She settled in a trice. She bedded down on Betty's settee and the next day launched herself into the cooking and cleaning, as Betty had never had servants in America and said she never would. But Della could see she was struggling, the house unswept and the laundry building up. They had it spick and span in a few days and Betty was grateful. They talked all the while, of America and school, of bicycles and husbands, of Broughtons and fathers, of flying machines and brothers; Betty talked, that is, and Della asked questions. Her responses were few but her mind was full of commentary.

Once the house was clean, they pottered about in furniture and junk shops, going to top town, over to Grimsby, seeking out bargains and splashing out at Bon Marché on Cleethorpe Road – a sturdy, round kitchen table free from woodworm, an embroidered footstool for Betty to put her bad leg upon

– she was in good health for a woman in her sixties, but her ankle got puffy at times and needed a rest – and a silver frame for the only photograph of Truman her aunt possessed – in sepia; the fisherman's straight back and plain gaze made him look honest. Seated comfortably at the new table next to the range, feasting on pikelets and goosegog jam, Betty produced from a drawer in the dresser a fresh ream of paper and some pencils, which she fell to sharpening with a penknife.

'I went to a stationer's before you moved in and ordered this for us. We're going to use it for sketches and plans.'

'What for?' said Della, reaching for a cloth to wipe her hands clean of stickiness.

'We're going to build a kite, you and I.'

'You can buy them. There's a shop on Alexandra Road.'

Betty shook her head. 'Would Broughtons rather buy one? Or design it and build it themselves? The latter, I think.'

Della watched as her aunt fetched in a newspaper and put it on the table. It was the *Liverpool Daily Post* – her aunt must have bought it when she came through the port on her way from America. Betty opened it to an article titled 'Our Friends in Flight'. It gave a potted history of the brave mortals who had taken to the air in one way or another.

'Look at this feller,' said Betty. 'Otto Lilienthal. He built quite a number of gliders and made many flights in them. See here – "Lilienthal averred that a man should become *on intimate terms with the air* before ever trying to fly in it." Excellent advice that, and something the Wright brothers knew well. Think about what I told you, that they tested dozens of wing shapes in their workshop in a home-made wind tunnel. That was before they built gliders. And they tested those for a long while before any attempt to fit a motor. They had to get the glider right first, and every piece of it – to be on intimate terms with it, like Lilienthal said. Poor man, he died for it. He crashed in a glider that killed him.'

'Gosh,' murmured Della and Betty added, 'Everyone used

to say, at Kill Devil Hills, those brothers will kill themselves one day. Those gliders will fly too high and they'll slide out, fall to their deaths. But they never did.'

Della read on, of men in America and France mainly, vainly struggling against the air to be lifted and conquer it. She read of Samuel Cody, who built kites large enough for a man to ride in and piloted a boat pulled by kites across the Channel. He was an American living in England and became the first man to fly an aeroplane in Britain, only last year. He tested his 'Man-lifter' in competitions all around the country. *So easy is the controlling or steering apparatus*, it read, *that Madame Cody makes frequent ascents.*

'A woman!' said Della. 'In the air!'

Betty nodded sagely. 'Read on.'

It went on to the Wrights, of course, and explained how they had travelled recently in Europe, demonstrating the flyer and wowing crowds. 'If only I could see the Wrights fly,' she said, 'like you did.'

'Maybe we will one day, or someone similar. There are aviators all over the place now. Anyone can get linen, wood. And with a sewing machine – and a Broughton brain – knock up the wings in their front room. Then you'd just need some struts, a plank of wood for the rudder bar, a stick or a wheel for steering. And you have your glider. Find a rich benefactor – or a newspaperman keen to make a name – and you can buy yourself a motor. Take it out on Cleethorpes beach, with those flat sands stretching for miles, just right for take-off and landing. Anyone with a mind for it could do that, Della. Even a woman . . .'

And Betty sat back in her chair, one eyebrow raised and a smug chin.

'Auntie, are you saying . . .'

'Let's build our kite first, shall we? Small steps, Della. Small steps.'

'What sort of kite are we going to make?'

'We might start with a flat one, for practice. But I'd most like us to build a box kite. Ever seen one of those?'

'I don't think so.'

'You'd know if you had. It's an extraordinary thing. Quite a young kite – a feller in Australia came up with it a few years back. It's so clever because to look at it you'd never think it would fly better than a flat kite, but it does. There's more lift, you see, compared to the drag. It's what Cody uses. We're going to make one of those. Now, if you go upstairs to my room for me and look in the drawer beside my bed, you'll find a book.'

It was titled *The Aeronautical Annual.* Betty opened it and read out the opening phrase: '*To ask questions of Mother Nature is delectable. If her answers be often non-committal, even such are lures to lead us into better questioning.*' Della leafed through it. She saw reproductions of mechanical drawings by Leonardo da Vinci – a design for a mechanical wing, made four hundred years before. An article by George Cayley from 1809 that read: '*we shall be able to transport ourselves and families, and their goods and chattels, more securely by air than by water, and with a velocity of from 20 to 100 miles per hour.*' There were sketches of the wings of birds, mathematical drawings of kite designs surrounded by algebra, diminutive men suspended from balloons and a diagram of the Wrights' flyer, which showed how the machine was the first in the world to work in all axes: nose up and down, directional control of the wings and the ability to bank to either side, neatly labelled as pitch, yaw and roll.

She pointed this out to Betty. 'That's what you were talking about, that first night. Control.'

'That's right.'

'But how . . . how could we do this with a kite? Where the strings are attached, I suppose, for stability, so it doesn't flap around in the wind. And the tail keeps it stable too, with bows on it to give drag . . .' She was looking up into the corner of the room, but she was seeing a kite, white in the broad blue skies above the Humber estuary, playing with the air, pitching, yawing, rolling.

Within a fortnight, they'd designed and built some diamond kites as starters and the first box kite was taking shape. They'd ordered all the materials from top town. The sails were made of linen, a fine cloth, also used to make the binding tapes. For the longerons and cross-stays they used bamboo, for lightness. The flying line and bridle were hemp, the bows ribbon from the haberdasher's. They had a local carpenter make the spools for them, two-handled for control, to wind the flying line around. Della stood examining their diamond kites at Betty's kitchen table before they left for the beach for their first flight. She ran her fingers carefully along each edge, ensuring the angles were correct, that the bamboo ran true. Betty was grinning at her. It was infectious.

'What?' said Della with a smile.

'You got the bug. The flying bug.'

And they grinned together, then went to fly their handiwork on the beach.

It was one of those March days, blowy and chilly yet sunny and glad, the sea froth and shells picked out brightly against the toffee-coloured sands like stars, the strewn seaweed messy in clumps and shining greenly. The sea was far out that day and before they unleashed their kites, they were drawn to it, Della striding forward carrying the two diamond kites, then hanging back for her great-aunt's much slower step. Far beyond the pier, there was an inch of water stretched flat for miles before it deepened way beyond them. They stood beside the edge of the water and saw their echoes in the mirror of wet sand.

'I'm ten years old again,' said Betty, beaming into the sunshiny air, lifting her head, grey tendrils playing about her round cheeks. 'Alfred would laugh to see his little sister all fat and old on our sands again.'

'It doesn't matter,' said Della, defensive of her aunt these days, yet beyond that, protective of any shade of difference in a person, anything that others might mock. Why should they? Who gave them the right? 'What you look like. How old you are.'

'True.'

'If you can do something, you should do it. Whoever you are.'

'You're learning, you're learning,' said Betty and reached out for her kite. 'Here we are, a good spot. We need a good, clear run and the wind behind us, no trees, no obstacles. Why the beach is best. Good offshore wind. Choice weather for kiting.'

Della wondered if they'd have to start running along the beach to get the kites airborne, and worried her aunt would never manage it. But Betty did not move, stood still with feet firmly planted, and let the wind blow into her face before turning against it. She held her kite in her right hand, the kite already starting to catch the breeze and lift. She held the spool in her left hand and once the kite caught the updraught, she let it go, hurriedly unwinding as she did so, the kite tugging at its tether, lifting, lifting. She did it with such aplomb, all her old skills from childhood returning, unforgotten. The kite ascended, swaying back and forth, tethered short as it was. As Betty let out more and more line, its stability improved and it flew straighter. Betty made it look easy.

Della tried the same with her kite, but it wouldn't lift. Just flopped. She tried again and again. She ran along with it and hurled it into the air with no success. Betty watched, directing her kite with ease, laughing.

'Here. Come here. Don't guess. Feel the wind, sense it. Where it's coming from, where it's going. Let the wind do the work. A kite is a deflector. It's not like a wing. It's using its tethered point against the wind to create direction. It's all about how it presents itself to the wind. So, we have to be on intimate terms with the wind, you recall? As I told you before?'

She handed her kite's spool to Della, who held it, feeling

the tug of the kite, alive in the wind above. The wind changed direction so abruptly, so often, it was a struggle to keep control. Betty's smooth piloting of the kite was again evidence of her skill, skill that Della had yet to develop; within a few seconds, Della's marshalling of the kite had ended with it crashing to the sand.

'Don't worry, dearie. The wind's fairly gusty today. A frisky breeze makes it tricky. But the wind gets stronger and steadier further from the ground, so your aim is always to work your kite to a higher altitude. Then you'll have more control.'

Betty started the kite off again, casual, skilful, letting it play in her hands, then releasing it to the wind, the invisible force that gave the kite sudden life. 'Here, take it. There, feel that pull? That's the kite telling you it's ready to go. This is what makes kite-flying so interesting. Constantly feeling the wind, the tug of it, the kite pulling at you, talking to you. It's a conversation with the wind. You just have to listen.'

They practised getting Della's kite aloft for quite a while. She improved steadily. Then, they turned to how the kite moves when it's high up in the air.

'You see, because we only have a single line, our kite is limited by the wind direction. We're at the mercy of the wind. What would happen if we had two lines?'

Della gazed up at the diamond, fluttering and buffeted by its element. How could you turn it better? 'If you had two lines, you could pull on one side and it'd swoop that way.'

'That's right. What about the tether, where you put it on the kite?'

'Well, if you changed the angle of the tether, you'd get it to move differently. Better. More stable.'

'Yes, so we experiment. These are our first kites,' said Betty, taking the kite spool from Della and winding it in, watching the diamond resist the pull, eager to escape. 'We'll try different designs, make them better. More stable, more manoeuvrable. Make them dance a better dance with the wind.'

When she brought the kite in, Betty spooled up the line by turning the handles, then placed the kite on the ground, heaping sand over one pointed end to stop the kite lifting away again.

'It all started with kites, you see? Those Wright brothers said to themselves, Let's build ourselves a kite that's strong enough, and light enough, with enough surface, that we can put a body in it and lift it on the wind. A glider, if you will. Just a kite without a string.'

And she picked up Della's kite and got it in the air again, handed it to her niece and the two of them spooled out their kites and watching them take on the wind.

A kite without a string, thought Della. A memory came to her of a story she'd read aloud to Puck in their younger days, from an old Victorian children's compendium of Pop's, of a kite broken free that had a gay old time before it came crashing to the ground, trodden into the dirt by the hooves of a cow, never to fly again. It was called something like 'Pride Must Have a Fall'. She'd always hated that story. Now she understood why.

4

Puck was well again by April and Della could visit him. She found him sitting up in his bed, surrounded by new books and toys bought during his confinement. He'd lost weight, his face a bit pale and his brown eyes enlarged and darkened; his hair, uncut, was long over the ears. But his spirits had not been diminished, nor his delight in chatting.

'So glad you're back. It was awfully stupid of them to send you away. Oh, I suppose it was to make sure you didn't get sick. That's important, I suppose. I mean, it'd be awful if you died. I wouldn't really care if Midge died, or Gertie. I mean, they're much older and they're hoity-toity with me. But not you, Del.'

He was bored of the toys but loved the books, especially anything about nature, and desperate for her company to relay what he'd found out. She was always his sounding board, that way. He never stopped to ask if she were interested or not. He just assumed and he was usually right.

'Listen. Did you know that it's only boy crickets who chirp and they have ears on their legs? And lady mosquitoes drink blood only so they can lay eggs? They're not evil, just doing it for their babies. And bees are to be found on every continent on earth except the icy bits. And there's a beetle that can carry ten elephants?'

'That last bit doesn't sound right.'

'I mean, oh, you know what I mean! If he were a man, he could carry ten elephants. Like a flea could jump over St Paul's Cathedral, if he were a man. And dragonflies have four wings and can move each one separately?'

'I didn't know that. Why do you think they have four wings, instead of two?'

'I don't know for certain. Maybe it helps them fly backwards. They look topping, don't you think? I love watching them. All flying things really.'

'Me too. All flying things. I've been designing kites, Puck, with Great-Aunt. She knows all about them.'

'With mad Betty?'

'She's not mad!' She frowned. 'Where on earth did you get that idea from?'

'Pop told me she's touched. A bit loony. That's why she went away.'

'But Puck, that's not true.'

'But Della,' he said in a sing-song way, 'Pop said it so it must be true.'

'Not everything Pop says is right.'

'Well, it is to me. He'd never tell lies to me.'

The results of being a favoured child, she thought. Not Puck's fault, not really, that arrogance. Pop's fault though, spoiling the child, the golden boy.

'Auntie Betty is very clever actually.'

'She doesn't look it. Just looks like a fat, old cow.'

'Oh, Puck!' she snapped. He was exasperating today, she thought with annoyance. And surprise. When had Puck become so young? Such a blasted child, all of a sudden?

She was about to say, 'Wouldn't you like to come to the beach, when you're better, and fly kites with us?' But something stopped her. She didn't say it and she didn't tell him any more about kites or their plans. She felt obscurely that battle lines were being drawn and that Puck would not be an ally. Not an enemy, perhaps, but not neutral either. And she wanted to keep her kite-flying for herself, for her and Betty and nobody else. Nobody else, until Dudley, that was.

Della was summoned home that month and came with a heavy heart. Betty too was grumpy at the news, yet they made a pact that the kite work would continue, when Della had the time away from helping Mam in the house. When she came back with her carpet bag, Mam kissed her face four times and pinched her nose delightedly. Della felt a pang of guilt about being so loath to come home. But it was like a return from holidays, pleasure at her old things in her room, her own bed, but a yearning for the new life she'd made in those few weeks, and mostly the new way she looked at herself, thought about herself, which Betty had given her and Mam did not know. *I ought to tell her*, thought Della, watching Mam deftly tie up her apron strings, ready to make pastry for a celebratory pie. But she didn't know how to explain it, what had happened to her, how wholly she felt changed inside. The truth was she didn't understand it herself. Couldn't find the words. And somehow, didn't want to. It was her secret and she cherished it. Deeper down, there was a part of her felt Mam never understood her like Betty did, that Pop was a tyrant and didn't care about her, that if she could, she'd leave her home tomorrow and live with Betty, without a second thought. But she was ashamed of those feelings and pushed them down further, burying them beneath loyalty and love.

By early summer, they had two box kites, a small one for Betty to manage and a larger one for Della. Despite being slight, Della's arms were pretty strong and she soon grew frustrated with the little one. When they flew them, they were sometimes watched by sunburnt, wandering children or a curious perambulator, come to see the two odd females on the beach: one with a stern, old countenance and a big hat whatever the weather, the other one young, rather plain of face, yet elegant and lithe, getting better by the day at manoeuvring her kites and making them dance in the air. If the wind dropped and the kite hurled itself towards the ground, Della was expert at twisting its leash and flipping it back up into another air current, sailing it up, up again into the wide sky.

'A good recovery!' Betty would cry. 'Excellent rescue!'

'Can I have a try, missus?' beach kids would whine at Betty and she'd chase them off, big feet flapping on the sand, arms shooing them as if they were greedy gulls. Della was softer and might pass them a diamond kite sometimes to mess about with, but never the boxes. The box kites were their pride and joy, and not toys, certainly not.

One day of particular summer loveliness, the sun high in the sky and plump cotton-wool clouds careering across it, a great flying day with strong, regular winds, Della was lost in her kiting and at first didn't notice the boy with the book, sitting off downwind, watching them seriously for over an hour. He didn't ask for a go, he didn't talk to them. Just rested his palms on the sand, a satchel beside him, and watched. He held the book up to shield his eyes sometimes, following the kites' movements with his head, now and then looking at Betty or Della as they stooped to retrieve a kite or muttered to each other. Finally, he approached them, half-sideways, nonchalant, as if by accident. When the kite came down heavily and Della crouched to check for damages, the boy appeared by her side and said, 'Is it all right?'

She nodded, so as not to be impolite. A Yorkie, that unmistakeable twang of his Yorkshire accent marking him as a tourist as surely as any bucket and spade or ice-cream moustache.

'You're an excellent flyer,' he added.

'For a girl?' said Betty, hands on wide hips, scowling at the interloper.

'Uh, no, madam. Actually, I'd say the best I've seen. Boy or girl.'

'Well, of course she is. She's my great-niece, isn't she? All the Broughtons are skilled. We made the kites ourselves. Designed and built them, her and me.'

'Gosh! Truly? That's very impressive indeed.'

Della could find no more excuses to fiddle with the kite on the ground, so stood up and sneaked a look at the boy, found him to be inches taller than her with a long face, long legs and long arms, long all over really, with long grey shorts and short green sleeves, topped by a tweed cap. She saw her aunt regarding him curiously; yet a lopsided smile was beginning on her hard-edged face and Della saw he was charming her. Yet he didn't seem conscious of it. It was just his way, perhaps.

He removed his cap and revealed ink-black hair slicked back, lifted by the wind in crow-feathery clumps. 'Mrs Broughton, Miss Broughton, it's an honour to meet you.'

Della and Betty looked at each other and giggled.

'I'm Mrs Perry. My great-niece is Miss Dobbs. And who are you, young man?'

Cap still in hand and a confused expression made him look very young, Puck's age even, and Della wondered if he was younger than his height suggested. She looked down and noticed the book he held was by Charles Dickens. *I never read story books*, she thought.

'Dudley Willow.'

'Willow,' mused Betty. 'You bend with the wind, then.'

He smiled, and it was an improving smile, making his face rounder and his eyes friendly.

'I try,' said Dudley Willow and popped his cap back on. 'I'm very interested in the wind. And flying.' He picked up his satchel, slid the book in there, retrieved a magazine and held it up in two hands, to stop the wind ripping its pages. *The Aero*, it was called, written in flowing font, graceful and fluid, dated Tuesday, 29 June, 1909. Its headline read 'The Coming of the Monoplane' and beneath it was a photograph of a Blériot aeroplane, one long oval wing spanning the picture, atop a cage of wooden struts, a tail plane behind and two wheels below. In the midst of it sat Monsieur Blériot himself guiding the elegant machine.

'Crikey!' muttered Della and looked to her aunt. 'Look at that. Only one wing. How does he get enough lift?'

'Astonishing, isn't it!' said Dudley Willow. 'Monoplanes don't seem possible. But then flying doesn't either. It's just deflecting air, that's all. It's preposterous, really.'

Della stared at him. This lad knew about aeroplanes all right.

'Please, take it,' said Dudley and offered her the magazine. She thanked him and held it between herself and her aunt. They hungrily turned the pages for more news.

'Look, Della,' said Betty. 'Here: "Small Motors for Flying Machine Models". That'll be next, after the glider. Glider first, then a model with a motor.'

Della was lost in the pages of up-to-the-minute words straight from the horse's mouth of aviation: current aeronauts, their ideas and designs, and their hopes for new challenges. The magazine was a marvel and certainly not available where they lived. She had forgotten briefly that they were being watched, but now she hushed her aunt and regretted their talk of engines. It was their secret, because it had to be. After all, what would people say, if they knew a fifteen-year-old girl and her American great-aunt were planning on building and flying their own aeroplane from Cleethorpes beach? They'd be mocked mercilessly, become local figures of fun and derision, and if word reached Pop, well, that would be the end of it, the end of everything. They had never spoken to anyone about it and now this boy, this stranger, had heard of it. But he had a nice expression, and he was smiling, and she thought his long face looked sincere; but then she rejected this. Everyone knows you can't judge a book by its cover. She closed the magazine abruptly and handed it back to its owner.

Dud took it and put it away in his satchel, saying, 'You know, that box kite you've made. It's smashing. But, have you seen Mr Cody's designs? He adds winglets – like bat wings – on either side, to give it more lift. You might want to try that next.'

How presumptuous this boy was, to give them, the brilliant

Broughton kite designers, advice about their craft. But he said it in such an amiable way that she didn't really mind – and actually, he was right.

'Obliged,' she said and went back to her kite, readied it for flight and sent it upwards, striding backwards away from him as it caught the breeze. She saw the boy converse a while with Betty before he gave a brief bow and wandered off down the beach, ambling along for a time, staring out to sea. Then he turned inland and walked briskly shoreward, with purpose, his long thin legs cutting the air like scissors towards his destination. *I wonder where he's off to?* she thought, then shook her head to dismiss it.

Dudley Willow came back the next day. He had two more back issues of *The Aero*, said they could keep them, said he'd read them cover to cover. *That was kind*, thought Della, interested but wary. Betty was taken with him and invited him to join them. They all had lunch – a simple picnic of pork pie, haslet sandwiches and apples – which they shared on the sand. He told them about himself. His father was a textiles manufacturer in Bradford. He'd come for a summer holiday to Cleethorpes on the train, staying in a guest house with his nurse, his father still at home. He didn't mention his mother. He said he liked to run long distances, was a fledgling radio ham and fascinated by anything mechanical. He was eleven years old.

'That's a bit young,' said Della, thinking out loud and surprised to hear her own voice say it.

'A bit young for what?' said Dudley, smiling. He smiled all the time, a small smile. Maybe it was just the way his face was innocently made, like a dolphin.

I don't know, she thought. Two years younger than Puck. But seemed to have years on him.

'People often think I'm older,' he went on, 'because I'm tall.'

'It's more than that, boy,' said Betty. 'You have a way about you. You're an easy-going kind of feller.'

'Probably because I'm an only child. Always in the company of adults. Makes you grow up early, I suppose.'

Della felt her cheeks grow hot. She found people talking about themselves intensely embarrassing.

'Isn't it time we were going?' she said to her aunt.

'Oh no, indeed,' said Betty, placing her palms on the sand to help shove herself up to a standing position, ungainly as ever. 'I'm off to get us some ices. Do you fancy one, Dudley?'

'Do I!' he cried, turning to Della, who was all but scowling. 'But only if Miss Dobbs does?'

Betty didn't stay to discuss it, lodged her cumbersome bag filled with all manner of useful and useless objects under her arm and walked off towards the promenade. Della resolutely stared out across the estuary towards Hull, thinking of her sister there, married with children. How did she talk to boys back then, when she was Della's age, when she was young and stupid like Della? But nobody in this world could have been as much of a tongue-tied idiot as Della believed herself to be, sitting on the sand, hugging her knees, with this boy beside her, and nothing to say. Nothing.

'I live in Bradford Street,' she tried.

'Oh yes?'

'And you come from Bradford. Funny that.'

'Yes.'

Hopeless.

A pause.

'Your aunt is a character.'

She thought, *What can* that *mean?*

Dudley went on, 'I've been reading *David Copperfield*. Have you read it?'

She shook her head.

'Well, there's a part in it you might like. David has an aunt called Betsey, funnily enough, who is a real character too.

And she has a friend who lives with her called Mr Dick. And he's writing a memorial but keeps getting messages in his brain from King Charles I's head. So, he writes all of these messages on paper and makes a huge kite out of it and flies it high up in the air, to get rid of all the bad thoughts in his head. To begin with, David thinks he's touched, you know, a bit mad but—'

She interrupted, 'What are you trying to say about my aunt?'

Her chest felt tight and her face hurt from frowning. Not another one, like Pop and Puck, casting slurs on Betty. Why can't a person be different without being accused of insanity, for heaven's sake?

Dudley's face fell. 'Oh . . . well, nothing really. I was just going to say, Betsey Trotwood in the book defends Mr Dick to David and to everyone, and relies on his advice in all matters. His brother tried to put him in an asylum but she thinks his ideas are remarkable. And so do I. I mean, what a brilliant idea that is, to take whatever is troubling you, fix it to something that flies and launch it into the air.'

She thought for a while. She expected Dudley Willow to pipe up again with some new interesting fact. But he didn't. He waited for her, waited ever so patiently. And it wasn't even awkward any more. Just a comfortable silence between two people, surrounded by the brisk wind across the flaxen sands, the chattering gulls above, the dunlins and oystercatchers way out at the edge of the sea, pottering about and digging with their beaks for treats. Betty came back, they ate their ices and the three of them talked about birds and aeroplanes and wings and things, there on the sand, until dusk. Then, the tepid summer rain came and sent them skittering across the sand, laughing and hurrying old Betty, damp and abuzz with the lowering clouds and electricity in the air.

They parted at Ross Castle, Della going left to home, her aunt right to her house, and Dudley asked if he might

accompany Mrs Perry, as his guest house was in the same
direction. Della went her own way, then peeked back at
them. The boy loped beside Betty, the two of them chatting.
Then Dudley turned and before she looked away, she saw
him crook his arm in the air, a stiff kind of wave to her.

They didn't see him again that summer.

'He didn't even say goodbye,' muttered Della to her aunt
one day.

'He didn't need to,' answered Betty, mysterious. But Della
could not draw her out and was left to wonder about it, and
about Dudley Willow, though he was only some boy, some
Yorkie who was too tall and too young. But she wondered
about him, all the same.

5

Summer ended and the tourists straggled away and left Cleethorpes to breathe again. Della liked reclaiming her home town and was cheered by the colours of autumn each year. Mam usually agreed, but those days she was so tired. The last time Della had seen her like that was a few months ago, when Puck was ill. She trudged from room to room and trudged upstairs and down. She stopped going to her musical evenings with friends, as she had been wont to do, an opportunity to indulge the musical part of her personality that had been submerged by motherhood and wifedom. When all the siblings were still living at home, Mam used to play the piano in the house to entertain them, and the others would sing along and Della would listen. She had tried to teach them all at one time or another and still gave Puck lessons but he never practised; Midge was a natural musician as well as an actress, could play anything, just like her mother; and Gertie could play well and teach her children to play too, a useful skill for a genteel mother. Mam liked to tinker about with a Bach invention or a Mozart slow movement; nothing too noisy or dramatic, or it would disturb Pop. He hated noise, retired to the bed in his study early each night, at eight-thirty, and everyone knew he wore earplugs to block out the house's sounds. But these days Mam had left off playing even for herself. Even that tame activity that gave Mam such peaceful pleasure had stopped and Della was worried about her mother.

Their cook, Mrs Butters, seemed to know something and she often scolded the maid, Harriet, telling her to hurry up and help Mrs Dobbs and do more and more around the house. It came to a head when Della found her mother vomiting into the basin, helped her clean it up and sat with her on her bed, noticed her wan, drawn face with alarm and stroked her wavy chestnut hair that was scored through with grey.

'What is it, Mam?'

'I may as well tell you. There's a baby on the way. I didn't think I had it in me – or Pop for that matter. I mean, I'm past forty and your father is in his fifties. I thought it was the change coming but I suppose for men, nothing changes.'

This revelation and the unwelcome details of her parents' private life – the unsavoury thoughts and associations they raised in Della's mind – were almost too much to be borne and Della struggled with the urge to run from the room and hide. Only her mother's obvious distress kept her there, so she put her arm round Mam and thought of something to say.

'I'll help.'

'I know you will, love. It's going to be a boy, I think. It feels the same as Puck did. So that'll make your pop happy, mm?'

They sat and stared at their shoes, contemplating this unlikely occurrence, that anything could cheer up Pop. But another boy might do it. And Della realised how much her mother would need her, not only during her pregnancy but after, when the baby came, and most especially, if it were a girl; that Della's dreams of escape to Betty's for their secret project would sink beneath the wet sand of responsibility. And she resented it – the fact of it, but the child itself too. Even Mam, even lovely Mam, she resented a tiny bit, getting herself into this, so late in life, when she should have been free, when Della should have been free too. Then she felt a stab of guilt about that and scolded herself inwardly, knew it wasn't true, not really.

'At least Shakespeare made up plenty of characters to name it after,' said Mam, and Della smiled; they both did.

'Betty will help too,' said Della. 'Being a midwife and that.'

'Of course. If your father allows it.' Mam sighed heavily. Della looked at her mother, saw the grey hairs and the bags under her eyes, and though she possessed scant knowledge of precisely how babies came into being, she knew enough to realise that she actually blamed her father for this – in fact, that somehow something told her it was his fault, at the base of it. With that realisation, she felt a surge of love for her mother, protective urgent love and an impulse to shield her and the baby inside her from the world; she felt a solidarity with her she had never felt before and wished the baby would be a girl. Mam caught Della looking at her pityingly, and so she took Della's hand and held it to her belly. 'Another Dobbs in the world. And I think it will be a mighty little soul, given how sick it's making me. Must be a boy.'

A day later, Della cycled to her aunt's house, and was ready to gossip about Mam and the baby when Betty handed her a letter, postmarked Bradford. It turned out Dudley and the old woman had a secret arrangement that he could write to Della via her aunt. Nothing was said, but Della knew it was something to do with hiding it from Pop, about corresponding with boys for a start (even those as young as Dudley), but also about the subject matter – the letter mostly concerned aviation, a topic that Della never mentioned at home. And she was awfully glad Puck wasn't around to rib her about the letter too.

'*Dear Miss Dobbs*', it began and she thought, even before she'd considered whether or not to write back, that she must tell him to call her Della. '*I hope you don't object to this letter, but your great-aunt assured me it was all right and I must say it would be smashing if you wrote back.*' It was all about flying – the best pilots, the latest aircraft and a long meditation on Monsieur Blériot's Channel crossing from July, with finely drawn sketches made in ink. '*It makes you think,*' he wrote, '*that with the arrival of aviation to our shores that any chap from Europe – with wings and intent – can land here whenever he likes.'*

He writes like a grown-up, Della thought, and reflected on how much younger than this her brother seemed, even though Dudley was the younger. She almost felt herself younger than this mature young person, especially in her writing style, of which she had never been proud, being both a quiet person in speech and never one for writing much. He signed off, *'Kind regards, Dud'.* Della read it in secret and hid it at the back of a drawer in her room. Thereafter, they wrote about once a month, always 'c/o Mrs E. Perry', always *Dear Della* and *Dear Dud.* She worried her letters couldn't live up to Dud's, but he didn't seem to mind, often writing *'Do reply soon'* and *'Keep in touch, won't you?',* which made her smile. It would have done no harm to tell Mam about it. But she didn't. It was part of her secret life and she treasured it.

The baby was due in June of 1910. By the end of March, Mam was exhausted, suffering with constant heartburn and desperate for the last couple of months of pregnancy to end. She was under the local doctor's care, arranged by Pop, as he didn't want Betty in the house if he could help it. Sometimes Mam went for a walk with Della to see her aunt, who gave her midwifely advice, the things about being in the family way and what the baby would need that she'd forgotten, seeing as it was thirteen years ago she was last like this, with Puck. But this time around it was so different, Della heard her mother confide in Betty; she was so tired, too old for all this. Della had all but given up on kites and aeroplanes, in practice anyway. She'd not spent much time with Betty at all, as she had been running her mother's household for weeks. Yet Mam couldn't relinquish control willingly and kept waddling into the kitchen to direct affairs and getting told off by Mrs Butters, who was helping with the evening meal four days a week now. Della cooked the other three evenings and went to bed weary every night, wondering when the day would come that she could be free of all this. For once the baby came, there would be even more work, and her mother would need her more than ever; those days she had before the idea of the baby had come into being, those days in the sun on the beach with Betty and Dudley, felt like another girl, another life, like something in a story, even if she could feel the sun on her face from those kite-flying days, even now in the rainy early months of the year.

One day in April the weather was like the end of the world: ice, fog, glimpses of the translucent sun, rain, hail and snow-flakes sweeping across the estuary, closed by an apricot-jam sunset. Something in the air. It was a chilly night when Della turned off the lamps and closed the lower-floor doors then ascended the stairs, sleepy yet light-footed. Dud had sent her the latest *Aero* and she had it ready in her room for reading when she had the chance, and already she had visions of Deperdussins and Blériots and Farman biplanes soaring in her head, lifting her mood into the skies, her cares and responsibilities falling like feathers. Mrs Butters and Harriet had gone home, Puck was away at school and Pop was snoring in his room. The house was hushed and Della would have a bit of time before sleep took her to lose herself in aviation talk. Then, a tremendous crash came from Mam's room downstairs. Della hurled herself about and took the stairs two at a time. She burst in to find her mother on all fours on the floor, her ewer and basin smashed in pieces on the wooden floor, and a shockingly scarlet stain of blood like murder across the white bedsheet.

'Get the doctor,' her mother gasped through gritted teeth. But first Della helped her up and got her to the armchair in the corner, saw the blood and fluid like a gash down her leg and across the front of her beige cotton nightgown. Della blundered out into the hall to the telephone they'd had installed that year, spoke breathlessly to the operator who put her through to the doctor, whose wife said he was out and she'd tell him when he came back in.

'But there's blood,' said Della and the wife said she couldn't magic her husband out of thin air, but she would send a boy to fetch the midwife down the road and what address was it again? And all the time Mam was yelling in the other room like a trapped animal and Della's ear ached from the hand held against it to hear what this damned doctor's wife was saying.

She raced back to Mam and found her on the floor again, crawling round and moaning like nothing on earth, and pulled the sheet from the bed, got two bath towels from the cupboard and laid them out, soft and clean, on the stained mattress. She crouched down and talked to Mam in swift low words, cajoling her up on to the bed and to lie on the towels. Her mother's face was a boiled beetroot and her eyes were rolling back in her head, her body heaving in its misery.

'It's too early, too early,' she moaned. 'The baby's too small.'

Della's thoughts twisted and turned like a bag of snakes and all she could think was that she should have hot water in a bowl, and a flannel for Mam's head. She suddenly remembered her father – his presence at night was so absolutely silent and absent, she had forgotten he was even there. She shouted and shouted for him, but of course, his stupid earplugs kept him sleeping soundly. Yet she daren't leave Mam, just prayed and prayed the doctor or the midwife or Pop or somebody would come soon and she could relinquish sole responsibility and just help around the edges, as she felt most comfortable doing in life.

Mam was grunting and moaning and writhing as in the throes of a fit, her face growing deathly white, almost green. Her mother's hand had been in hers, squeezing it tightly with every new contraction until Della thought her fingers would be crushed, but abruptly Mam's grip and face slackened and she fell back on the pillows and her eyes fluttered and shut.

'Pop!' Della screamed, 'Pop! Pop!'

A door opened and Pop's shuffling gait was heard thumping down the hall. Della was stroking her mother's face – 'Mam, Mam, wake up, Mam. Your baby needs you. Your baby needs you. Wake up.' Della looked up and finally, finally another person was alive in that world of white and red and pain and silence.

The second Pop saw them, he rushed awkwardly to the bed and bent down to his wife, his good hand cupping her pale cheek.

'Lucy,' he whispered. 'Lucy, it's Stanley. Wake up, my darling.'

Mam was still, so still. Della looked up at her father, had never heard him speak like that before. But then a sound, so faint both of them cocked their heads like birds to hear it. Mam moved her mouth; a tiny moan came from it. She was still alive, just.

'I've rung the doctor. His wife said he was out. She said she'd send the boy to get the midwife. But nobody's come.'

'Della, get on that blasted bike of yours and fetch your great-aunt. Go, go as fast as you can, Della.'

The night was chilled and the air clear as ice on a frozen fountain. Della had no coat, had not thought of it, but she didn't feel the cold and rode double-time along Kingsway, pedalling hard up the incline and freewheeling down again before thrashing the last bit to Betty's house. She threw the bike on the pavement and started yelling for her aunt before she'd even reached the door, upon which she banged so hard her fist crumpled, her fingers flailing. But she felt no pain, only intent, that the door would open, that Betty would be there, in all her solid midwife self. When the door opened and Betty appeared like a surprised spirit, all white hair and white nightie, Della's words tumbled out and Betty said, 'Go to the Dolly and wake them up. The owner has an automobile.

Tell him he's taking Betty Broughton to Bradford Street. I'll dress and get my bag.'

Della ran over the street to the Dolphin Hotel and saw light emanating from the narrow window above the front door. She lifted the knocker and rapped it several times, before she heard someone shouting within, 'What's the hurry?'

Della didn't know if she'd need to argue the case; she thought, *Why would they raise the owner of the hotel just for my queer old great-aunt?* But the call was made and when a man with a large handlebar moustache appeared from upstairs smoking a cigar and was told Betty Broughton needed an emergency drive to Bradford Street, he galloped downstairs, passed his smoking cigar to the night porter and rushed out into the night. Della followed and saw her aunt coming across the street, boots and coat on, no hat, hair wild and bag in hand.

'Betty,' the man shouted familiarly, yet urgently. They must have known each other from the old days. 'The car is down the street in a garage. I'll fetch it round and meet you here.'

'Get on your bike and get home,' her aunt said to Della as she stepped onto the pavement. 'If your mam's awake, do everything you can to keep her that way. Smelling salts or open the windows. Go!'

Don't let her be dead, Della thought over and again as she rode home. *Don't let her be dead by the time I get there.*

'Let her live,' she said hoarsely into the air streaming over her. 'Let her live!' she shouted to the winds and the road rushing beneath her wheels and the sea roaring beyond, implacable, out of reach.

She whisked round the back, leapt off her bike, which crashed into the yard wall, and she ran into the house. Silence. She stumbled into Mam's room to find Pop holding her hand, his back blocking Della's view of her mother's face. Della stopped dead. But then a cry came from Mam, so piercing it split Della's ears and filled her with joy, that her mother was alive, that the baby was coming. Mam arched her back, threw her legs open and snorted like a horse.

Pop turned his head to see Della, his face a picture of terror – and yet there was a light of exhilaration in his eyes.

'Betty's on the way in a car.'

'Cordelia, Cordelia!' cried Mam and Della rushed to the bed, shocked at the sound of her formal name being screamed by her mother. Mam looked crazed, dropped her husband's grip and grabbed her daughter's hand and said, 'Get this man out of here. I can't have men in here when I'm like this. Get him out!'

'All right, all right!' Pop laughed nervously, then checked himself, puffed out his cheeks and shook his head. His expression conveyed that he'd never imagined himself in this situation and couldn't quite believe he was in it, and he said, 'Now you're here Della, I'm going to find the doctor and – God help me – once he's done with Mam and everything's all right, I'm going to murder him!' And off he went, limping but determined.

'Oh, Mam,' sobbed Della and dropped her forehead onto her mother's hand, 'I thought you were dead.'

But Mam took her hand away and grasped her knees, puffing, puffing and yelling again, her eyes squeezed shut and hair plastered across her cheeks. Della had no idea what to do, but thought she ought to look – down there – to see what was happening, to help her mother, give her some encouragement. Gingerly, she stood and peered round the edge of her mother's nightie and saw it – a dark dome, the baby's head. She could not take her eyes away. There it was, her mother's child, there it was, coming into the world. Her chest expanded and she was filled with the wonder of it and the acid fear that it could be hurt, that she must do everything she could to see that baby safely into this world and through it, all its life, all her life.

She rubbed her hands soothingly on her mother's calves

and said, 'The baby's coming, Mam. I can see the head. It's got dark hair, Mam, black as anything.'

Mam uttered a throaty 'Ha!' then puffed, threw her arms back and braced herself against the brass bedstead behind her and pushed with all of her might. In the noise of it, Della did not hear her aunt arrive, but saw a figure in the doorway throw off its coat to the floor, and underneath it Betty was still in her white nightie. She rushed around and looked between her niece's knees, grabbed her bag, placed it at the end of the bed and opened it up to reveal a row of instruments shining and clean – she must have been prepared, just in case – dear Auntie Betty – and pushed up her sleeves.

'Go and fetch clean towels for the baby and get some water boiling,' she told Della. 'We're nearly there. Come on, Lucy. Come on, girl. Let's get this baby born.'

Della stood up straight and nearly fainted, put her hand to her head and shut her eyes. Betty was shouting words of encouragement, Mam was screaming again and the world seemed to be toppling, but Della willed herself to open her eyes, to be strong and help her. She ran to the cupboard, took out four clean towels, the softest ones, and brought them back to the room, put them on Mam's dresser then off to the kitchen, where she found the man from the Dolly boiling water in a pot on the stove.

'Had five of my own,' he said, good-humoured. 'Always need to boil water.'

'Thank you!' gasped Della. Thinking feverishly ahead, she said, 'When the water's boiled, could you pour it into jugs and basins so that it'll cool down. We'll need it to wash the baby. And my mother.' And now she was giving orders to the owner of the Dolphin Hotel – the strangest night of her life.

She rushed back down the hallway to Mam's room and came in to find her arm flailing, as if shooing away imaginary wasps, and Della took it, and stroked her hand as Mam pushed her head back into the pillow, gasping.

Betty was at the business end, hands on Mam's knees, saying, 'One last push, dearie, and that'll do it. One more push, come on.'

And it all happened at once, Mam's loudest yell yet, her feet lifting off the bed, and the reddish form flopping out on to the towel Della had laid, Betty cradling it up, clamping the umbilical cord and snipping it.

'Towel!' Betty snapped and Della flew to the dresser and grabbed one. She came back to the bed and saw the baby properly for the first time. It was tiny, so tiny. A tiny little girl. Della felt a glow of relief, the girl they'd wanted. But the baby wasn't moving, her mouth and eyes shut. Della spread the towel on the bed and Betty lowered the meagre thing onto it and wrapped her carefully in the towel. First, Betty opened the tiny mouth with a finger and peered at it. Then she picked the baby up, sat on the edge of the bed, placed her tummy-side down on her knees that were sloping slightly downward, the head held just off the knee in one hand, while rubbing the little back with her other hand. After a while of this, she turned the baby over and took her across to the dresser, shoving Mam's things aside to make room. Della came with her, glancing back at Mam – who had collapsed on the bed but was breathing heavily, as if in a restful sleep – then Della moved some bottles and Mam's hairbrush on to the floor to make plenty of room for the package in the towel resting on it. Betty was bent over, her head close to the baby's; she was whispering to her and rubbing her chest. 'Come on, little one,' she was saying. 'Come on, come on. Live. Live. *Live.*'

But the baby wasn't moving, her face was still, only jiggled falsely by Betty's fingers, trying to rub life into the tiny chest. Della turned away and stifled a sob, then went to her mother and held her hand.

'Born too soon,' she heard her aunt say, in a low miserable voice. 'Born too soon.' *The baby's dead*, she thought, *after all this. The baby's dead.* Her mother's lips were forming words, though she had no energy to voice them.

'What is it, Mam?'

'Baby. Where's my baby?' she whispered and Della could not bear to speak. Her mother stopped breathing a moment, as if to wait for the answer, and there was a spell of pure, empty silence in that room.

An animal sound, a tiny whimper like the dying things Puck brought home sometimes, but it got louder and stronger, and it was coming from the baby.

'That's it,' whispered Betty, 'that's it, little one. You tell us all about it.'

And the baby was moaning, a whine climbing higher and higher, until a full-throated wail came out of the tiny red mouth and the room was filled with life. Della laughed, how she laughed and squeezed her mother's hand. Mam opened her eyes and searched the room for the source of the sound, Betty coming towards them proudly with the tiny bundle in her big round arms. She held out the child and placed it with infinite tenderness in the arms of its mother.

'It's a girl,' said Betty, beaming, and they all grinned together. The face was in repose now, the baby safe on her mother's chest, her jet hair – so much of it – sticking up in all directions, white waxy stuff on her cheeks and forehead, wrinkled and red from bawling. A serious old newborn face, petite and flawless. A matchless moment of stillness as the three women, three generations, gazed upon their new addition.

The front door banged and Pop came into the room, saw Mam and the baby. Della watched her father's face alter, awash with relief.

'I couldn't find the doctor,' he muttered, but his face showed that none of that mattered now, now he could see his wife alive, awake and come back to him, and the bundle in her arms was breathing and red-faced and here.

Mam looked up. 'Sorry, love,' she said. 'A girl.' A hint of

a frown, but then the clouds lifted and Pop smiled, as if determined to make the best of it. So many expressions on his face Della had never seen in her life, and now she was seeing them all in one night.

'I've not washed her yet,' said Betty, but Pop said, 'Never mind that,' and Mam lifted the bundle towards him and he took it, looking down upon his fifth child with unmistakeable pride.

'She's a fighter,' said Mam.

'Weeks early,' added Betty, 'but she came out ready for life. It was touch and go, Stanley. But that girl was born to survive.'

'A mighty little soul,' said Della, echoing her mother's words all those months before.

'Ophelia?' said Pop, passing her back to Mam, as the mighty little one started to whimper. 'Or Desdemona?'

Mam shook her head and looked down at her new daughter. 'Not one of those wet weekends,' she said. 'This one needs a name that befits her better than that.'

They were all lost in thought.

'Cleopatra,' said Mam. 'Cleo for short.'

For the first three days of Cleo's life, she fed voraciously and Mam barely moved from the bed. But something changed on the third evening and she started to cry. She cried all night and into the fourth day. Mam couldn't soothe her, nor Della. Pop didn't try. He retired to his room, put his earplugs in and wouldn't be seen, except to have meals brought by the maid or Della. Betty came and she couldn't soothe her either. Cleo was on the breast for hours, sucking away then falling asleep, only to wake after a half hour or so and scream again.

Then on the fifth day, she stopped crying. Della surfaced from sleep as if from a variety of madness to hear silence again. Peace. But Cleo stopped sucking too. She would not feed. Her face went grey and she slept too much. Mam was at her wits' end. Della had no idea what to do, went to fetch

Betty again. They coaxed and stroked Cleo, crooned and sang. They tried a bottle with a rubber teat, they tried water first, just to get some fluid into her, then tried milk, but nothing worked. Cleo lost weight, became listless and barely made a sound. The doctor was brought. He told them she was born too early, that there was nothing to be done, that the best they could do was to keep her close and let her slip away. Della, Mam and Betty were sitting on Mam's bed, Cleo wrapped tight in a blanket between them, sleeping, snuffling, but in a deep repose from which she was unable and unwilling to ever awaken. And the doctor left. They heard Pop mutter with him in the hall and show him to the door, thanking him. The front door clunked shut, heavy and final.

'Lucy, you're not going to listen to that fool?' said Betty, standing up, hands on hips.

'It has nothing to do with you,' said Pop, appearing at Mam's door. 'That man is a well-respected doctor of many years' standing. He knows his business.'

'Does he heck.' Betty scowled. 'That baby needs extra sustenance. She won't suck but that doesn't mean she doesn't want food. We need to start with spoons, get them sterilised in boiling water, then give her milk a drop at a time.'

'We've had enough Broughton interference,' said Pop in a low voice, his eyes intent. 'You're giving my wife false hopes. The doctor knows best and that is that. Please leave.'

Della looked to Mam, certain she would defend her aunt, but Mam's face was as grey as the baby's and she had no will left to fight, nothing left but exhaustion. She stared at the bed and said nothing.

Della swallowed hard and spoke up: 'Pop, I think Betty's right.'

Pop glared at Della. 'You pipe down, child. Nobody asked you. Must I explain this to you? Our doctor is an experienced medical man. If there were any chance, he would know. Men of science would offer us the answer, if there were one. But he did not. There is nothing more to be done. We need to carry out his instructions. And be left in peace. Not subject the baby – and your poor mother – to more interference and fuss.'

Della felt herself up against an implacable wall of male logic. But men said a lot of things, and they weren't always right. And this was not a point of honour, this was life or death. 'We should try it, shouldn't we, the spoon-feeding? Anything to help Cleo? Please, Pop.'

'This is what comes of allowing that Broughton woman into our lives, the Broughton disgrace! Well, no more. I should've put my foot down about this months ago. I am the master of this house.'

'But Pop, if it weren't for Betty, Cleo would never have lived at all. Betty saved her, she got her breathing. Betty saved her life before, Pop.'

'That woman did not save our baby. God did.'

'With the help of a midwife,' snorted Betty.

Pop turned to her and lifted his chin, his good hand, balled in a fist, held straining against his stomach, his neck tense. 'Leave my house now. Leave us to grieve in peace.'

'For Christ's sake, Stanley, she's not dead yet!' cried Betty and Mam cried out too and collapsed forward on the bed, weeping beside Cleo, who lay still, impervious.

'Get out!' screamed Pop and took a limping step towards Betty, as if he would strike her. Della saw in her face that she knew there was nothing left to say. She turned and left, the front door closing soon after.

Pop was shaking as he turned to observe Mam still sobbing on the bed. Della saw him raise his fist and hold it briefly to his bared teeth, holding back a tidal wave of grief about to erupt from deep inside. He held himself together and left the room, as dignified as his bad leg would allow. Della heard his door close. She waited by Mam until she quietened down, her eyes barely open in her exhaustion. She soothed her mother and told her she would put Cleo in her cot, that she would watch her for the night. Mam curled up on the bed like a child in the womb. And slept.

But Della did not take Cleo to her Moses basket. Instead, she cradled the grave mite in her left arm and went to the kitchen. One-armed, she went about her business, the baby so light on her arm she barely felt her. She boiled a pan of water and dropped three teaspoons in, the smallest she could find, then removed them with tongs onto a clean cloth. She took a bottle of boiled water they had prepared earlier and warmed it through in the hot pan, mixed it with some cow's milk and poured it into a bowl. Then she sat by the range, cosy yet wide awake, held the baby more upright and brought a spoon of the mixture to her mouth. Cleo ignored it. Della nuzzled the baby's lips with her little finger and the rosebud opened slightly; she slipped a drop of the mixture onto the bottom lip and watched it slide into the mouth. Cleo's eyebrows contracted, then relaxed. But she didn't cry. Della tried another bit, and another, only drops at first. Then, Cleo's eyelids fluttered and opened a slit, moving from side to side. But still she did not cry.

A noise at the back door. Della swivelled her head as far round as she could, not wanting to disturb the baby. A figure was lurking, just out of view. Della put down the spoon and stood nervously, took a step forward and saw Great-Aunt Betty in the backyard, grinning at her. She went to the back door, Cleo starting to snuffle on her arm, and turned the big old key in the lock.

'Clever girl,' whispered Betty. 'Milk and water. Is she taking it?'

'Yes!' said Della in delight, nervous of sound, but remembering Pop's earplugs.

'Good. You carry on. We'll start with that. Then, we'll go on to pap. Milk and water with a little flour or bread mixed in, just a tiny bit at first. Where's your mam?'

'Sleeping.'

'And your pop? I think he'll murder me if he finds me here!'

'I think he will!' said Della. To be unafraid, like Betty. What a marvellous thing. To care about nobody's opinion, to be beyond the pale. There was a freedom in it, the bridle removed. Now she'd seen it in her aunt, Della could not imagine going back to the way she was in the days of her silence and meekness. The stable door was open, and she knew her spirit was about to bolt. First though was the baby. They had to save Cleo. And life would come later.

6

'Samuel Lidgard, at your service! Step in, ladies, do.'

'Oh, shut your trap, Sam,' said Betty and ushered Della into the back seat of the shiny automobile. Then she sat in the front beside Mr Lidgard, the moustachioed and red-cheeked owner of the Dolphin Hotel and of the chugging Napier in which he was to drive them that day to the Burton upon Trent aviation meeting.

Cleo was five months old by then and – despite not sleeping much and always yelling for milk and attention – was fighting fit, when a letter from Dud told Della that a 'lady flyer' had been invited to the Doncaster meet, and that Della must try to see him there, as his father was taking him and together they could witness this pilot flying for the first time in British skies. After telling Mam, who asked Pop if Della could go, there followed three full days of argument and bad temper, when Pop ordered Della to go 'nowhere near those *damned dangerous* machines' and banned her from ever going anywhere with 'that *blasted Broughton* woman'. Even when his blood was up, Pop – ever the actor – liked to use alliteration to drive his point home.

The cat was out of the bag. Della had told Mam of her aviation obsession a week or so before, as well as explaining about her correspondence with her friend Dudley. After Mam chastised her for having secret 'doings' with a boy, Della flourished the letters and invited Mam to read them, saying, 'All we do is talk about flying, really. Help yourself!' Mam had a bit of a read and came to the conclusion that it was all quite innocent and, quite rightly, pigeon-holed Dud, from what Della said of him, as being a 'really nice boy'. He had recently revealed to Della that his mother had passed away giving birth to him, which poignant fact she passed on to Mam, who promptly felt very motherly towards him, poor lad. Now Mam was firmly on his side, which only served Della better; somehow her aviation fancy was given solid ground by Mam's regard for this poor dear boy who'd lost his mother.

So when Dud's latest letter came, Mam tried her best to persuade Pop to support his youngest daughter's interests, but to no avail. She told her daughter that, in life, you had to choose your battles carefully, and this one was lost before it began. Della wrote to Dud that it would not be possible to meet him there and please to report back all the wonders he had seen, which he did; it was rather a short letter as, on the day he went, much of the flying was rained off by the appalling Doncaster weather. But he also told her the interesting news that the Belgian flyer in question, Hélène Dutrieu, was going on to the Burton upon Trent aviation meeting and hoped to fly there – and even carry passengers . . .

'You've done enough for your mother these past months,' said Betty. 'It's your turn now.'

Della began that sunny September Wednesday by lying to her mother. She came downstairs fully dressed at first light, to find Mam nursing Cleo beside the kitchen range while Mrs Butters prepared breakfast and cooed over the baby. Betty hadn't been well yesterday, Della fibbed, and she wanted her great-niece to come and help her with the housework. She was to go before breakfast, in order to use the whole day. Mam told her how kind she was and Della blushed, with guilt, not pride. She had no idea when Mam would tell Pop, but assumed he would have sparse interest, apart from insisting she come home by a decent hour to help her mother with the evening meal.

Della cycled to the Dolly and met Betty and their fellow conspirator Mr Lidgard outside it. After his key role in the Cleo birth scene, Betty had revealed that Sam Lidgard had been a childhood friend of hers – and perhaps something more once upon a time, but no more details were forthcoming. It had become clear to Della that the widowed hotel owner still carried a torch for her aunt and looked for any excuse to do her a favour, of which this was the latest. All three were soon on the road to Burton, to Della's first aviation meeting, to see true aeroplanes fly – if the weather held – and behold that rarest of rare beasts, an aviatrix.

They arrived in the town on the Trent after lunchtime, having eaten along the way a haphazard picnic prepared by Betty. There was no problem in the fact that Mr Lidgard did not know the exact location of the show, as every man and his dog were heading in one direction and that was the show-ground itself. They left the automobile on a crowded side street and walked the rest of the way, following the throng under bunting strung across streets, with flags decorating the street furniture, limp in the sultry, windless air. Della kept her eyes on the skies, while boys and young men were seen sitting on roofs and walls drinking beer and eating pies, as if this were a normal occurrence in Burton. The impression was that nobody in town had a minute's work to do that day. Instead, everyone was sky-gazing.

'They must have called a half-day holiday,' said Betty, struggling on in her long, thick skirt, her face growing redder and shinier as the walk went on. 'I've never seen so many layabouts.'

As they approached a bridge, the crowds thickened to the point of deadlock, all craning their necks for a view of the flyers, while Mr Lidgard, who had secured three tickets for the event from a contact he had in Nottingham, lifted his hat and waved it before him as if swatting flies, not people, while calling out, 'Coming through! Ladies and a gent with tickets, coming through!' There was at one point a minor kerfuffle, when a keen boy tried to jostle Mr Lidgard and thereby relieve him of said tickets from his inside pocket, but the hotel owner was having none of it, and pushed the boy hard in the chest and used some ripe Cleethorpes insults on the Staffordshire lad.

In the heat of that moment, a sound arrested all movement as everyone threw back their heads, hands over eyes to shield them from the hot afternoon sun, at the rumbling whine of an engine approaching. And there, appearing from behind a gasometer, a great machine flew skyward. As the crowd around Della gasped, she heard herself gasp too, and it was if all breath had left her body, as if time were suspended, as the aircraft flew over them and the crowds turned as one to follow its progress, holding on to their hats and pointing.

'It's a Goupy biplane,' said Della.

'Yes!' answered Betty. 'The chassis looks like the bonnet of a motor car.'

The pilot, most definitely a man, and not Mlle Dutrieu, was boxed up in his seat behind the engine. Raising his hand to give a wave as he passed by, he was an aristocrat of the air. The crowd cheered again and, as one, raised their arms and waved excitedly back. Calls of 'Hallo, hallo!' rose from the people and more gasps issued as the aviator turned sharply with skill and grace, circling the aerodrome and heading back to its landing ground, disappearing behind the surrounding buildings. Della and Betty looked at each other, mouths and eyes wide open with delight, and laughed, clasped each other around the arms and shoulders and, lost for words, cried, 'Ha ha!'

Then, with renewed vitality, they pressed onwards and at last reached the entrance gate, where Mr Lidgard proffered their tickets, and then they were in, sanctioned and exclusive, the space around them slackening and the air buzzing with aviation fever.

To one side, Della saw rows of motor cars in an enclosure, drawn up to the boundary ropes, thus acting as a grandstand for the motorists who stood and sat in their leather seats. Itinerant musicians wandered through the crowds on squeezeboxes and penny whistles, collecting coins, while a band played a way off, their toots and trills riding on waves across the thick air and the hubbub of thousands of excitable spectators. The flying area was marked out by whitewash on large sections of the turf. The ground was bordered by the sparkling River Trent without and encircled within by white tented hangars. Before each one stood a flying machine, surrounded by lines of onlookers, dotted with umbrellas used as parasols, wide-brimmed ladies' hats and mostly flat caps for the men, heads and hats and excitable faces bobbing and swaying in a sea of gladness and gossip.

Mr Lidgard – 'Call me Samuel, dearie' – handed Della a programme and she read the List of Aviators, topped by number one: *Mademoiselle HÉLÈNE DUTRIEU (Farman Biplane)*. There were six other pilots, all male – Bruneau de Laborie, Paul de Lesseps, Julien Mamet and others – listed with their machine names in brackets: Blériot and Hanriot monoplanes, Goupy and Farman biplanes – a strange poetry with a hint of Gallic charm. Each name was followed by the colour of a pennant; Dutrieu's was to be white. Further down, it was explained, each aviator's pennant would be hoisted on the mast at the Judges' Box when about to fly and each machine itself would sport the same coloured pennant. Della scanned the crowd and spotted the flagpole; the pennant was black and white.

'Look, Auntie,' said Della, pointing to the programme. 'It says here that someone called L. Beaud is flying next. Let's find his hangar and his Farman, and watch him take off.'

But the engine was up and running and the biplane rolling forward by the time they got near and Monsieur Beaud was up in the air in a trice, maintaining a good speed and very low height, swooping over the heads of the spectators in a tremendous demonstration of low-flying, describing circles and figures of eight only perhaps thirty feet or so above the

ground. The crowd cried out and applauded as if at a fire-
works night and Della watched the whole display with her
hands clasped and held against her mouth to keep her heart
inside, as the flying was so spirited, so adept, so dangerous.

As Beaud turned towards the whitewashed turf to land,
he touched down neatly enough but further on than perhaps
he had planned, as he was soon in great danger of running
into the sparkling river beyond. But Beaud was not to be
fazed and athletically leapt out of his machine, sprinted ahead
and grabbed a strut, helped by a team of mechanics who
had predicted his problem and come running, and together
they slowed the progress of the machine and brought it to
a stop. The onlookers went wild, yelling and hooting and
clapping, as if the pilot's oversight had been an elaborate
part of the fun.

Della, Betty and Samuel strolled around the whole park,
consulting the programme and naming the aviators, Della
noticing characters she'd seen in Dud's *The Aero* magazine.
If only Dud were here, she thought. *How he'd love it!* And he'd
know every pilot by sight. There was Ladougne with his
gorgeous moustache, dressed in neat collared and buttoned
overalls, and the obligatory airman's flat cap turned backwards.
Here was Bruneau de Laborie, standing chatting nonchalantly
beside his Farman in homburg and monocle, fully suited with
waistcoat and high white collars, looking like a gent on his
way to the theatre, rather than one who would grapple with
the oily machine beside him. The aviators stood around a lot
and talked between flights, smoking and drinking the local
Bass beer, with an air of fairy dust surrounding them as if
their prowess in the skies was evidence of a deity; all eyes
were turned to the pilots and even the mechanics seemed to
stoop beside them.

But Della was impatient to see one person in particular, who
she had not glimpsed as yet; perhaps she was lounging in the
back of her marquee, not content to stand before the crowds

as the other aviators were. So Della and her companions waited beside Mlle Dutrieu's marquee and Della watched the entrance with a fierce gaze, willing the aviatrix to appear. Approaching teatime, Della saw Beaud appear from the hangar he shared with Dutrieu, and then behind him came a white woollen jersey, a white cap and there, a dark-eyed, dark-haired diminutive woman strode out and approached her machine. Hélène Dutrieu – variously described as the Human Arrow from her daredevil bike-racing days and the Girl Hawk from her latest career – was pint-sized and humble of face, not milking the crowd at all and quite the ordinary figure, standing near the Farman she shared with Beaud as if she were a shopgirl waiting for an omnibus home. Della stared and stared at her, as if by looking she could inherit the woman's skills and all at once take a seat in that beguiling biplane herself. Dutrieu's very ordinariness gave Della a thrill. *If she can do it*, thought Della . . .

Never the speaker, Della willed herself to say something but could only hold out her hand, which Dutrieu took firmly and shook once. She was about to turn away when Della spluttered, 'I want to fly!'

'*Je vous demande pardon?*' was the frowning reply.

'I want to fly, like you. I want to be an aviator.'

'Ah.' Dutrieu nodded. 'If you want very much, then it happens.'

Then with a quick *Merci*, she turned away and her head dipped as Beaud murmured to her and they went to the machine and were lost in their mechanical world, lost to Della who stood, mouth open, hat askew. That is how Betty found her when she came puffing, saying, 'Don't wander off, dear!' But Della was unresponsive; in her head, she was soaring away from them all.

Just then, one of the officials stepped forward and called for the crowd to give a special round of applause for the Girl

Hawk, and everyone who had heard him did. Then he made one more announcement: 'And now, our lady flyer will be taking up a passenger! Yes, that's right, a passenger, ladies and gentlemen!', after which he turned to speak to Dutrieu, but she had gone and the official adjusted his white cap and perused his fingernails to save face.

Della turned to her aunt, her face a picture of hopeless supplication.

'It'll be some local dignitary,' said Betty, as indeed the official asked an aide, 'Where is Lady Colwick?'

There was some low talking and shaking of heads. It appeared as if Lady Colwick, whoever she was, had been taken ill. Betty wasted no time but strode forward to the white-capped official and said, 'My niece is designing and building her own aeroplane. She would be the perfect passenger for Mademoiselle Dutrieu. What do you say?'

But the official was stiff-lipped and unimpressed, glancing back to see the aviatrix appear again from the marquee, approach her machine and look around for her passenger.

'If I may,' interjected Samuel, thrusting out his arm and shaking the official's limp hand, 'I am the manager of the Dolphin Hotel in Cleethorpes and you and any guest of your choosing would be welcome to stay at our establishment free of charge for a night or two –', at which Betty poked him in the side. He winced. ' – or a week? All beverages and bar meals provided?'

Della watched the official pat Samuel on the shoulder. She could've kissed Samuel! He was such a thoroughly good egg. The official strode over to the Girl Hawk and said, 'Mam'zel, here is your passenger. Miss . . . ?'

Della stumbled over and said, breathless, 'Dobbs. Miss Cordelia Dobbs.'

Dutrieu simply said, '*Allez!*'

She climbed on to the wooden shelf that served for a seat in the Farman biplane and gestured for Della to climb in behind. Della took one last view of her aunt and dear Samuel, who willed her onwards with their keen eyes. She took Dutrieu's offered hand and sat down. She was surrounded by wires pulled taut in all directions to keep the wings rigid. She stared at the controls over the pilot's shoulder and saw Dutrieu's hands pat them lightly, as if for luck.

Once the machine was readied and released, they rushed off across the field, bumpy and jolting. Della's left hand flew to her seat to grab on to it, a reflex that she knew would do little to protect her, but she had no choice in it. Her other hand was patting her chest, again involuntarily, as if it were comforting her for having put herself in this mad and dangerous position of sitting upon a flying box. In a trice the machine lifted and all resistance from the lumpen ground was gone and they were aloft, rushing towards the horizon. Della gazed down and the white faces of the onlookers shrank to dolls' heads; then the roads, bridges and railway tracks became a scrawled drawing upon the earth, as the machine climbed higher and higher, like a ship sailing upon the waves of the air.

Fear. It clutched at her chest. Like an alarm bell clamouring through her body: *get me out of this! Get me back down to earth!* The certainty that there was nothing to stop her falling out of the sky. Over and over in her mind a voice said, *Let it be over.* And the sharp taste of disappointment, that it wasn't stunning and awesome and all the things she'd wanted it to be. That it was her fault, that she had failed the test by being terrified. She wanted to cover her eyes, curl up in a ball until the nightmare was over. *Get me back down on the ground and I'll never do anything so bloody foolish ever again.*

She closed her eyes, yet she couldn't escape the rushing wind and deadly speed besetting her on all sides. But another voice came, the one that had been waiting for this for months, a deeper self that had been biding its time all her shy life. Instead, it said to her, *Open your eyes. Look around. Look left, look right. See where you are and what you are doing. You're here now. Don't squander it.* With her eyes open, she forced her head to turn about and see. The first thing that struck her was by focusing on the ground, she felt almost stationary. They were so high up that the ground was moving past as gradually as if they hung there in the sky. And then, something mysterious happened. Now that her body had had time to adjust, and the same for her mind, once she realised she wasn't going to drop from the air she was suffused with elation, streaming out of her fingertips and toes and hair and eyes and she just couldn't believe she was there, up, up, up, above the world. It was so beautiful, so beautiful!

Fear had dissolved, replaced by wonder. There were so many things she could see from the air that she couldn't have imagined on the ground. The serpentine pattern of tractor tracks in fields. Sheep like polka dots. Lakes as small as silver puddles that glittered like brooches, and as they passed over them, she watched the sky moving past in the mirror of water, as if looking through a high window. When the sun shone directly on the water, there was a blinding patch of white light, bordered by sprinkles like flour on the glaucous blue, a pleasing contrast to the green and beige countryside around it. The patches of water looked like a cut-out from the paper of the ground. Hedgerows bled across the dark lines of field boundaries in black fringes.

In fact, the world from the air revealed itself to be a jigsaw, completed by a great hand from above. Dark shapes blotted the perfect patchwork: the shadows of clouds. She saw that these cloud shapes and then the clumps of trees looked from this distance like almost identical obscure patches. Not easy for navigation. But what occurred to her most keenly was that the earth from up here was a map; that maps were simply what birds saw. How much easier it would be to find your way from here to there in the air than on the ground, blocked by obstacles. This was the way to travel, above the flattened,

still earth. But not all was static; something was rushing along
beneath them at precisely the same speed. Of course, it was
the tiny shadow of their aeroplane fleeting across the land,
their twin silhouette.

Looking up, she saw the clouds above sail past like galleons,
and thought how strong the wind must be up there to blow
them so hard. But, she realised sheepishly, they weren't rushing
over her, she was speeding below them. Further away, the
clouds hung over the land, beams of sunlight streaming down
between them like a luminous fan. It was even more exquisite
than she could have fathomed. She was shaken out of her
reverie by a sudden bump, turbulence in the warm air, at
which her pilot turned the craft back towards the airfield.

Focused entirely on the wonders around her, Della had
forgotten Dutrieu altogether. She concentrated now on the
aviatrix sitting before her, placid yet focused. The controls,
simple as they were, responded so delicately to Dutrieu's
touch. Della discerned some of the qualities that made for
good flying. It wasn't about strength, or power, or any manner
of fanatical bravery. It was about finesse, delicacy and calm-
ness. A daredevil would break wood sooner or later, but a
calm, methodical yet natural flyer – female or male – could
learn to charm the air.

The wind rushed all about them at every angle, as there
was no protection for aviators or their passengers, only a seat
and nothing to secure them apart from the air itself, whose
force held them pressed back against the machine. Despite
the summery day, the rushing air was cold and she shivered
in her jacket; yet she shivered too down her spine, knowing
this was her place, the only place for her was in the air. A
lifetime of awkwardness banished. The air was her element.

All too soon, Dutrieu pitched downwards and cut the engine,
the aeroplane gliding towards the whitewashed ground. The
world grew large and solid again as the machine met it, the
wheels hopping, the field sliding beneath them, the sound of

the applauding crowd filling the air, and Della knew she hated the ground as fiercely as must swifts and swallows, was nervous and unsure of it, wanted with every fibre of her being to swoop back up.

The aeroplane came to a stop and she climbed out, Dutrieu behind her. Della's legs were shaking, her body glad to be back on firm ground, a sense of relief to be down and of achievement that she'd done such an extraordinary thing. But the loudest voice in her mind was shouting, *Again, again!* The fear remained clear and stark in her, yet the joy of it was so overwhelming that she knew she would do anything it took to become a pilot and make the sky her home.

7

The beach at Filey was golden and broad, backed by brooding umber cliffs, striated by the wind and weather of ages, so different from the flat lands and estuary acres of shining wet sand and seabirds Della knew from home. It was quite a journey from Grimsby – Samuel drove Della and Betty to Hull, from where they took the train up the coast to Filey, followed by a horse-drawn omnibus to Primrose Valley, where the beach in question lay, and where, early that year of 1911, the Blackburn Flying School had established itself on the tow-coloured sands.

On arrival at the school mid-afternoon on a Friday in August, Della had not known what to expect. A flying school was an unknown quantity and she imagined a classroom and black-board for the instruction of aerodynamics, perhaps, something she had no aptitude for. She hoped it was more practical than theoretical skills they had in mind. To her surprise and delight, there was no such thing as a classroom, the only buildings being a hangar containing two Blackburn monoplanes and a low bungalow on higher ground. Della and Betty must have formed a quaint sight, negotiating the rocky path to the hangar in their long skirts, Della carrying their overnight bag. Indeed, a pair of fellows in greasy overalls appeared outside and watched them with amused expressions, one shaking his head. Della noticed and tried to steel herself for their reception – and the battle ahead. After flying with Dutrieu and seeing how delighted the Burton crowd were with the lady flyer, she had developed a false sense of the world's acceptance of female aviators. In fact, Betty had written to Mr Robert Blackburn's office soon after to request that her great-niece have a flying lesson or two, only to receive a curt dismissal from a clerk claiming (falsely, as it happened) that no school in England would be caught teaching girls to fly. Betty, a woman for whom the word no was always an invitation to fight, circumvented the clerk and instead wrote a colourful letter directly to Mr Robert Blackburn himself, citing her illustrious brother's career as a railway engineer, her niece's mechanical mind and their own experiments with box kites, upon which she received the brief directive to 'come up and see what we can do'. That was enough for Betty, and for Della, though Mam was uncertain and still smarting from having been lied to about Burton; but as ever with Mam, she was forgiving and any strife soon forgotten.

Pop, however, was a different matter. After the magical flight, the trio had begun their late drive home from Burton at dusk and by the border of Nottinghamshire the sky was dark and the Napier had broken down. They arrived home late afternoon the following day, after a stay in a south Lincolnshire guest house and with grimy hands from fixing the automobile, to a raging Pop grasping the morning telegram Betty had sent explaining their whereabouts. Della imagined he'd been apoplectic on receiving the news, but by the time she got home there was less wind in his sails. He threatened that she would be cut off without a penny if she continued to defy him; but Della knew the money was Broughton-made, so she wisely apologised and begged Pop's forgiveness to keep him sweeter, but made no resolution to change her ways, knowing too that Mam would give in to keep her child happy, always her way. It was wise to let the dog bark, but stay out of range of a bite, so one could carry on regardless.

So, here they were in Filey, standing before a handsome Blackburn monoplane, its white wings outstretched, its alloy panels gleaming in the sunshine. Della stared at it, wide-eyed and delighted to see in the flesh an English aeroplane, designed in England, built in England. *Just like me*, she thought. And such a beauty too – unlike herself, as she saw it; the kingpost above the fuselage crowned by a constellation of wires all stretched to their limit to hold the one wing as taut as the squarer design of the biplane. Monoplanes were lovelier, she felt, more like the birds they aspired to be, and she could not quite believe she stood beside one now, and if these dratted mechanics – one tall and one short, lending them a slightly ridiculous aspect – stopped shaking their heads and smirking, perhaps she would be allowed to fly in one. She left the talking to Betty.

'We were invited by Mr Blackburn himself,' said Betty, proffering the brief letter to one of the men, who would not look at it.

'Flying lessons only at dawn. Come back tomorrow.'

They couldn't argue with that and, to the sound of derisory laughter issuing from the hangar, the two women retraced their steps and set about finding a nearby hotel in which they could stay the night.

They returned the following morning, to be told there were no flying lessons at the weekend, so they took a walk and sat on a bench up on the cliff path watching the Blackburn make flights all that morning and the next, the same man as pilot each time, his head encased in leather flying helmet and goggles.

'It flies better than a Blériot,' said Della. She noticed it was more manoeuvrable and it could cope with the light winds there were that day, whereas it was said the Blériot was flummoxed by the slightest breeze. She was drinking it all in, ready for her chance inside it, if it ever came.

Monday morning, the women were there before the mechanics had arrived, ready and waiting in the darkness. The first to appear at the glimmer of dawn was the pilot himself – Della recognised his profile – who visibly jumped when Betty emerged from the dimness of the hangar and thrust out her hand.

'Are you the flying instructor here, sir?' she asked, shaking his uncertain hand with gusto.

Della appeared from behind her and the pilot squinted at her in the faint light.

'I am. Benny Hucks, though people call me B.C. Pleasure to meet you. And your . . . daughter?'

He's thinking, granddaughter, but he's too polite, thought Della, herself too tongue-tied to speak, as being in the presence of aviators still caught her star-struck. His hair was parted neatly in the middle and his flying jacket was tan and belted at the waist, his trousers conclusively creased. Everything about him spoke of precision. Betty put Blackburn's letter in his hand, brooking no refusal for her great-niece this time, and the instructor Hucks eyed Della briefly before saying, 'Well if Mr B. says yes, so do I.'

The women both grinned, Betty clapping her hands before retrieving the letter from Mr Hucks.

'This machine is not ideal for teaching,' he said, 'as it's only one seat, but I can let the young lady sit in the cockpit and feel the controls. I think that would be a good start.'

'Yes, please!' enthused Betty and turned to Della. 'Come on, dearie.'

The early light grew as the sun rose, spreading a rosy glow reflected in the monoplane's alloy panels, casting it in a feminine light. Hucks wheeled out a set of steps and set them up beside the aeroplane, then unbolted a strip of wood that lay across the cockpit, and lifted it up ready for an inhabitant. He gave Della's figure the once-over and said, 'Good. Glad to see you've sensible shoes on.'

'She's sensible inside and out,' said Betty.

Hucks held his hand out to Della, who took it firmly and ascended the steps. She wished again for a less female mode of dress – how easy the step into the cockpit must be with trousers on! – as she hitched her linen skirt higher to allow her right foot to plant itself firmly on the seat, a rounded metal shelf that looked like an adapted bucket. With some difficulty, and thanking Providence for giving her short legs and a narrow behind, her left foot joined her right in standing on the seat and then, knees bent, she wriggled herself down to a seated position.

'What's your Christian name, Miss?' asked Hucks, standing beside her halfway up the steps, their faces level.

She said it, low and quiet, and he had to ask her again. 'Cordelia,' she said louder and looked at him this time, his round face quizzical, a trim moustache above an amused mouth. He lowered his head and whispered, 'Perhaps it's your great-aunt's wish to fly, is it? Are you just along for the trip?'

'Oh no!' said Della clearly. 'Not at all. I flew with Hélène Dutrieu at the Burton Aviation Meeting.'

Hucks's eyebrows jumped and he said, still with that little smile, 'Did you, now!'

'Yes, as a passenger, I mean. And I read *The Aero* and we're designing our own aeroplane. I want more than anything to be an aviator. I mean, an aviatrix.'

'So, you *can* talk, when you're on the right subject, eh?' said Hucks, lowering the wooden spar across her as he spoke and bolting it into place. 'That keeps the aeroplane together. Now, eyes front.'

She looked up and took in the range of controls. Her hands rested on a narrow wooden wheel that was mounted on a stick, connected to a bar across the cockpit. Before her was a wooden board, fitted with three mysterious instruments.

'Right, the controls first. The thing is with aeroplanes, they're different from autos on the road. More like fish underwater, moving in three axes. There's pitch – nose up and down. There's yaw – turn left or right on the horizontal. And roll – wings down one side, up the other. So you need controls for all three. Here, the wheel pitches like this – you lower it or raise it, to move the elevators at the back, see, on the tail? And the nose will go down or up. Next, rotate the wheel left or right, you get a roll left or right – look at the wings. They warp up or down to roll the aeroplane. Now then, if you move the whole wheel left or right, that's your yaw control. It's a new idea this, putting all the controls in the wheel, instead of having a rudder pedal. Blackburn calls it the three-axis control system, all of the aircraft's move-ment in one place. Simple as that. Pitch, wheel up or down. Roll, wheel twists left or right. Yaw, shift the whole wheel sideways. Got it?'

She nodded resolutely. She pulled the wheel up, pushed it down, heard the elevators click at the back. She turned the wheel right, saw the right wing's trailing edge warp up and the left wing's warp down. She saw that the aeroplane would turn towards the up-going wing, as that was producing the least lift. She shifted the wheel to the left and turned round to watch the vertical rudder flap on the tail's fin turn towards her back on the left. She pictured herself yawing that way, in a blue sky, the clouds above, the sea below. If only she were up there now.

During this explanation, Della heard Betty greeting someone behind them. The two mechanics had arrived. One glance confirmed her fears that they were not pleased to see them.

'Best get on, B.C.,' called one of the mechanics to Hucks. 'Lot of work to do.'

'All right, chaps,' Hucks called cheerfully back. 'Time to step down, Cordelia.'

He took her hand and she reluctantly climbed out, back onto the blasted ground. It was a wrench to leave the Blackburn. It felt like home there. Della noticed a mechanic shaking his head, grumbling.

She turned to Hucks and held out her hand, which he shook good-naturedly. 'Thank you, Mr Hucks. When can I start my flying lessons?'

A guffaw came from the hangar. A voice said, 'The Wrights had it right. A woman with wings is a dangerous thing.'

Hucks laughed, but glimpsed Della's serious countenance and corrected his face. 'Ignore them. They're only joshing.'

Doubtful, thought Della.

'Listen,' Hucks went on, 'I believe we're getting a two-seater next month, beginning of September. Why don't you come back then?'

Della looked at Betty, who was scowling towards the hangar but turned her face all sweetness and light to the congenial pilot who had helped them. 'Mr Hucks, you have been a true gentleman and we will never forget that. Thank you.'

He amiably shook hands with them both, then walked into the hangar. Della and Betty heard more laughter from there as they took their leave, though both hoped it was the dastardly mechanics who mocked them, not Mr B.C. Hucks.

Early in September, a letter came from Dudley:

Dear Della. Life goes on here as usual. I'm writing from school as usual. You don't know how fortunate you are to have left school early and spend your time at home. I dream of that, I really do! But my father would never hear of it, of course. He tells me nobody from my station in life could leave school aged only 13 (which sounds like rot to me and I'd rather fling 'my station' to the winds if that's what it brings me!) He says I must be properly educated in order to go on to study textiles at university and take over his business. It is a fine business, I'm sure. I will grow into it, I suppose. But school must be endured first. Boarding is all rather horrible and the boys can be rotten, bullying and beating and so forth. I'm sure you don't want the grisly details. Suffice to say, it's all a bit miserable. The only good thing is the horses. They have horses here and yours truly is allowed to tend them and ride them every weekend during term time. I'd be there every moment if I could. Something about a horse is peaceful.

Anyway, enough of me. There is aviation news we must discuss and I'd honestly rather write about flying than anything else. Your Mr Hucks made a bid for the Daily Mail *Circuit of Britain contest last month, but sadly had to retire early. Shame. But he sounds like a ripping flyer. Terrific for you that he's your teacher. Also, you must know by now I think that the first English woman has gained her pilot's licence! It said in the newspaper that she was married to Maurice Hewlett, who writes novels. It didn't give her name. Mrs Hewlett, I presume! At last, women take to the air. It's an open road for you now, Della! Or rather, open skies.*

Della hadn't known that and the news was momentous. For her to hear that a woman had now officially learned to fly and been sanctioned by the Royal Aero Club itself was stunning news and spurred her onwards with greater passion than ever. She told Pop, who merely said, 'They do not even give her name.' *Surely the newspaper's fault, not hers,* thought Della and shrugged off Pop's disdain. Betty of course was delighted: 'She's the first. Let's make you the second.'

The next week, up they went again to Filey and watched the mechanics – there earlier this time – laughing at them as they approached the hangar at dawn. Hucks had been right – a brand new Blackburn stood before them, with two seats. The pilot appeared, face indistinct against the burgeoning light.

'Mr Hucks?' called Betty as they came closer.

The pilot looked up.

'Not Hucks,' he said. 'He's moved on. I'm Oxley. What's it concerning?'

'Benny's got one of 'em in the family way,' quipped the taller mechanic, whose partner fell about laughing and added, 'Both of 'em!', at which Oxley chortled too. The two women stood, waiting for the laughter to subside, still, calm, backs straight. Then Betty spoke: 'Are you the Chief Flying Instructor of the Blackburn Flying School?'

'I am. Hubert Oxley, madam. And who might you be?'

He was a young man, in his mid-twenties perhaps, dapper. The way he stood, his subtle swagger, spoke of the conceit of youth and manhood. Della wished him away, to be replaced by their amiable Hucks. But Hucks was not here and Oxley was, and even a superior swaggerer like this was not going to stand in her way, not now they'd come so far and the two-seater Blackburn stood before them, waiting for her to step in.

'My name is Cordelia Dobbs,' she spoke up, cutting off Betty who was about to do the honours. Others had spoken for her before, many times, all her life. Now she was ready to speak for herself. 'I know how aeroplanes fly. I have been a passenger at Burton upon Trent with the Girl Hawk, Mademoiselle Hélène Dutrieu. I am designing my own machine, with my great-aunt here, sister of the great railway engineer Alfred Broughton. Mr B.C. Hucks has talked me through the controls, so I understand how they work. I wish to learn to fly here at Filey on a Blackburn aeroplane. Our money is as good as the next man's and we have enough to pay for four lessons, agreed by letter from Mr Robert Blackburn himself. So, if you would inform us if today is a good day to fly, I would like to begin.'

Never had she heard herself speak this way. During the whole speech, she stood outside herself, watching a refined and confident young woman addressing the world. She looked taller to herself, she felt taller. Her ambition had given her inches. She felt she could leap into the air right then and fly with her own wings.

No laughter ensued from the hangar. Oxley stood, hands on hips, his smirk removed. 'All right, then,' he said. 'Let's get started.' He called to the mechanics to get her ready, meaning the Blackburn, and pointed out the passenger seat, into which Della climbed. He was in front, her behind.

In minutes they were up in the air, high above the amber sands below, the gulls wheeling ahead watchful of the machine in their element. But Della saw none of this, intent as she was on the controls before her. They were connected to Oxley's, so she watched them move of their own accord, as if manipulated by a ghost. She watched the wheel turn and the aeroplane answer, banking, climbing, now diving and up, up again. Oxley was very adept, every movement sure and confident, though once, as he began his dive, the air rushing and pressing hard on the back of her head, she looked over the side to see the sea come hurtling towards them until he pulled up and banked into a turn, and she wondered if the man were careful enough to be a teacher. She decided there was no choice – Oxley it was and there was no other; and oh my, he was a super flyer.

That first lesson he took her up twice, speaking on the ground in between, explaining the vagaries of turning. 'In the early days,' he said, as if Blériot's cross-Channel feat had been two decades ago, not two years, 'pilots would turn with the rudder. Many still do. They yaw right or left with the rudder. But that's a hangover from boating, just like the wheel there. Should be a stick really, much better than a wheel, more manoeuvrable. And a rudder bar for the feet would be better than this three-axis wheel. Perhaps Blackburn will alter it for the next model. Anyway, what I do is bank into a turn – use the wing-warping – have you ever cycled?'

'Yes and I repair cycles too. And I race them,' she added. 'On my own.'

But Oxley did not laugh at her, instead going on, 'Then, you know exactly what I mean. When you want to turn a corner on a bicycle, you lean into it. It's the same with an aeroplane. Bank into the turn, don't just do it with yaw, use the wings, then add a bit of yaw and pitch up the nose a little, just to keep it balanced. You see?'

Everything he said she understood, first time, as if he spoke her mother tongue, as if she had lived all these years in a foreign land, and only now was she home.

She was eager to jump into his seat and try it for herself, but he said it must be next time. She thanked him and went to Betty, who clasped her hands between her own, chucked her cheek and beamed. On the train back to Hull, Betty said, 'I'm getting too old for all this travelling, Della. You can come by yourself next time.'

Della was startled at the thought and frowned at her great-aunt. Betty patted her knee. 'You don't need me any more, dearie. You don't need anyone, only your aeroplane, the sky and the wind. You're an aviatrix now.'

Della came for three more lessons with Oxley, each time being allowed only to observe. She enjoyed the flights, yet became impatient to take the controls – it was a long journey to Filey just to sit and watch – but he told her she could take his seat if she paid for more lessons after Christmas. In December, her aunt showed her an article from a Yorkshire newspaper, sent to them both from Bradford by Dudley. It was a short piece, giving scant details, just saying that on the sixth of the month, two Yorkshire airmen flying in a Leeds-built double-seated Blackburn monoplane had been dashed upon the sands at Filey; the pilot was thrown from the aeroplane, landed on his head, broke his neck and died instantly. The passenger was pinned beneath the wrecked machine and died of his injuries within an hour; he was a Mr Robert Weiss of Dewsbury. The pilot's name was Mr Hubert Oxley.

8

By September of 1912, the Blackburn Flying School had decamped to Hendon, down south. Della read about the new airfield there; it was built by the dashing aviator Claude Grahame-White and anybody who was somebody in aviation was flying at Hendon now. They also had a flying school and gave lessons: fifty guineas for tuition on a monoplane or biplane; seventy-five guineas for both.

'My finances are such,' said Betty to Della, 'that I could manage the fee. But you'd have to find lodgings, get yourself a job and pay for your upkeep. Talk to your mam first. See what she says.'

Della had not told her mother about Oxley's death. How could she? Della had heard of aviator accidents and even deaths – they were alarmingly common – but the death of an aviator she had actually met changed her, made her fearful. For months, almost a year, she'd stopped all talk of more lessons; she tinkered with aeroplane designs at her aunt's kitchen table from time to time, but that was all. Instead, she immersed herself in Cleo growing and changing. Her youngest sister rarely slept for long and from her earliest days treated the traditional infantile amusements of dummies and jangling keys as beneath contempt, instead demanding human interaction and babbling constantly. Della carried her around on one arm, *The Aero* magazine in the other, trying to read, reading it to Cleo sometimes, just so she could do both at once without her younger sister revolting. By the age of two and a half, Cleo's devotion to Della was almost as complete

as that to her mother and, in fact, her first word was DehDeh
– for Della not Dada – though Mam came next and Pop
down the line, after Bubba for Mrs Butters. She played
endlessly with Cleo, taking her for walks on the beach, and
as Cleo had turned from baby to small person, with unruly
dark hair that never succumbed to the comb and small, active
eyes that saw everything, they spent hours planting seeds in
soil and making salt-dough for modelling.

All of this time taken up with her sister pushed to the side
of Della's mind the ever-present thoughts of flying, the dreams
of designing her own aeroplane, of building it, and beyond
that, taking it into the air. Every time she thought of flying
it, or any other machine, she saw Oxley's head crunching into
the Filey mud and it haunted her, his smashed body, the
moment he must have known, before impact, what his fate
would be, the sand rushing towards his face, the knowledge
of cold, wet death about to strike you, life gone just like that.
All to fly a machine through the air, to ape the birds but fail,
stupidly, head first, in a flash of clumsy, idiotic hubris.

Then one day, Dud sent her an article from *The Aero*, where
Blackburn himself gave the verdict that it was pilot error. Della
felt this must be true, believed she'd seen it in Oxley, his love
of diving, that daredevil streak. And understanding why it had
occurred gave her confidence to carry on. She had come to
realise that flying was not about blind courage, but instead was
about risk, assessing it, approaching it logically. She knew she
was living through the age of aviation and any new age needed
its pioneers. And pioneers are learning on the job and thus will
make mistakes. And they might pay with bones and blood and
their lives. Anyone who is prepared to push the boundaries has
to accept that they may well die. So, she realised, once she
made her peace with that, then she could fly and not be crip-
pled by fear. It was about knowing your machine inside out,
about trusting your hands and feet, your body and your eyes,
and, just as that early lesson from Betty had taught her, being

on intimate terms with the air. All that, and in April that year
of 1912, Harriet Quimby, the American aviatrix, crossed the
Channel in a Blériot monoplane, the first woman to do so.
Della's hunger to fly was rekindled. If Hendon was the best
place to learn, then to Hendon she would go.

But first, she must march up to the cannon's mouth and
have it out with Pop.

'I would forbid you to go, Cordelia. But I see that you are
intent on this foolish course of action. What can you possibly
hope to gain by learning to fly these machines?'

Della stood before her father as he sat in his throne before
his desk, the rough sea beyond thrashing about, distracting
her eye but not her intent, which was iron. *You might forbid
me to go*, she thought, *but it's Broughton money that'll pay for
it, so it's not really your decision, Pop.* She'd never say that,
though. No point in poking the lion.

'I'm good at it,' she said simply.

'But how do you know that? Your mother tells me you
haven't even flown solo yet. How can you leave your home,
your family, on a whim?'

'It's not a whim. It's going to be my career.'

'A woman cannot make a living at such a thing. We are not
rich, we cannot afford to indulge in expensive hobbies. What
on earth possesses you, child?'

'It's the one thing I know I can do well, really well. I've
always learned by doing, not reading. It's a very practical
thing, flying. You have to be observant, good with your hands.
And you're mostly on your own. It suits me.'

'But there are scores of other activities one could say that
of, such as gardening, or cooking, or even throwing a pot or
painting. Something artistic, like Miranda, or even look to
marriage and children, like Gertrude. Something on the ground
at least, for heaven's sake, where you mustn't rely on damned
machines. You can't trust them, Della. Why can't you choose
something . . . safe?'

In his face there was something tender, a glimpse of the
Pop she'd known as a little girl, before his accident, before
they'd lost him. She was accustomed to his anger now, his
fits of temper, his negative and unreasonable stance on anything
that gave her joy. But his look now told her he did care, he
wanted to protect her. Perhaps he was not a tyrant, but simply
the most misunderstood man in the world.

'I'm at home there, in the machine. It's not alien to me.
It's like . . .'

Della hesitated, intent on proving her point. She knew what
she wanted to say, but feared Pop's stern countenance. Yet
her ambition spurred her on and she said it: 'Didn't you feel
like that on stage, Pop? Like it was your home?'

Pop's eyes clouded, he turned his face away and stared at
the sea beyond. An acre of silence stretched out between
them. Della waited – had she gone too far, saying that,
reminding him of his loss? But it was the only way to make
him understand. After a long time, he simply said, 'Go, if you
must.' But he would not look at her and he did not say
goodbye.

Mam had written to Della's elder sister Miranda – known
to everyone but Pop as Midge – living now in Clapham, the
successful actress with her own lodgings. Having left home
so many years ago and barely returned, Della's sister was a
mystery, an alluring one. But there was a note of envy in
there too, that Pop was so proud of Midge's theatrical success,
following in his own footsteps. Della wondered if they'd get
on, the two sisters, so different from each other, or even if
Midge would agree; Della imagined the flamboyant actress
might find her little sister lodging with her a bit of a bore.
But Midge did agree, replying that of course Della could stay
with her, though a settee would be her bed, if that suited. It
did suit Della – a wigwam would suit if it meant she could
fly – and by January 1913, she was kissing Mam goodbye and
trying to stop her own tears at the sight of her mother's

coursing down her cheeks, and the thought of leaving the elfin Cleo, about to turn three years old, was almost more than she could bear. But aviation called and Della's will to fly was stronger than almost anything else, even her mother's tears or Cleo's hot grip on her hand.

Midge's place was a flat in a well-kept house overlooking Clapham Common. Another actress occupied the downstairs and Midge the first floor, where a balcony painted white jutted out over the street. Here Midge would sit and smoke after shows. Her life on the stage appeared to Della unbearably glamorous. The sisters had not spent time alone together since Midge left nine years before, off to stage school aged fifteen and then on to her blossoming theatre career in London two years later. Now she lived alone, a New Woman with an independent income, answering to no one, except her cadaverous landlady, Mrs B. (Della never learned her full name). Della was timid with Midge, perplexed that Pop had such respect for this daughter when she was defiantly female and independent, and yet for herself wanting to forge her own path, he had nothing but disdain. Seeing Midge again, striding along the platform at St Pancras, a broad-brimmed fashionable hat upon her coiffed hair and sleek monochrome coat cinched at the waist, Della recognised with a shock how much Midge resembled Pop – those large, alluring eyes, coffee-brown hair and inner confidence brimming over every step; or how her father once was, at any rate.

'Oh, Della, darling. All grown up. Look at you.' Midge spoke in blunt phrases, her voice low and certain. After a brisk hug and cheek-kissing and arms linked, they travelled by omnibus back to Clapham and the red-brick terraced house with the black railings around a neat front garden. Midge talked most of the way, entirely about herself without stopping to ask a thing about Della; she rattled on divertingly about her theatrical friends, her writer friends and her artist friends, the conceited wash of words bathing Della in nostalgic comfort as they were shoved up against each other on the omnibus seat, just like they used to snuggle in their childhood bed.

'I don't know anyone who flies,' said Midge. 'To think of Pop. His youngest gal a pilot. Ha! He must've given you the full King Lear!'

'He's so sad,' said Della.

Midge pursed her lips and gazed off into the middle distance, studiously pensive.

'Yes. We'll think on that. Something needs to snap him out of it. Will Cleo do it, do you think?'

Della smiled. 'Maybe so.'

One thing made settling into Midge's place infinitely easier than living at home: her father's despair was not hanging over it. The weight lifted from her was a physical release, as well as a mental one. It reminded her of those weeks spent at Betty's when Puck was ill, which comforted her further and made Midge's place have the scent of home, somehow, yet without the oppression of Pop's moods seeking out every corner, stifling joy. For Della, this was always followed by a dull twinge of guilt, that she shouldn't resent his moods, his anger, as he had suffered, he had lost so much. But she felt other people's misery was tiring when it was endless, however sympathetic she intended to be. And on the rare occasions he'd look her in the eye, there was often accusation in his stare, that she was fit and able, she was able to be happy, and then her guilt would be muddied with reproach, which made her feel more guilt still. At home, Della would be laughing with Mam and Mrs Butters in the kitchen about something silly, and Pop would call out from his study, and all light would vanish from the room. Like walking under a thundercloud. Well, now the sun had come out.

First things first, Della asked Midge's coiffeur to chop all her hair off. The hairdresser wouldn't go that far, but he did cut it down from long Victorian tresses wound in a constantly unwinding bun to something just brushing the shoulders, something thinned out and light, that she could tuck behind her ears and not bother with. The weight all gone induced an intense feeling of liberation. She'd wished she'd done it years before. Pop wouldn't be pleased, but who cared about that now? She was in London and she was free to follow her own course. Indeed, she went back a week later and asked to have another two inches off. The air around her neck was delicious. She felt ready for anything now.

The Hendon season began in February and stretched to November, so her aunt had signed her up for lessons to begin in a month, at the end of February 1913. Before that, Della had to start earning her way. Midge had explained by letter that she had found Della a position in the box office of the New Royalty Theatre in Dean Street, Soho. She was a girl-of-all-work there, selling tickets and also bringing food, drink and messages for the actors, sweeping the stage, finding props and so forth. Sometimes, she would sit in the wings and observe the action. Here all was artificiality, black shadows and coloured lights, the dark unreality of the theatre; up there in an aeroplane it was the blue escape of the skies. Polar opposites, which underscored the differences between herself and her father the actor more keenly than ever. Yet, she thought of Pop, his forsaken career, and she found a spark of pity kindling for him. For herself, she couldn't think of much worse than being an actor, the anathema of everything she was and wanted, but for Pop it once was everything and she pitied him its loss. If someone said, You can't fly, you'll never fly . . . She shuddered and willed that day never to come. Watching the handsome players strut about and make their pronouncements under the inspection of the crowd, she knew the stage might be her idea of hell, but the rest of the theatre was fun to be in and to exist on the periphery of, as she was accustomed to in life. It was a lively job with lively people,

yet where she hardly needed to talk, which suited her well.
The only drawback was the late nights, as she would need to
be at Hendon early for flying lessons. So she planned a system
whereby she could sleep in the afternoon, work all evening,
a few hours' nap in the night, then on the early train straight
to Hendon first thing. Only a driven person could keep this
up, or rather only a driven *young* person. Her youthful energy
was her best ally and she hoped it would hold out. It simply
must, she told herself, and let that be an end to it. She was
too young to understand the optimism of youth and in her
first week found herself yawning all day such that it was like
a yawning disease, but the walk to Clapham station for the
journey to Hendon that first time was bracing and cured the
disease, temporarily.

Hendon village had a pretty aspect, with the Burroughs
Pond at the centre. The approach to the aerodrome was that
of a country road called Colindale Avenue, muddy and
potholed, which one walked along comfortably enjoying the
rural aspect of farmers' fields and acres of pasture stretching
out on either side, bounded on one side by a railway embankment. Hedgerows haphazardly bordered fields dotted with
trees and cows. Before long, the airfield grew on the horizon,
the hangars bobbing into view and the famous Hendon pylons
she'd read about – conical towers of alternating dark and
light wood topped with a T-shaped structure upon which
signals would be hoisted indicating flyers and progress on
race days. An unfeasibly tall ladder rested against each pylon.
The grounds were surrounded by white railings, barbed wire
was strung along the outer paling and tall wooden fences
surrounded the enclosure. There were rows of hangars with
pointy white roofs, the nearest of which was emblazoned
with the name GRAHAME-WHITE, in case you didn't know
the star of the show. Before this were large huts fronted by
pavilions with stepped seating for race days. Nearest to the
airfield was a building bounded by balconies on the ground

and first floor with steps up to a lookout post surrounded
by flags and topped with two signs:

EVENT NO. and STARTERS.

The airfield itself was oval and looked to be around two
miles in circumference. The contrast with Blackburn's solitary
hangar at Filey was sharp. Clearly, this was the cutting edge
of aviation.

At the entrance gate, she gave her name to a supercilious
middle-aged man, who looked through his list and shook his
head.

'There's no Cordelia Dobbs listed here. There's a Cornelius
Dobbs, but no Cordelia.'

'That's me – rather, there has been a misunderstanding.
Regarding my name. But that is me.'

Della wondered if the name change was a deliberate ploy
on her aunt's part to ensure Della's acceptance for lessons. *I
wouldn't put it past her*, thought Della, and smiled at the clerk
who, after harrumphing and complaining, could not think of
a sound reason not to allow the young woman to pass, so did
so, begrudgingly. He motioned towards the row of hangars
and said, 'The first hangar. Mr Grahame-White is there.'

She approached the wooden-walled hangar, its open front
allowing her to see that it was cluttered with aircraft paraphernalia: parts of dismantled aircraft scattered here and there,
including wheels, fuel tanks, rolls of linen, wing frames, skids,
propellers, tail planes, rudder bars. Around ten men and some
boys were there, flat caps, dressed in overalls, some with
scarves against the chilly early-morning air. All turned when
she walked in, stopped what they were doing, stood still and
stared.

Della had to steel herself. Her heart was strong with the
ambition for flight but her mouth was dry with shyness.
Nobody spoke, just stared. One boy, losing interest, turned

back to his work wiping oil from a sheet of linen, but the men stared on.

'Is Mr Grahame-White here?'

'Stepped out,' said a gruff voice, though she could not say which mouth beneath heavy moustache had said it. They all looked alike to her.

'Will he be back presently?'

'Hangar Three,' said another voice and Della took her leave, grateful to escape the male gaze. A smattering of laughter and murmuring followed her, yet she was accustomed to this now and it hurt her feelings less each time she heard it. She realised that, despite her nerves, she was slowly becoming immune to ridicule.

She walked purposefully past the second hangar, seeing on her way a Farman biplane waiting patiently for its next flight. Beyond, the line of hangars revealed glimpses of other aircraft nosing out of each hangar entrance into the cool air: a Deperdussin, a Blériot. She knew them by sight, even from a glimpse of the nose. Those hours of reading *The Aero* had paid off. She felt like an expert in her field, though it was mostly theoretical. Now, today, this moment, she would be tested to see if her practice could live up to her theory. She found herself crossing her fingers in a throwback to childish pleas to whichever god would listen, the god of playgrounds or fairgrounds or having cake for tea, and she willed herself to be lucky today, to take to flying as she hoped to. To return home, tail between her legs, Pop's smug righteousness flung in her face – it was more than she could bear. She simply must succeed.

At the front of the third hangar sat a curious contrivance: a Blériot-shaped aircraft, yet the wings were far too short. They looked mutilated and could never fly. Beside it stood a tall man, dark hair slicked back from brooding eyebrows, a long nose and full mouth. He was dressed in an all-in-one flying suit, large buttons down the front and white collar poking out around his strong neck. He held a chequered cap, which he slid onto his head as she approached, the peak backwards so it cast no shadow on his face. And that face, so impossibly handsome that Della thought she might be sick.

He looked up at her and frowned, clearly expecting Cornelius but suspecting Della, so she impelled herself to speak to this apparition, her tongue a dead jellyfish on the beach of her mouth.

'Mr Grahame-White?'

'That's right,' he said, jovial and curious, 'and you are . . . ?'

'Miss Dobbs. There was a mistake. Cornelius.'

'My name's Claude, not Cornelius.'

'I know. I mean, I'm not.'

'Not what?' He was smiling at her. He was enjoying this.

'I'm not . . . a man.'

'I can see that.'

'I have paid for a series of lessons. May we begin?'

Grahame-White's expression switched from amusement to testiness.

'Miss Dobbs. I run a busy, thriving business here. I don't make time for timewasters. Did someone put you up to this? You don't have a chaperone or anyone to recommend you. Are you certain you know what you're doing?'

Della stared at him. Was that a refusal? Was this an interview? She felt she must say something, or he'd send her away forthwith.

'Please sir, let me assure you that I am very serious about learning to fly.'

He observed her, frowning, as if assessing her and finding her wanting. 'But you are a woman, Miss Dobbs. And I'm afraid I'm yet to be convinced that the air is the place for a woman.'

She swallowed her nerves and began to speak on a subject – that of women's fitness to fly – that engaged her mind and her tongue like no other: 'I believe that women are nimble in the way they move and think, as much as any man. Perhaps more so. Also, we can take it when we're told we're making mistakes. And you don't have to be strong to fly a plane, not in your body anyway.'

He was not frowning so much now and he had unfolded his arms, that had been crossed across his chest, so his hands were on his hips. 'I will admit to you that a good friend of mine, the journalist Mr Harry Harper, is a rare champion of women in aviation, and after much discussion, he has swayed me somewhat.'

Seeing his softer demeanour, Della tried another tack: 'And women are safer by nature than men, surely? We don't have that foolhardy, daring streak so common in a man. And you could say, a woman's body has extra padding against the cold.'

Grahame-White laughed – just as Della hoped he would – and replied, 'Look, it is the case that I have agreed to women being taught here at Hendon. But I must warn you, many of my colleagues actively despise the idea of women flyers and you must run that gauntlet if you wish to achieve your pilot's licence. For some, it is perhaps a misplaced chivalry, that does not wish to see a lady put in danger's path. For others, it is a deep belief that a woman's mind and body are too feeble to acquire the necessary skills for aviation. But I've been persuaded by Harry that indeed the woman's temperament is possibly most likely to have prudence, which the man who is in a hurry does not possess and which will be his downfall. As long as women stick to aerodrome flying and do not attempt the rigours of cross-country flying, I think we can say that a woman – suitably skilled and qualified – may fly at Hendon.'

Della thought he was a bit pompous, pontificating like that, but at the same time her excitement grew at being spoken to seriously by this hero of aviation and she grinned, biting her lip. Grahame-White noticed and his face softened.

'Got the flying bug, haven't you,' he stated.

'I do, I mean, I have. I read everything, sir. I've flown in a Farman with Dutrieu. I met Hucks at Filey and he showed me the controls of a Blackburn. I flew as a passenger in a two-seater Blackburn with Oxley, several times, before . . . uh, before he . . .'

'Yes, a bad business, that. Well, it happens. But you know, in many cases, it needn't have happened at all.'

'Why is that, sir?'

Grahame-White gave a small smile, regarded the serious young face, then went on, 'You can dispense with the "sir", you know.'

'As you wish,' replied Della, meekly.

'As I was saying, there are undoubtedly accidents in this flying business. Of course, we are dealing with machines and machines can malfunction. But what I've learned is that more often than not, it is the pilot's character that can cause an accident. On the technical side, he must be able to judge speed and distance accurately. Any man who drives a motor car well has made a good start. Do you drive, Miss Dobbs?'

'No.'

'Do you ride horses?'

Only the donkeys on Cleethorpes beach, she thought, though didn't voice this ridiculous image.

'No. But I do cycle. I race my cycle – only against myself – but I can cycle very fast. And I can fix bicycles. I fix them for everyone in my neighbourhood.'

'That's good to hear. Cycling is almost as useful as horse-manship, for a budding pilot.'

What horses had to do with aeroplanes, she couldn't gauge, but he went on: 'All of these things are useful for the physical experience of flying and manoeuvring an aero-plane. But the most essential, I believe, is the disposition of an airman, his essential character. In flying, one finds two sorts of airmen: one careful and the other impatient. A good pilot needs a certain amount of dash, but a great one must be cautious. Up there, the smallest mistake could be the end of you.'

Della thought of Oxley, certainly a man with 'dash', diving without caution and landing on his head.

'I believe that is what caused Mr Oxley's death.'

'I agree with you. So, what type are you, Miss Dobbs? Though I think I can guess, by your demeanour.'

'I believe I am methodical and thorough in everything I do. I have a capacity for action and a good memory for details. I have quick hands and eyes.'

'Miss Dobbs, let me make myself absolutely clear. I have taught many women to fly and I regret it. My experience has shown me that the air is no place for women. If any of my female pupils get into bother in the air, and when they panic as they are wont to do, I would feel personally to blame if anything tragic should happen to them. And that is not something I wish to live with.'

Della swallowed her nerves and answered him, 'Mr Grahame-White, I love flying and I love everything concerning flying and aviation, from the wood to the linen to the air itself. But I'm not reckless. I value my life. If my life were over, I could not fly any more. And I live for flying.'

Grahame-White considered, holding her future in his gaze. Then he held out his hand. 'Then, you must climb aboard, Miss Dobbs, and let's get you started. This is a Blériot trainer. As you can see from the wings, it cannot fly, yet we use it to train novices so that they become accustomed to the controls and to taxi around the airfield to practise turns and suchlike. We will use a standard aircraft to take passenger flights, and only once both stages have been completed to my satisfaction will a pupil find he is allowed to go anywhere near the controls of an aircraft and hope to fly one.'

Della stepped up into the trainer, his hand firmly guiding her. Once seated, she thought of Dutrieu, the fine movements with which she steered her aircraft, and thought perhaps the woman's body – as well as her mind – might be more suited to flying. After all, a tall man's huge clumping feet on the rudder bar might be too heavy, while her own petite feet, nestling now on the wooden bar, must be capable of more finesse than that. *Yes*, she thought, seated and snug in the Blériot, *this could have been made for a woman. This is where a woman should be*.

9

10th March 1913

Dear Dud,

I'm at Hendon every day now. I reckon that sounds like heaven to you. But it's not as easy as all that. Mr Grahame-White is not around much. He has a bit of a glamorous life off at aviation meetings and competitions and such. He was all right about me flying, after a bit of persuasion. But the other men in the hangars are _awful_. They won't speak to me. Only grunt a bit.

There are two tutors – Mr Gordon and Mr Jessop – they know their stuff and are quite helpful. They assign their pupils numbers and call them for instruction from first to last. I am always last – _always!_ – however early I arrive or however long I've been waiting. The other pupils are not always horrible to me, but hang about in little groups and smoke and use blue language – even the posh ones! I heard one say (behind my back, not to my face), 'The only reason a woman comes to an airfield is to make eyes at all the chaps. And if she must come, she ought to be a damn sight prettier than _that_.' Some are nicer but will only talk to me about the weather, or what I'm wearing. They can't imagine that I'd want to talk about technical matters. And there's no 'ladies first' here. The woman must wait.

Those days when they let me get near an aeroplane, I'm allowed to taxi slowly around the airfield in a Blériot trainer and practise the controls. They call it 'grass-cutting'. It is useful, because you get used to the *controls, and I'm finding that my hands move quicker than I can think it. I've gone up in quite a few passenger flights, because they say I ought to get used to the speed and the noise of the motor and the rushing wind. But you know I'm used to this, from my Blackburn days, but my tutors think they know better. I'm <u>dying</u> to get my hands on the controls not on the ground, but in the air. Once, they let me hold the stick while my tutor directed the controls, which drove me <u>mad</u>, as I was itching to get my hands on it properly and direct the machine myself.*

Anyway, that's me. I hope school is not too rotten. And I hope they let me go up in something that actually flies soon, or I will go <u>barmy</u>.

All best, Della.

Soon after she had sent her letter, her plea was answered and they let her have a go in an airworthy Blériot. The first time she stood next to it, she ran her fingers across its side lovingly. Her hand smeared with oil, which she rubbed off on her sleeve, staining it. Her flying clothes would be saturated in the stuff, and she had to ask Betty for more funds to buy two sets of clothes, so that one could be scrubbed and left to dry while she wore the other. Midge wouldn't allow her to keep them in the house – they stank so of rancid and burnt engine oil, fuel and general muck, a stench unique to aviation yet also reminiscent of rotting vegetables cut through with scorched toast – so she had to hang them to dry in Mrs B.'s shed out the back, used for keeping a few chickens. Between the stink of burnt oil and chicken droppings, she had to admit her life as an aviator was far from feminine.

Yet she revelled in that, even the stares she'd get on the journey home, her face grimed in oil spatters and smudges. These Blériot lessons were another level of vexation, as she was only permitted to make short starts off the ground before bumping down again; the engine itself was doctored so that it would not give enough power to fly higher than a hop, even if she'd tried. Thus, they called this stage the 'grasshopper'. At each hop, her chest would empty, she'd lose her breath and then, bumping down again, her breath would come back in a rush. It was exhilarating, those stretches off the ground, but it was also frustration embodied.

Her next few lessons were very brief, only a few minutes in the air each time. But they were at least more satisfying, flying in a straight line a few feet above the ground across the airfield, then alighting again before turning to the left. Once she was facing back towards the hangar, she would rise again into the air and fly straight, before alighting once more at her starting point. She learned about the precise stages of take-off and landing, how to manipulate the throttle and the fuel lever, how to use the blip switch on the stick to land smoothly. Her tutors were surprised at how adept she was and encouraging, in a crotchety way.

Walking to and from the hangar, she would hang about and watch the other flying schools that were based at Hendon. There were instructors, mechanics and pupils of many different nationalities: American, French, Belgian, Italian, Swiss, Russian. But the languages did not matter so much, as they all spoke a new one: aviation. It was a long way to come for a few minutes in the air each time, but she revelled in her time at Hendon, listened to the others and watched them, asking the odd question. She found there was a slow but steady and grudging acceptance of at least her presence, if not her right to be there. Her queries were answered, although some were more cordial and keen than others. Some would allow her to get her hands even more dirty and tinker with the engines and other parts of an aeroplane. She was learning about the mechanics of the thing and found she had a great aptitude for it, from her bicycle-fixing days and her Broughton brain. This gained her more respect from the men who surrounded her, and those who laughed at her still did so, but were fewer and quieter than before.

She was fiercely impatient to begin the flying proper, yet reminded herself of Grahame-White's warning, that impatience was the aviator's enemy. But the weeks stretched on, through March and into April, as some days she would arrive at Hendon to find the weather had turned, the wind was up or rainclouds had moved in, and they wouldn't even let her sit in an aeroplane, let alone go grass-cutting, hopping or low-flying. To come all that way only to be sent home with nothing was almost insupportable, and she cursed the weather, especially the wind, her new enemy. But her ambition shone through the grey skies and she knew she would keep tramping over to Hendon, as many days as it took, as many frustrated hours; that one day it would be her day and she would fly properly, up above the hangars and the pylons, towards the clouds, away from the earth, the jeering mechanics and the doings of men. In the sky, free as the birds, the earth a plaything beneath her wings.

One May morning, Grahame-White had informed her that today would be her first proper flight at the controls of an aircraft, one with a fully powered engine and full-length wings, high above the aerodrome. At long last. And with Claude! He looked as dapper as ever, wearing tweed trousers with suede patches behind the knees, tucked into patterned long socks, smart shoes and grey jacket, and his customary cap turned backwards. The very picture of a gentleman aviator.

'Show me your gloves, Miss Dobbs.'

She pulled them from the pockets of her woollen coat and held them out. Her flying clothes had progressed as she realised what was needed. Warmth was the main objective, warm yet malleable, so that the body would be snug yet able to manoeuvre without restraint. She had seen a photograph of the French aviatrix Raymonde de Laroche with a thick woolly pullover on – which seemed bulky to Della – while the American Harriet Quimby wore a custom-made all-in-one purple flying suit. She could not imagine herself so glamorously attired, but compromised with layers, wearing a man's long-sleeved cotton vest beneath her chemise, corset, camisole and blouse; her jacket was quite thick, as were her stockings beneath her drawers. Her long skirt was woollen, not too tight-fitting and yet not too voluminous – she didn't want her skirt flying up during flight, entertaining the onlookers or worse, obscuring her vision – and her close-fitting beret-style felt hat she wore low down and tight on her head to keep it safely on in flight and protect her ears. Strong, fur-lined boots encased her feet, as they were just as important as the hands for controlling the aircraft. Her gloves, made of leather and lined with thick wool, were both durable and toasty. Her aunt had sent them recently, anticipating her needs, as she often did.

'Good! Those are excellent gloves. Even in the spring, the high air can become cripplingly cold and once the fingers are cold, then there is desperate danger that a pilot's hands will become so numbed that his fingers will refuse to move.'

He glanced up and down her figure. 'All in all, a very functional attire, Miss Dobbs. Well then, let's get started. We're going up in a Bristol Boxkite. You'll be at the controls and I'll be sitting beside you, ready to take over if needs be. Are you ready?'

'I am,' she asserted, though her chest was filling with moths.

The Boxkite was a monstrous biplane. She'd read that they called Cody's aircraft the 'flying cathedral' and this was no different. She estimated that it must stand about twelve or so feet high and the wingspan looked to be almost three times that. It was long from front to back too, longer than the width even, with the tail plane and propeller behind, making it a 'pusher' aircraft. The canard section jutted far out at the front and the whole thing was mammoth, the endless wires strung here, there and everywhere between the massive wings like a taut cat's cradle. Grahame-White saw her gazing up at them and said, 'They say if you can set a canary free inside and it escapes, you don't have enough wires.'

This made her smile and allayed her fear a touch. Yet at the edge of her vision, she realised that the ground engineer, mechanics, tutors, pilots, pupils and sundry boys were gathering nearby to watch the woman fly. There was a carnival atmosphere in their looks, laughing and pointing and chuntering on, a general shaking of heads. *They want me to fail,* she thought. *That'd make their day. Well, sod them.*

'Come on, my dear,' said Grahame-White and gestured to where she should climb up to where there was a wooden plank for a seat, with just room enough for two. Again, she was glad she didn't have a wide behind, and it was pleasurable too to be snug alongside Mr Claude Grahame-White, a bit of a thrill to feel his thigh pressed against hers – where else could one sit so close to a man? Apart from the omnibus, but that was with strangers. His very nearness was an unwelcome distraction, she realised, and scolded herself to concentrate. One can't be a pioneer while simpering, she knew that, and she wished he were not quite so inviting to look at. She pulled on her gloves and sat in place, the controls before her.

'Place your hands on the stick.' It was tall, the top of it opposite her face. 'The Boxkite uses a stick, as you can see, not a wheel. Push the stick away from you to pitch down, pull towards you to pitch up. Left to right operates the ailerons. This aeroplane rolls using a kind of aileron – look. Those flaps on the wings are hanging down now, but when the chaps start her up, they'll come up. Now, your feet. The rudder bar yaws left and right. Understand?'

Della said, 'Yes. All of it.' She swallowed more words; she'd wanted to blurt out, 'I know all this!' but she held her tongue.

'See this string hanging down in front of you? That's to help keep you straight. If the aeroplane yaws one way or another, the string will point to one side, you see? So, while we are flying, you must try to keep that string level.'

This was a new addition, yet it made sense to her and she nodded.

'Now, today, as conditions are perfect – an absolute flat calm – we're going to fly up above the aerodrome at around five hundred feet. We'll fly straight forward for a minute or so, then make a left turn, head back to the aerodrome and land. One last thing – I've had such good reports of your technique from the other instructors, I'm going to let you control the rudder bar. But if at any moment I feel you are making a hash of it, there's no room on this seat to shove you aside, so I will be thrusting my leg over the top of yours, and taking control of the rudder. Do you understand?'

The thought of Claude Grahame-White's thigh thrusting anywhere near her own was rather wonderful. But she certainly didn't want him taking over. She wanted to fly this machine herself, from take-off to landing.

'Well? Are we clear?' he said.

Oh, how she wished she could scream, 'Yes, yes! Let me at it!' But there was to be no screaming, no female nonsense. It was enough they were letting a woman into the air at all. They would never let a hysterical woman go up. So she nodded instead, firmly.

'Well, then, Miss Dobbs, show me what you can do.'

She reached for the brass fuel cock and turned it through ninety degrees, thus allowing the fuel to flow into the engine. She took both throttle and fuel levers and moved them all the way forwards, opening the floodgates of fuel, from zero to ten on the quadrant. There were mechanics behind them, and the ground engineer, positioned at the back of the aeroplane. The ground engineer shouted, 'Fuel off!' She'd stood there before, watching another pilot about to take off, and had seen the fuel dripping from the engine. Now, she brought the fuel lever back to zero and the throttle about halfway down. The ground engineer turned the propeller, squirting fuel from a can into each cylinder, priming each one. He shouted, 'Throttle set!' and Della ensured the throttle was indeed set, about halfway up, at four on the scale and answered,

'Throttle set.' The engineer shouted, 'Contact!' and she found the toggle switch, which must have been pilfered from a Victorian light switch, and clicked it on. 'Contact,' she replied.

Two men behind swung the propeller to spin the rotary engine over, the magneto sparked and the fuel was fired. The engine burst into life – the aeroplane juddered, now a live thing, inanimate no longer. Immediately, she began to move the fuel lever slowly forward until it was just ahead of the throttle, around five on the scale. She'd got it just right and the engine continued chugging. She waited while the engine warmed up, about half a minute, listening to the sound of it sweetening, feeling the beast wake itself and prepare for flight. Then she pushed the throttle carefully forwards, allowing air into the mixture. The revs increased, the aeroplane was pushing up against the chocks before its wheels, eager to go. The engine roared and she took note, as she'd been trained to do, of exactly where the levers were – the throttle at seven, the fuel lever around four and a half. This could change from day to day, according to the weather's moods, and these were today's positions for maximum engine power, when the engine was at its loudest and giving the most revolutions per minute.

Grahame-White beside her made her jump as he shouted into her ear, 'Listen to the engine.' Her other tutors had taught her well, as she knew what he meant. You had to be on speaking terms with the engine, you had to empathise with it. You could hear when it was at the right pitch, if you knew it well. If it were too rich, if there was too much fuel in the mixture, black smoke would issue, but you could hear it too; it would tell you the mixture was unhealthy. The right mixture would sound sweet to the ear. Hers was laboured, so she eased back the fuel lever only half on the scale to four, and the engine sang.

She looked behind and saw a number of men and a couple of boys hanging on to the back of the aeroplane now, keeping the brute subdued. One boy's cap blew off. *He'll not wear that next time*, she thought. But from where she sat, the propeller and engine behind, there was no air in her face, no wind, as the day was calm; Grahame-White would not have let her fly otherwise. The mechanism beneath her was shaking and whirring, straining at the chocks. It was time to go.

She moved the throttle back to three, allowing the engine to continue to run, but at its slowest. She noted this position, as she knew that's what she'd need to set it to when she came in to land: this was her throttle back position, the engine idling lumpily. She pushed the throttle up to four, running at fast idle, ready to go. The men at the back ran round to the front and grabbed the chock ropes, staring at her, waiting for her to thumb the blip switch, which killed the thrust momentarily. She did it and on each side they deftly pirouetted the chocks away from the wheels and pulled them out. The aeroplane rolled forwards. The forward motion was release and panic all at once. Before, the damned thing had been an infernal contraption, screaming and jolting and buzzing at her, but now it was motion and movement and life, life moving forwards, wanting to escape the ground – and soon it would do just that, at her command.

Now it was responding to her. She moved the throttle gradually up to seven and they gathered speed. Airflow in her face increased, the machine bumping speedily across the ground. She looked to the side and saw the ailerons lift on both wings, tightening up the control cables and stiffening the stick. It had been floppy before, but now it was tautened by the wires. She was bouncing over the grass now, the land well cared for yet natural, rutted and unsmooth as any natural thing is, but now no more bounce, no more ruts; the world had smoothed out, and at that instant, she knew the wheels had left the ground and she was up, up in the air. No time to savour it. She had to inspect the attitude of the aeroplane. With the propeller spinning left, the Boxkite wanted to go that way too, leaned into it, so she had to nudge the rudder to level it. The breeze was strong in her face and she had to concentrate, manipulating the stick and rudder carefully.

She had only flown a few feet from the ground, so now she had to climb, something she had never done before. She had to pitch upwards, bring the stick closer. Grahame-White's hands appeared and grasped the stick below her own. He was shouting something but with the roar of the engine and the rushing wind, she couldn't make out a word. A peep at his face – at the alarm there – and she knew. The nose was coming up a shade too rapidly, and the aeroplane could stall, and drop from the sky. He helped her ease it up gradually, a moderate climb, the stick trembling within their grasp, her brain overloaded with information, her ears and eyes and body assaulted by the sensations of flying, the trees and buildings rushing away from them at crazy sliding angles. This was the most frantic five minutes of her life, a blur of noise and action, a screaming rush into the unknown. But as the aeroplane levelled out and they reached five hundred feet or thereabouts, the throttle at seven, the nose straight, the climb was done and calm achieved. Now, now was the moment she'd dreamt of; above five hundred feet, the aeroplane steady, she could at last look about her and see her place within the kingdom of the air. The wings were behind her, so she had a magnificent view. They were flying at around thirty-five miles per hour, and at that speed, at that height, she felt almost stationary, as she had with Dutrieu. She was used to the noise now. She was walking her aeroplane through the sky, nudging it with stick or rudder, keeping it on the straight path. She could finally enjoy it. A pause for serenity. She could look upon the earth and see what God sees.

Della now fixed her attention on keeping steady. She kept glancing at the string before her and the canard beyond, keeping the same view on the horizon, keeping it constant, and manipulating the controls with very fine movements to keep that same view. At some point soon, she knew, her tutor would want her to turn, but for now she was enjoying herself, seeing Hendon's fields and hedgerows, teeny farm animals and box-like houses parade beneath at a stately pace. Above, the wide blue sky, the clouds seeming so near and within reach that it was tempting to reach out a hand and try to grab a candy-floss handful, though she knew she couldn't.

The wonder of it, the beauty of it, the humming of the wires played by the wind the most harmonious sound imaginable. She glanced at Claude and he was smiling at her. He nodded. She didn't need a translation. He knew she was smitten with this world and he felt it too. Only aviators and other flying things knew it, their secret world of the skies.

She wanted to fly straight forever! Turning required thought, and she wanted to empty her mind, become one with the air. But it couldn't last forever, one couldn't fly on forever, just as when she would race her bicycle down long, straight roads back home and build up such a speed it had felt like flying, a species of freedom born from speed and escape; but the end of the road would come, a turn or a corner, and responsibility would beckon. Up here, there were no roads, but there was fuel and oil to run out, time and her tutor, the pull of the earth. But how tempting it was, to fly on and never come down.

The time to turn came too soon. Claude prodded her and made a left turning motion with his hand. He shouted in her ear; again, she couldn't hear the exact words, but she did hear 'rudder' and knew what to do. A gentle touch with her left foot on the rudder and nothing happened. Was I too gentle? she thought. Or is it not working? She was about to press it again, harder, when Claude held his hand up, forefinger extended, just as her old schoolteacher would do when signalling that a child should wait . . . And wait she did, and in two ticks the Boxkite started to turn to the left. *So unresponsive,* she thought. This monster of an aeroplane takes its time to make its move, she realised, and noted that for the next move.

Now she was fully in control of the aeroplane, she realised it was not as easy as she had imagined. It was hard, in fact, it should be hard. She'd thought of the Boxkite like an animal, she'd watched it so many times she thought she'd got the size of it. And she'd thought that, like an animal, it'd trust her. But she knew now it was different to be in control, to actually touch it and move it. It over-reacts here and under-reacts there. You might have all the textbook knowledge in the world, but each aeroplane has its own character, its own moods. You must strive to know it better.

She remembered what Oxley had told her about turning, that you could use the ailerons or wing-warping to turn, and use the rudder to balance it. Hendon taught the opposite, but she found that keeping the nose up, using balance from the Boxkite's ailerons and the slow rudder, all three together made a controlled turn, and she felt no panic as she saw the picture before her alter, the new view coming into alignment. She nudged on the rudder, nudged on the stick, then brought the stick back to the middle, waiting for the craft to yaw to the left, which it did, faultlessly. The wings were absolutely steady.

She realised that she could feel the alignment in her body, could feel it in her behind on the hard seat, in her sides, in her ears, in her very blood. Every part of her felt unconsciously linked to that creature's equilibrium, and if it was about to slip out, her hands and her body responded unconsciously too: the muscles and sinews simply knew what to do, what minor adjustment was needed. She found she barely looked at the Boxkite's string, or even the canard out at the front. She could feel yaw in her bones.

Soon, the airfield was in view again, as she'd successfully turned the aeroplane around to face back the way they'd come. Claude's hands came into view, motioning that they were to prepare for landing. Now, the real world came back with a slap. Her mind ran over the sequence: she positioned the aircraft to aim at the airfield. She pulled both levers down to reduce the power. She lowered the nose, gently, gently, aiming at the landing point on the field ahead. The wires' hum began to slide upwards, to a high-pitched whistle, a high squealing. Claude's voice in her ear: 'Ease back!' he yelled, and she brought the stick back a tiny amount. The squealing lowered in tone but grew louder. A weight grew in her chest, her blood drained, a sinking feeling. The aeroplane was very draggy, not so smooth now.

She put her thumb on the blip switch at the top of the stick. She held it down, using it as a throttle, delivering power to the engine in a pulse, now a spot of thrust, now nothing. That characteristic sound of a blip-switch controlled aeroplane coming in to land: a soft, sighing chug, chug, chug, like a raincloud sneezing. Her descent was controlled, smooth, the whistle of the wires now smoothing out into a sigh, yet panic was rising in her chest as the ground grew closer, and growing it was, the field broadening out so fast, so wide, the panic of the earth's solid weight that could save you or smash you to pieces. Though her mind raced and her heart fluttered, her body was calm, it knew what to do. She felt the wheels touch the earth and she was down, easing the throttle back to its idle position at two on the scale. She taxied the aeroplane across the field and came to a neat stop a few feet from the waiting crowd of men.

Claude, laughing, said to her, 'That was bloody well top-notch! Excuse my language, but I think you'll forgive me.' Then, turning to the assembled crew of mechanics, pilots and boys, he shouted, 'She was damned good, lads!' And they all broke out in applause! Della laughed too. Claude nimbly climbed out and the ground engineer came to him and they slapped palms and shook hands vigorously. She felt a wince of resentment, and thought, *Is that congratulations on being a good tutor, or surviving a woman pilot in one piece?* But she dismissed it – what did it matter? What did anything matter, now she could fly? Claude swung round and offered his hand to help her clamber down. She felt she did not need it, but she took it, as to feel his hand close around hers was wonderful, and she realised then that she was shaking all over, from relief, from joy, from heaven knows what, but she was shaky and actually she welcomed his help. The ground engineer said, 'She's got hands all right,' and Claude agreed. Standing close to her, he said, 'I hardly had to do a thing!' Then he turned to her and there was a precious moment of connection she knew she would never forget – an image of the great aviator gazing down at her, her body still shaking from the shock of it all as she looked into his eyes and his delight with her shone from them, and he said, 'You've got it, Della. You've got the touch.'

10

'How lucky! How lucky I am!'

Della talked aloud to herself these days, but only when flying alone. The wind and the aircraft would confer. Or they'd argue, fight and it was out-and-out war. But always a bond there, a kind of dance. Everything she did in an aircraft was a dance with the wind. And she must be one with her aeroplane, to take the wind as her partner. It was partly physical, but was mostly mental. An aeroplane was sensitive; in every movement she made there was a prime position of balance that took no energy from the aeroplane. She was not pushing it or dragging it. She and her machine were one, the sky and its birds her only companions.

'Far from the madding crowd,' as Pop used to say.

Only now, only there, looking down upon the land, she had an inkling of the world in which she lived. How small it was, how vast it was. How small she was, and yet how transcendent, in this sky. A Christmas carol sung at school spoke of angels, and here she was one of them, winging her flight over all the earth, in the realms of glory.

She had been flying solo for some weeks. Her first solo flight had been an exercise in terror. She had begun her take-off, glancing beside her at the empty seat, and at the moment she had left the ground, no instructor, on her own to live or die, the phrase had popped into her head and she'd said it aloud: 'You've fucking done it now.'

This wasn't her usual way of talking, but she'd heard an understudy utter it in the wings one night at the New Royalty

Theatre, an old hand who'd been kicking around for years. Their King Lear was taken ill and the understudy was up and petrified. He'd huddled beside the stage grumbling to himself before he went on, and as Della passed by she heard him say it. (Backstage profanity was on a par with that she'd hear in the Hendon hangars, so her ear was well attuned to it by now, if not always her tongue.)

Flying an aeroplane alone was something for which she had devoutly wished for so long, she could only recall her pre-aviation life with difficulty; but then, with no Claude or other tutor on hand to save her skin if she messed up, the idea was outright treacherous. Yet she could not refuse it, not come this far and turn back. She must go on. She would prepare thoroughly, check every inch of the aircraft before flights. She'd consider the weather and mentally factor in everything this might mean to the manoeuvrability of that particular aeroplane on that particular day. After that, it was up to her hands, her eyes, her ability, and the hours and hours of practice in the air and, almost as crucial, in her mind: on the omnibus, she would climb to the top deck and stare at the sky, mentally describing flight paths. Seated in the railway carriage on its way to Hendon, she'd stare at the horizon and watch herself negotiate turns and imagine freak wind gusts and how she'd deal with them. It was all preparation, mental or physical, it was there to form muscle memory, so that it was so ingrained in the body that the mind need not concern itself. Her learning, she hoped, would give her a fighting chance of escaping her own stupidity.

It was still fearsome though, if you thought about it too much. All the things that could go wrong. There was pilot error for a start, and the field of human idiocy was vast, limitless. Merely taking off was fraught with possibilities: the briefest lapse and she could start an uncontrollable turn on the ground that wasn't corrected soon enough, or she'd forget to put the elevators in the right position, or perhaps she had too much back stick so it'd be producing so much drag that the aeroplane wouldn't even get airborne. Or she could get it airborne, but then mismanage the mixture and the aeroplane wouldn't fly above thirty feet and there'd be a fence or a shed coming at you and what are you going to do? If you're lucky, there might be a gap in the hedge, but at some point you're going to have to turn and make your way back and where is there going to be room to do that, at thirty feet? So you could crash and take your chances and the wrath of your tutors, the engineers and the aircraft owner, or you might try to land again within the airfield but touch down awkwardly and rip the undercarriage off. Never mind the vagaries of the aircraft or the air itself; one could pull the wrong lever; she could be landing and pull the fuel lever back, but get the mixture wrong and the engine might burst into life just when it should be idling and then whoosh, you'd smash into a building, or a hedge if you were lucky, or some onlookers if they didn't shift in time.

And that was just take-offs and landings. Up in the air, her problems were now three-dimensional. There was wind to worry about, but also trees and other obstacles – aircraft were this extraordinary invention, yet they were inordinately fragile and wont to crumple in the air at the slightest touch, just like a paper aeroplane. Della had heard of numerous scrapes aviators had been lucky enough to survive. A recent bizarre mishap involved a chap called Reynolds in Oxfordshire, who was flying along in his Bristol when it turned over completely upside down, whereupon he fell out of his seat, landed on the inverted top wing, and stepped off onto the ground before the machine smashed into pieces. It'd be hilarious if it weren't so hazardous. It could easily have been another Oxley head-cruncher. Not so funny. In the case of the Bristol, the pilot survived, but there were many more stories where they hadn't. All pilots knew that with every flight there was a chance of snapping wood, of accident, of death.

Since that first solo flight, throughout her apprenticeship at Hendon, she had made a few mistakes: a broken wing, a crushed propeller. But as yet, her training and her skill – and yes, perhaps her luck – had triumphed. After thirty-three lessons and around three months of flying both biplanes and monoplanes, she was awarded her pilot's licence: on the twenty-fifth day of May 1913, on a Grahame-White biplane, at the Grahame-White School, Hendon, Aviator's Certificate 492. She was only the 492nd person in the United Kingdom to receive that honour. And now there she was, on a peerless June afternoon, the only aviatrix to be flying solo at Hendon that day.

As she directed a Deperdussin monoplane towards the aerodrome, the fields and homesteads around Hendon came more sharply into view, their secrets guarded by roofs but not their garden fences; the aerial viewer sees beyond such walls. The crowds that day were heaving at the airfield boundaries. It was a race day. Women were not permitted to compete in races either at Hendon or anywhere else in England; the hustle of competition in the air was considered too demanding for the ladies. But at least Claude had let her fly at a proper aviation meeting, with other pilots known widely and adored, with thousands come to watch.

The multitudes came early down Colindale Avenue, filling it with their slow, contented bulk. Some of the locals would sell cuppas and snacks along the way, while street vendors shifted picture postcards of handsome aviators, programmes, toy lead aeroplanes for the kiddies and other souvenirs. Once inside the aerodrome, there were splendid tea pavilions – red and white tents scattered about, each with a wooden floor and dainty tea services set out invitingly. The spectators observed the fine flying and the fashions too, watching each other almost as much as the skies. Some sat in the hundreds of chairs, others in their automobiles where an excellent tea was brought over by waiters for a very moderate charge. Some of these cars were topped by boys in caps and long socks, defying their small stature by perching on the car roof. Perhaps there is no finer vantage point than the roof or open back seat of an automobile, to recline among the cushions and watch all manner of biplanes and monoplanes rise to thousands of feet and cheer the aerial thrills performed by Hendon's feted pilots: Samuel Cody, Tom Sopwith, Alliott Roe, Gustav Hamel, Benny Hucks, the Farman brothers Maurice and Henri, and Claude Grahame-White. And now Cordelia Dobbs herself, Hendon's dear girl and Claude's star pupil.

As Della came in to land, she saw numerous hands raised within the enclosure, pointing at the lady flyer, while ticketless men and boys climbed up and perched atop the wooden fences, many of them waving at her too. She raised a gloved hand and waved back, which always thrilled the crowd. Somehow, once pilots were up in the air, they were of another world, so to see one wave at you was as if a god leaned down and touched you. The landing was smooth, without incident, and as she taxied to a halt she was delighted to see Claude – always swamped by adoring fans on days like these – waiting to meet her and introduce her around.

She'd met by now most of the well-known aviators who flew at Hendon. It was a real pleasure to see Benny Hucks again – her first tutor at Filey – and now she had her very own pilot's licence to show him how far she'd come. They spoke of the golden beach at Primrose Valley and the superior qualities of the Blackburn aeroplanes, how brilliant was their design and how well-balanced. And what a thrill to speak with the flamboyantly moustachioed Sam Cody and his wife, of whom she'd read all those years ago at her aunt's table, of his Man-lifter kites and his wife's ascents. Some of the pilots did bring their wives along with them, while others were free and single. Claude had married the year before after a shipboard romance, to Dorothy Caldwell-Taylor, the impossibly stylish and wealthy socialite. She swanned around the aerodrome in the latest and dearest frocks and hats, knew everyone and everyone knew her. She called her husband 'Claudie'. Mrs Grahame-White was the first person in Della's life she could honestly say she hated. Oh, how she despised her. And what a stubby little donkey she saw herself beside this preening thoroughbred with the glossy dark hairdo. But she had one thing over Mrs G-W: she was a pilot. In fact, it was rumoured she hated flying, having tried it once and nearly strangled her husband in fear until they were back on the ground. This woman might own hats more expensive than Della's entire course of flying lessons, but she wouldn't – and couldn't – fly.

As Della climbed down from the Deperdussin, she was glad to see that Dotty – as Della sneeringly called her (but only to herself) – was nowhere to be seen. Della had Claude to herself. Every day that passed, she knew that her time at Hendon was ending. Her tuition was paid for and done and her position here was reliant on Claude's goodwill; he gave her opportunities to fly, but only when he was around, which was increasingly rare. As his fame spread, he himself was spread more thinly, and she saw him less and less. The other pilots and engineers were either paid or self-financing, and despite the respect she had gained with her licence, nobody but Claude would allow her to fly for free. Her wage at the theatre was pitiful and her great-aunt had told her in a letter the week before that there was little more capital to spare for flying time and certainly not enough to buy her own aeroplane. And there were no jobs for women as mechanics or engineers at Hendon or any other aerodrome; she knew, as she'd approached several that month and been soundly repelled at each one. It was one thing for a girl to kill herself in an aeroplane, but she wasn't to be let loose having a hand in someone else's safety: 'We only take men, of course,' said an engineer at Brooklands, polite, uncomprehending. Her days at Hendon were numbered and soon she would be out on her ear: no more flying and no more Claude.

'That machine is beautiful,' he said, admiring the sleek lines of the Dep. It was not much better to fly than a Blériot but my, it looked good. 'And you handled it beautifully too, Della. Well done. Come and meet some folk.' She beamed as she removed her helmet and goggles, following him into the melee. There in the Private Members' Enclosure were the great and the good of London society – bankers, industrialists, automobile manufacturers, department store owners, various toffs – some of whom took the slight hand of the diminutive aviatrix and cooed over her. This was hellish – speaking to strangers and lots of them – but she did her duty, to please Claude.

'I do enjoy the sight of these aviatresses,' she heard one pompous old sot say, addressing himself not to her, but in her general direction and to a few fawners standing about. His fat wife did at least look at her, but only to say, 'But their outfits are quite . . . outlandish! A little woman all greased up like a minstrel! Does she wear a corset, do you think, under that get-up?' *I'm not deaf*, Della longed to say. *I'm not a foreigner or a child. I can hear every word you say.* But they spoke and inspected her as if she were a friend's exotic pet, oblivious to criticism, a faintly idiotic curiosity. A short man about her size in a bowler hat was shaking her hand and talking to her about something or other while her eyes sought out Claude, surrounded by fans, drifting away from her towards a table where he began to sign programmes and laugh with the mostly female entourage. He loved the attention as much as she disliked it. His face glowed with it, but was soon obscured by a bobbing wave of broad-brimmed hats and trembling feathers.

'So then, Miss Dobbs, what do you say? Are you game?'

The short man had gained her attention again and she started, wondering what on earth she'd agreed to when saying *Yes, yes* distractedly while her thoughts were else-where.

'The tour would all be paid for, sponsored by the Johnson and Miller Press, and your aircraft would also be purchased under your instructions – any machine of your choosing – nothing's too good for our little Della Dobbs.'

After only a few weeks of press attention, she had already tired of the novelty of the fame she was gathering as one of the few aviatrixes in the country. The way people like this chap called her Della as if they knew her, and 'our' as if they owned her.

'I'm sorry, I didn't catch that. What tour is this?'

The man laughed and shook his head. 'Head in the clouds, eh? Well, you can be forgiven for that, I'm sure. What I'm proposing is a cross-country tour, with all the towns being destinations in which the Johnson and Miller Press own local newspapers, you see. Of course I'm sure you're aware that Mr Johnson and Mr Miller own the *Grimsby Gazette*, as well as a range of other provincial papers across the British Isles. We'll start in Sussex, then Kent and Oxfordshire, on to Bedfordshire, then Lincolnshire, ending at your home town of Cleethorpes, where we'd like you to land on the beach. It'd make a tremendous show. We'd start in July and end at the far side of August. Lots of flights, lots of people to meet and chatter with, and photographs to pose for; even a custom-designed, *exclusive* flying suit for the modern lady flyer – everything a girl could want, eh?'

'An aircraft, purchased under my instructions? Is that what you said?'

'That's right. Any machine you desire, though of course it remains the property of the Johnson and Miller Press, but we'd paint your name on it and it would be for your *exclusive* use, during the tour. A generous daily wage for yourself. And all your expenses paid, staying in the finest establishments. With the proviso, of course, that you speak to no other newspapers than ours and give us *exclusive* rights to all interviews and photographs for the duration of the tour and some other sundry details regarding your name and so forth that we can discuss at a later date. So, what machine will you choose, Miss Dobbs, to be your personal craft for the duration of the tour? What are the best aeroplanes, in your opinion?'

Della stared at the red-cheeked newspaperman. 'Well,' she stuttered, 'Blackburns are splendid.'

That night she arrived home, exhausted and begrimed, to find Midge on a rare night off, curled up with a box of liquorice allsorts and *The New Freewoman* magazine on the daybed in the front room. After stripping off her clothes – stiff with filth, oleaginous – she gave herself a wash and brush-up and relaxed into her baggy pyjamas, a striped flannel pair she'd bought from a men's outfitters, the smallest size they had. (They were snugger than nightdresses.) Midge made her a much-needed cup of tea with lots of sugar and she collapsed on the armchair by the fire. Midge was well aware of Della's financial problems and the soon-to-be-realised and devoutly-to-be-avoided booting-out from Hendon, so Della's news was greeted rapturously.

'Oh Del, what a coup! I can't believe it! Aren't you over-joyed? You look like a right sourpuss.'

'Of course, yes. I am. I can't believe it either.'

'What's up then?'

'I don't want to leave Hendon.'

'Well, I know, but it doesn't matter now. You've got this tour and you don't need Hendon any more.'

'I do,' muttered Della.

'But why? What can Hendon offer when you'll be the star of the show?'

Della stared gloomily into her tea. How had it come to this?

'I'm in love.'

'With that poncey airman?'

'He's not a ponce! Just look at his glamorous wife.'

'You don't need some fop – and a married one at that – and just look at what he did marry! That says a lot about him.'

Della contemplated her own scruffy flannels and her thick hole-ridden socks, ran her fingers through her cropped and scruffy hair, noticed the black muck forever under her fingernails. *Plain and shy, plain and shy.* She sank deeper into her chair and sighed.

Midge leaned forwards and Della caught her expression. It was soft and understanding, which surprised Della.

'Listen, love. I'm not made of stone. I live alone, but I have my male companions, you know that. I know what it is to be lonely. And I've had first love – long time ago now – but I remember it like it was last week. It's a powerful thing.'

Della looked away, stared at the flickering fire, and she welled up – how ridiculous! – but how else could she feel, when her whole body hankered for him? She'd never felt such craving, never knew it existed. She yearned for a glimpse of him. Her day was made when he said a kind word, her whole week ruined when she learned he was away on tour. She knew every nuance of that handsome face and it delighted and troubled her equally. To want something that one could not possess, the exquisite pain of it. And what did she want of that face? She imagined scenarios where they would be alone – they were never alone – away from the crowds, the pilots, the engineers and the wife, and it'd just be the two of them, and he'd take off her helmet and goggles, so fondly, and raise her chin and kiss her with that lovely full mouth, and oh . . .

'It's all hogwash, you know,' said Midge, her face back to its usual hardness. 'I'm sorry, darling, but you need to know. Love, and all that. Passion. It's worse than novels. It's *lies*.

Especially for men. It's all about one thing. And you know what that one thing is, don't you? Once that's done, they lose interest. Believe me, I KNOW.'

Della thought of Claude and all his female fans. They all wanted something from him, but what was it? To be adored? To share in his fame, be touched by his glitter? She wanted more. She believed she had met her true love, projected their lives forward as if across a wide, pink-blue sky at dawn, two pilots flying into their future, ecstatically happy as he'd found the only girl in the world for him – an aviatrix who had the touch! – and she'd found her man, who was kind to her, and valued her, praised her and looked down at her and smiled, as no other man had ever done. It was so right. How could it possibly fail? All he needed was to know it. And if she went away, if she left Hendon and him, how could she show him? She knew she would never, ever tell him in words – she'd sooner land on her head – but by being there, by flying for him and impressing him, he'd slowly come to realise she was the one, and he'd ditch that stupid cow and sweep her off her feet and marry her. Happily ever after.

'Oi! I'm still here you know, Dolly Daydream!'

'Sorry, Midge.'

'You have got it bad, haven't you?'

A single tear escaped and rolled down Della's cheek, fell on her hand. It was good to let it out, good to share it, but at the same time she was afraid that voicing her love and airing it would destroy it. It had been immaculately preserved in her thoughts but now it was crumbling into dust as the tomb was opened, and she instantly regretted it.

'You don't want to hear this right now, Della. But it needs saying. This sort of wishy-washy love, it's all fantasy, it's all mist. You imagine all sorts of possibilities are hidden there, depths and profound feelings and such, but the mist clears and there's nothing. Nothing, except emptiness. Or traps. You don't need a man right now, love. You really don't. For heaven's sake, girl, you're a trailblazer! Look at what you're doing! A female pilot, going on tour, showing the men that what they can do, we can do, and a darn sight better. I'm not saying we don't need love. But I am saying you should never let it stand in your way. I'd eat my hat if it were true, but if he does by some miracle love you, a bit of absence will do you good. Heart grow fonder et cetera. But darling, in my view, that'll never happen. And you'll sail off into your future with a sponsorship deal – there are theatre companies I know who'd sell their legs for that! – and your life is only just beginning. You're so young, Del. You have so much to look forward to! It's going to be divine!'

11

'What the hell's wrong with it?' Della asked Ronnie. 'It was fine on the way here.'

The engine had started up well but within seconds she saw the Blackburn's oil pressure gauge sink alarmingly; black smoke poured out from the engine and with a loud clunk it stopped forthwith: no warning, no petering out, just bang, dead.

She jumped down and together they inspected the engine, the prop, the fuel tank, the oil tank. There was sand on the oil tank, embedded in the glutinous mass all over it, but then there would be – they were on the beach at Camber Sands after all. But once Ronnie had taken a closer look, he said, 'Bloody hell. Someone's put sand in the oil tank.'

'Sand's got into the oil tank? Blown from the beach?'

'No, no – look. There's loads of it. Some bastard's heaped it in there. Destroyed the engine. The debris's been pumped through the bearings, they've gone molten and the whole thing's melded itself solid. What a damned mess.'

Della's cheeks flamed. There was no way she'd fly for days now, much less today. A whole new engine would need to be ordered. She'd have to wait till the next step on the tour. There were two other pilots there that day and they'd taken off from the beach a few minutes before, heading back to the airfield. They'd all stayed in the same Rye hotel the night before, ignored her at reception, ignored her at dinner, ignored her at the bar. They'd have a smoke and laugh with Ronnie – everyone got on well with Ronnie – but when he tried to include her in the conversation, the others turned their backs and shared crude jokes and laughter rang out against her. Despite Ronnie's protestations, she gave up and went to bed early, flying in her mind her route from the airfield to the beach and back, the route she had walked that afternoon to look for landmarks and make a mental map in her head. A lonely business, this.

'They hate me.'

'Who?' said Ronnie, though she knew he knew.

'The other pilots.'

'Don't be daft.'

'It's true. They hate me. They did this.'

'You've no proof of that. Don't start shouting the odds. They'll have you up in court. Slander. Just shut up and let's get a telegram off and get a new engine delivered to Tonbridge. Hell's teeth! Why did I ever agree to tour with a bloody woman? I must've been mad.'

'Don't blame it on me!' spat Della. She was fit to burst. 'It's not my fault they sabotaged my machine.'

'It's your fault you're a woman,' he said and she glared at him, to see him smirking.

'Oh Ronnie, you're a stinker.' Hopping mad still, but it was a relief to laugh with Ronnie. He was a foul-mouthed grease monkey – as they called mechanics in the American magazines – but they got on like a house on fire. He worked with his brother Jim, who didn't say much but knew every-thing there was to know about Blackburns. He was shy of Della but always obliging. He loitered behind while they argued, fending off boys running over the beach and up to them, begging the flying lady for rides. These two Cockney mechanics hired by the newspaper company kept her aero-plane running sweetly, travelled with her, ate and drank with her, joked with her.

They were both tall with huge feet, so would be hopeless pilots, she imagined. They were so similar in age as to be almost twins, except that mouthy Ronnie had sandy hair, thick like a scrubbing brush, and quiet Jim had wispy hair that was light blond, nearly white. Both were strong and hard-working, surprisingly dextrous with their stubby-fingered hands and skinned knuckles smeared with muck and blood, and they could read an engine like an alphabet. In between flights, Jim in particular patiently taught her more in a day about aircraft mechanics than she'd have learned in a month at Hendon, and Ronnie would randomly test her with mechanical quizzes. Thank heavens for them.

Between the three of them, they took the aeroplane to pieces, ready for moving it on. They worked efficiently, in silence, intent on their job; accurate, ordered, mucky-faced. When they were done, Della gazed out across the sand dunes, the tussocky grass still, as if waiting, the light blue sky beyond.

'Perfect flying day too,' she said. 'Flat calm.'

Ronnie shook his head. 'No point going on about it. Done now. Maybe it was those lads. You don't know. When you were signing all the autographs and that. We were chatting with the other engineers, we weren't watching the aeroplane. Could've been one of those boys.'

'I bet it wasn't,' piped up Jim. If Jim spoke, it must be important.

'Next time,' said Della, 'one of us should stay with the aeroplane at all times. Never leave it for a second.'

Ronnie glared at the aeroplane, lying in pieces. He twisted a rag around his hands, threw it on the sand and kicked it viciously into the still air.

The three of them tramped back to Rye, Ronnie and Jim going off to arrange for a truck to haul the wounded aircraft pieces from the sands, while Della visited the post office to send the telegram asking that Johnson and Miller arrange for the new engine to reach Kent as soon as possible. They'd been incredibly accommodating, all the Johnson and Miller people, providing her with the loan of the Blackburn, the services of two ace mechanics and full board and expenses. All she'd had to do in return was fly where they told her to fly; she was happy to oblige – but took less happily the stage name they'd dreamt up for her: *Meggie Magpie.* The forename came from the local term for Cleethorpes people, the Meggies. And the magpie was there as a suitably alliterative bird, represented in her five custom-made black and white flying suits. As she approached the post office, she took in her stride the amazed scrutiny of passing women and the whistles and laughter of men at the sight of an oily-faced gal in a monochrome all-in-one flying suit. The Girl Magpie was the star of Rye, of Lewes, of Hastings, and would surely be the star of every town she visited. The photographs of her with her new name – her stage name, as Midge pointed out – were splashed across each Johnson and Miller newspaper front page; her transformation into star aviatrix was complete. 'Oi Meggie!' they'd call at her, at the airfield, at the beach, on the street. It always took a while before she recalled that they were shouting at her.

Back at the hotel, the pilots were in the bar chatting up local girls and both glanced at her over their pints as she walked in. Della was about to rush up the stairs off the reception to hide in her room. The sooner she left this place the better. But she took a step – and found her feet had made a decision for her. They were planted directly before the two pilots, one of whom turned towards her with a look of contempt and triumph.

'Problems?' called the other one, smirking. The pretty local girls stared at her. One began to titter and another joined in. One girl looked uncomfortable and slanted her eyes away.

Della stared at each airman in turn. What could she say? How could she prove it? She could not. But she had the nerve to look at them, at least. To look and look and not look away. *I know you*, she tried to say with her look. *I know what you are*. Eventually, one pilot turned and fiddled in his pocket for his pipe tobacco. The other turned his back too and cleared his throat. The giggling had stopped. The uncomfortable girl watched Della.

'May I . . .' she began and held out a cardboard beer mat to Della and a stick of red chalk from the dartboard. 'Will you sign it, to Vi? From Meggie Magpie?'

She did sign it: *To Vi. Thank you. From Della.*

That's how it went, on the tour. A new town, new people gawping, star-struck kids, smirking men, some cordial words, some insults. Jim wordlessly defending her, Ronnie blustering through, Della flying well and the Blackburn's new engine running up to par. Reporters, photographs, autographs, dinners, a tour of the local factory, a tour of the local football ground, the local this and that, gratified that Meggie Magpie had come to town. *Meggie, where do you get your stylish flying suits? Meggie, how do keep your nails from breaking? What do you put on your hair to keep it nice, Meggie?* A scandal at Witney when it was rumoured she wore no corset beneath her black-and-white suit. She was asked directly: *If it's not too personal a question, Miss Magpie* – (Miss Magpie!) – *what are the arrangements for your undercarriage?*

At Luton, after her show flights and once the autograph hunters had died down, she was approached by a smart yet conservatively dressed woman with deep-set, intense eyes and a determined mouth, who introduced herself: 'Mrs Hilda Hewlett. I make aeroplanes.'

Della shook her hand delightedly. 'Mrs Hewlett, I'm so happy to meet you! I know your name, of course. I remember hearing when you became the first English woman to gain her pilot's licence. It really encouraged me!'

Hilda smiled modestly. 'Well, you're certainly flying the flag for aviatrixes everywhere, my dear. I never really took to flying myself, but I love aircraft and so I build them now. I set up a flying school with Gustav Blondeau at Brooklands. Tom Sopwith was one of our first pupils and we were the first flying school in England to graduate a fully fledged pilot. Now we have our own aeroplane-building business in Battersea. And next year we're hoping to expand and move here to Luton.'

It was awe-inspiring to learn of all the achievements this woman had managed in the male worlds of both flying and construction. Della had heard of the Hewlett-Blondeau school, but cursed her stupidity for not putting two and two together and realising that the Hewlett flying school and the wife of Hewlett the novelist who gained the first licence were one and the same person – the same *woman*, that is. If she'd known this last year, would she have gone to Hendon at all? Probably not, as it would have been vastly preferable to learn at a flying school owned by a woman. But then, she'd never have met Claude. *Good thing too*, she imagined Midge saying. 'It's an honour to meet you, madam. It really is.'

'Do you have some time to talk?' Hilda went on. 'We could take some tea and discuss things. It's not often two female flyers have a chance to meet. It'd be good to know you more.'

Della readily agreed and they went to the tea tent, ordered cakes and sandwiches and shared anecdotes of learning to fly in a world of men.

'How did you come to it, this flying lark?' asked Hilda, and Della told her about Auntie Betty and the Wright brothers.

'I never thought I was good at anything,' recalled Della. 'Until my aunt told me about her side of the family, what good hands we had and these mechanical brains. I'd already found I loved racing bicycles and fixing them.'

'Ah, me too! I was always interested in engines and how they worked. Yes, it's tricky for a girl to discover these things, if all she's taught is needlework. I learnt some practical crafts when I was younger. I knew what women could do, if they were only given the chance.'

'How did you come to flying?'

'It was the Blackpool Aviation Week in 1909. I saw Hubert Latham fly his little stunner, that white Antoinette monoplane, and, my word, it was like a slap in the face. I woke up. I knew this was the future: aviation. I met Blondeau and he became my business partner. He was a brilliant engineer and together we bought a Farman and went to their airfield in France to await its arrival and learn everything we could about aeroplanes. They let me tinker about, because I spoke French and they could see I knew my way around a motor. Do you know about that, dear? You should, you know. No point in flying if you don't know how it works, or what to do when it goes wrong.'

Della assured her she knew her way around aeroplanes now, thanks mostly to Jim and Ronnie. 'I tried to learn what I could in the hangars at Hendon, but they didn't make it easy for me. I was always the trespasser.' She told Hilda more about the snide laughter, the mockery and disdain, even Claude's disparaging comments to begin with.

'Yes, well, we all know Grahame-White is no champion of women – flying ones, that is.' Della blushed but luckily Hilda didn't seem to notice, and went on, 'I've seen it all, dear. But one must persevere. And you certainly have. Be proud of that. They do say any apprenticeship is largely about character-building.'

Della told her about the sand in the oil tank episode.

'Yes, I've heard this kind of thing before. One day someone's going to get seriously hurt. I've heard of a German aviatrix whose fuel tank was drained just before a flight once, for a malicious joke. So of course you must check your aeroplane even more thoroughly next time. And surround yourself with good men. You have to seek out the ones you can trust.'

'My chaps – Ronnie and Jim – they're the salt of the earth.'

'That's good. And my business partner, he's a good one.

But it was hard to find him and to be taken seriously, especially in England. The rotters don't make it easy for us. It's worst in England, I believe.'

'I can't even fly in competitions here. The Royal Aero Club won't let me compete against men. It's so frustrating.'

'Yes, but you can in France. No rules about female competitors there. Yes, you still get the odd man who doesn't like women to fly, but there seemed to me to be a much more libertarian attitude, as you'd expect from the French, I suppose. Why not go over there and tour the competition circuit? I have a few contacts I can give you, particularly at the Farman aerodrome. Or Germany. There's a very good international community there. And that German aviatrix I mentioned? She is a great flyer and building her own aeroplanes now. Her name's Melli Beese. I'll be happy to make the introductions, via letter or telegram. I'd think about it, dear, I really would. In the meantime, if you ever need my help, or want an aeroplane building for you, here's my business card. Just drop me a line.'

They talked on for an hour, before Ronnie began loitering outside the tent and giving her looks to chivvy her on to more interviews and nonsense. She could've sat with Hilda Hewlett all day.

'Mrs Hewlett—'

'Hilda, please. We're friends now, aren't we?'

'I do hope so. I can't tell you what a tonic it's been. With other pilots, you can talk shop, but there's not many other people who can talk about it with you. And there's certainly no women to talk to about it, not one I've found anyway.'

Hilda chuckled and said, 'Oh yes, in any social situation, aviation is a real conversation-stopper. So you keep it to yourself, you keep it under wraps. You can't let it out. With my husband, he was supportive and interested to a point but would get bored of it. He came to a few shows to begin with, but not many. I learned to keep quiet for an easier life. It was so enjoyable to meet you too, dear. Keep in touch, won't you? And do think seriously about going over to France or Germany. It might be just the thing for you.'

The tour went on, the gravy train rolled on, and she began to hate the sound of Meggie Magpie, her publicity-courting alter ego. She was always desperately glad to close the door to her hotel room and wallow in the bath, dwelling on the madness of it all. She was tired of the merry-go-round; sometimes after a flight she'd get a mild dizzy spell, which she could control if she'd been given a minute of peace to breathe, but it was always on and on, to more talk and attention. She would never say this to anyone on tour, as it seemed ungrateful. It was nice to be admired, nice to be praised, but for heaven's sake, she didn't belong to the public. And she hated being the centre of attention. She spoke to Midge about it when she came to an aviation meeting in Bedfordshire – Midge, the voice of reason: 'Look, it's expensive, mucking about in flying machines, and you have to pay your way. If you haven't got money or a rich husband, that means you have to tart yourself about as a freak. So what? You know the truth, deep inside. You know why you're doing it, and you're lucky you have the talent for it. You're in the entertainment business now, baby. That's how you get back at them, for the harsh words or the bad reviews – you have the talent and they don't.' (Of course, Della realised, Midge was also ranting about her own stage career.)

As well as the carousel of the tour, Della's bath-time thoughts inevitably strayed to Claude. Did she still miss him? Hard to tell. When she had first left Hendon, the pain of separation was acute, an almost physical throb deep down. But it soon passed, and because she was so busy she had minimal time to dwell. And after all, he had often been away from Hendon for days at a time, sometimes weeks, and she'd had to endure that for so long, it was part of the pattern of her feelings for him. Separation in this case, though, had not made the heart grow fonder. Comments by Midge and now by Hilda, and the distance from him giving her a chance to observe in a more detached fashion, allowed her to conclude that their parting actually was probably the final nail: she'd told him she was leaving to do a nationwide tour, and instead of the congratulations she'd expected and desired, he frowned and pouted, asking if it would include cross-country flying as well as aerodrome flights. She answered yes, it would, and she was most excited at the prospect, of learning new map-reading skills and how to walk a route mentally and look for landmarks. At this, he'd almost scowled and had replied: 'It must be remembered that women's efforts in aviation have mostly been confined to aerodrome flights, which is a very different proposition to cross-country work and the hazardous achievements undertaken by men. I strongly urge you to decline any of those more dangerous aspects of the tour, Della, and confine yourself to exhibition flights at aerodromes only. Women are simply not up to the job.'

Only a few months ago, she had bought every word of his as gospel, hung on each and swallowed it whole. Only a few months later, and she felt as if she had aged years, and now her gaze narrowed at the great aviator and something snapped inside as she regarded that handsome face. She thanked him for his advice and said she hoped they would part as friends. At which he shook her hand roughly and stalked off. That was the last time they had spoken, and it had haunted her for weeks. Was he angry with her for leaving him? Was that proof of deeper feelings? Or did he simply hate to be proven wrong? The lack of faith in her talent was the most hurtful thing. But it did her good. It almost cured her (though the longing in her body didn't go). She was sad to put her infatuation away in a drawer like an old beloved toy, but relieved too to be free of the reminders it had given her of her callow youth. She realised that he was her first proper crush, her first great love really, and yet it was not only what she wanted from him that fuelled it – desire, adventure, love and passion, marriage even – more than that, he was her mentor and her aspiration. She looked for his approval the same way she would from a father figure – after all, her own father had doled out only large helpings of disapproval, certainly in recent years, and a pointed lack of interest before that. Claude had approved of her, had praised her and was proud of her. She had wanted him, but more than that, she had in some way wanted to *be* him. Now she was on her way, he could only hold her back. She was free of it now, more or less.

Thus, since Luton, her bath-time thoughts rarely alighted on Mr Grahame-White and instead now wandered curiously across the English Channel, to Europe . . . So, every night, after a bath and room service, if she could avoid the state dinners, she'd lie in bed flying figures in her head, then deep sleep till the next morning, and back to the hubbub and all the people, people, people; never her strong point, small talk. But she couldn't complain, not really, as she was being paid to fly, actually being paid to do it! And not in any old aeroplane, but her absolute favourite aeroplane: the Blackburn. It was quite improved since 1911, and the balance was even more pronounced. A privilege to fly. She so looked forward, more than she could say, to the end of the month when she'd be landing it on her home town beach, to fly into Cleethorpes where the local residents, her people – the Meggies, from whom she'd got her nickname – would cheer for her, their girl, to swoop in, and when she'd see Mam and Betty, Puck and Cleo, perhaps even Gertie and the boys, and Midge might come up, all standing on the beach and waving. Maybe even Pop might leave his room, for that. And to add to the joy, even Dudley Willow was coming. He'd persuaded his father to let him escape to his old holiday haunt for a few days. Now he was fifteen and she hadn't laid eyes on him since that day he walked away with Betty four years before, in 1909, he aged eleven, she fifteen. How different they'd look! How

good it would be to see her penfriend again and talk aeroplanes. Something to look forward to. First, Lincoln. Then
home.

There was a breeze at Leadenham, a big flat airfield near
Lincoln, but nothing she couldn't handle. It was to be her
longest cross-country flight yet, flying over to Lincoln, to
circle the cathedral and the castle, then back again. It was
also her biggest air show since Hendon, with eight other
pilots. As usual with the men, they were engaging in some
competitions from which she was barred. But, as the girl
star, she was given the honour of being the only one flying
to the city and back, and she took pride in that. There were
murmurings that the other pilots were put out that only she
was to fly cross-country. *Well, they can't have everything,*
Della thought. Arriving at the field and settling in their
hangars, there were so many people milling around, inspecting
the Blackburn and asking questions of Ronnie and Jim, more
local news people turned away by Johnson and Miller Press
(she was exclusively theirs; she belonged to them), that there
was an atmosphere of muddle Della did not like. She wanted
to escape and have time to think. So she went to her aeroplane and lay down on the hangar floor, beneath a wing.
The best place she could think of to get a modicum of peace,
and it worked. It looked to others as if she might be engaged
down there with last-minute preparations, so they left her
alone. She had studied the route on a map the day before
and marked up in dark pencil the landmarks to look for.
She closed her eyes and flew it in her mind. She considered
the cloud base that day and the strength of the breeze, the
prevailing wind direction, and how it might affect the
Blackburn. She couldn't plan for everything, but she could
try.

She felt a tap on her boot, tipped her head sideways to
look and saw Ronnie beckoning her: 'Lady flyer wanted for

Lincoln Star photograph.' And he leaned in closer: 'Come on, you lazy cow.'

Disgruntled yet resigned, she scrambled up and put on a cordial face for the waiting photographer on the grass outside the hangar, glancing at Ronnie and Jim who were showing off the Blackburn wing camber to a clutter of pilots and strangers. They did love to brag about it. So did Della, and she was honoured it was hers – well, Johnson and Miller owned it, of course, but hers to fly. She spoke with a reporter about her flying suit, then when she turned back to her aeroplane, Ronnie and Jim were not there. Instead, she saw them on the grass nearby, pointing at the sky. There was another Blackburn at the show, just taken off, a slightly older model than hers, and they were shaking their heads, obviously comparing the two and finding it wanting. Finishing her interview abruptly, she went back to the aeroplane and started to make her last-minute checks. Within a few seconds, her mechanics were beside her, doing their double and triple checks as well. She looked at the prop to see that all eight bolts were there and tight; checked the wires to see they hadn't been slackened, that the cable lengths were equal and the aeroplane balanced; the stick and rudder to see they were securely connected to the wires; the tail plane and elevators to see they were intact; the oil and fuel tanks full and free from debris; the wings to see there were no tears in the skin, no cracks she could feel in the braces, struts, ribs and spars; the wheels, to see the tyres weren't slashed and that the wheel nuts were all there – she saw that the axles were newly covered in fresh grease, so she could see they'd been given very recent attention. There, all done.

'Have you checked everything?'

'Yes, miss,' Ronnie scowled.

'Check,' added Jim.

The Blackburn was positioned outside on the grass, the

crowd stepping back and Ronnie and Jim doing last-second fiddles with this or that, dabbling to the end.

'Time to go,' said Della and climbed aboard, at which the crowd gave a cheer.

Fixing her helmet and goggles, Jim popped his white-blond head close and said, 'Long flight this. Be careful. Break a leg.'

'Will do, Jim.'

The take-off was bumpy, but the ground was rutty, which would explain it. She was relieved to lift into the air, but the moment she did, something felt odd. She looked behind and saw with horror that a wheel was falling through the air, hurtling towards the ground. She did not see its impact, but she knew it was hers. A lost wheel was a disaster. Trying to land with only one was dangerous in the extreme. The under-carriage would be ripped to shreds and when the aeroplane stopped, it could be flung forwards on to the prop and tip over on to its back, then she would be trapped beneath the aeroplane, the fuel would pour out of the tank and ignite on the hot engine and it would be death by fire: every aviator's worse fear. It was all bad, whichever way it happened. Her only chance was to land it and not flip over, which would be good fortune only. And had she lost only one wheel, or had she just seen only one fall and the other had fallen before? And which one was it? That mattered – if she were to try to land on one wheel, she'd have to know which side to lean towards. She climbed above the trees and swallowed the panic rising in her tight throat. She looked out across the fields on both sides, scanning the landscape for water. A duck pond, that's what she needed. Best with a missing wheel to land in water, if you could. But she looked on and on and could see nothing. So a field it must be. She needed the flattest one she could find; stubble or bumps or ruts would only make it worse and the added risk of more damage could be lethal. After some minutes of searching, she remembered that she'd seen a recently mown patch of grass not far from the airfield, quite sizeable and not on a hill. She'd noticed it as a hare had been scooting across it when she flew up. She turned cautiously; every move felt wobbly now, every second her confidence eroding, a sandcastle against the tide. Heading back the way she came, she looked desperately for the field and feared she'd forgotten where it was, or imagined it. Everything before she'd lost the wheel was like a dream, a distant dream of safety, and she'd fucking gone and done it now and was going to get herself killed.

'There it is,' she said to calm herself, the yellow-green mown patch coming into view. 'Flat as a millpond,' although it wasn't, quite. But it'd have to do.

The sun flared from behind a high white cumulus and temporarily blinded her, yet when she was able to see again she noticed her shadow speeding alongside the aeroplane, moulding itself to every curve and furrow of the land beneath her, and there, at just the right angle, a lucky angle, she saw that one wheel was still intact, the left wheel. So, the left it would be, as she prepared to go down, keeping the balance steady.

'Easy, girl,' she said and a memory of Claude's voice in her ear during their first flight sent a shiver up her spine, but now she was alone and she'd have to save herself. She was gliding – volplaning, Claude used to call it – and she tried to slow down the aeroplane as much as possible; the slower the descent, the less chance of fatal impact, but she had to keep the speed up enough to give enough lift to the right wing. The ground rushed towards her, opening out. She thrust left with everything she had, to keep the left wing down, the right wing up and all the weight on the left wheel. The second it touched the ground, the whole craft swung violently to the right, whipping round in the direction of the lost wheel, pivoting around it. She was pitched forwards at a terrifying speed and shut her eyes as a colossal crunch took out her propeller and the aeroplane tipped up on its end. There was an authentic moment of balance, where the aeroplane stood neatly on its front end, where physics took a breath of indecision and could have gone either way. It teetered for a split second – seeming to her like a score of seconds or more, in which her brain had time to compute that she was indeed going to die when it fell, horribly crushed or burnt to death in agony by the explosion – until the aeroplane thankfully slipped backwards and landed with a crash on its ruined undercarriage.

Almost immediately, it seemed, hands were about her. Men from the airfield, strong arms pulling her out, shouting and muttering, and then Jim's face, talking to her, but it was all jibber-jabber and she turned her head away, a pain searing through her neck as she did so. She might have passed out, but then she was awake and wanted to get up, get away from all these fellows. Jim was holding her hand and Ronnie's raised voice was saying, 'Give her space, give her air.' His voice was cracked and shrill, like she'd never heard it before.

'I'm all right, Ron,' she murmured.

Ronnie's terrified face loomed over her. 'Oh Jesus Christ, Del, you could've died.'

'But I didn't, Ron. I didn't.'

His grimy face stared at her. There was oil and grit in his sandy hair and his eyes were white and round amid the muck. 'Cos you're such a bloody good pilot, that's why. That's what saved you, landing on one wheel. Bloody brilliant. They couldn't take that away from you, Del. They can't beat you on that.'

'Not now,' said Jim and scooped her up like a doll and carried her back to the hangar. They laid her out on some tablecloths brought from the tea tent and put a picnic rug over her. Someone was fetching a doctor from Lincoln, but it'd be a while. Jim held her head and gave her sips of milky sugary tea, just as she liked it. She was moving each finger and each toe, bending each knee a touch and each elbow. Everything was working. Her head ached and her neck was sore. But, thank the stars, she'd survived. She slipped in and out of sleep, waking for a sip of tea then dozing again. Her thoughts strayed to the wrecked aircraft itself, her beautiful Blackburn, crumpled and ruined.

'Sorry about the aeroplane,' she said.

'Don't be daft,' whispered Jim. His voice was low and soothing, but there was a shrill sound coming from outside the tent. It was Ronnie, shouting, then another voice, a low man's voice yelling back, angry.

'That's murder, that is. Attempted murder, you rotten bastards.'

Jim shouted, 'Don't, Ron!'

The other man's voice now: 'What are you saying, mate? You accusing us of murder? Where's your proof? I'll have the law on you, bloody cheek. Say that again, I'll get the police on you.'

'It's a fucking outrage!' yelled Ron. 'I'll beat the shit outta yer.'

She wanted to say, 'Ronnie, come away,' but her throat hurt too much.

Someone else said, 'Get them out of here. Go see to your pilot. Bloody Cockney troublemaker. You didn't check your aeroplane right, don't blame us. Mechanic's fault if the wheels fall off.'

'Ronnie,' croaked Della and his face was there, before her.

'I did check the wheels, Del. I did. I know I did. I'm sorry, Del, I'm so sorry. Those bastards – the split pins were gone. Someone took the split pins.'

And Jim raised his voice to his brother for the first time ever in Della's hearing, and he said, 'NOT NOW, RON!', then fell to stroking her hair. And then it was as if Mam were there, talking soothingly to her, not to worry, sleep now, pet. And she did sleep. The next few hours passed in a blur of half-waking, half-sleeping, the exhaustion from weeks of touring and the shock of the accident knocking her out almost cold.

*　　*　　*

She awoke in a hospital bed, in Lincoln. It was morning and they said she'd been there one night. Nothing broken, but severe bruising, whiplash and concussion. Nothing serious, and she'd be out in a day or two. If they could get another aeroplane, she thought, she'd still have time to make it to Cleethorpes for the end of the month. But then it came home to her that she had nearly died, that her beloved aeroplane had nearly killed her. Could she fly on regardless? Could she ignore such a warning? The short answer was, yes. The long answer was, yes indeed. She hadn't come this far to give up now. She didn't have to think about it much before her decision was made. The best response was to thumb her nose at the saboteurs and the naysayers and carry on flying, getting better, learning more, and outfoxing the lot of them.

On the second day, Jim and Ronnie came and sat with her. First, she asked them to send a telegram to Mam, to tell her she was all right and not to worry. Della was worried that her family might read something in the press before she could get a message to them. Ronnie filled her in on what the local papers had to say that morning about the brave aviatrix who stepped out of her aeroplane after a near-fatal smash. They said they'd had to shove their way through journalists and photographers to get into the hospital. Everyone wanted the real story.

'And what is the real story?' Della asked. 'What's all this about the split pins?' These held the wheel onto the axle, smothered in grease; you wouldn't necessarily notice them if they weren't there. But without them the wheels would fall off, no doubt about that.

Both brothers looked about suspiciously, as if the nurses might be spies.

Ronnie said, 'We didn't think you'd remember that.'

'I remember it all right. And I want to know who you were shouting at, outside the tent.'

'I can't prove it. It's just like before. I can't prove a thing.

But when you were resting with Jim, I had a good look at the axle and I saw it. The nuts were there, the collars, axle grease freshly on, all that. But the split pins were gone. There's no way we'd've forgotten 'em. Someone took those pins.'

'You don't know that,' said Jim, quietly.

'I know it wasn't us. The only logical explanation is someone – and not any old thug – it'd have to be a mechanic or even a pilot, who knew exactly what he was doing. What he could get away with, what wouldn't be spotted. And what'd be most likely to ruin your flight. Some bastard took those pins and they probably just wanted to teach you a lesson. But you could've died, love.'

Della lay in silence for a few seconds, gazed out of the window beside her bed and watched a cloudless square of sky, blank, unhelpful.

'Why do they do it, Ron? Why do they hate me so much?'

Ronnie sighed and wiped a hand over his face. He looked tired, haggard even. *Maybe he's had enough of all this*, thought Della. Maybe working with an aviatrix is just more trouble than it's worth. But then he folded his arms and looked her in the eye. 'They're jealous. They don't want a woman making it look easy. If a woman can do it, what does that say for the size of their cocks?'

'EXCUSE ME!' A white-capped nurse stood stiffly nearby, her face flushed with outrage.

And all three of them burst out laughing, but oh, it did hurt her insides. It hurt like hell.

12

It was magic hour, that brief time before darkness where everything glows. She approached from the south-west, from a modest airfield near Waltham, flying high into the darkening sky. She flew a two-seater Blackburn, a replacement for her wrecked one, brought up in pieces on the railway from London at Johnson and Miller's expense. For her first night flight, Ronnie and Jim had outlined her wings with electric lights and she carried a powerful searchlight, to wow the crowd when she came closer. She continued north-east towards the estuary and the waiting crowds. The street lamps along the Kingsway were strung with coloured bulbs just switched on, while the promenade was filled with jostling tents, glowing with the golden hues of lamplight, and bustling people buying food and drink and chatting away in the sultry August night of 1913. The carnival atmosphere was heightened by a brass band on the pier, as well as roving groups of instrumentalists collecting pennies in their hats. The sun was setting over the broad Humber estuary, the glow of dusk reflecting pools of gold from the puffy clouds and streaks of amber across the lapping tide. A grand evening for the Meggies, those Cleethorpes residents out in force, eagerly awaiting the local girl flyer to swoop in.

There was a section of the beach marked out with torches where she could land and, as she'd asked, it was almost directly opposite her front door. As she came in, she flicked on the searchlight and swooped it over the crowds, saw them pointing and waving, did two circuits over the beach, then came in to land. The first to reach her was a local mechanic, hired by Johnson and Miller to watch the aeroplane while she did the rounds.

He waved at her and asked, 'All well?'

'Yes, thanks, flying well,' and she added, 'Don't leave her for a second, will you?' He shook his head and patted the aeroplane's flank, as though it were a favourite horse.

Next to arrive were Puck and Cleo, Puck waving his arms like a hooligan and trailing a gang of excitable lads all around his age, shouting 'Hie, hie!' while Cleo was screaming, 'Della! Della! Della!', incandescent with excitement, hopping manically to try to get up into the aeroplane. Cleo, now nearly three and a half, had shot up and looked unfeasibly tall. Della felt a pang about how much she had missed by being away, but it couldn't be helped. Puck too had grown and filled out, at last looking all of his seventeen years – in height and build if not in behaviour, which was still characteristically silly. Puck picked Cleo up and Della reached down and hauled her in. The lithe, leggy body on her lap was an absolute tonic – to feel her sister's warmth and to see the pride in her face was like medicine after a long illness. 'My favourite sister!' cried Cleo and nuzzled into her neck. How Della had missed her family. And her home.

Next to come were Mam, happy tears making her eyes glint in the lamplight; Auntie Betty flanked by Sam Lidgard, arm in arm; Midge and a male companion both dressed up to the nines; and even oldest sister Gertie had come from Hull with her husband and three boys, though the boys were playing chase and largely ignoring proceedings. Della passed Cleo to Mam and climbed down, to the sounds of whoops and cheers from the crowd. A chant began of 'We-love-Meg-gie! We-love-Meg-gie!' Cleo wriggled down from Mam's arms and flung her own around Della's legs, leaving Mam to hug her pilot daughter and say into her ear, amidst the chanting and the yelling and the madness of it all, 'So glad you're down safe.'

A huge hug next from Auntie Betty, whose face was a picture of pride and appropriation – 'Look at you!' she crowed. 'My girl aviatrix!'

'Thank you, Betty,' Della replied, her voice muffled in her aunt's mammoth embrace, her throat rather choked from this occasion of vindication, where the two women who had fancied flight on this very beach, sailing kites like dreams in the sky, were now hugging beside Della's Blackburn. 'Thank you for everything.'

A kiss then from Gertie, blonde hair pinned back in fashionable Grecian style, curvy in a summer frock – how pink-cheeked and well she looked! – standing beside her older husband Eric, grave and embarrassed at all this fuss, his vivacious wife patting Della's cheek with pride.

'Aren't you clever!' Gertie cried. 'And I love your magpie outfit.'

Another hug, from Midge this time, all louche and proprietary; dressed in the latest, figure-hugging gown and enormous feathered hat, she said to anyone who was listening, 'I taught her everything she knows – about the entertainment business, that is.' And a solemn handshake from her foppish companion. Puck bumped into him as he showed off to his rowdy mates on the beach, who were hopelessly trying to impress local girls – 'Sorry old bean!' said Puck, who received a scowl from Midge's man but, unaffected by others' disapproval as usual, clapped Della on the shoulder and said, 'Bloody proud of you, sis. Brought some chaps from school to watch. Bloody impressed, I can tell you.'

'Puck! Language!' cried Mam, as ever.

Della asked her, 'Where's Pop?'

But Mam didn't say, just looked across the beach, across the Kingsway to their house and shook her head. Pop hadn't come.

Midge overheard and said, 'I tried to get him to come, Del. But the stubborn so-and-so said his leg was aching him and he wouldn't shift.'

Della looked over to the house and saw the curtains were closed in Pop's study. He hadn't even watched her. All at once, she was filled with the bitter taste of failure – and resentment too, that Pop would make himself the centre of attention by not coming, and so try to steal her moment from her. Puck could please Pop with a dead worm, but Della landing a flying machine on to their very beach was not enough.

Then, the *Grimsby Gazette* reporter and photographer muscled in and Della was on publicity duty for a while. She was introduced to local dignitaries, but was much more interested in the crowd of so-called ordinary people, the ones who mattered to her far more, in fact, who came up and loitered behind the great and the good, between whom Della would thrust a hand to shake and sign people's event programmes. She recognised some faces from schooldays, the local shops, friends of friends – and there was Mrs Butters, for whom Della excused herself from dignitary talk and gave a big hug. Then she saw that Harriet, their maid, was right behind her. Harriet said, 'Can't believe it's you, Miss Dobbs.'

'Don't be daft,' said Della. 'It's Della, not Miss Dobbs.'

'It's Meggie Magpie actually!' joked the *Gazette* reporter, extricating her for more photographs, remarking, 'In 1900 there was scarcely a motor on the road and Icarus was still considered the representative flying man. But now, even girls can fly!' There was talk of some passenger flights, there and then, for some of the illustrious guests, but Della said that night flights were not safe and she would do it in the morning. Then there was talk of a dinner, even though it was past ten at night. Della was trying to say she needed to get the aeroplane back to Waltham and then go home and see her family, if that was all right with everyone, when a tap on her shoulder made her turn around to face the chest of a very tall young man.

He was dressed in white shirtsleeves and beige trousers,

with a matching jacket slung over one shoulder. He was smiling down at her – so very tall! – and he held out his right hand and she shook it. That face. She knew it, but a younger, softer version of it.

'Dudley Willow,' she said and a broad grin took over her face. 'Well, I never.'

'I watched you fly in. Stunning aeroplane that Blackburn. And your flying? You're a marvel, Della.'

And you're a man, thought Della. How the skinny tall boy of her memories had transformed into this confident young man, still towering over her, but filled out and just as relaxed in his own skin as he had been all those years before. The crowd buzzed and jostled around him, yet he was unaffected by it somehow, as if he were apart, thinking his own thoughts. Was it possible he was only fifteen? But he was always old for his years, Dud. Wise owl. Oh, if only the crowd would evaporate and they could wander off and talk.

'I can see you're busy,' he said and his face changed as he was jostled by some lads, crowded by the others around him. 'I just wanted to say hello.' He turned to go, but Della put her hand on his arm and said, 'No, wait! I mean, can you wait around a bit?'

'Course I can,' he said and stepped aside, while Della took her leave of the press, making arrangements for passenger flights from Waltham in the morning, alongside other photo opportunities and meetings with VIPs later that day. The journalist said he'd send a car to the Waltham airfield for her now and she could take it back to Cleethorpes whenever she was ready. Gertie's boys and Cleo were starting to flag at the late hour, so Della wished them goodnight and said she was flying back now, that a car would bring her home in an hour or so and please don't wait up. She retrieved her flying goggles from a sleepy Cleo in Mam's arms and turned to look for that tall boy. Where was he? He was over by the Blackburn, of course, inspecting it in all its glory, chatting avidly with the mechanic and pointing to its wings. She went over to Dudley and said, 'I'm flying back to Waltham now.'

'Yes, I thought so. It was marvellous to see you, Della. Do keep in touch.'

She looked at him and smiled. He smiled back.

Della leaned in and said, 'Do you want to come with me? Or do you have to be somewhere?'

Dud looked shocked, then replied, 'Nowhere. Nowhere at all.' He slipped on his jacket, clambered briskly up into the passenger seat at the front and Della climbed into the pilot's seat behind him. She could see he had some difficulty manoeuvring those extremely long legs into the cockpit, poor chap. The mechanic did the honours and swung the prop, and before long they were up in the night sky above Cleethorpes beach, leaving behind sand and sea, guests and gossiping: who was that beanpole Yorkie that Meggie Magpie took for a ride in her aeroplane that night?

She glanced down and saw the seafront's lights shrink to a glistening sprinkle as she ascended. Dud kept turning his head this way and that, scanning the streets below and giving the odd excitable wave to curious late-night pedestrians, even though in all likelihood they could not see him clearly. It moved her very much to see her home town from the air – to see it from above, humbled as a doll's town. She changed her course to fly over the streets she knew well before turning south again towards Waltham. She flew them high over dark, looming shapes of mysterious trees and across secretive fields, no people or creatures in sight. The veiled landscape was one with the night. Della felt as though she and Dud were the only souls in the sky. All the birds' heads were under their wings and other flying things safely stowed under leaves and in crevices. Yet Dud pointed out two bats dancing in the air beside the spire of Humberston Church. He turned his head to her, his face lit up by the lights strung about her wings, but also by joy, his first flight, and a night flight at that. Her chest swelled with pride that it was her who was giving him that gift, honoured that he trusted her to keep him safe. Her childhood friend, her compatriot and correspondent in all things aviation, Dudley Willow.

Just before they reached the appointed airfield, they saw the static white sails of a windmill. Dud turned his head to watch it as she passed. Coming in to land, she saw her trusty mechanics standing outside the hangar, waiting for her. Once she'd stopped the aeroplane and was climbing out, Ronnie said, 'All good?' and she gave him the thumbs-up, at which he began to remove the lights from the wings. Jim stood with arms crossed, staring at Dud, whose face as he climbed out was glowing from the cleansing wind and happiness.

'That was incredible!' Dud cried and laughed. Della laughed too. She remembered her first flight with Dutrieu, the delight bordering on ecstasy. It rather thrilled her to think of him feeling overwhelmed with it all, and she its architect.

Ronnie said to Della, 'Aren't you going to introduce us, then?'

'Ronnie, Jim, this is an old friend of mine, Dudley Willow.'

'Doesn't look old,' muttered Jim, but held out his hand, which Dud shook with alacrity, Ronnie's too.

'It's an honour to meet you. You're Della's engineers, I take it?'

The brothers finished removing the lights in silence, Ronnie smirking and Jim glowering, but Dud went on unfazed.

'Course you are. Well, you've done a grand job on this Blackburn. What an aeroplane! All those years ago we used to bang on about how good Blackburns are and now you're actually flying one, Della! It's magnificent!'

Ronnie said, 'You know your aeroplanes then, lad?'

'I do. I'm an aviation fanatic.'

'He really is,' added Della. 'We've been writing to each other for four years. He's a whizz with aeroplanes. Knows everything about them.'

'Doesn't fly then,' stated Jim. 'Doesn't look old enough.'

'No, sadly,' said Dud. 'And with these clodhoppers and heron's legs, perhaps I never will. I was always fascinated by the mechanical side of aeroplanes, the engineering of it. Like with this Blackburn, the way that the various weights are arranged – the fuel, oil, pilot and passenger – gives it the perfect centre of gravity. So clever. But I've never been a passenger till tonight. And now I might just cut my legs off to fly again, if that's what it takes!'

Ronnie said, 'What's your current top three aircraft then?'

'For speed or manoeuvrability?' asked Dud, eyes narrowed in thought.

'Both!' cried Ronnie. 'Look, I'd offer you a cuppa, lad, but there's no facilities here. Come and take a pew in the hangar though and we can chat.'

Della excused herself to find the car waiting for her beyond the airfield gate, where she asked if the driver would wait for a while. He said it was no skin off his nose and he'd wait all night if necessary; he was getting paid by the hour after all. She walked back to the hangar and the four of them chatted for an hour or so, sharing thoughts and ordering aeroplanes in lists of favourite this and worst that, disagreeing and arguing, handling various bits of kit, laughing and shouting each other down. Even Jim chuckled. Dud had that effect on people. Put them at ease. Not an awkward bone in him, just affable.

Ronnie said it was nearly midnight, so they brought the Blackburn into the hangar, and Jim said they must be getting back to their guest house in the village. They'd see her in the morning for the passenger flights, and was her car still waiting? She took a peek outside and saw it there in the dark, the friendly driver probably hunkered down behind the wheel and snoozing, enjoying his ever-increasing hourly wage ticking by. So, her two mechanics left her and Dud, Jim glancing back suspiciously, Ronnie smiling knowingly.

'They're great chaps,' said Dud, his hands mucky from

handling aeroplane parts, greasy smudges down his trousers and once-crisp white shirt.

'Your lovely suit,' she said.

'Oh, I don't mind. Though Father would spit if he saw it!'

They talked of their fathers. Dud's father was still determined he would be going to Leeds University to study textiles and then to come into the family business, just as he had done at Dud's age. She told him how Pop let her down, how it was all getting her down; how sick she was of England and its disdain for female pilots, about not being able to fly competitively here, but worse, the sabotage; how she was seriously thinking of going to Europe, France first, then perhaps Germany.

'I'm more than thinking about it. I'm determined to go. And go soon. I'll probably go to France next month.'

Dud looked gutted, then recovered and said, 'Jolly good idea. It's far and away the best thing for your career, I'm certain of that.' But his face showed how torn he was and he looked as if he longed to go with her, trapped as he was by his school and university and his father and the textiles business he had shored up like four high walls around him. And she felt lucky that she had a choice, that her future had a shape to it and she was the one who would shape it, not her father or anyone else, but herself.

'I don't speak French though,' she said.

'Oh, I do it at school. I can send you a phrasebook and you can get practising before you go.'

'If only you could come and be my translator.'

'Gosh, yes,' he gasped. 'If only.'

She looked at him with sympathy and he was staring at her intently.

'It's such an honour to know you, Del.'

'Oh, don't. It's just me.'

'I know that. But you are a remarkable person. You knew what you wanted to do and there were so many things in your way. But you did it anyway.'

'I just knew it was the thing for me. There didn't seem any choice, somehow.'

Dud sighed and said, 'I don't know what that thing is yet, for me.'

'Maybe it's flying,' she said and immediately regretted it.

There was a pause, then she asked, 'What do you love doing, Dud? I mean really love?'

'Horses. You know how I love horses. Riding them. Looking after them.' He gazed off into the far distance and she could see that look in his eye, the one she had had at his age about flying. 'I feel like I know them somehow. That they know me. That must sound stupid.'

'No, it doesn't actually. When you ride them, you become one with them.'

'Yes! That's it! How did you know? You've never ridden horses, have you?'

'It's just the same with aeroplanes. And I used to get that on my bicycle. It's like you fuse, somehow.'

'Yes! And for me, it's as if when I move my horse forwards or backwards, it's my legs I'm moving. I don't have to ask it or even think it. It goes beyond that, it's quicker than that.'

'I know exactly what you mean,' said Della and he was gazing at her, so young that face of his, so young. She wanted to kiss him, but he was only fifteen. That was wrong, wasn't it? She imagined what some might say: that it was immoral, that she was a young woman and he was barely a man. But Della was only nineteen herself, only four years' difference, so did it matter? If they had been in their twenties or thirties, nobody would care. But surely it's beyond that with Dud, after their years of letters. It's true friendship and how old they are and who's older than who doesn't matter, does it, surely? That handsome young face, so starry-eyed towards her, the glamorous pilot. What rot, she knew that. But if he loved her, if she kissed him now, he'd love her even more. A cruel thought entered her mind: what a pleasant tit for tat it would be on Claude, to have her own adoring fan to follow after her, as she'd done for him. That noxious little fact ruined the moment and made her turn away.

'We'd better go, Dud,' she said and gathered her things. 'I'll drop you off at your digs.'

Della padlocked the hangar doors and they walked without speaking to the car, the field sodden with dew beneath their feet. They woke the driver with a start, and he pretended he hadn't been sleeping and started talking nonsense about his job, driving this person or that person about and who said what and how funny it was, and all the time Della was looking away from Dud and feeling she'd sullied something very important but it was too late now. And before she knew it, they were back in Cleethorpes and Dud was telling the driver where to drop him, and he was getting out. He held the door open to say goodbye and she said, 'I'll send you my address from Europe, Dud. Will you write to me?'

'Course I will,' he said and smiled. 'I always will.'

13

She had never known cold like it. The cold-in-your-bones kind of cold induced by long-distance flying was insidious and depressing. She was dressed in warm layers under her leather jacket; no more of that silly black and white outfit she had to wear on her British tour – now she was in France and flying under her own name at last. Despite these layers and a helmet and fur-lined boots, she still felt as if ice-water encased every muscle, every sinew and nerve, so that her movement was laboured and even her mind felt frozen. So bundled up against the cold was she, and so cold was the air, that she had brought no food to eat on this cross-country trip, as she couldn't have retrieved food from a pocket if she'd tried. It would have frozen solid by then anyway, and she wouldn't want to eat frozen sandwiches, hungry as she was. She'd been flying for ninety minutes, her teeth chattering involuntarily on and off the whole time, and she felt weak from hunger. She never liked to eat before a flight, as it made her nauseous, but now she cursed her stupidity at missing breakfast. And she couldn't land and grab a bite, as tempting as it was, for then her bid to win the Coupe de La Rochelle would be void, and she'd come this far. The prize of 1,000 francs would be awarded to the pilot who made the flight from Poitiers to La Rochelle on the coast in the best time.

Flying cross-country over long distances required a whole new bag of tricks. Firstly, there was the endurance of it, the ability to keep focused and sane for hours of flight, to stand the cold and keep your mind and body active. Then, there was a different set of problems concerning navigation. Watching out for the odd lake or farmhouse wasn't enough when you were flying a hundred miles. Tools were needed: at the very least, a compass (usually fixed within the aeroplane) and map. But where do you put a map, bundled up like an Eskimo in a windy cockpit with no cover? She'd talked to other pilots and gleaned some tips. She had rolled her map in a telescope case strapped to her leg. Yet removing it was difficult, so it was largely there for emergencies – that is, when she was hopelessly lost. She had memorised most of her route from Poitiers to La Rochelle. Navigating from the air on a good clear day, she always felt like a giant stepping through a model village. She could see the land's future rolling towards her: from only a thousand feet she could see fifty miles away. She followed the railway lines from Poitiers to Niort. From Niort, she followed the canal, La Sèvre Niortaise, that meandered in a higgledy-piggledy fashion through the heart of marshy country known locally as Venise-Verte, or Green Venice. She was very pleased with her neat navigational system and it worked well – until the fog came up just beyond Niort, that was.

Flying above thick fog was like trying to wake from a nightmare. With no sight of the canal or the land surrounding it and even sound being muffled, it was as if the world had melted, leaving only cloud forever and ever. Absolutely alone in the firmament, she had to keep her head and focus on the compass.

Then she saw a hole in the fog ahead, a chance to catch a glimpse of the ground. She headed towards it with glee, seeing snatches of the ground that made her long to go down to it. But the moment she reached it, without warning her Farman biplane dropped a hundred feet. *What on earth?* She struggled with the controls to avoid a deadly side-slip into oblivion and tried to turn into a gradual arc, but dropped again. There was nothing for it but to try a measured descent and land somewhere. After an hour and a half of flying and the Coupe within striking distance, it was to come to a bumpy end, and if the fog didn't clear in a matter of seconds, she knew it could be all over for her, full stop. She volplaned down, telling the blasted fog, 'Clear, you bugger, clear!' and this time it did, revealing farmers' fields surrounded by a complex network of canals, rushing at her aeroplane at an alarming rate. She edged towards a furrowed field that looked reasonable and hoped for the best. The aeroplane came down with a bump, a lump in the ground caused it to hop back into the air for an instant and then back down to earth with a smash, and she heard a crack underneath her, then something splintering behind. The impact had driven soft brown earth up in a cloud, which rained on her head. Her eyes were protected by goggles, but her mouth was open. She spat out soil and tasted blood. The rest of her body was so bundled up she felt held together by her clothes. The fog began to descend around her again, as if it had waited patiently for her to gather herself. Soon she was encased in white. If she weren't so raw with cold and her ribs weren't aching so much, it would have been restful. Time passed in shock and unwillingness to move; her body was so relieved to be earthbound again, it refused to budge, like a spoilt cat in a heavy sleep. Yet her mind was spitting with anger, that her attempt at the cup had ended like this all because of the old enemy, weather. If there had been no fog, she'd be on her way to La Rochelle by now, and perhaps even a longed-for record. Oh, how she wanted to break a record: distance, altitude, speed, she didn't mind. In these days, when new machines were made almost daily, records were made and broken almost by the day too, but it would be grand to hold one, even if only for a few hours. But it was not to be and, she told herself, 'You're alive. And the Farman is fixable. So, stop whining.'

She was answered by alarmed French voices, and faces

were around her, looming out of the fog like phantom balloons. There were three or more of them, country people, patting her arms, her head, talking at her, smiling and staring at the broken contraption around her. One woman stroked her cheek and crooned. Della saw blood on the woman's fingers as she withdrew her hand. Then the woman removed Della's goggles and helmet, upon which the gathering gasped in one voice.

'*C'est une femme!*' crooned the woman, echoed by others – '*Une femme? Une femme!*', succeeded by some guffaws, more gasps and even a solitary round of applause from a pair of unseen hands. To see an aviator crash in your field must be quite the event, but to find a female pilot even more fun. Two burly men pulled her from the aeroplane and tried to lay her down, but her legs, though shaky, were all right and she pulled herself upright and said, '*Merci, merci,*' to the gathering group.

'*Ça va? Ça va?*' people were asking.

She gathered herself and focused her mind on Dud's French phrasebook, of all the hours spent practising the foreign words with Betty and Mam before she left. '*Oui, oui. Bien, bien merci,*' she said and then asked, 'Telephone? Telegram?'

The small crowd clustered about her, around ten strong now – *where do people appear from at every crash?* It always surprised her, but she reasoned it was of course the sound of the aeroplane passing over that caught one's attention. A flying machine was still a novelty for many and miraculous for some. Perhaps these French country people had never seen one, who knew? She was so accustomed to the wonder of flight that she forgot at times that it was alien for many, and still viewed with a religious distaste by some who believed that God never meant man to fly – and certainly not woman.

'*Oui, télégramme, là-bas. Allons-y,*' said a woman and took her arm.

'*Merci, mais, un moment, s'il vous plaît,*' she said as politely as she could, stepping aside to look at her downed aircraft. A quick check told her what she needed to know: some minor repairs were needed beneath and to the front, but nothing too bad. The rest seemed fine. All of this was accompanied by mutterings and fascinated gazes, hushed tones and subtle gasps, as onlookers watched the woman inspecting her machine as if an angel had stepped down into their field.

The group escorted her across the field and as the fog waxed and waned, she caught sight of a village beyond, not far to walk. The French chatter around her was friendly and comforting, though the series of questions frustrating, as her efforts at learning some French before she came served her well enough for getting about but didn't extend to complex conversations. She found herself saying sorry a lot: *Je suis désolée*, to which everyone always shook their heads and appeared genuinely pleased she'd tried any French at all. Beyond the field, a strong farmer's hand helped her over a stile and on to a road down to the village that was filling with people – how had word travelled so fast? – many of whom were shaking their heads in wonder. The words '*fille*' and '*femme*' bubbled around her like a brook, and one little girl even stepped nervously before her and handed her a messy bunch of weedy flowers hastily plucked from the roadside.

The fog was less thick in the village and she could see it was surrounded by the canals she'd spotted earlier, and that the name of this pretty place was Coulon. There were a number of facilities, including cafés, a hostelry, at least one hotel and, thankfully, a post office of sorts, though it sold vegetables too; there was a mound of pumpkins at its door. Here she removed some of her bulky clothes and stretched, to the postmistress's evident distaste. Della's ribs sent a shooting pain through her chest when she raised her arms. Other than that, her body felt relatively unscathed and she considered herself very fortunate. She sent a telegram to her French mechanic Luc at Poitiers, telling him of the damage to the aeroplane and requesting he come in a car with replacement parts and tools. She knew it would probably be several hours before he arrived; he may even have left for La Rochelle himself to meet her there, so wouldn't receive the forwarded telegram until later. There was a chance she would have to wait until the next day for him and for the repairs. So after allowing herself to be shepherded to a restaurant, she determined to relax and enjoy the hospitality. The owner, a tall dark man with a heavy moustache, was delighted with the aviatrix supping at his establishment and chuntered on to her as if she could understand every word. He brought her a dish of heated water and a cloth to clean her muddy, oily and blood-smeared face (she realised she had bitten her tongue on impact, hence the blood). He then brought wine, and hot chocolate too, followed by bread and gooey goat's cheese and a rich, red stew of autumn vegetables. All of these hurt her to eat, ravenous as she was, yet the red wine, full and comforting, slipped down easily like good medicine. Then, the village physician was summoned, who thankfully spoke English.

The doctor was courteous and unhurried, telling her to please finish her food before he examined her. Her chest ached as she breathed. When she accompanied him to his surgery afterwards, her self-diagnosis was confirmed – a cracked rib. But that was all, so she was relieved. The doctor kindly took her to the nearby hotel, checked in and allowed her to go to her room in peace.

While peeling off her clothes, she spotted her map and removed it from the telescope case. She spread it out on the floor and looked at the area where she had come down. What had made the aeroplane drop so suddenly like that? Simply the weather, the machine itself, or could the map solve the mystery? She scanned the square inch where it had happened and found no answer. She remembered that the air had seemed suddenly empty of resistance, as if flying over a great fire. Perhaps there was some industry down there, producing heat. Who could tell? She hoped it wasn't the aeroplane's fault, or hers.

Not quite satisfied, she crawled tentatively on to the bed, cradling her sore chest and curling up on her side, and before sleep stole in she thought first of Dud, then Cleo, and she wished for England. But thoughts of home inevitably led to Pop and how he had acted after her night flight to Cleethorpes. She had spoken with him the next day; after a round of passenger flights and more local honours, she had finally managed to knock on his study door. The first thing he had said was, 'My God! You've chopped off all your hair!' She had begun to tell him about her flights and he had seemed to be listening, but when he had said, 'Short hair does you no favours, Cordelia,' she had lost heart. She had asked after his leg and he had delivered a long monologue on pain. She had looked at him curiously, without feeling. It had been a cold moment; something had clicked in her mind, and Della at that point had given up on her father.

Thus, not everything in England had been rosy. She had been in France for some weeks now and found it had its fair share of charming people. French aviators were some of the world's best, as were their graceful aircraft. Female pilots were largely welcomed and treated well and it was a pleasure to meet two aviatrixes of whom she'd read all good things – Marthe Richer and Hélène de Plagino – and see them fly with skill and flair, despite the fact that both had only just achieved their licences, on the same day in June. French food was delicious and the wine delectable. Her mechanic Luc was very handy and skilful, polite and hard-working. But he did not speak much English beyond aircraft parts, and she did not speak much French, and after all, he was not Ronnie and he was not Jim. She'd tried to persuade them to come to Europe with her, but after her British tour had come to an end they had found very good positions at Farnborough airfield. She knew even as they said no that she was asking too much, that in financial terms, her life on the continent would be as erratic as the weather. With her substantial earnings from the Johnson and Miller tour, she had bought herself a Farman Shorthorn aeroplane – on Hilda Hewlett's recommendation – ordered from the Farman aerodrome itself at Châteaufort.

It was a good machine, worked well and did what it was told, mostly. (Not a patch on the Blackburn, but you can't have everything.) The Farman brothers themselves were considerate, highly knowledgeable and supportive, introducing her to Luc and assisting with finding a number of contracts for her to fly exhibitions and competitions around the country within her first month of arriving. In other words, she could not complain.

Her mechanic Luc was a stocky little fellow with a permanent shadow about the chops and rather bad teeth. He was a decent mechanic and very able at the technical side of things, but he had no interest in friendship beyond the aviation meetings, and would disappear between events to heaven knows where. Perhaps he had a family, a girlfriend somewhere, but between his natural reticence and the language barrier, Della could glean little of him beyond his job. Between shows, she would venture out into whichever French town or city she found herself in and wander about, seeing some sights; at these times, she found some measure of happiness, that her career had brought her here, to this foreign land she had only read about and dreamt of while growing up (mostly in aviation magazines, rather than stories, but still) – and now she was here, seeing a cathedral here, a château there with her own eyes, paid for by her own success. But she felt a continual pang in her chest at her own singular company. Seeing elegant places alone was a mixed blessing: time to contemplate their loveliness in peace, but no one to share it with, nobody to say, *Look at that!* or *Remember when* . . . *?* She'd retire to her digs and drink wine alone, writing letters home about the sensational things she'd seen, but it wasn't the same. And she never told of her accidents in these letters, which were perhaps

read by a few in the family, but were always answered by
Mam; she didn't want to worry Mam unnecessarily, or Betty
(and there was a perhaps misguided pride, with Betty; she
didn't want to admit any sort of failure to her early mentor).
When she wrote to Dud, she found herself being much more
honest about the hard times and admitted every smash and
mishap she had had, then descended into moping about how
miserable she was, for which she always apologised, keenly
aware of how envious Dud must be of her continental galli-
vanting. But she told him anyhow, she told him it all, and it
was a pleasure to write in English after struggling with a
foreign tongue all through the long days. It was hard, not
being able to speak the language fluently (though in truth her
French was getting better). In short, she was just plain lonely.

But the worst of it was that the competition circuit was not
quite how she had imagined. The idea of competition – of
flying at speed for prizes around a circuit or across open
country against talented pilots from all over the world – had
sounded thrilling and the epitome of freedom, everything
she'd sought to escape by leaving England and coming to the
continent. But in practice, it was quite something else. She
wrote about it to Hilda Hewlett, the only person she knew
who had first-hand knowledge of such things and who, being
a woman, would truly understand.

4th October 1913
Dear Mrs Hewlett,

*I hope you don't mind me writing to you. I don't think
you will, as you were so kind to me that day in Luton.
You'll see from the postmark that I'm now in France. It's
better here than England, that is true. And I'm earning
my way around the competition circuit.*

*But it's not all plain sailing (or plain flying). First, the
contracts are not good. I'm paid less than the male pilots.
And many of the prizes are for men only.*

The aviation meetings have big crowds and I'm learning
a lot from seeing aircraft and pilots from every country
you can think of, from Norway to Russia and further
afield. It reminds me of that international flavour there
always was in my Hendon days. You know Claude
Grahame-White once told me that women were not suited
to competition flying, that the 'cut and thrust of it is
unfeminine'. That annoyed me at the time and I really
wanted to prove him wrong. But what I'm finding is that
competition flying doesn't seem suited to aviation itself,
that flying too close to other pilots and their machines is
foolish and downright <u>dangerous</u>. The change in airflow
when another aeroplane flies over or under or behind or
before your own can be very choppy indeed, or even <u>disas-
trous</u>! As another aeroplane passes you by, the turbulence
from its prop wash is enough to make you side-slip or fall
from the sky.

I've seen four accidents now where air congestion had
caused an aeroplane to come down or at least be put in
difficulties. They fined those airmen and we all complained,
but the truth of it is that the more aeroplanes there are in
the air, the more the crowds cheer! The organisers know
what butters their bread! I've started avoiding competitions
that are oversubscribed, particularly those stuck within an
aerodrome. I'd rather do cross-country where the air isn't
crowded. I keep telling myself that Claude was wrong
about women and competition, and that I'm just being
sensible. But the feeling that I'm proving Claude's point
really rankles me!

I've come to the conclusion that I was spoiled by my
Johnson and Miller tour. Everything was laid on for me,
with nice hotels and all expenses covered, and Ronnie and
Jim my mechanics looked after me a treat. Now, I'm my
own boss, my own accountant and sponsor and promoter
– something I thought I wanted, but the truth is, it's all a

*bit exhausting and – sorry to sound a bit whiny – I'm
really and truly <u>fed up</u>.*

*Any advice you have would be very welcome, Mrs
Hewlett – or if I may, Hilda.*

Very best regards to you,
Della Dobbs

November 6th, 1913
Dear Della,

*How nice to hear from you. I was very sorry to hear of
your less than pleasing experiences on the competition
circuit in France. I do understand why you may feel at
times that aviation is not for you. I was never a keen flyer
but always much more interested in the engineering side of
things, as I told you. However, I believe that you are a
highly gifted pilot, a natural, if you like. I also believe that
you would feel something hollow at the centre of your life
if you were to give up on it completely. That is your choice
and one you can always change later on in life if needs be.
However, perhaps instead of giving up, you might consider
staying within the world of aviation yet absenting yourself
from this dicey pursuit of competition flying. That is where
much of the danger lies. If you were to consider aircraft
design, manufacture and also flight testing, then you might
find the balance you seek. I know you have the mechanical
mind necessary, from our discussion that day at Luton. You
may feel that this area of aviation is even more biased
against the female than flying itself, and you would be
right in most cases. But there are some women out there
– I would hope to include myself in this scant group –
who are carving out careers in this male-dominated world
and indeed, making quite a success of it.*

*With that in mind, since you are over in Europe, I
suggest you go on to Germany and visit the aviatrix Melli
Beese, of whom I have spoken to you before. She and her*

husband Charles Boutard are currently designing their
own aircraft and are based in Berlin. If you visit them, it
might show you a way of life that you could use as a
model for your own. They are young and ambitious, much
like yourself. My situation is somewhat different from
yours, being older, with an established marriage and being
a parent, whereas you have all that to come, of course. So,
although you are always welcome to visit me and observe
our work here, ask questions and so forth, I do feel that
some time spent with these two young people would benefit
you more aptly.

If you would like me to, I could write ahead to them
and make the introduction. I would be happy to. If it will
help you in some way, I would like to ensure that this new
science of aviation does not lose another of its far too few
females. There are several I know of already who have
tired of this manly atmosphere, let alone the inherent
danger, and have retired too early for my liking, and for
the future of women in aviation. Thus, we need pioneers
like yourself to fly the flag for female pilots everywhere.

Please do keep in touch, my dear, and very best wishes
to you in all your endeavours.

Yours sincerely,
Hilda Hewlett

14

In Neukölln, outside Berlin, in December 1913, Della shook the gloved hand presented to her and said, 'I'm sorry I don't speak a word of German.'

'It is no matter,' said Melli. 'I have always had some talent for languages. I speak several, even Swedish. I studied in Sweden as a sculptor, in my youth.'

'I only speak a bit of French. Foreign languages are not something that're encouraged very much in England.'

'And aviation, in England? Is that encouraged?'

'Yes, to a point. Well, for men, it is.'

'Ah, yes. Is there a country in the world where women are welcome in the air? I've yet to hear of it.'

Melli was dressed in an extraordinary get-up: a full-length fur flying coat with fur hood and fur knee-high boots. Fabulous winter flying gear. Della thought, *I must get myself some of those!* They stood in the Neukölln aerodrome, where Melli and her husband Charles had based their aircraft construction business. Beside them was the Beese-Taube aeroplane, the aircraft of Melli and Charles's own design, which was a sleek, one-seater monoplane. Della was itching to try it and tickled pink when Melli offered her a go.

The aircraft took off so swiftly it made her gasp. The difference between this powerful engine and her Farman Shorthorn – stored back at Châteaufort for safe keeping – was astonishing. The motor was a French air-cooled model and felt at least twice as powerful as the ones she was used to. She flew carefully, but allowed herself the joy of letting it go in the free air, and delighted in its roar as she turned about the skies over Berlin. It banked gracefully, it flew fast and true, it felt as if it weighed no more than a handful of feathers. Oh, it was a beauty! A true bird. Della was sorry to come back to earth, though again impressed at the speed and control of its descent.

Helmet and goggles off, she was so overcome with enthusiasm she clapped her hands on Melli's shoulders, then immediately drew back, embarrassed with herself. But Melli laughed and seemed delighted that the English aviatrix approved.

'It'd be terrific for flying stunts,' said Della.

'Yes, I agree. And reconnaissance too. It's so light and manoeuvrable.'

'Yes! So, how many have you sold?'

'None.'

Della was staggered. A beauty like this?

'Come with me and we will have a drink, some food. I will tell you all about it.'

Melli changed her clothes to a smart suede flying jacket, with a white collar and black necktie like a man's. Though her clothes were fairly masculine, her femininity was very much in evidence. She cut a striking and stylish figure and Della felt frumpy in comparison. In fact, she was so impressed with the German aviatrix and everything about her, it brought on an attack of shyness, which she forced herself to overcome. Melli took Della to meet Charles – a head taller than his wife, with an immaculate pointed moustache and clear blue eyes. They were newlyweds, only a few months married, and it showed. Their hands were often about each other, resting on an arm, nestled in the small of the back. They smoked the same cigarettes, sharing them from the packet. As they seated themselves in a local restaurant, Della felt as if she should excuse herself, to leave the couple be. But that was only her shyness, and she knew it. Melli and Charles appeared very happy to host her and particularly to have a good moan about their situation here in the German aviation world.

'It is because I am French,' said Charles. 'I am an alien. And now we are married, my wife is an alien too, in her own country.'

'No, Charles, it is because I am a woman. They cannot conceive that a woman could help to design and build an aircraft and that it would fly.'

'Perhaps it is both,' sighed Charles and stared dejectedly into the ashtray.

Melli went on, 'Observers came from our country's military, a few months ago. We could see they were impressed.'

'Who wouldn't be?' said Della, shaking her head.

'But they did not pursue it further. So, no German military pilots will have the chance to see the aeroplane, let alone fly it. We need contracts from the government to survive. They introduced a fund, the Flying Donation, but since we married, we are exempt – as Charles said, we are not German.'

'That's terrible.'

Melli stubbed out her cigarette and forced a smile. 'But you know, we are not to be beaten, are we, Charles? We have a new project. Very exciting! Will you tell her, Charles, or shall I?'

Della looked curiously at Charles, but he had not yet recovered sufficiently from his depression to comment.

'It is a boat-plane,' said Melli, triumphant. 'What do you think of that?'

'A flying boat?' cried Della. 'Excellent!'

'Yes, of our own design, with help from another. It has many new ideas, excellent ideas!'

Melli explained its intricacies.

It sounded superb, but Charles still stared downward and did not comment. He looked up and caught Della looking at him. 'We have put all our money in that flying boat. If it does not sell, we are finished.'

'But it will sell, Charles,' Melli went on, never fazed. 'Don't you think, Della? It is the future!'

Della said the right things. But she could not get Charles's down-turned face out of her head and hoped heartily that his despondency was proved wrong and Melli's prospects were securer than they seemed. Perhaps Hilda Hewlett had heard a glossy version of this handsome couple's life. The truth was that nothing was definite, their country was against them and the future was uncertain.

When Melli excused herself to the ladies' room, Charles watched her go and then leaned in conspiratorially.

'I would not say this before my wife, but things are not good here.'

'I'm sorry to hear that,' said Della, embarrassed and longing for Melli to return, though admittedly rather fascinated by what her husband was about to say.

'The situation regarding my French nationality threatens us more each day. What Melli omitted to mention is that the government observers that came to look at our aeroplane? They are part of a huge military push here in Germany. The Germans are arming themselves up to the eyes. And why, you ask? Why?'

She shook her head. The politics of Europe was of no interest to her, unless it got in the way of her flying.

'Friends have been warning us for months. Charles, they say, you must go back to France. But Melli won't listen. She is driven only by her ambition. She does not see what is coming. I've told her, you should divorce me. Become German again. Just for the time being, not forever. But for now. It is not safe here. For you too, Della. You should go back to England, soon, very soon.'

She was alarmed. 'Why is it not safe?'

Charles glared at her. 'They are preparing for something, don't you see? Gathering aeroplanes about them like armour. For what reason could they need so many aeroplanes, hmm? Can't you see?'

She glimpsed Melli returning blithely, making her elegant

way between the tables. Charles just had time to say in a hoarse whisper, 'War! You will see, soon enough. There will be war.'

On the train back to Paris, she thought gravely about what Charles had said. Was war coming, to Europe, to England even? She had heard talk of it, but hadn't quite believed it. This Frenchman seemed so sure. But Melli didn't seem bothered about it, hadn't even mentioned it. Perhaps Charles was overstating the case. Della thought of the two of them and realised she was overwhelmed by envy of their relationship, even though it was troubled. But it was only troubled by outside forces – clearly they loved each other. They were setting up this endeavour together and that was so appealing, especially to her lonely heart. She moped that she hadn't yet found her soulmate, someone who could fly with her. For them both to be pilots must be joyous. Della thought of how she had seen them fly together and how delighted they were with each other. She decided they were a genuine union, each other's rock and support, no matter that one was French and the other German. She was so jealous of them. Hilda's suggestion to visit Germany had been an eye-opener, a vision of what Della's flying future could be, but it was blotted by prejudice and poverty, and the threat of war.

Della got back to France on Christmas Eve. On her return to her hotel near Châteaufort, the manager handed her a letter from England. Mam's hand. She climbed the stairs to her room, looking forward to hearing all the family news. But why was this letter so much briefer than usual?

Dear Della,

I'm sorry to write with bad news, but it's not been possible to reach you any other way. Dearest, your Auntie Betty has passed away. She had a stroke a week last Tuesday and went quickly. She didn't suffer. I'm so sorry to

*give you this news as I know how very close you were and
how much you looked up to her and how fond she was of
you. Please be comforted to know that when I saw her only
days before she died, she was talking of you, how proud she
was of your career and your wonderful talents. She was full
of it, she always was, and mentioned your name almost
every time we spoke. Any news from the little one? she'd say.*

*She was buried in a quiet service at Cleethorpes
Cemetery. I'm sorry, love, but we couldn't get hold of you
in time. Gertie came and Puck too, as he was home from
school (though Pop's leg was bad keeping him in bed and
Midge couldn't get away from London). Mr Lidgard was
there and was a bit of a mess, keening at the graveside,
poor man. He told me he'd asked Betty to marry him,
many times, he said. Did you know? But apparently she
said she'd only had one husband and only wanted one
husband and that was her Truman. Her solicitor tells us
she did make a detailed will some years ago, so we shall
discover what her intentions were when things have gone
through probate, which may take some time as these things
do. There's no need for you to interrupt your tour and
come home. You get on with what you need to do. It's what
Betty would have wanted, I'd say.*

*Anyway, don't be too sad, love. Remember that she lived
a long, full and very happy life and died ever so
peacefully. Really, it's something to be glad about. Don't
take it to heart too much.*

Your loving mother,
Mam

Della spent Christmas Day lying on her bed, not eating,
not sleeping, though she was tired from her travels from
Germany and the hotel guests were celebrating the season
with roast goose downstairs. She clutched Mam's letter and
read and reread it. Betty, her mainstay, her mentor, was

gone. How Betty had believed in her, how much Betty had taught her, the money she gave to fund her flying, the ideas she planted in Della's mind that cold January night in 1909, where it all began. She owed her so much and now could never repay it.

But perhaps being here was enough, flying her way around Europe and being paid well to do so, showing the other pilots – especially the male ones – that she could do it too, that she was worthwhile and, more than that, talented and skilful, with her Broughton hands and brain. Mam was right, she should finish her tour and prove to the world that an English girl could fly her way around Europe. Betty's unwavering belief in Della had paid off in spades. Rest in peace, Betty Perry.

Just after Christmas, Della won a prize for flying the fastest from Douai to Arras and back. La Brayelle airfield near Douai invited her to try a day later for the Coupe Fémina at their aerodrome. She was gratified, as this most prestigious competition gave 2,000 francs to the woman who flew the longest distance entirely alone, without stopping, before sunset of the last day of December. Her early heroine Hélène Dutrieu had won it in both 1910 and 1911, flying around 160 miles the second time she triumphed.

There had been no award the previous year and Dutrieu was not flying much this year, and neither was another star of the French aviation scene, Marie Marvingt. Therefore Della felt she was in with a good chance. She arrived mid-morning, starting early, as there was to be an exhibition day at the airfield after lunch and she needed the space and time to complete as many circuits of the airfield as she could in order to compete for the Coupe. She was welcomed by Louis Bréguet, the talented aircraft designer who had constructed the airfield some years before, a good chap with a stupendous moustache. A few other pilots and plenty of ground crew were about, with whom Luc immediately began to banter, leaving Della to tinker with her Farman, making last-minute checks, but really just finding something to do to cover her shyness.

'Good luck with your flight today.' The voice was French, speaking English, an uncommon sound to her ears.

It was a male pilot, short of stature – in fact, almost exactly her height – with fair hair and friendly eyes, wearing a smart, tan flying suit. He held out his hand and she shook it.

'My name is Jérôme Montague and you are Miss Cordelia Dobbs of England.'

'I am.'

'It is a pleasure to meet you. Please, will you call me Jérôme? We are about the same age, I think, and perhaps should not stand on ceremony.'

'Pleasure to meet you too,' Della said, anxious to get back to her machine and think about starting her flight. But the friendliness of this young man arrested her, unaccustomed as she was since coming to France to much conversation.

'The pleasure is mine to meet such a talented aviatrix. Everyone is talking about you.'

'You speak English very well.'

'I try, I try. You do not speak French?'

'A little. I try.'

'Ah, with a French mechanic, that must be difficult for you here in France.'

'Well, it hasn't always been easy. But I get by.'

'I toured in Russia earlier this year and did not know a word of the language. I thought I'd go mad! Nobody to talk to.'

'Well, yes. There is that. You went to Russia? How interesting!'

'It was fascinating and I won many prizes! But it was lonely, you know?'

'I do know,' said Della.

Luc had appeared beside her, so she made her apologies and took her leave of Jérôme. Something about him made her smile as she climbed into her aeroplane, but now she must concentrate. She wanted to win this cup dearly, as to hold a record here in France was her most recent and most consuming passion.

The day was first-rate for flying, cold with plenty of lift, only a steady light breeze. Best of all, there were no crowds to distract or annoy her, apart from a few lads hanging over the gates on one side of the airfield, larking about, shouting and bragging about something. All else was quiet.

She went up smoothly and began to turn, flying over the boys. She thought she'd give them a treat by waving. They were watching her intently as she went up, until she lifted her arm to wave and the three of them each hurled something towards her aeroplane. An ear-splitting bang behind her told her something had hit the propeller. Everything juddered and then there was silence. Quicker than thought, she threw the stick forwards to get enough speed for flying. She looked up, wanting to choose a place to land, but the boundary fence rushed up at her like a train and she smashed into it. A great splintering sound assaulted her ears and she was thrown forward, landing on the ground on her side with a thud. Shaken but not aware of any pain as yet, she hauled herself up and scanned the scene, checking to see that nobody had been in the aeroplane's way when it came down, and that the engine wasn't about to catch fire. Before the ground crew reached her, she saw, beyond her machine, the same boys, roaring with laughter as they threw more sticks at her aeroplane and then ran away hooting.

Luc arrived first and Jérôme Montague was right behind him. Luc touched her carefully on one shoulder: 'All right?' he said, visibly worried.

'Yes, yes. I'm all right.'

There was fussing and questions, but she brushed them aside, hot and shaking with anger at what those little bastards had done to her aeroplane.

'Did you see?' she spat. 'Those boys threw sticks at my aeroplane. They could've killed me.'

Luc shook his head and Jérôme said, 'Yes, it was seen, please do not upset yourself. One of the crew has been sent to fetch the police.'

'Good. Thank you,' puffed Della. She tried to calm her breathing, but staring at her stricken machine filled her with hate. She could see it would not be fixed today, and they were moving on tomorrow, so there went the Coupe. There were only a few days till the deadline, and she would not have time to try again. She was so angry she wanted to wail bitterly, but she couldn't let the men see her like that. So, she breathed in deeply and that cracked rib ached again and she exhaled miserably.

'Come, Miss Dobbs. Hot coffee for you, plenty of sugar,' said Jérôme. While Luc and another mechanic began to look at the broken wood of her Farman, she let herself be taken to an enclosure, where she drank the coffee and shared a cigarette with Jérôme. Cigarettes were not something she usually partook of (she thought they tasted grim), but the hot smoke calmed her as it filled her lungs, despite it clawing at her rib. She ached down her left side and knew there would be bruising there, but she was otherwise intact. Another lucky escape. But how many lives could this cat have? she wondered.

'I still can't believe it,' she sighed. 'What were those boys playing at?'

'I remember throwing stones at a cow once as a boy,' said Jérôme, with a sparkle in his eye. She couldn't imagine him doing anything horrible. Such a refined face. 'Boys do cruel things. And there's something about watching us fly that turns people crazy.'

'How so?'

'Some of these crowds at aviation meetings. One must never trust them.'

'I've seen them climb over boundary fences and suchlike, but I must say they're quite well-behaved in England.'

'Same here, mostly. But in Russia they were terrible. They would run onto the field where the aeroplanes were coming in to land. And they actually enjoyed accidents, you could see it in their eyes. They loved a good smash, you know? Even here in France the crowds seem disappointed if there are no crashes.'

Della grimaced. 'That's appalling. What do they think we are?'

'They do not think of us at all. Only the spectacle, I believe. They call it in America a Flying Circus. Yes, that is what we are. A circus to them. Clowns of the air.'

'What a depressing thought.' Della frowned. 'But, I'm afraid I need them, as it's their money that pays for me to fly. So they have their uses.'

'True, for some perhaps. I am lucky, I will admit this. I have no need of money. I fly only for pleasure.'

They talked on, of their family backgrounds, how they had come to flying. Jérôme's family were from Paris and clearly very wealthy, his father something in shipping, with a house in the city and another in Nice. They indulged him in this flying lark; it was a boyish hobby in their eyes, but Della could see how smitten he was with aviation. He had no plans for making any sort of business out of it – he didn't need to – but his obsession was to break every record in the book. He spoke of flying over mountains, over the Atlantic, over Antarctica and onwards.

'This new technology we have in aviation, even the sky is not the limit. One day, we will reach the moon, you will see.'

His face lit up with it. A picture popped into her mind of Melli Beese's vibrant eyes, speaking of her flying boat. How her own face must have looked to B. C. Hucks, to Hubert Oxley, and to Claude. And then she thought of Charles Boutard and everything he'd told her.

'What if war comes here, to France? Will you fight?'

But even talk of war could not dampen Jérôme's mood. 'Oh, if war will come, it will come. There is nothing we can do to stop it. But I will not fight on the ground, in the dirt. Never. I will fly for my country, fly above the earth and serve France from the air. We will have the best flying force in the world! If only you could join us!'

Jérôme's enthusiasm was a tonic. She thought about how his buoyant disposition must have stood him in such good stead in this crazy aviation business, especially traipsing around Russia. On long-distance flights too, where a merry character might resist the despondency and irritation of facing ordeals through grim weather and breakdowns and delays. When he had to go and prepare for the aviation meeting she was sad to see him go, but they arranged to meet later that evening for dinner. This thought imbued her with a pleasant sensation of warmth, like slipping into a bath.

She went over to the hangar where her Farman had been taken, to find Luc working on the aeroplane. She told him she felt much better now and set to work with him. The crowds were gathering for the show and the atmosphere was buzzing. She stepped outside to look for Jérôme, and saw him at a hangar across the way, talking and laughing away with his mechanics. She looked up at the sky and saw storm clouds gathering in the east. The wind was picking up. She was quite glad she was not to fly again today. But it was not too bad and should hold for a while. There would still be plenty of time to see some good flying today.

She took her leave of Luc for a while and headed over to the main hangar, from where she wanted to watch the racing. Hundreds of spectators had gathered around the airfield and some of them turned to stare or point at her as she walked by, the woman in a flying suit. But she'd disappoint them today by staying earthbound. Jérôme was nearby and she caught his eye, waving and grinning. He ran over to her and she reached out to shake his hand.

'*Bonne chance!*' she said.

'I do not need it!' he crowed. 'I am the best here by far! I will prove it!' and, full of a young man's pride, he sped back to his machine – a smart Bréguet Type IV – and jumped into the seat. Della watched him with interest, wondering if his actual skill would live up to his bravado.

Jérôme took off effortlessly and ascended apace to a great height. He produced figures of eight, sharp turns, dives and swoops, and it was clear that he had a sure and instinctive judgement of speed and distance. Undoubtedly a born aviator, with bewitching hands. Oh boy, could he fly! Such precision and delicacy of controls as she had rarely seen; it was a thrill to watch him. He came in low and skimmed across the crowd, the people gasping and cheering as he swept over them, then he arced up gracefully over the trees and did that same low-flying again and again. The crowd were in the palm of his hand and Della was astonished at his skill. She couldn't wait to talk to him about it, what a delight it would be to pick his brains, perhaps even to fly with him tomorrow, if he didn't mind. She was sure he wouldn't mind. He banked and came round again for another swoop past a copse of trees and curved over a wooded hill, then dipped down low and disappeared.

An almighty smash rang out, the horrendous screech of shattering wood mixed with shrieks from the crowd around her, and then all was still. Della ran and ran, almost blindly, vaulted the boundary fence and ran on, over the field by the hill and round its edge, to be met by the sight of the Bréguet aeroplane collapsed in on itself, inverted and crumpled to a heap of splinters. She rushed up to Jérôme's small body beneath it, and saw his pallid cheek, his head turned at an unnaturally sharp angle to the left, his chest crushed by the engine atop it, his arm flung out, bent, with the humerus poking out by some inches through the torn flesh and shredded leather jacket, the bone white and alien, fringed with blood.

She fell to her knees and sobbed. Within seconds, the thudding of other feet was all around her, not friendly feet but spectators, shouting and jostling. Legs and arms and coats and backs loomed and she was shoved aside. She jumped up and saw a woman steal Jérôme's cap that lay beside his ruined head.

'What – what are you . . . ? Della gasped and reached across to try to stop her. She saw that the woman was flourishing Jérôme's bloodstained cap and Della lunged at her, wrestling with all her might for that precious object.

'*C'est à moi! C'est à moi!*' screamed the woman, holding firm to the cap and wrenching it away. She then flounced off with her companions, shouting French obscenities in Della's direction. At last some of the ground crew arrived, including Louis Bréguet himself, and a trace of order was restored. Della watched as they drove the crowds back and remonstrated with them. Another pilot checked the body, but it was hopeless, they all knew it was hopeless. They stood and stared at the broken thing with the broken boy inside. It was as if they could not look away, as if the sight of it were telling them, *Look at it. See what flying costs us.*

Della doubled over and vomited on the churned-up, bloodied ground.

15

Swerving around a fire engine on her motorcycle, she nearly hit a nanny and perambulator crossing the thoroughfare, the nanny gaping as Della rode on. Weaving on down the Strand, she turned a couple of corners and then into John Adam Street (turning corners always reminded her of flying, the way you'd bank into a turn) and pulled up outside the Little Theatre. Dismounting, she patted the handlebars, just as she had in every aeroplane she'd flown since getting her licence, just as she used to do to her bicycle, all those years ago. Bicycle, aeroplane, motorcycle: no matter which, it was her steed and she trusted it, far more than she trusted anything else in this world. It was a world that had been confusing and restless at the best of times, but now was a world gone mad.

Removing her motorcycle goggles and climbing the steps up to the office, she heard a boy shout the latest war headlines down the street, and with a lurch in her throat she thought of Puck. Dud wasn't quite old enough to join up yet, thank heavens, and with any luck, the war would be over before he came of age.

Inside, the offices bustled with women scribbling, typing, talking on the telephone, handing out papers, receiving envelopes, shifting boxes of supplies. Women of different backgrounds – quite a few were suffragettes before the war, but now had laid down their suffrage pamphlets and taken up lists of accommodation for Belgian refugees. There were writers, duchesses, actresses – it was formerly the offices for the Actresses' Franchise League, after all – and in the midst of it swirled Midge, dressed in smart, pressed khaki, in her element. Bossy and busy, she was organising three ladies who had offered to run a canteen van to the Woolwich Arsenal, telling them where to buy the tea and buns, and from where to refill the boilers when they ran out. Midge was saying to these three young women with hobble skirts and wide eyes, 'You're in the Corps, now. It's not a picnic. You're going to work, really hard. You'll have to buy your own khaki. Yes, khaki.'

'Won't the boys need the khaki?' asked one woman. 'There are shortages, aren't there?'

'We are all here to serve,' intoned Midge. 'Be proud of that and don't take any nonsense about it. Some will sneer at you for that. If you get sergeant's stripes, you'll get men shouting at you in the street, "Kiss me, Sergeant!" but you must turn the other cheek. You are soldiers now. Women soldiers.'

Della handed in the answers she'd received from the messages she'd despatched earlier, and was given a new bundle to take out. Midge noticed her and nodded, with a sisterly smile that Della returned. They were back living together and now working together too, getting on rather well considering how much they saw of each other, day in, day out. At least most of Della's work was out of the office. She had gone back out on the streets, on her 'Trusty' Triumph motorcycle she'd bought with the money she'd made from selling her Farman, when she'd received Midge's invitation within days of the declaration of war: 'The Women's Emergency Corps needs drivers for its Motor Department,' Midge had written to Della. 'Buy a motorcycle, learn how to ride it and get yourself up here to help.'

To help. A siren call. Since Jérôme's death, she'd been lost. Floundering. She had months of flying exhibition contracts in France to honour, though all she'd wanted to do was go home. The very day Jérôme was smashed to bits, they'd carried on the show. They couldn't cancel, they said. She absented herself. She tried to talk to her mechanic, but he was blasé about it. It was difficult to tell his true feelings, as he was reticent and there was the language problem, but there was a general shrugging of shoulders and resignation about it. She went through the motions of completing her tour, but something had frozen inside her the day she saw Jérôme's poor dead body and she saw her love of flight perched on a knife edge, between beauty and death, and it was not a comfortable place to exist for long.

The minute she'd completed her final show, she was on the train to the coast, where she boarded a ship and made her way over to London. On her final leg, on the train from London to her home town, she went through the cabin to the main carriage, where a group of boys were gathered. As the train went on its way, it passed over several fog signals. At each signal it made a hefty bang and at every one the boys would shout, 'The Germans are here! The Germans are here!'

When she stepped down onto the platform at Cleethorpes, the July day was overcast and breezy, the beach packed with holidaymakers and the promenade likewise. If there is war here, she thought, will they come by sea? She realised that her home town – indeed the whole east coast – was very vulnerable, open to the continent as it was, to attack and invasion.

She realised the beaches would probably close soon and there would be guns and warships. Aeroplanes might come – aeroplanes of war, bringing what? A pilot shooting his pistol at dog-walkers on the promenade? She supposed they could drop something heavy and sharp; that'd do some damage. Perhaps they'd take photographs of shipping and so forth. Whatever uses the war found for aeroplanes, and surely they must, England would use them too. And that's why they'd need pilots.

She wrote to every major aerodrome in the country, she wrote to the local council, she wrote to the War Office. She wrote to the man in charge of the Royal Flying Corps, Brigadier-General Sir David Henderson. Nobody wanted her, not even as a tutor of civilian pilots, as demand had dwindled once young men started joining up; and anyway, they didn't want a woman teaching anyone. Letting them fly before the war was one thing, but letting them teach was another.

She wrote again to the War Office. She listed her training, she listed her achievements. After a third letter, she received a short reply from Henderson himself:

My good lady, please desist from your requests. Stay at home and assist your mother. Lord Kitchener himself does not approve of women fighting in any way. It is the male's job to protect the female. There will be no room for petticoats in our air forces.

Grounded. Home. Mam and Pop. Mam had gone out the day war was declared with Cleo's old perambulator and stocked it with sugar, flour, tins of meat, sardines and vegetables. She had been mocked by Pop and received disapproving comments from Mrs Butters about the evils of hoarding, but had been proved right, for within days flour had doubled in price and Mam had been smug in her wisdom.

Cleo and Puck had been beside themselves with excitement. Puck had joined up on the day after the declaration of war.

'I was born at just the right time,' he crowed, 'so I can be in the scrap from the start.'

Puck – or Pte Julius Dobbs as he soon became – rushed off to Clee Fields to start drilling with a bunch of his local pals, digging slit trenches and learning how to lob a bomb over. With his private schooling, he could've been an officer, but he wanted to be with his childhood chums. Before long he was dressed in surplus Post Office blue, due to a lack of khaki (the London girl was right). Almost every young man in the houses surrounding Bradford Street went to join up in those first weeks; there was only one they knew of who hadn't, but he soon did after an unnamed person strewed bloodstained bandages over the cherry tree in his family's front garden, a message for shirkers to do their duty and do it sharpish. For King and Country, they were all saying, as the 10th Lincolns were marched off to a country location kept secret (for about five minutes – everyone living near Brocklesby had seen the huts go up on the estate), in order to complete their training. The locals lined the streets on their route as the boys marched past, dressed in a medley of civilian hats or blue peaked caps, some with and some without badges, carrying white kitbags with their new identity stencilled on the side: *Gy BATTn Lincolnshire Regiment.* Some carried parcels from the family: home comforts, for their first foray into army life.

Mam didn't want Puck to go and wept at the door, wouldn't come to see him march. Pop was proud as Punch and for the first time in years left the house and hobbled up to Isaac's Hill to watch them pass by. Della wanted to stay at home with Mam but Cleo was desperate to see her brother march, so, after Pop had left, Della took her along the road and held her hand tightly to stop her flailing into the column as it came through, though Cleo nearly wrenched away a fair few times in her excitement and drew glares when she started screaming her brother's nickname, which of course could be misheard quite disastrously when squealed by a four-year-old. The mood was not one of joyous celebration, but of pride; yet also there was a marked lack of jocularity, and even the marching lads themselves expressed with their set faces the gravity of the situation.

Within days, Della was off to London to join her own Corps, but Pop had nothing to say about that and she asked him nothing either. Their impasse was complete. And it filled her with an irksome resentment she wished she could leave behind at home. It was easy to give up on a person and declare it done, but it was harder to live with the depressing truth of the mutual rejection.

Mam wrote regularly to Della and Midge – for they were sharing digs again for Della's latest London sojourn – about Puck's training at camp: heavy digging, campfire cooking, map-reading – *Puck will be in his element,* thought Della. *What a lark he must be having!* – and standing on guard, standing to prepare to meet cavalry, hand-to-hand fighting, bayonetting straw-filled sacks.

One day, Mam wrote after hearing from Puck, they were taken into town for a cinema trip and were given the glad-eye by all the girls and won the envy of all the boys and the respect of all the men. At last kitted out in their lately arrived khaki, they were proper soldiers now, at which Mam cried more and more, staining the letter with blotches of tears. Della knew Puck would be having the adventure of his life, like an extended Scout camp, and since everyone said the war would be over before the winter kicked in, she was sure he would never get further than Brocklesby.

But Christmas came and went and the war went on – joyfully on for those desperate to get abroad and join it. In May 1915 Mam wrote about Puck's battalion – now renamed the Grimsby Chums – and their passing-out parade, where every man, woman and child in the two towns stood to watch them strut by, cheering and waving handkerchiefs. The streets were filled with yelling and alacrity, the long, confident march around the familiar streets a parade of pride and joy, accompanied by cheers and laughter, bugles and drums. It was quite the occasion and lit up the towns for the evening hours.

Around that time, Betty's will was finally read. All her money had been dispersed equally, between her niece Mam and each and every one of Mam's children and grandchildren; so each received quite a small portion. There was an addition to the will: Betty's house was left to Della. But there were stipulations: it was to be kept a secret from the other siblings, to prevent bad feeling. The house must be rented out until Della was twenty-five, thus providing Della with an income; it must

be specifically managed by Mam and rented at a low rate to
a deserving family.

Betty's words, transcribed into the will, were:

*In order to encourage my great-niece to be adventurous, I
wish for the house to be held over until she reaches the age
of twenty-five. By this age, she will either be ready to settle
down with a husband, in which case she can live in the
house if she so wishes, or sell it to move elsewhere. Or she
may wish to use the money from the sale to continue her
aviation business – for example, beginning her flying
school – or if aviation has dried up, she can use the money
to begin again. The choice will be hers.*

What an extraordinary set of affairs. Only Betty, unconventional
and determinedly different, would write such a curious will.
There was an amount of money for Della to help her out as
and when, though not much; she'd have to keep working to
afford to live. And certainly not enough to buy an aeroplane,
that's for sure, though that was moot while the war still raged.
Yet when she was twenty-five, in four years' time, she would
have either a home or a boost to her career. Oh, Betty, what
a wonderful woman she had been! How Della missed her and
mourned her, wishing her aunt would show up at her door.
She'd gladly give the legacy back and her right limb in exchange
(as one can still fly with a wooden leg).

Della's days in London progressed with a new-found
security in the future. Feeling lost as she had these last months,
she now knew that in a while, whatever happened, she would
have the chance to start again. There was some guilt, that she
was receiving more than her siblings, but after all she had
been the one to befriend Betty when the others were less
interested. Puck, following Pop's example, had been positively
dismissive of her. So Della did not feel too bad about it, least
of all for her brother.

As for Puck's army progress, she heard that after leaving their home town he went on to Yorkshire for a few months, then down to Wiltshire. In January 1916, the Grimsby Chums left for France. Puck sent a letter home soon after, that Mam sent on to Della. After this Mam chose to send on every letter she received from him, and he wrote often. All the letters to Mam and Pop were chirpy, despite a few gripes:

I haven't washed for a few days – I can hear you gasp from here, Mam! Yesterday, for 3 hours we had a rotten bombardment from the Boche. But we were safe in our trench, never fear. It was such an almighty racket, I bet you could hear it in Meggies. We haven't captured an enemy trench yet, but when we do I'll try and find you a little German knick-knack as proof. When I come home on leave – I wouldn't hold my breath if I were you, Mam and Pop, but whenever that happy day comes – I'll bring it to you as a present.

Puck, the boy of action had also had some time to ponder things in the trenches, as this pensive letter showed:

The Grimsby Chums and I are doing marvellously and fighting the good fight. I am very high-spirited most of the time. Now and again though I do think on home and worry that I wasn't the best son I could be. You see, I am so very grateful for having such a good Mam and Pop. I want to extend my thanks to you both, for all you've ever done for me.

Della thought she'd never hear the day: Puck, grateful? His breezy selfishness was somehow part of his charm. Yet it touched her to hear him acknowledge his golden position at home and she was so glad he'd told Mam and Pop and

thanked them properly. That would bring them great pride,
she thought. Yet there was a note of concern in the letter
that struck her: perhaps events out in France were not so
breezy – what else could have sent Puck into such a forlorn
reverie? It chilled her to realise that it sounded as if her
brother was putting his house in order, before . . . Before
what?

After the first few letters had come from Mam, Puck started
to write to Della alone. The reasons for this were stated clearly
in the first letter:

> *I cannot spill the beans to Mam and Pop about what it's*
> *really like here, Del. But you and I were always honest*
> *with each other and I fear I shall go stark staring mad if I*
> *don't tell someone what's truly going on. I'd like to tell you*
> *what it's all about, but please don't show these letters to*
> *anyone else. They're just for you (and the censor).*
> *Especially don't show the old folk, obviously, but also*
> *Midge. She always looked down her nose at me and I*
> *don't want her knowing all my miserable business. So*
> *you'll have to hide these letters and keep the knowledge of*
> *them to yourself, dear Del, if you can bear it.*

She felt the privilege of the chosen one, yet she was also
alarmed to find out that the letters from home were not accurate. Puck had never lied; indeed, was known for his brutal
honesty. It was touching though to hear that he was protecting
their parents (and she got a thrill of sibling rivalry from
hearing that he didn't trust Midge). He went on:

> *It's wet and cold and rough as hell. It's a proper baptism*
> *of fire in the trenches and many have been hit in the*
> *head, sneaky wounds when the Boche sent a searchlight*
> *out over us and followed it with a stream of machine-gun*

*fire. Two chums were killed. We haven't even properly got
at the Boche yet. Most of the chaps out here say it will
end soon. I jolly well hope it does. Not the war we
wanted. Not at all.*

Not the war we wanted, thought Della. A curious phrase.
What would that look like then, a wanted war? Perhaps a
rougher version of Puck's rabbit-hunting days, but with the
Boche slammed on the table instead of bunnies. Surely this
boy she remembered could not already be a man, fighting
for his life with a bayonet? Della tried not to think about it,
tried not to picture Puck actually fighting at all. She imagined
him scouring the French woods for small creatures to shoot
at for fun. But perhaps there were no trees left there, no
animals, and soon perhaps all the boys would shoot each
other dead and there would be no more boys in France.
Then more boys would line up on English streets and off
they'd go, more boys gone and never seen again. Best not
to think about all that.

But she had no choice but to face it; Puck's letters became
increasingly candid.

*Del, it's bloody awful. All is mud and rain and more mud
and cold and misery. The rain turns the mud into soupy
brown rivers. Chaps drown in the mud or dugouts collapse
and bury men alive. Such stupid ways to meet your
maker. The rations are dreadful too. We are all so hungry.
There are rats and lice. We are infested. There is no comfort
and no rest from it. We sleep hardly at all. We are driven
mad by the noise and the fear. Not knowing when it'll be
your turn. A chum was horribly injured the other day, his
face shot to bits. I never could have imagined a sight like
that, before seeing it with my own eyes. Imagine yourself a
butcher, chopping up the faces of animals. Now picture
that you have to look at your friends that way, chums*

*you've got to know better than anyone you've ever known
in your life. To see them that way. It's too awful for words.
Don't tell Mam and Pop any of it. I couldn't bear for
them to know.*

Puck's secret letters to Della came thick and fast in those
early months of 1916. Every one of them pained her to read,
made her frown and worry and haunted her all day. She
would write back to Puck after each one of his, sharing minor
events of her days, trying to remind him what ordinary life
in England was like. But she felt sick doing it and guilty at
each cheerful word she wrote. Every time another letter came,
she'd be eager to rip it open and hear Puck's news, and then
feel a pang of guilt knowing that she would feel so low after
reading it that she almost wanted to put off opening it. Once,
she put a letter unopened in her jacket and carried it round
with her as she sped through the streets, its symbolic and
emotional weight a drag in her pocket. She eventually had
to pull over and read it, as she could go no further and hated
herself for figuratively making her poor brother wait. She
read the words of woe, put it back in her pocket and sped
off, trying with the wind in her face to obliterate Puck's
misery from her mind, the joy of motorcycle riding causing
her to forget it all, transiently. And again, always the guilt at
wanting this oblivion. He was living it and she was only
reading it, and even that she wanted to shun. *What a coward
I am*, she thought.

But at least she was trying to help, she told herself,
doing her bit for the war effort. She did her job,
despatching messages around the streets of London,
efficiently and gladly. It made her feel useful and she
became very adept at weaving through the traffic on her
motorcycle. She thought about racing it after the war
– what fun that would be! But again, there was that guilt
of thinking ahead, to after the war, with Puck up to his

neck in mud and danger. It seemed the height of self-ishness. But, she told herself, having happy thoughts was not really a betrayal of the troops. Surely it was important to try to stay chipper. What has misery ever done for anyone? She spent some free time with Midge and her theatre gals, whose actor colleagues and boyfriends were all off at the war. Shows with all-female casts were put on at local theatres and Della helped out in the box office, just as in her old life before the war. She kept up writing to airfields and the government throughout the year, pushing her case to be allowed to fly; she followed the reports of the ever-burgeoning new Royal Flying Corps and its action in France, and its many fallen pilots. But always the same response – *no, thank you, dear lady.*

She would look through the newspaper lists of 'Fallen in Combat', first and always looking for any mention of Puck and other Grimsby Chums; she would hold her breath in a wordless nausea until she was sure that Pte Julius Dobbs was nowhere to be seen on those cursed lists. Then she would go on and scan for RFC casualties. Once, she noticed a pilot from her Hendon days, killed in action. Not Claude, thank heavens.

She read in the papers that he was now Flight Commander Grahame-White, serving in the Royal Naval Air Service, as well as keeping the London Aerodrome at Hendon going for training military pilots and making aeroplanes for the war effort. She could not deny that she kept a kindling of first-love glow for him; though it was a little cooler now with time passing, she wondered if she would always have it, and marvelled at the power of first love to inhabit the heart for a lifetime. Her face felt hot scanning the lists for his name, but it was never there. Her feelings for him were all wrapped up with her love for flight; the two had been born like twins and were inseparable. And how she missed flying! Oh blimey – like a malady of the heart. At least with her motorcycle, she could feel the speed and the wind in her face that reminded her of it, but it was some time before she could stop imagining and wishing that her machine would speed off and up and above the traffic and into the skies.

She could find nobody to talk to about flying. She remembered Hilda Hewlett's words, that she'd bored her husband with talk of it. There were servicemen everywhere in London of course, on leave and looking for fun, and she went on evenings out, but they didn't like her talking about mechanical things and gave her funny looks. One chap called Cyril took her out for dinner, which was all right, but he wanted her to dance. She had two left feet and, for such a fine pilot, was surprisingly clumsy. He suggested she should wear lipstick (which she never did, nor any make-up for that matter).

On the way home, he pushed her up against a cold wall and stuck his tongue in her mouth, which was repulsive. She shoved him so hard he stumbled into the gutter. He swore at her and left her there, so she went home to Midge's place alone, shaken and baffled. She didn't tell Midge about it; she probably would have laughed, so au fait with such things she was. Della felt too ashamed to share the grubby little affair with her experienced older sister. All of Midge's many beaux were gentlemen, or so they seemed to Della.

Thus, her first kiss was a disappointment, if a kiss it was. Surely it didn't count. After that, the idea of blokes and kissing lost its sheen and as she offered no encouragement, she didn't get asked out much. It wasn't that she didn't want a boyfriend – she quite liked the idea, for company, and she thought about what proper kissing might be like, and things like that, from time to time. But Claude still loomed large in her mind, and all other men seemed too young or stupid or both, and she imagined not one of them would ever want to listen to her drone on about aeroplanes.

Dud was the only one who really understood about flying. Della could only discuss it with him, via his letters, and very welcome they were. Della was so jealous and angry about being rejected as a pilot. How much good she could do! She would moan about the stupidity of it in letter after letter to Dud. But it was no use whingeing to him, he could do nothing about it. Glued to the road she was, and so she piloted the cycle as well as she could, set herself time trials whizzing between London landmarks and, at rest, she tended it and cared for its maintenance with the love of a mother. There was nothing or no one else to watch over, after all.

On the fourth day of March 1916, a Saturday, she was asleep – off duty and treating herself to a rare lie-in – when she heard a heavy knock at the door. She was alone, as Midge had not come home the night before. Heaven knows where she was. Midge being in her late twenties and still defiantly single, one heard she was having quite the time with soldiers on leave in the watering holes of London nightlife. Della dragged herself off the settee, wrapped one of Midge's house-coats about her and – there was more insistent knocking – stumbled over and opened the door. There stood Mrs B., the landlady, with a face like thunder. Della glimpsed someone loitering behind her.

'A young man to see you, says he's family?' she said brusquely. 'I said, he couldn't come up, less he's family.' She stepped aside to reveal a very tall soldier, in full uniform, cap perched smartly on a long face with a gracious smile.

'Dud!' she cried and, with a flinch of embarrassment, her hand went to her hair, which she knew would be in a fearful state, but *Who cares really*, she thought, *it's only Dud and he never minds a thing.*

'Thanks, Mrs B. It's my brother.'

'Right you are,' snapped Mrs B. and stomped off downstairs.

'Hello, *brother*,' Della said with a wink.

'Hello, Della, sorry I couldn't warn you.'

'About coming or about this?' she said, pointing at his uniform. Dud in uniform, what a horrible thing. It did suit him, she had to admit, though the cap looked awfully big on his head – it did on all the boys' heads, she always felt. Older men filled it, but the youths made it look like their dad's hat. The sight of him togged up in army gear made her feel queasy. She was sure he'd escape it, only a few months ago she'd been sure. But a lot had changed in those weeks and the war they all thought would be done by now was dragging on, ploughing all before it, brothers and fathers and sweethearts. And friends.

'Well, I've joined up, yes. OTC training in Leeds. I'm off up there tonight. Been visiting relatives in town. I only have an hour or so. Is it all right to have a cup of tea somewhere, if you're free?'

'Have a cup of tea here, Dud. It's cheaper!' she said, laughing. To see Dud, how enormously nice it was.

But he looked stiff and said, 'Perhaps a modest little café would do the trick. It's a fair day out there, cold but sunny.' *A good day for flying*, thought Della, then corrected herself. She still assessed the weather for flight, every single day, even earthbound as she was. It'd become part of her marrow to think of it. Dud continued, 'I can wait out here, if that suits?'

'Oh. All right, then. I won't be long.'

Dud waited on the landing and Della looked about the clutter-strewn disaster that was her and Midge's shared digs. Whizzing around on a motorcycle only required a similar level of femininity and smartness as aviating. There must be a clean skirt here somewhere, she mused and threw a few things around. She found one of Midge's blouses, a little too fussy for her own taste, but under a waistcoat and overcoat, nobody would know. Suited and booted, and after an attempt at righting her knotty hair, she found a hat of Midge's that was suitably narrow and unostentatious for her own taste and went out to join Dud. When he saw her he smiled broadly, but looked away. *What's up with him?* she thought, but figured it must be the length of time since they were last together, and the somewhat heady atmosphere of that last meeting. It'd only take a few minutes of chat, surely, and they'd sink into comfort with each other.

They walked two streets over to a tea room Della knew, which served pretty good iced buns and strong tea. On the way, Della moaned again about her lack of success at gaining aviation employment, which Dud said was an awful waste. Once through the door, to see a spare table at the back they had to peer over many female heads, which all looked up with admiring glances, clearly approving of the lad in uniform and his girl.

Seated, with a teapot and some buns, they began to talk more freely, of family matters and of Puck's letters, but Della didn't give Dud all the details from her brother's private correspondence; she didn't want to frighten him. How much he knew of what was going on out there at the front, she didn't know, and she didn't want to ask. And Dud's youth, well, his being younger than her anyway, always made her feel protective towards him, in a similar way to how she felt towards Puck – his big sister, looking out for him. In his face, Dud looked even younger than Puck – which of course he was by a couple of years – but in his demeanour, his character, his way of speaking, he had years on her brother, always had. As Della stealthily took a handful of sugar from the bowl and surreptitiously poured it into her jacket pocket – well, it was hard to get hold of sugar these days – Dud raised his eyebrows but said nothing, then took a napkin to dab his mouth delicately, smoothed it out on his lap, coughed and said nothing.

'You all right?' she said and felt her cheeks go hot, though she wasn't sure why.

He looked up at her and cleared his throat again. 'Della, I – uh – I want to ask you something.'

'All right,' she said and her mind raced.

'I'd like to – I'd like to be – what I mean to say is . . . I'd like you to be my girl.'

'Oh Dud,' she began and smiled, but he wasn't smiling.

'That came out wrongly,' he went on, his cheeks reddening, his napkin now clutched in his hands. 'I mean to say, Della, I want you to be my fiancée. I want us to be engaged.'

A dozen thoughts scurried through her head, bumping into one another, a chaotic conversation. *He's so young, like a boy. So young. I can't marry anyone. No, that's not right. I wanted to marry Claude. I probably still would, if he asked me, if he turned up right now and asked me – would I?*

Dud took her silence well and went on, bravely. 'I know it might be a shock to you. But it's not to me. I've thought about it very carefully. I've thought of little else. I'm eighteen now and after this war business, I've a good future ahead of me in textiles. And, well, you know all that. But more than that, Della, more to the point that is . . . Well, the truth is, Della, that I love you. I've always loved you.'

I know that, she thought. *I've always known that.*

'Oh, Dud,' she began, but couldn't look at him. Why couldn't she look at him? Her friend, her best friend in all the world. Her only friend, she felt, beyond family. A good reason to be with a man, to be best friends, but the rest? To be lovers? She was so unsure of that side of things, had never been kissed properly. Would it be Dud, her first real kiss – should it? Her best friend?

'I quite understand,' he said, clipped, and pushed out his chair, and half stood up.

'Oh no, Dud, please! Please stay,' she said, and some women nearby looked up and there were whispers. Dud sat down and stared at the table. 'Listen,' she said in low tones. 'It's not what you think. I'm so . . . You . . . You're my best friend, Dud.'

He looked up at her then, a smile, his eyes shining. 'Yes, and you're mine. That's what makes it so perfect.'

'I'm not sure about that. I think I'd make an awful wife. I'm probably rather selfish and . . . you know, driven. And I'm so – I'm such a fool about love and all that. I don't know a thing, honestly.'

Dud was still smiling. 'Me too. Again, we're alike. We can work it out together.'

'But it wasn't – When I've thought of marriage, which I haven't much, it's always been an older man I'd imagined, someone who knew more about it. I feel such a novice about these things and I always felt I'd need that, someone with experience to teach me how . . . how it all works.'

She had no idea what she was talking about now and felt herself cringe with embarrassment, yet after his initial nerves, Dud now seemed to be basking in something beyond her, some innate confidence, that muted confidence she'd always admired in him. And she felt, though she was the older one, the one with more experience of life, the one being asked, that she should be the one sitting quietly confident; but she was not and it irked her.

'I understand, I think,' he said. 'I think it might be about having someone to rely on, an older man, like a father figure.'

'Well,' blustered Della. 'No, that's not—'

'I mean, you know,' Dud went on, quite sure of himself, yet stepping carefully, 'your father. It must have an . . . effect. The way he is, the way he's been with you. So . . . cold.'

'Now then,' she said and felt herself squaring up, but why? Why? She more than anyone agreed with every word – but it wasn't anyone else's place to say it, to say a bad word about Pop. That was her job, and certainly not Dud's.

'That's not what it is at all,' she snapped, garnering more whispers behind. 'Look, can we get out of here?'

'Of course,' muttered Dud. He paid the bill and she stalked outside, angry, feeling foolish for being angry, yet annoyed with Dud. Flattered too, yes, flattered. And confused.

He came out and stood before her on the pavement. He

was so very tall. She looked up at him. He had such a nice face, a nice mouth. She thought of Claude's mouth and how she'd yearned for it. And however nice Dud's was, it would never be Claude's. *Oh God, I'm still in love with him*, she thought with a dull sinking. And then she thought of Jérôme and his lambent blue eyes, and she felt sick. What a muddle it was, in her head. She wouldn't wish it on Dud, or any man.

'Dud, I behaved badly, I'm sorry.'

'No, no. It was my fault. Let me walk you back. Please.' Again, Dud the sensible one, escorting her like a gent and taking the blame like a gent. But he did say those things about Pop and what right, what right had he? And what was he trying to say, anyway? That she wanted to marry her father or some of that head-doctor nonsense you hear about these days? They walked in silence, but she knew both their minds were busy, busy.

'Dud, it won't work, I don't think. Do you?'

She thought he'd be devastated, but he was quite calm. 'I do, actually. I think it'd be glorious.' He said it very calmly, like a fact, and she saw that way he was always smiling and she felt a great urge to be fifteen again, running along the wet sands of Cleethorpes beach and flying kites with him. Not here, in these clothes, in this city, in this bloody war.

'I think more than anything,' she said, 'I can't bear to lose you as a friend and if we were married, we wouldn't be friends any more. It'd be different.' *It'd be ruined*, she thought.

'I think it'd be better. Like being friends, but even better. The best married couples are friends as well as . . . well, you know, other things.'

'Well, I wouldn't know,' she said. 'My parents aren't like that, they're not friends at all.'

'Perhaps they're not the best model.'

Oh, here we go again, she thought. 'They do their best,' she said, irritably.

He stopped walking. They stood in the Clapham street, opposite each other on the dirty pavement, busy people stepping round them. 'I apologise, again,' he said. 'Oh dear, this hasn't gone at all well. I've upset you and insulted you. I should never have come.'

'No, please don't say that. I'm so glad you came.'

'I can only say—' he said, then stopped. He looked away, up the street, then let out a heavy sigh. 'That I don't think a girl – a woman – anyone – should have to be talked into loving someone.'

'Oh, but I do!' she cried. 'Of course I do.'

He shook his head. 'Not in the same way.'

Her eyes welled with tears. He looked at her and his face crumpled. 'And now I've made you cry. Oh, God.' He fumbled for a handkerchief and pressed it into her hands.

It's not what you think, she thought, wiping her stupid eyes. Crying! By saying yes, she had feared she'd lose her best friend. But by saying no, she now knew she had. Oh, what a bloody mess.

They reached her building and stood outside it. She went to hand him back his hankie, wet and crumpled.

'Keep it,' he said, considerately. But she pushed it into his fist, just so she could hold on to his hand and make him look at her.

'Dud, please. I'm the one who's sorry. I told you I'm a fool about such things. I'm the one who made a hash of this, not you.'

'No,' he said firmly, gazing down at her. 'No,' softer. 'I never should have pressed you like that.'

'Please, if you are my friend—' she began.

'You know I am,' he asserted and squeezed her hand.

'Can we still be friends? Always be friends?'

'Of course. Lifelong friends.' He smiled his crooked smile, and she glanced down at his uniform and realised something. Lifelong doesn't mean the same to him now as it did before.

He doesn't have all the time in the world – or at least, he must feel he hasn't, that his time may run out, be cut short. And all he wanted to do was tell her how much he loved her. And she ruined it. But maybe that's the only reason he asked her; because he was a soldier now, and she was the only girl he'd known, really known, and he thought it was something to hold on to, going off to war. This boy, the kite boy, Dudley Willow. Going to fight the Boche.

'Is it because you're going away, is that it? Is that why you wanted to . . . you know, have something certain?'

He shook his head, sadly. 'Perhaps. Clever Della.' A rueful smile.

'But us being friends, you know, Dud. That is certain, the most certain thing I've ever known.'

'Apart from flying,' he replied.

'Well, yes, it used to be. Now I'm not so sure.'

'True. Now nothing much is sure any more.' And there was that young face again, eighteen years old and the weight of the era on his narrow, slim shoulders. 'I must go now or I'll miss my train.'

The thought of him gone was like a hollow in a winter tree, letting in the cold.

'Will you write? Please write to me, Dud. From Leeds and from wherever you go after. I couldn't bear it if you stopped writing.'

'I should think so.'

What? I should think so? He pressed the hankie into her hand and smiled soberly, but didn't wait to say goodbye, turned on his heel and walked off briskly down the street. No more chat, no farewell. She was about to call after him, but he turned the corner of the street and he was gone.

She turned the key in the lock, pensive, regretful, and opened the front door. Immediately, a strange noise assaulted her, a curious whining, like a cat in a stand-off. She went to the stairs and peered up, trotting upwards until she found Midge sitting on the top step, her head resting on one hand, the other hand clutching something. The whining was coming from her throat. Then it stopped and she heaved a great sob. She was holding a telegram.

'Oh God,' said Della. 'Oh God, oh God.'

16

Mam showed her the buff-coloured envelope with OHMS printed on the outside. The envelope offered no clue as to its contents, so she could only imagine the hurried dread with which Mam must have opened it; indeed, the opening had not been done as usual with Mam's letter knife stored in a pot in the kitchen; the envelope had clearly been ripped open by hand. Inside was army form B.104-82B. *It is my painful duty to inform you that a report has been received from the War Office notifying the death of Pte Julius Dobbs* et cetera. The sympathy was offered of Their Gracious Majesties the King and Queen as well as the regret of the Army Council.

Cleo told Della in a quiet moment that when Mam had opened 'that letter' her face went deathly white and she collapsed to the floor.

'Is Mam having a baby?' asked Cleo.

'No, pet. Why d'you ask that?' said Della.

'Harriet says when ladies are expecting, they swoon a lot.' Cleo was nearly six – chatty and curious, lively and mercurial – and seemed to have no conception of what had actually happened to her only brother. Della dreaded the moment when this would sink in.

There was also a letter from Puck's platoon officer. It began in standard fashion, like a vicar's bland comments about the deceased at an average funeral: sadness at the loss of Pte Dobbs, that he was one of the best in the company and would be greatly missed. The letter went on to describe Puck's manner of despatch, that '*the firing was rather brisk*' and that Puck was '*hit on the chest by a bullet that passed through his heart. He did not speak a word as death was instantaneous and could have felt no pain.*' It ended with a line that read a little more engagingly, that touched Della and clearly also Mam, who mentioned it often, mouthing it sometimes to herself when she thought no one was watching: '*He was held in affection by all of the section.*' Its rhyme made it easy to recall, like a prayer.

That letter was much read and took on a worn, shiny patina. Mam wrote back to the officer, thanking him for his kindness and offering her prayer that he himself would be spared the terrible blow her only son had received. Her only son. Her collapse when first hearing the hateful news was the only outward sign of Mam's distress. She held herself together with precarious effort and fought never to betray her feelings, even to Della.

Pop was quite a different matter.

There was no body to be sent home, as Puck was buried out there, so once Della and Midge had arrived at the family home the day after they'd received the telegram, there was nothing to be done. No funeral arrangements to be made, no wake to organise. Just a void, an emptiness in the house that could not be filled by activity; no elaborate mourning rituals to fill the days. The hours dragged and weighed heavy and silence reigned.

Even feisty Cleo began to comprehend the gravity of it. Ever since the outbreak of war, she had been ferociously knitting scarves for soldiers and one day, sitting beside the kitchen fire, her needles clacking away as Della wiped down the table, Cleo said to Della, 'Does being dead mean you never come back?'

Della knew the moment had arrived and swallowed hard, her mind working to come up with the kindest reply. 'Puck is in heaven now. It's the loveliest place you can think of, so everyone stays there forever.'

Cleo frowned. She stopped knitting and would not pick it up again, with no explanation, just a hasty shaking of her head. The next day, Della found all of Cleo's needles and wool in the dustbin, tangled in a vicious bundle, and Della wept and wept, her head low over the bin. The red and white yarn and its sorry mess had been turned filthy by the rubbish around it; it seemed a terrible crime somehow and a pathetic waste.

She knew it was important not to cry in front of the others, especially Cleo. She would wait until night-time and whimper in her bed, as she imagined Mam did. Pop they heard lamenting at least once a day. He wasn't noisy about it, but the house was so haunted by dead air that the tiniest sob could be heard through the walls and floors, and their ears were tuned to grief and listened for it despite themselves.

From the day Della and Midge arrived, neither had been allowed to see Pop at all. He now never left his room. He used chamber pots, which Harriet the maid emptied during the day; but Della knew Mam emptied them at night, and felt angry about this, really furious. Mam lost her son too, she would whisper to herself, and the last thing she needs is to be carting Pop's shit about along with her own troubles.

Pop's grief – never leaving the room, not speaking to anyone, the sobbing, albeit restrained – was all more fuel on the fire of Della's resentment at his selfishness. From sympathy, to resentment, to bitter disappointment, now was added a steadily burgeoning anger at Pop's behaviour and an increasing diffi-culty in holding back her disgust with him in front of Mam. Della did it for her mother, though, in a way as a thumbed nose to Pop for causing Mam so much trouble. He wasn't the only one to grieve, you know. And as if he was the greatest sufferer, as if the greatest sorrow was exclusively reserved for him, everyone tiptoed around him. Except Cleo. Daily, she would bang on Pop's door and shout at him – *Come out, Pop. Don't be silly, Pop. I don't want to play hide and seek any more.*

Come out this minute, Pop. He always ignored her. Mam or Midge would drag her away, but Della wouldn't. She stood and watched the gutsy firecracker tell Pop what was what. She revelled in it, in Cleo's innate audacity, something Della wished she herself possessed but felt she never had in the past. But maybe flying had given her a taste for it. She certainly did not care what Pop thought of her any more, of what anyone thought of her, really (apart from Mam. And Dud). And Cleo had the excuse of being a small child and thus was immune to impropriety. So no, she did not stop Cleo from banging on Pop's door. But it made no difference anyhow: Pop went on with his stately mourning as if he were the only one who mattered. But the truth was, of course, that they'd all lost Puck.

Things got worse when Midge left. She had already had to find understudies for several shows as she'd stayed on longer than planned to support the family.

The great successful actress that she was, the family seemed to assume and accept that she was needed in London – there was only one Miranda Dobbs in the world. Della, however, was only a motorcycle rider for whom there would be suitable and willing replacements, and it was expected that she should stay at home to help Mam. In fact, she wanted very much to stay with her mother, and found some comfort in being able to ease Mam's long, weary days. But she resented the assumption that Midge was 'required' elsewhere while her own war work was unimportant and expendable. And she recognised Pop's selfishness in Midge, that she was so easily able to assert her need to leave and do it post-haste, without any angst on her part. There they were – Pop and Midge, two egotistical peas in a pod. Once Midge had left, though, Della missed her life and motion. That was the thing with flamboyant people – they filled the air with the heat of their character; it could be suffocating but, once gone, there was only the cold air left.

Within the silent prison of that haunted house, how the urge to fly gripped her, more than ever before. All the fear she'd suffered after Jérôme's death had dissolved with the absence of flying in her life, and now she hungered for it, felt starved of it. Alone in her room, she would whisper incessantly: *I want to fly! I just want to fly!* to the point where she felt like a madwoman. She was trussed in skirts and blouses, helping out endlessly in the kitchen, now Harriet had left – Pop's chamber pot had been the last straw for a young woman beginning, in the war, to see the new possibilities of work that did not involve shifting for middle-class lazy buggers and instead could be an escape from the domestic trap and a life of service.

Della was mired in domestic responsibility in a way that took her straight back to 1909, when Betty came and she first began to dream of kites. Oh, how she missed Betty. And Puck. And flying. And Dud, oh Dud. No letters yet from Leeds, only a black-edged card of condolence for the news about Puck, sent from Clipstone Camp, Nottingham, where he must have been training. She wrote straight back to him there, pouring out her apologies about their last meeting and her grief for her brother, but there was no reply, which hurt her sharply at first. So, she wrote again and there was still no reply. Her upset moulded itself into a dull, cold realisation that she had lost her best friend now as well as her brother. She could do nothing about any of it, had no say in death or absence. She used to feel that she had a hand in her destiny: when flying aeroplanes, you were the ultimate master of your own future, battling against the elements and against physics itself to survive. But out of the air, on solid ground, at home in wartime, she had no control, no power whatsoever. She was like a baby in a basket floating downstream, whichever way the current and the wind would take it, reliant on the charity of outsiders or on blind chance.

Frustration, resentment and anger combined with grief was

the headiest of mixtures and was bound to cause an explosion eventually. It came when Mam fell ill – a nasty bug, all head-cold and aching limbs. She'd tried to struggle on but Della sent her to bed. She was closing the door to Mam's room when she saw Pop's door open; the chamber pot appeared, followed by Pop's arm. He placed the pot on the hall carpet, his arm drew back and the door closed. The waft of faeces mixed with urine swept over her. And that was that.

She stomped down the corridor and pounded on Pop's door. No reply. She did not wait. She turned the handle and threw it open. Pop was about to sit down in his study chair and he stopped, mid-bend, and stared at his daughter, who crossed her arms furiously.

'How dare you!' he said in a low voice.

'How dare I? HOW DARE I?' She was shouting. 'How dare YOU, you selfish, selfish man.'

Pop sat down and gathered himself, his face showing the stubborn determination not to lose his cool as she had.

'Leave this room this instant.'

'Not until you've dealt with THAT,' she said, pointing out the door.

'What did you say?'

She was incandescent now. No fear, no regret, just driven by fire and rage.

'Get off your lazy fucking arse and pour your own shit down the privy.'

It was a joy to curse in that hushful house, it was bliss to see the blow her words had caused, the shockwave that rippled through this Victorian man's very soul at hearing his own daughter speak to him so, and speak of such things, to such as he.

And it gave her such joy, she couldn't stop herself. 'I'm not cleaning up your shit any more and neither is Mam. You need to grow up and stop expecting everyone to kowtow to you like some kind of emperor in your own house. You treat Mam

badly. You spoiled Puck because he was a boy and Midge
because she was an actress and Gertie because she was pretty.
But you neglected me, you ignored me, because I didn't fit
into anything you considered worthwhile for a girl to be. And
no one has had the guts to stand up to you, except Cleo. But
if you could only see everything you have, you would amaze
yourself. The love of Mam, the love of four daughters – despite
your behaviour, despite everything, they still love you. Yes,
you've lost a son, but we've all lost Puck. Start thinking about
the women in your life for once and realise that if they weren't
here, you would have nothing. Nothing at all.'

Pop listened implacably, as if this were a script he knew
well. He did not react in the way Della was expecting – or
desired. She wanted him to argue and fight, but instead he
grew icy cold.

'Cordelia, you have always been a bitter disappointment to
me. You were not a boy, to begin with – not your fault, I grant
you, but I was disappointed nonetheless. Then as you grew,
it became clear to me that you were dull and of little interest.
You were too shy for the stage and too plain to be married.
You have no skills, nothing that makes you special. You persevere with this flying nonsense knowing there is no future in
it. And in that way, if I am selfish, then you are my mirror,
for your obsession with flying above all else shows your own
brand of self-righteous selfishness that you are too stupid to
see in yourself. You could never speak up for yourself and
yet now, now that you have found your voice, you use it to
denigrate the memory of your dear brother – passed from us
before his time, to heaven, where he belongs with the other
angels—'

He stopped, choked. Recovered, he went on, '– and you
choose to speak the foulest profanities to me, your father. If
you had an ounce of humility, you would see the weakness
of character in yourself and would humbly settle yourself to
a life of quiet spinsterhood, helping your mother and serving

your family. But no. You stride gaily on with your ridiculous short haircut, assuming you are an important figure in the world and in this house. But you are not. You are nothing. You are not liked here. And you are not wanted here. If your mother chooses to allow you to stay, then I concur for her sake. But I never wish to see you or speak with you again. Now get out.'

Della rushed out, and on her way knocked over the chamber pot, which spilled the lumps of shit and the amber puddle of piss all over the front hall tiles. Behind it was Mam, spectral in her nightie, coming towards the door with her hands over her mouth, as if she had heard every word. She cried out, 'Oh!' but Della leapt over the mess and ran up the stairs. In her bedroom, she went to her drawer and found the cash in her secret purse, then took out the black-edged card Dud had sent and pushed both into her pocket, ignoring the calls of 'Della? Della, love?' from Mam, her voice sirening up the stairs.

Downstairs, to the sound of Mam and Pop having words: 'What have you said?' 'What have I said? You should be asking your daughter.' 'Your daughter? She's your daughter too!' They turned to her as she came downstairs, leapt again over the grisly puddle, grabbed her coat and hat from the hook and ran through the empty kitchen to the back door. She didn't look at her father's study window as she passed, and she walked briskly with barely a breath all the way down Kingsway and around to the railway station. It was an hour for the next train towards Nottingham; she paced the platform as she waited.

She could not sit down; she had to keep pacing, thinking. She felt worst about the mess on the floor. Now Mam would have to clear that up, because Pop never would and Mam would never let him. She felt rotten about that. But she firmly blamed Pop. *I can't stay in that house,* she thought. *I can't stay there any longer.* But what about Mam? She couldn't think of that now. At least she could have a bit of a breather. She was waiting for a train, thank heavens, to get away, at least for a short stretch. Clipstone Camp was near Mansfield, she believed. She'd have to change trains, perhaps find a bus when she got there. But she'd manage it. She'd navigated her way across the French countryside, for heaven's sake, so she could certainly find a large army camp in Nottinghamshire. Yes. But, what was she doing?

The Nottingham train pulled in and she found a seat. Sitting waiting to go, she considered her plan, such as it was. She was going to see Dud, simple as that. She wanted to see him, she needed to see him. She couldn't explain it really, but there it was. As Pop's icy words cut into her heart she had known she had to run, to get the hell out of there. And Dud was the only person she wanted to see.

On the train, she remembered Pop's words as if she were sitting in the wings of her own life and watching an actor mouth them. Some words leapt out, as if Pop had shouted them, rather than spoken them so coldly in his low, calculating voice. *Dull. Plain. Selfish.* Fleetingly, Della recognised this egoism in herself, her obsession with flying, but then she dismissed it as not being in the same league as the egoism of her father or elder sister. She thought, and thereby fooled herself, that she was cut from a different cloth. Yes, she was just as driven, but she was nicer about it. She did long to fly, thought of it every day, now more than ever, and yet she wasn't going to leave Mam and pursue it, not now. She saw herself as a martyr in this regard (yet she spent little time considering that all civilian flying had been banned when war broke out and that nobody would hire a female pilot anyway).

So, she was selfish. About flying. But she was a nice person, wasn't she? She'd always done her best with Mam, and with Betty. She didn't have friends really, but that was because she was shy, not because she wasn't nice to people. She always tried to be nice to Dud; it was just his proposal took her by surprise, a hell of a shock, and it wasn't the right time. But now, now she felt differently and wanted to see him, more than anything. But her refusal then wasn't cruel, not deliberately cruel. Surely it'd be more cruel to say yes when you weren't sure? Oh, she didn't know. She didn't feel herself a bad person. Couldn't believe it, not through and through. Obsessed with flying, yes, all right. If that's the worst you can say about someone . . .

But that was not the worst of it:

You have no skills, nothing that makes you special.

You are not liked here. And you are not wanted here.

You are nothing.

That was not true. *Not true, dear Father*, she thought. Mam loved her, Cleo loved her. Even Harriet and Mrs Butters chatted away to her, the latter giving her a hug now and then. And Midge and Gertie. And Puck. Puck had loved her and written secret letters to her, poured his heart out. And her public, when she was flying, they flocked to see her. Well, they loved Meggie Magpie anyway, or Della Dobbs, lady aviator. And those personalities were part of her own, part of her.

And Dud loves me, she thought, the train swaying round a long, stretched bend. Or he did, once. She thought mournfully of the famine caused by his halted letter-writing. Perhaps he didn't write because he was embarrassed, she wondered. He didn't want to bother her, if she didn't want him. Yes, that was it. Or perhaps not; maybe she had ruined it that day. Perhaps the lack of letters was a sign that his love had died for her at her refusal, that his interest had moved on. He could be writing letters to another girl right now, from Clipstone Camp. *Dear Ruby* or *Dear Dolly* or whoever, *I am so very glad you're my girl and*— Oh, please no. Not her Dud. *And he is mine*, she thought, *he's always been mine. And I'm his.*

Either way, even if he turned her down, she was on her way to him now and she simply must see him, and tell him that she loved him. Maybe he was right about her; maybe she was too wrapped up with her father and what he thought of her. Well, today had put the kybosh on that, that's for sure. She certainly wasn't looking for a father figure now. The idea disgusted her. *The future belongs to the young*, she thought. *And the old are jealous and hate us for it.* And another idea occurred to her, quite a revelation at the age of twenty-two – that her parents and indeed everyone older than her did not, in fact, as she'd always assumed, know everything. They were splashing about in the shallows just like herself and when the big waves came, as they always did at some point in everyone's life, it was how you faced the wave that counted. Let it wash you away or try to ride it out. Perhaps that was the only rule there was. There was no magical moment when you assumed the mantle of adulthood and knew what to do. *Gosh*, she realised, *I'm an adult too. I could even have had two or three kiddies by now. And I have no idea what I'm doing. And neither does Mam or Pop.* What a turn-up!

The train was full of soldiers, entraining and detraining, from various billets, home visits and camps no doubt. They had the odd leering look or word for Della, but not too much bother. At Mansfield, she asked about and found a bus going to Clipstone village that went on to Forest Town, near to where the camp entrance lay. On arrival, she stepped down into a road that led away to dense forest in the distance, and down which were marching what could only be described as hordes of soldiers. They were very well-organised hordes though; in formation, smartly turned out. There were hundreds of them, perhaps even a thousand or more, snaking away down the forest road and around the corner so that it was impossible to tell how long the snake might be. The tramping of feet on the road was an unearthly sound as it thumped past, and all along its length, excitable children – mostly boys

– bobbed up and down, stared and pointed, joined in the march – or some solemnly saluted, perhaps thinking of their own fathers or older brothers.

Della stood and gazed at them, the sea of male faces bobbing along in time to their feet. She scanned every one she could, madly looking for the one she sought. It was mad, she knew that, but she couldn't help herself. Who knew; she might be lucky. But she saw only strangers, so in the end she left them behind and, following directions given by the clippie girl on the omnibus, found the camp entrance. Beyond it stretched acres and acres of identical huts in rows going this way and that, each hut topped by a chimney emitting a long thin stream of smoke, the scent of which, along with cooking smells and a hint of latrine and sweat, wafted on the breeze to the outside world.

She peered along the dusty road leading away from the gate into the heart of the camp and noticed the odd knot of soldiers around and about, even a spot of garden here and there. She had not known what to expect, but when she thought of a camp it was always Puck's training that Mam had described that she had in mind. Not this industrial approach to army training, row upon row of well-built huts, like a town beyond this village, a town of strangers, of fighting men, of brothers and fathers and cousins and pals, stretching away towards the forest where they say Robin Hood once roamed, an awe-inspiring sight. She approached the hut at its side, manned by a stern-looking soldier trying to look dignified in the tiny shed where he kept guard. The day was dull and the sky was troubled as she walked up to him and smiled. He did not acknowledge her, so she spoke up.

'Excuse me, I've come to visit a friend of mine.'

He turned to briefly size her up, then looked back at the road he'd been studying. He was watching the column file past and looked at it longingly as it disappeared down the street. Perhaps he'd rather be with his mates than in this shed.

'I bet you 'ave, love. Now, off you go.'

'No, really. Please. It's a matter of importance.'

'You should've written first. Arranged it with 'im.'

'There wasn't time. You see, it's a . . . family emergency.'

His face softened. 'Concerning what?'

'Well, it's a private matter, you see. A . . . death in the family. Our brother. Killed in action. I'm . . . his sister.'

Oh, she felt awful lying about it. What a stab in the back it was for Puck. Perhaps Pop was right about her and she'd do anything to suit herself. But she didn't know what else to say, what else this tyrant would listen to. And she thought, Puck wouldn't mind, he wouldn't mind at all. He was always up for a wheeze like this.

The soldier was fooled and said, with newly found respect, 'All right then, miss. What name was it and what unit?'

'Dudley Willow, King's Own Yorkshire Light Infantry, 4th Battalion, Reserves.'

The soldier frowned and muttered, 'KOYLI, 4th. Yes, that's right. They've gone, miss.'

'Gone where?' *Marching*, she thought. So, he was there after all, on that road just now.

'Off. You know. Gone off. To the continent.'

A sickening gulp stuck in her throat.

'Are you sure?' The clippie girl had told her there were thousands of soldiers at the camp. How could this one lad know all the battalions?

'Quite sure. My cousin's in the KOYLI, you see, that's how I remember, different battalion. Shipped out two days ago. 4th went too; well, they're the 8th now they're in the Expeditionary Force. But anyway, they've all gone. You've missed 'em, I'm afraid. You'll have to write your news to your brother. Awfully sorry. Oi, miss, you all right? You look a bit green.'

She didn't faint. She wasn't sick. But she felt all her faith drain from her. How sure she'd been that she would see him, how certain. Since finding her love of flight, she had come to believe that if you wanted something badly enough, and you put enough effort in, then it would eventually come to you. That had happened with getting her wings, though she'd learned it didn't work with love, not with Claude, anyway. And now, Dudley was gone and there again was this horrible feeling, just like in the moments after hearing the news about Puck, when Midge was wailing on the step and Della grabbed Mam's telegram and read the awful words. A drowning sensation, that nothing was solid, nothing was sure, everything was at sea and forever changed, the ocean currents running on and on, washing away your expectations and certainties, beyond your reach. That was how she felt: neither on solid ground, nor up in the air that she loved, but adrift and aimless, hopeless and alone.

17

'I know you,' the man said.

'Well, I'm local,' said Della.

He leaned his elbow on the side and sort of smirked at her.

'No, I mean I know your face. I've seen it in the papers, haven't I?'

'That's right.'

'You're that flyer girl. That Meggie Magpie.'

Della finished off the receipt with the stubby pencil she kept in her overalls' front pocket. 'Yes, that's me.' *Or it was*, she thought. *A long, long time ago, as they say in fairy tales.*

He came closer and leaned on the counter right next to her.

'I bet you could tell a tale or two, eh? I bet you've been around.'

Even though they were talking about flying, it was clear they were actually talking about something else, something suggestive, even smutty. Della sighed. She was so bad at all this double talk. The man had ten years on her at least – not a problem in itself, but she happened to know he had six kids and a wife down the road. Harmless banter maybe, but the way he was looking her up and down stirred something in her and made her feel ashamed, somehow. Then she thought of Dud in France and a warm wash like summer air swept through her and she sighed again, woebegone, that this fellow she loved was away and she couldn't even write to him, her best friend in the whole world. She shook her head to rid herself of the dream. Bad habit, that. Daydreaming. *Flying*, she thought. *Flying cleared out the cobwebs. God, I miss it like . . . like the blood in my body. I can't do without it. Or Dud.* The bloke was frowning at her and she realised she'd been standing there chewing on her pencil and staring into space for a while now. *He thinks I'm a bit touched,* she thought. *Oh well, probably best. He'll run a mile now.*

'Receipt,' she simply said and, handing it to him, she turned back to the garage and looked at her next vehicle. She heard the man go outside and start up his Morris and drive off. Back to work. Another motorcycle to fix, a Triumph just like the one she used to whip around London on, except this one had a dodgy gearbox.

Weeks before, coming back from Clipstone on the last train with her tail between her legs, she had stolen into the house late at night and had tried to sneak up to her room unnoticed. Mam had appeared at her door, nose chapped and raw from sneezing, eyes red from the same – or from crying.

'Oh, love, so glad you're back. I was so worried about you.'

She had gone for a hug but Mam had warned her off. She hadn't wanted Della to catch the virus, a really nasty one. But she had wanted to talk to her and had beckoned her inside her room. Della had taken off her coat and hat and sat on the edge of the bed and Mam was wrapped up in her dressing gown, leaning on the pillows. Della had started snivelling. Mam reached out but then held her hands up: 'No, I mustn't. I'll have to comfort you from here, pet. What is it? Is it Pop? Those things he said? Where'd'you go today? Is it that upset you, too? Tell me, darling. Please.'

Della had a little cry, her mother's hand massaging her leg half up on the bed and Mam sniffing and sneezing as she did so. Della wanted to tell her something, but she knew it would break her heart and couldn't bear to say it.

She spoke almost inaudibly. Mam had to ask her to speak up: 'I can't stay in this house,' muttered Della. 'I'll have to go.'

'No, love,' said Mam, shaking her head. 'No.'

'I'll have to, Mam. I can't stay here . . . with him.'

He doesn't mean it, he's—'

'He said awful things to me. Terrible things. You don't know.'

'I do, I heard. Well, the end of it anyway. You said some rather ripe things yourself.' Mam smiled, but Della was in no mood for it.

'I'm sorry about the pot,' said Della.

'I know. It's all right.'

'Pop . . . he said I was—'

'I know. Let's not repeat it again. Words have a horrible power, like a spell. Once said, they're there forever. So we won't give those words more space and time in this world. We'll banish them, you and me. Della, look at me.'

She did. Mam was ill, but her eyes were still bright with meaning and love. She took her daughter's hand and held it firmly. Warm and clammy though it was, her grip was strong.

'You are my darling girl. The only one who really understands me. My favourite. There, I've said it. I know you won't go blabbing it to your sisters. I know you can keep your mouth shut. You've had years of practice at that. But listen, darling. Your spirit, your brave but quiet spirit, is something I had once. You know how much I used to love playing the piano. Well, you don't know this, but I used to write music once. Yes, a long time ago, in another life, before your father. I studied music and went to see orchestras. I wanted to be a composer, write piano concertos and conduct them – yes, I wanted to be the fellow standing at the front waving the stick.'

'Oh, Mam. Did you try? Did you write one of those things? A concerto?'

'No, I never did. I tinkered about with tunes on the piano. But you never saw girls' names written on music, only men's: Johann, Antonio, Robert. No Johannas, no Antonias or Robertas. And you never saw women up there, only men, always men in their black frock coats. So I just assumed, well, a girl can't be a composer then, or a conductor. It's just not possible. And I was a quiet girl like you, so I didn't speak up, and I never told anyone my secret hopes.'

'I never knew, Mam.'

'Nobody did, really. It seemed too ridiculous to tell. And then I met your father, and he was handsome and ambitious, and I loved him very much. And I loved having children, oh how I adored my babies! And because I never spoke of my secret hopes, never practised them again, put down my pen and the idea of waving a baton before a great orchestra . . . well, they withered and faded and then I put them away as a girlish dream.'

Della was crying again, though she wasn't sure why. She was just so unhappy, so sad about Mam and her dreams like dried flowers pressed between the pages of a heavy book. About Dud, about everything. Mam threw caution to the wind and reached out and held her, and Della cried against Mam's nightie and felt better after a while, snuffled and blew her nose, wiped her eyes.

Mam said, 'But when you started up with kites and flying, I saw you had that same itch in you, a pure streak of ambition. Oh, I was so proud of you. I still am. Midge had it but she turned it outwards somehow, looking for praise, for followers. Gertie had a bit of it, but she had my love for kiddies more. That's all she really wanted, a safe home to have her chicks in. But you, you're like me, you just wanted it because you wanted it. You loved flying for its own sake, not because it brought you anything or gave you anything, you just loved it for itself. That's how I was with music, how I still am. Oh, my lovely girl. It's such a joy for me to see myself in you.'

They hugged again and laughed a little, the tears dried and almost forgotten. Then they heard Pop shifting about in his room, the door open and close. He must have left some unwashed crockery out there; a whiff of cabbage and cold gravy drifted up the hall. Della was brought back to earth and crossed her arms, frowning. Mam sighed.

'Your father is a complicated animal. He seems all bad to you, because you don't know him. And that's his fault, to be sure. He's never let his children know him. Even Puck – *his* favourite, as we all knew – never knew him, not the real him. I'm the only one who has that privilege.'

'But Mam, he treats you so—'

'No, darling. As much as I love you, I won't hear you say those things about him. I can't explain a man like your father to you now in a few choice phrases. It would take years. Just keep in your mind that he's almost a broken man, broken by bad fortune and now grief. And his parents – you never knew them – showed him little love, that's true too. But he has deep vaults filled with love you don't know about. Somehow, we need to find a way to reach him. Something to break him free. But I haven't worked it out yet.'

Della remembered a throwaway comment Midge made on an omnibus once, that they had to get through to Pop somehow, and that maybe Cleo could. She understood that, knew some of what he'd been through. But, it was so hard to forgive cruelty. And cruel is the word she would use, if Mam had let her speak of it.

'Now then, I hope that one day, when you're ready, perhaps you'll tell me where you went today and what you found there. But for now, will you think about staying? I need you, pet. I need you like water and I can't do without you just now. Since Puck . . . well, I was almost broken too, like your father. Almost broken into tiny pieces. And seeing your nice face and having your help every day, it's been more of a comfort than you'll ever know. You are wanted, Della, you are needed and you are loved. So, if you could see your way to staying, just for a while, it would help me more than you know.'

Mam's eyes were desperate. And how could Della refuse? Actually, she didn't want to refuse. Pop never came out of his damn room anyway, and she just couldn't bear to leave Mam like this.

'I'll stay,' she said and Mam beamed, a watery, tired grin subsiding into relief and then exhaustion.

Mam answered softly, 'I'm tired now, my love, and I want to sleep. It's past midnight and you must sleep too. I've some sugar hidden in the cupboard and we'll have pancakes with lemon in the morning and sprinkle it on, eh? How does that sound?'

Mam made the best pancakes.

So, Della had stayed. But she decided that, in order to remain sane, she could not be imprisoned in the house forever, not even for Mam's sake. So one day, she fetched her motorcycle overalls from her case stuffed under the bed, pulled them on, slipped out of the back door unnoticed, climbed aboard her trusty (and rusty) old pushbike and cycled down to a local garage on Sea View Street.

A neighbour had told her that the owner and his son had both gone off to France, and the owner's wife was doing her best to keep it open but really struggling; many of the local lads had just come of age and joined up. *Time for a visit*, Della thought.

She found the garage – Lancaster and Son – closed up and the front door of the next house open. A woman was huffing and puffing, dragging a rug out to beat it. Della gave her a hand, for which the woman thanked her, but then she eyed her in her overalls and drew back, as if Della were cursed or hideously ugly.

'What's your game?' said the woman.

'I'm a mechanic,' said Della.

'And I'm Kaiser Bill,' said the woman and shook her head.

'Listen, Mrs Lancaster,' said Della and filled her in on her work before the war. 'Ever heard of Meggie Magpie?'

Mrs Lancaster gasped and touched her cheek. 'That you? Oh, I see it now. Course it is! Your brother—'

'Yes,' said Della, a slight shrug. 'How are your husband and your boy?'

'All right, I suppose. I don't hear much. Listen, can you really fix things? Engines, I mean?'

'Yes, I can. If you're willing, I'll open up the garage for you. They'll be funny about it to begin with, I should think, a woman doing the fixing. But we could throw a bit of an opening day, with a bit of food and a drop to drink. Make a bit of a splash. And put a notice in the paper, perhaps. Get some custom in. What do you say?'

Mrs Lancaster's eyes widened and then narrowed. 'I can't afford to pay you much, only what I paid those boys.'

'That's all right. I can manage.'

'All right, then! Let's give it a go! A woman mechanic, I never did!'

So they did. Mam made sandwiches and from somewhere Mrs Lancaster magicked up sugar and eggs and made fairy cakes, and a few people came by and stared at Della and ate what was on offer. The *Grimsby Gazette* remembered Della and gave her a spot for free, making it into a feature about how the plucky pilot had turned her hand to helping out the local industry, filling the place left by two brave soldiers away at war. The article was adorned with a picture of Della pretending to tinker with a spanner, dressed in her overalls. They said she was like those ladies of the Women's Volunteer Reserve garages, doing their bit for the war effort. In the news again, she mused. Earthbound, but still making the news. She didn't care about it, as long as it spread the word. Customers began to turn up, at first having a good stare again, but soon they started to hand over money. And then it all became normal; they saw she knew her stuff, what a good job she was doing, and before long she was the mechanic in Sea View Street, where you took your car, van or motorcycle (if you could get enough petrol to run them) and also your bike if it needed a fix, and the gal in the overalls would see you right.

It kept her out of the house, away from Pop, yet she was still home in good time to help Mam with dinner and play with Cleo after tea and do her bedtime stories, which Cleo loved, especially now they could share the reading, Cleo being six years old and a precocious reader, doing all the characters in different voices. Perhaps she'd be an actress like Midge. She certainly had the nerve for it. Pop still never came out of his room, but Cleo carried on bashing on his door and demanding his presence. She missed her father – she was just a child and her daddy was never to be seen. It was quite ridiculous if you thought about it and eventually Cleo had simply had enough.

One evening, while Della was sitting by the fire in the kitchen, reading back issues of *The Aero* and reminiscing about the old days, Cleo sneaked downstairs from bed, lay in wait beneath the stairs and, when Pop opened the door to eject some detritus or other, she rushed him like an ambush and charged past him. Della heard the commotion and came out to look, saw the little minx shouting at their bemused and flustered father – 'Why have you been hiding, Pop? You know I like to play hide and seek but you've been very silly and been hiding too long. You're a very naughty daddy. A very naughty man.' Della stifled a laugh and listened with glee, as Cleo finished with, 'What have you got to say for yourself?'

After this, Della was amazed to hear from Mam that Pop had agreed to allow Cleo into his room after she came back from school, just for a half hour. What they did or discussed was as mysterious as Pop himself, but it was a good sign, everyone thought that. Della did too, yet there was a seed of envy there, that again Pop had picked his favourite, another chosen one to enter the sanctum, while she was left outside in the cold. She told herself she didn't care, but she did, a little. She thought of Dud often, and his silence was almost unbearable. It made her so sad and became a weight she carried. Funnily enough, she bore him no ill will, blamed only herself.

He was a thoroughly good person, Dud, she knew that. She didn't tell Mam about it, even though Mam was waiting, she knew. She didn't tell her because she was ashamed of her own part in it, her stupid feelings of superiority over Dud she'd once felt but which now seemed the height of foolishness.

Soon after Cleo broke through the invisible wall of Pop's seclusion, Mam received a letter from Della's eldest sister, Gertie. Her husband Eric had been working for the War Office dealing with shipping in the Humber, but now he'd been transferred down to London and so she and their three boys were alone – apart from the servants – in their large, comfortable house in Hull. Gertie wrote that Eric would feel much happier if they weren't in the city any longer, as it had been and could be again a target for zeppelin raids. So, she was thinking of moving the boys to Cleethorpes, into a rented house near to Mam and Pop, where they could all help each other. She admitted in the letter that she was lonely and that it'd be fine and dandy to be close to Mam again.

'She only needs me when she needs me,' said Mam.

Within weeks, Gertie and the boys were moving in to a tall thin house on Albert Road, empty since the owners' sons had died fighting overseas and their parents had removed themselves to the countryside, to escape memories, one supposed.

'It's haunted,' whispered Cleo when they all went round to visit, bringing home-baked bread and some curtains for the boys' rooms that Mam had run up on the Singer. They all felt it, that the house was somehow hollow at its heart; the boys were subdued and Cleo clung on to Della's sleeve the whole time. After a day, Mam was saying to Della, 'What would you think if Gertie and the boys moved in here? She could share with you and the boys could sleep in . . . they could have . . . the spare room.'

'What does Pop say?' asked Della, not that she cared, but she did wonder.

'I haven't told him yet, or anyone. I wanted to know what you thought first.'

'I think it'd be smashing.'

'Really, love?'

'Yes, I do. But, are you ready for . . . do you think you'll be all right? Seeing them, you know, in *there?*'

She'd raised her eyebrows to indicate the room they both knew they were talking about, Puck's room, kept like a shrine to him these past months and dusted daily by Mam, with not a thing changed. Della guessed she went in there not to shift dust about but just to sit, to be with his things, smell his old smell, breathe in the shadow left by her son's absence.

'Yes, I'm ready. Do you mind sharing with your sister? We can get a new bed in there, there's just room if we move the chest of drawers out.'

'I'd love it,' said Della, genuinely. She'd been a lonesome thing since Clipstone and her eldest sister's company was more than welcome. She hugged Mam, murmuring in her ear, 'You're very brave,' whereupon they squeezed each other more tightly.

On the day of the move, the boys tumbled into the house amid great hilarity. Cleo shrieked with glee and attacked them joyously with a woollen snake Mam had made for her last birthday. They called her a Hun and chased her round the house shooting imaginary pistols at her back while she squealed uncontrollably. The noise was shocking, riotous and fantastic, filling the house with a life it hadn't seen for months. Della shook her head, laughing, linking arms with Gertie and walking to the kitchen, where the two sisters and Mam made tea and ate cheese scones at the table, the children running in and out for snacks in between launching further assaults on each other upstairs and down.

Pop actually surfaced from his room to see what all the rumpus was about. He actually smiled. Thereafter, the boys were allowed to visit Pop – one at a time – in his room at set hours during the day. Laughter was heard from the study. Other improvements to the general mood included Mam playing the piano again, to entertain the boys – polkas and mazurkas and suchlike, to which the boys and Cleo would dance together, in the manner of hoodlums, but still. It made Mam laugh too. Also, Della was cheered up a treat by spending nights chatting with Gertie in bed.

She knew Gertie as vaguely as she had known Midge before they lived together. Gertie had left home at eighteen, when Della was only ten, off to marry the older Mr Eric White, and she started having babies almost immediately. If Midge was exotic, Gertie was somehow holy, for her ability to catch a handsome, wealthy man and produce so many fine boys. In both cases, her older sisters were a cut above and a lifetime away from the young Della, so it was a surprise to talk as adults now, gossipy in the moonlight, as Della had with Betty all those years ago.

One night, up came the subject of Pop, and a few home truths came out.

'What's it like being married, Gert?'

'Ooh, it's just swell. I've got a nice one. You've got to find a nice one, Del, one who'll be kind to you. There's plenty out there who are cruel, cruel for the sake of it, mind. You have to be careful.'

'Like Pop,' muttered Della.

'Steady on, dear. I wouldn't say that about Pop.'

'I would. He is cruel. He's selfish, treated Mam like a slave sometimes. And he said . . . well, he said some awful things to me, unforgivable things.'

'Like what?'

Della filled her in.

'Oh, he's done that to me too. That's just Pop.'

'I didn't know that. Like what?'

'Like when Eric and I were courting and he disapproved

because he was so much older – not that it ever bothered me, but he called me a Jezebel and a hussy and said I was whoring myself about for an older man and had I no shame and all that nonsense. I told him to keep his opinions to himself and he got ever so angry but I just laughed at him. He's all mouth and no trousers, believe me. He's said the most horrendous things to Midge too, especially when she started getting good roles.'

'Really?' said Della, incredulous. Surely Midge was Pop's favourite, after Puck.

'Oh yes, that she was a terrible actress and would never amount to anything. They had some fearful rows.'

'I never heard those. Where was I?'

'I don't know. They often had them at the theatre, or you were out walking, like you used to do all the time before you got your bike.'

'I had no idea.'

'Yes, well, you're not the only one, lovey. Puck was the one who escaped all that. And Cleo, Mam tells me. Cleo can do no wrong. But then, she does have a Puckish quality about her, doesn't she? Like my middle one, George. Ooh, a little tearaway. Pop dotes on him most of all. He certainly has his favourites, does Pop.'

'Don't you think it's appalling, though, Gert? The way he lords it over everyone?'

'Oh yes, but that's just him, isn't it? You need to accept that about him and move along. It's not worth blighting your own life with his silliness. He's a grumpy old bugger and that's that. You just need to not take it personally and make your own life. Also, he's jealous of you. You do know that, don't you?'

Della sat upright in bed. 'No!' That was ridiculous, surely.

'Course he is. He sees you out there doing this extraordinary thing. You're this heroine, famous, for being talented, a trailblazer. And there he is, sitting in his study, his glittering career long over, writing all these plays that no one will read, let alone put on a stage, and your stage is the sky and you own it. He's so jealous of you he can hardly breathe. And it makes him mean.'

Della shook her head with the shock of it. Could it really be true? 'I'd never have thought of that. But surely parents shouldn't be jealous of their children. That's unnatural, isn't it?'

Gertie snorted with laughter, then sighed, a careworn sigh of long experience. 'Yes, well, parents feel a lot of unnatural things at times. When George was a baby and wouldn't sleep and cried all the time, I seriously considered hurling him out of the window. I could picture myself doing it, throwing him out in a graceful arc and then the noise would stop, and oh, the relief it would be! You'll find out, when you have your own. It's not like it is in the magazines.'

Della was dumbstruck, that exemplary mother Gertie could think to murder her own son? *How little I know of the world*, Della thought. Gertie's home truths were disturbing her so much she almost disliked her sister for them. But to hear such honesty, in a house of whispers and secrets – Della began to realise what a tonic this was, how necessary and longed-for it was for her, for all of them. But it was still hard to swallow.

'I'd never have imagined in a hundred years that Pop thought enough about me to be jealous.'

'That's because you have such a low opinion of yourself. You always did. You couldn't imagine anyone would envy you, especially the mighty Pop. But that was always you all over. Always down on yourself. But you must simply let it go, all this Pop stuff. Move on. That's what Midge and I did, and you're doing it too, making your own way. Don't let his stupid words stop you. But you wouldn't, would you, eh? Good girl.'

And with that, Gertie turned over in bed and said, 'Night, night' and was soon snoozing, sleeping the sleep of the blissful mother who could finally sleep a night without waking at every sound, as her own mother was on hand, and after all these years the burden was shared at last. Della, however, lay awake for a long time, mulling over these revelations and deciding if she thought they could possibly be true.

Gertie's presence was to offer another gift to Della. One day her elder sister met one of her boys leaving Pop's study and used the excuse to pop in herself and see her father. Della would never know what was said in that room, but Mam told her after that there were some raised voices in there, though they were short and sharp, so nobody heard precisely what was said. But that very evening when Della returned, greasy from her work at the garage, coming in the back door to the kitchen dressed in her cruddy overalls, Gertie told her she'd been summoned to Pop's study as soon as she was home.

'He can whistle,' said Della. 'I'm not going in there again.'

'Oh, don't be daft, Del. You're as stubborn as him. Get in there and hear what the man has to say.'

Della looked furiously at Mam, who was rolling pastry. Mam glanced up and gave Della a nod, then went back to her dough.

'Oh, all right then,' huffed Della and stomped along the corridor, looking down at her grimy clothes. She was glad to wear them, a working woman, helping the war effort. It gave her the courage to go in that room and give him what for if he tried bullying her again.

She knocked loudly once, then went straight in. *He's not the bloody King*, she thought. *I won't bow and scrape.* What a joy it was to not be frightened of him any more. She hardly recognised the girl who used to tiptoe in. That girl was long gone.

'What is it?' she barked, arms crossed.

Pop in his customary chair. His face was hard to read, serious yet lightened somehow; there was a peace there she hadn't seen for years, not since an early day in Cleo's life when she was past danger and sleeping in the crook of his good arm. She'd seen that look on his face then and had wondered at it. *Had he ever looked upon me like that, when I was a babe, before I became a disappointment?*

'Cordelia, I believe this talk is overdue.'

A short silence. She had no patience left for him. 'What does that mean?'

He breathed in and went on, 'I have left it too long to say . . . to say . . . to apologise.'

He hadn't said the word, he couldn't say it: *sorry*. But he'd said the next best thing. But she wasn't going to let him off that easily.

'Apologise for what?' Let him feel uncomfortable for once, let him suffer for her, why not?

'My conduct was not that of a gentleman or of a good father. I must explain to you. The state of mind of a man, of myself . . .'

Words were failing him. His face frowned, he opened his mouth to speak, but no words came. There was an ounce of pity inside her, Della realised, maybe more.

'Pop, I know Puck—'

'No,' he said firmly, then she saw on his face that he regretted it. Clearly, avoiding his usual bullying stance was hard work for him and she appreciated that. 'No, we shall not speak of . . . that.'

He'd gained her sympathy, he really had. But she saw this as her chance to change things and she had never had much patience, just like her brother. 'But yes, Pop, we must say his name. We must speak of him. If we don't, it's as if he never was, and that's wrong. Puck. There, I've said it. Puck. Our lovely boy.'

'No, Cordelia,' muttered Pop and he turned his face from hers, and she could see he was weeping and trying to hide it, unsuccessfully. Oh God, to see Pop weep, to hear the tiny sobs, was cracking her heart.

'Pop,' she said faintly. 'Pop, I'm sorry.'

'No,' he said again, and straightened himself, wiped his eye with the back of his hand, held it up against his cheek like a shield to hide from her. A small voice came from behind it. 'You have nothing to apologise for.'

Della felt a sea-change had come in that room. She looked away from him to the waves beyond, crashing on the shore, perpetual. A sense of long time washed over her and she felt a slackening, a relaxation in her bones.

She placed her greasy hand on his back; he did not shrug it off, or shun her, as she had expected.

'Thanks, Pop, old chap.'

And she turned and left the room, pulling the door to behind her.

Gertie and Mam were hovering in the hall.

'What happened?' whispered her sister.

'Nothing,' said Della. 'Well, everything.'

But she didn't want to talk about it. It was just for her. And Pop. She wasn't cured of it, her anger. There was too much bad blood for a simple fix. His words still rankled. And his years of lordship. She still didn't like him much; but it changed things, that talk. For the better. The next few weeks in that house turned into springtime without and within, sunshine lightening the dark corners, for the first time in, well, ever so long.

In April 1917, Della came down early one morning, ready to leave for work, and heard the postman's knock. He handed over only one letter and it was for her. Postmarked Bradford, her name and address written in an elegant, Victorian hand she did not recognise. She tore it open and looked immediately down at the signatory: Mr Arthur L. Willow.

Dear Miss Dobbs,

I am writing to you in my capacity as Dudley Willow's father. I want to inform you that Dudley has been gravely

*ill from influenza, yet thankfully he has now recovered
from this illness. He was sent home from the continent on
the HS PRINCESS ELIZABETH in January, whereupon
he was transported to the First Southern General Hospital
in Birmingham. After this, he came home.*

*However, he has had somewhat of a relapse. This is not
in his lungs, but instead, his mood and personality seem to
have changed out of all recognition. He was sent to
another hospital in Harrogate and is there now. The main
problem is that he is not talking to anyone, and I don't
mean he is a little quiet, I mean it quite literally. He has
not said a word for months now. I am at my wits' end, I
don't mind telling you. They say it's something to do with
the war and that he will come round eventually. But the
days pass and still he says not a word.*

*I looked in his room at home to see if I could find
something to cheer him up and take him out of himself.
While doing this, I found a box full of letters from your
good self. I have to say I was surprised as he has never
mentioned your name to me. However, please do not
concern yourself as I did not read a word of any of your
letters other than the beginning of the very first one, sent
back in 1909 when you were both young folk. This was
only in order to get some grasp of who this friend of my
son's might be, and I'd hazard a guess that you may be a
very important one. As I say, I can see that you are at the
very least a devoted correspondent of my son's and
therefore I would like to ask if you might help us at this
difficult time. His mother died when he was born, as you
may know, and it is only myself and some school chums
who are able to visit him. But, as you may imagine, many
of those school chums are now away in the war. Thus, I
find myself writing this letter to a stranger – that is, a
stranger to me though clearly not to Dudley, who has kept
your letters in apple-pie order. Here we come to the crux of*

this letter. Would it be possible for you to visit Dudley at your convenience? If this would be agreeable to you, please reply to this letter and I will forward you the details of his hospital in Harrogate. I do hope you can forgive me this imposition, but I am writing as a rather desperate man, I have to say, you see.

  Yours sincerely,
  Mr Arthur L. Willow

18

When she saw Dud's face, it wasn't his face. Some ghoul had come and taken it and now stared out at her with black eyes. There was an odd moment when he turned to look at her, and the eyes were all she saw, dark and ever-widening, threatening to take over his pale face completely, eat away at it. She had to look away, then hated herself for it and looked straight back up. He still stared at her. She came promptly then, covering the grey linoleum floor between them in a few strides. He'd been left in a room alone, the door shut behind her to give them some privacy for her first visit. 'Don't try to touch him,' the doctor had said. 'You don't even need to speak. It might be too much for him. A greeting, perhaps. But that's all. Just your presence will be enough, this first visit.'

Della thought, *We'll see about that.* But she had to admit, seeing Dud now, that face, those eyes that were not his eyes – her bravado popped like a soap bubble the instant she saw him. And she welcomed the doctor's advice and thought she should follow it, she should do what she could, whatever she could, to help him.

She pulled up a chair, her eyes locked on his, and sat beside him. He was staring at her, as if amazed; the eyes were dead yet intent – there was some life there, something of him. Then, as she gazed at his face, trying to find something more of Dud, he opened his mouth. She could hear the dull click of his tongue touch the roof of it, and was sure it was a D; D for Della. But nothing issued, and he was left with just a sigh and he closed his mouth again. Now the eyes filled with a veil of tears, not enough to tip down the white cheeks but enough to show that somebody was home, that Dud was still there.

'Hello, dear,' said Della, forcing a smile. 'So grand to see you.'

Dud kept looking at her, intently, like a child concentrating on a puzzle, entirely inside its own head. It broke her heart to look at him, but she impelled herself. She thought dolefully of her dead brother and felt somehow she'd let Puck down – unknowingly and inexplicably, but there it was. She wouldn't do that again. She'd meet Dud's gaze, she'd sit beside him and hold his hand, talk to him, love him. For as long as it took. She knew that.

She sat with him for a while like that. He stared at her the whole time, she looking at him, or glancing away at the placid grounds beyond, two horses grazing near a stable block, one placed here, one placed there, like a painting. Tall trees were waving lazily in the light breeze. It was peaceful, to see that, to sit with Dud. The horror was fading now.

That was the first visit. The doctor said she was allowed to sit with him for twenty minutes at a time, once a day. Any longer would be detrimental to his recovery. Dr Till was well-mannered, probably in his thirties, a bit military but with a benevolent face. He told Della about a condition that some soldiers were suffering with. They called it 'shell shock' but, he said, 'It's a misleading term, really, as lots of chaps get it when they've never been near a shell or a bombardment or anything of the sort.'

'Do you think that's what Dud has? Shell shock? Why he won't speak?'

'We don't know what happened to your friend, but he was ill to begin with. Influenza. Sent to a Casualty Clearing Station, and his commanding officer was there, checking on his wounded men, and he told us that in his delirium, Second

Lieutenant Willow went on and on about a Canadian. But it was a Canadian CCS, so it was thought to be only that. His CO wrote to me, saying he'd been in a nasty bombardment and then captured a German trench, staying several hours in it before he was found. We don't know what happened there.'

'What do you mean, what happened there?'

'Well, it was said they found him in that Hun trench and his mind was gone. But he had a ragingly high temperature and that's when he was sent off to the CCS. Fever, they thought. And he raved a lot in the CCS. But once the fever went down, he stopped talking altogether.'

'So he stopped speaking, out there, in France?'

'Yes. That's right. Bit of a mystery.'

Oh Dud. To think of him, in that German trench; she could picture him, as if she were flying high above the land and looking down upon him, so small, so alone.

She paid for a week in advance at a local guest house and came back the next day. Her visit was a copy of the first. So was the third. Each time the twenty minutes were up, the doctor would appear and Dud would sink back behind that soulless stare and Della would lose him.

On the fourth day, she decided enough was enough. She reached out and took Dud's hand. It was cold and his fingers were floppy, like he wasn't home there either. Empty, is what she thought, like he'd slipped away from this body, this life, like he had in London that day, walking off down the pavement in Clapham and not looking back. But just to hold his hand was such a comfort. And the feel of it – though cool, it was beginning, very gradually, to warm up.

The fifth day, she held his hand again, and on the sixth he squeezed hers, a good firm squeeze that gave her a thrill of hope, and she gasped, before it relaxed and the death look crept over him again. It was as if his soul came swelling in sudden waves, washing through his body and over her, then was just as soon dispersed and gone, empty once more.

On the seventh day, her patience was slipping; she longed to speak with him. His gaze, his presence, even his hands were not enough. Was she being selfish? She wasn't sure. But to feel that hand, Dud's – how she thought she'd lost him, as a friend, as a fiancé certainly, but perhaps even forever, as she'd lost Puck, taken by war. Yet to think he had come back and he was safe. Thank God, he was safe. His body was, at any rate, though heaven knows where his mind was. How to reach it, that was the challenge. But she wanted the challenge, felt she deserved no less than to be forced to work for his love. And by Jove, she'd bloody do it, if it'd bring him back. *So*, she thought, *talk to him. Talk like you used to write. Bring all the letters you once wrote into his ears now and bring him back.*

'Dud, it's been rotten without you. There were times when I worried ever so much that I'd never see that nice face again.' She didn't know the right thing to say. She thought perhaps there was no right thing to say. Best to speak the truth and be done with it. 'I missed you, old boy. I really did. I missed your letters. All my fault, dear, absolutely all my fault.'

His fingers moved. Tightened ever so slightly around her own.

'I came to see you at Clipstone Camp, you know. But you'd gone. You'd just gone one or two days before. Gone to France. I wish I'd come sooner.'

A little tighter. A tiny sound from his throat, a breath, but a breath with some substance to it. His eyes wider.

'I'm so sorry for what happened that day in London. It's hard to explain. I did . . . love another man once. An older man. But I can see it was a schoolgirl crush and I've grown up now. Something about the war. But before that too. When I saw that French boy die. That pilot. And then . . . Puck.'

Dud was shaking his head now, slowly from side to side. Again, a murmur from deep within him, but it couldn't reach daylight. His mouth turned down in grief, his eyes filled with it.

'Death,' whispered Della, then louder, 'It's death, you see. Too much death. I shouldn't say that, maybe . . . I mean, I can't imagine what sights you saw, Dud. What Puck saw. And I've had only a tiny share of it, not a thousandth of what you've seen. But my portion of death . . . it's forced me to grow up. I don't need my father, or an older man, or anyone else. I feel like an island now. But that doesn't mean – well, I do need love. Or, I *want* to love. And . . . I realised after you'd gone, what a fool I'd been. You were right, you were right about us.'

His fingers were warm and tight around hers now.

'*I love you, Dud*. Not because I need to, or because you love me, but just because I do, because you're my best friend, you always have been and you always will be.'

She saw the tears splashing onto his hands where they'd fallen from her face. She saw his eyes were filled too.

'Oh Dud, will you ask me again? Will you?'

He opened his mouth, but no sound came. Just a dry rasp in the throat. It pained him, she could see that. He dropped his head.

'It's all right, love. Shall I do it? Shall I do it for you this time?'

He lifted his head and his lips became the ghost of a smile. And he nodded. Just a slight movement of the head, but most certainly a nod. Assent. Yes. There was briefly peace in his eyes, before the deadness came back. But his hands were squeezing hers so hard, her fingers felt numb.

She bent her head close to his, brought her lips to his ear and whispered, 'Yes, Dud. Yes, I want to get engaged. Yes, I'll be your fiancée. Yes, Dud. I'll be your girl.'

Their arms went about each other, awkward, half out of their seats. He was shaking. She soothed him, stroked the back of his head. Friends all these years and she'd never felt his hair. It was soft, thick. Short but luxuriant in its thickness, like a cat's winter coat. She felt his head droop, rest on her shoulder now, his body less tense, folding into hers and she into his. Never had she felt so complete. She thought an aeroplane completed her, enclosed her and became one with her. That was true. But it was not human and this was. It was union, a pure blend of two people who loved each other. They had become one.

The door opened and someone stepped in. Dud flinched and pulled back. The doctor, the bloody doctor. Dud had gone back into himself, flopped down in the chair, his arms pleated across his chest, his legs twisted, his eyes down.

'It's all right, Dud,' Della whispered to him, reaching across and touching his hair again, brushing it away from his face. He let her do it but wouldn't look up.

'He doesn't like to be touched,' said the doctor, too loud.

'I'll be back tomorrow,' she said quietly to Dud, but he would not release himself from his twisted prison of a body, and didn't respond.

She got up and passed Dr Till, who held the door for her and followed.

The doctor stood before her in the white corridor and threaded his fingers together, lowered his head and used his most conciliatory voice.

'I'm concerned the visits may be upsetting Second Lieutenant Willow,' he said. 'He's always much worse after you leave, closed down completely. You see?'

Della jutted her chin out. 'That's because I've gone. Because he misses me.'

The doctor raised his eyebrows; he'd been expecting consent. 'Miss Dobbs, I don't know the precise nature of your relationship—'

'He almost spoke today,' she interjected. 'I heard a sound in his throat, more than once. He shook his head. He nodded. He even smiled, Doctor. Yes! He actually smiled! And then I put my arms around him . . .' She felt her cheeks colour, but she pushed on, not ashamed, certain she was right. 'And he

put his arms around me and we wept. He is in there, Doctor.
He's in there. And I can bring him out. I just know I can.'

'Well!' Dr Till looked briefly impressed, then professional
doubt swept in and he sighed. 'It would have been useful if
I'd seen that for myself.'

'But you won't,' said Della. 'Because he doesn't like you.'

A cough, the doctor's hands laced tightly together.

'Don't take it personally,' she went on. 'But it's true. Dud
and I love each other, you see. To answer your question, about
the precise nature of our relationship? We love each other and
we're going to get married. So, I think I know what's best for
him, don't you?'

'Well, I must say, Mr Willow, the patient's father, wasn't
entirely certain of the nature of—'

'Well, I must say, Doctor, that Mr Willow didn't know about
us, about the precise nature of our relationship.' *I didn't even
know about the precise nature of our relationship,* she thought,
until I'd lost him, like a fool. 'But Mr Willow asked me to come.
And now I'm here. And I'm telling you that Dud is coming
back to us. Very slowly, but surely. But not when you're in
the room. Agreed?'

'It is rather . . . unorthodox.' But he was smiling crookedly
as he said it, half a smile, half won over. She was nearly there,
she was sure.

'Well, that's me all over. Did you know I was an aviatrix
before the war? So, as you can see, a girl who ploughed her
own furrow. But to sort out Dudley, I need your help, your
advice and your expertise. Will you help me get him back?'

She'd done it.

Thereafter, she was allowed to come in the morning and
stay all day. Dud came and went for various therapies –
massage, a talking cure, bed rest – and while he was busy
Della walked in the green grounds. Civilised and peaceful it
was there – except when another patient passed by. Every

damaged man there weighed heavily on Della's mind, as she watched them being helped to a bench or trying to walk. There were some injured men with bandages on an arm or the head, a visible, identifiable sign of harm that was healing. Others were injured invisibly, in their minds, and these lost souls stumbled about the place in their blue uniforms with a frightening list of foreign ailments, shocking and revolting, pitiful and horrible. One walked as if he were on ice; another as if he were battling against an invisible wind. One poor bastard had a type of hysterical dancing motion as he walked, as if his legs and feet were joyous, but his face was constricted in frustration and humiliation. Every time one of these men came by, Della met their presence with a smile. It was the least she could do. She heard some talking to nurses or their visitors, stammering uncontrollably or shouting in impetuous rages, then collapsing into reveries, staring away beyond the grass, the trees, the fields and the horses, to something inner and beyond them all, some horror that played over and over in the mind, like a cruel pianola. One man hid from it under a bench and they had to leave him there for a while before he was dragged out by some orderlies, stiff like an unwilling toddler, eyes clamped down, desperately oblivious to it all. Only once he was gone did Della turn her head away and shake it, eyes shut, to stop herself from sobbing.

After another week of daily visits, she knew her time was running out. Mrs Lancaster had been awfully patient so far about Della going away and leaving the garage, but she couldn't afford to keep it closed for much longer and Della would lose her place soon, she was sure. And it was pricey staying in the guest house – the cheapest she could find nearby – and her savings from her war work were dwindling. She wouldn't be able to stay here much longer. She felt the urge to push Dud, to encourage him more. She asked Dr Till if she could take Dud to see the horses – how he'd always loved horses, before the war (that mythical time from the dim past). But the doctor said they'd tried that and he had shrunk from them, frightened of them; had almost run away. Other people had the same effect on him. He was more or less completely isolated here, liked to look at the view but didn't even want to go outside and wanted nothing to do with the people. *Well,* thought Della, *I can quite understand that.* The other patients, the chronic ones – who she heard the doctor term as 'noisy mental cases' – were upsetting her so much. Of course one would never say that, but it's what she felt and she thought they must be having the same effect on Dud. If only she could get him home, to look after him properly. Walk on Cleethorpes beach, even fly kites – well, why the hell not? What could be better therapy than kites? She thought of Mr Dick from *David Copperfield,* what Dud had told her all those years ago, sitting beside her, luminous in the summer beach light: 'What a brilliant idea that is, to take whatever is troubling you, fix it to something that flies and launch it into the air.'

So the next day, she asked her landlady for directions to the nearest library, and secured a copy of *Copperfield.* She started reading it to Dud that afternoon, holding his hand while she read out the first line: 'Whether I shall turn out to be the hero of my own life, or whether that station will be held by anybody else, these pages must show.' *The hero,* she thought. *Heroes.* What does that word even mean nowadays? Dud squeezed her hand, his body visibly relaxed, and turned his gaze out towards the grass, his face a picture of tranquillity. *Thank you, Dickens,* thought Della.

In between bouts of *David Copperfield* that smoothed Dud's moods like balm, she started telling him stories about her flying days, the sights and sounds of the air, the many flights she'd done, near misses and triumphs, the qualities of the different aircraft. All things he'd like. He'd sit up and listen carefully, looking almost gladsome, even in the shroud of his silence. And every now and again, she'd ask him a question.

Rhetorical to begin with: 'Can you believe that, Dud?' Progressing to more direct requests: 'What do you prefer, Dud? Blackburn or Deperdussin?' And one day, without warning, he cleared his throat and spoke.

'Della,' he croaked.

Della's mouth dropped, she leaned forward – 'That's right, Dud. It's me, Della.'

A strange little noise in his throat proved how difficult it was for him. 'It's all right, love,' she said, stroking his arm. 'Try again tomorrow.'

'No.' He shook his head. 'I want to come home with you.'

'Do you, Dud?'

'Yes. Get me out of this sodding place.'

He couldn't have made it any clearer. She put her arms around him gently and held him. He softened at her touch and let himself be held, buried his face in her hair. She lifted her face and found his mouth. A kiss, so tender. They were shaking, both of them, but not from shell shock, not from an illness of the mind, but from love and joy. They stopped kissing and looked at each other. And they laughed. Dud was laughing, and wiping his eyes, and kissing her again. Then, he stopped and turned away. Went in on himself and stared out at the grounds, the horses and all that, and she'd lost him again. But his kisses, his mouth – he was hers now, she knew in her heart, part of her. A piece of him had been lost, somewhere out there in France. But she would help him find it. And help him bring it back.

She told Dr Till gleefully about Dud's talking. They took him away and did tests. A considerate nurse came back to tell her, 'Though I'm not really supposed to disclose it, miss, I can't help it, you two being so romantic and all. You're quite the love story amongst us nurses, you know!' Anyway, she went on, Dud wouldn't speak a word to Dr Till, so in the end he brought in a couple of nurses and he would talk to them, so politely, 'Oh, he had us all in a flutter. Such a nice chap.'

'He is!' said Della, her eyes heavy with tears, glad, grateful ones.

'Yes, so he would speak to us, but not the doctor. So they thought it might be about men or maybe just the doctor himself. So we tried the gardener, a jolly one from a local village, an older man. And your fellow talked to him, about the horses. So, I suppose it must just be the doctor. I can't see why. We all love Dr Till.'

I don't care why, thought Della. *But it's time to get him out of here.* She went to find the doctor.

'He wants to leave here. He told me so. He must come home with me.'

'He is a Second Lieutenant in the British Expeditionary Force. He doesn't belong to you, I'm afraid.'

She scowled at him.

He went on, 'I didn't express that adequately. What I'm telling you is that he is either in a military hospital recovering, or he must go back to the front.'

Della explained that she couldn't afford to stay here much longer; the rent at the guest house was clearing her out financially. If only she could take him home . . .

'Look, I don't do this kind of thing for everyone, but I can see that Willow is making progress. But only when you're around, I grant you that. So, I've a possible solution. I've made some enquiries and it turns out there is a military hospital at a stately home not far from where I believe you reside.'

'Where?' Della's hands were clasped tightly.

'A place near Grimsby. Weelsby?'

'Yes, yes! I know it.' Not far, not far at all! Their old maid Harriet lived there. She used to walk to work. It wasn't home, but it was a darn sight better than here. 'Can he go there? When?'

'It will take a few days to sort out the paperwork. It's a convalescent home, where he can have time and space to recover fully. He won't have access to the same range of therapies he's had here. Yet I can see marked improvements in the last couple of weeks. And beginning to speak again is the most important one and a real breakthrough. I think he's ready to transfer to such a place as Weelsby. With your help.'

'He'll always have that,' she said. 'Till the end of days.'

Dr Till looked sympathetically at her. 'I believe you, Miss Dobbs. I truly do.'

Weelsby Old Hall was to be found down Weelsby Road, a broad lane bordered by high, thick hedges, cushioning the homes of the wealthy beyond. The house itself, owned by the Grant-Thorold family and turned into a military hospital for the duration of the war, had a broad facade topped with tall, slim chimneys, thronged in ivy, perforated with rows of windows; the architect must have loved light to let it stream inside so. The house was set in lush grounds, olive-green grass dotted with a collection of tall trees of many species, stretching away up a slope, there thickening into dense woodland.

The soldiers recuperating there were much further along the road to recovery; some of them were quite placid, others cheerful and good fun. There was card-playing and a piano, quite good food and company for Dud. When she came each day at lunchtime, escaping from her work at the garage for a precious hour, Della and Dud would link arms and stroll through the trees, see squirrels skittering away up to safety in the thickening tapestry of new leaves. The grounds were studded with clusters of geraniums and Canterbury bells, foxgloves in the hedges, with mind-your-own-business greenly creeping along the boundary stone walls and onto the paths.

Dud was talking now, to everyone. Only with officers of a higher rank, he would stumble over his words. Della never spoke of the war, never asked him what he saw, what he went through, what happened in that trench. Maybe nothing had happened there. Maybe it was an accumulation of horror,

silting up until full, breaking the surface. She heard some
shell-shocked soldiers went blind, others deaf, all with no clear
physical cause. As if the body had split itself from the mind,
had seen too much, heard too much and simply shut itself
down. She didn't know if Dud had spoken about the war to
Dr Till in his talking therapy, but she didn't want to raise it
here, in this vernal paradise.

Yet one Sunday, they had a whole splendid day to spend
together. After a period of silence as they walked deep into
the darkening, winding forest paths of the Weelsby woods,
Dud said, 'All my friends were gone. I'd not a soul to talk to.'

Della tightened her clasp on his arm, leaned into him as
they walked, waited for his next words.

'I wish I'd written to you, like Puck did. I was a bloody
fool.'

'No,' she said firmly and stopped, turned to him. 'That was
my fault, all mine.'

He tried to smile, a pained, skewed smile, but it was gone
as soon as it came. He stared at her blindly, stared through
her, as he spoke.

'When you see so much death, you think it'll be you next.
It's as if . . . your eyes are *infected* by death. Like watching
a thousand deaths in a moment. Not enough room in your
eyes for all that murder. It's a fear of death that infests you,
down to the bones. If I hadn't had a command, I could've
run away. I thought I might, at times. I feared that more
somehow. Almost worse than the fear of death is the fear of
being afraid.'

The tree canopies were closed overhead, the green gloom
of the woods held them and there were secrets in the small,
low hollows of trees.

'I've been an awful wreck, I'm sorry.'

'No,' she said, softly. 'Never be sorry.'

They linked arms again and walked on, turned the curve
of the path and found themselves skirting a field of young

wheat. Its wide expanse arrested them and they stopped to gaze across it.

'I'm getting better,' said Dud.

'You are!' she said and turned to him, beaming. But his eyes were wide with the fear he'd mentioned and his body stiff with it.

'But when I'm better, I'll have to go back. And I must go back. I must, to serve. To serve as others who served, who gave their lives for it. I've been away far too long. But . . . but . . . I can't . . .'

He crumpled then, head in hands.

'Dear, my dear,' she said and held him.

'Oh, God!' she heard him mutter, then he stood tall and stared at the wheat field again, full of green life, waving in the slight breeze. 'It's the mud. I can't go back to that damned mud. I can't, I can't. It'll drown me, Della, I've seen . . . oh, the mud—'

He was crying. The first time she'd seen him sob like that. She held on fast, listened to him try to stifle it. If she wasn't here, how he would howl, like a deranged animal. She could almost hear it, beyond his grinding teeth and the intense effort of damming a tidal wave. His head was on her shoulder, which was not easy when they were standing up, he so tall and she so small.

'Unforgivable,' he muttered, ashamed.

'Not at all,' she whispered. She held him while he came to himself, wrung out of tears. She looked up beyond the field to the sky, the wide Lincolnshire blue skies of her childhood.

Then she grasped his shoulders and pushed him upright.

'Then, don't go back to the mud.'

'But I—'

'Go to the skies.'

'What?' He wiped a hand across his nose.

'Learn to fly and join the Royal Flying Corps.'

'They wouldn't take me,' he said, shaking his head. 'It's all rich lads.'

'How do you know? They're desperate for pilots. Don't you read the newspapers?' She thought, *They're desperate for pilots because they're all dying.* But she dismissed it. He removed his cap and stared at it, fingered the peak. She waited.

'Will you teach me, Della? Teach me to fly?'

She grinned. 'Of course I bloody will!'

He laughed, wiping his eyes. 'I'd rather die in the air than in the sodding mud!' Then his face fell. 'Oh, sorry, darling. That sounds defeatist.'

'No, just honest. I know flying is dangerous, heaven knows, I know it more than most. But it's freedom too, away from the mud and . . . the trenches.'

A shadow passed over his face, as clear as cloud shadows sweep across a wheat field. 'Oh yes, to escape from . . . them. Yes. I'll apply for a transfer to the RFC, straight away. As soon as we're back at the house. That's the answer, my love. You're brilliant!'

He turned to her, his eyes full of love and light. They kissed and kissed there, undisturbed; ran their hands over each other, and she wanted to lie with him, how she wanted to. And his urgent hands showed how much he desired it too. But not here, not now.

He pulled away and they studied each other, gloriously.

'Will you marry me, Della? Now? Soon?'

He was smiling, her Dud, the old Dud, like the boy on the beach.

She was smiling too. 'Course I bloody will, Dudley Willow.'

19

To be flying again was ecstasy. Like being in heaven. She looked down and saw the shapes of the past in the landscape below, the lines of ancient strip farming in this field, the outline of a sunken village in that meadow. She'd forgotten that far-reaching sense of perspective that flying gave her, not only through space but through time too. She could see the history in the land. Surely it was the greatest human achievement, to have taken to the air? And to be here again, after all these land-bound years, was better than before, better than ever. This Type XV trainer – or whatever they were calling it this week – was basically a slightly updated Boxkite from the old days, a bit of a clod to learn to fly in, but she'd have flown a milk crate with wings if it'd meant getting aloft. When she taxied out and began to accelerate across the rutted ground, Dudley sat snug before her, his head turning this way and that with excitement, she herself had an inkling of fear. Fear that she was blinded by hubris, more than anything – that she thought she could fly again after so long without it, and have no practise goes, no further instruction. Well, like they always said about riding a bike – it's like riding a bike. And it was. Her hands knew what to do, her eyes, her head, her muscle memory, all slotted into the old patterns in a heartbeat. It was only her emotions, the unpredictable, unreliable parts of her that hesitated. But she knew of old to ignore all that and rely on her body and instinct. That's what flew for her, that's where she felt it, deep inside, in her muscles, her blood, her very bones.

The July day was scorching. Dark patches of ground, created
by copses of huddling trees, produced broad thermals, each
topped by cloud streets like celestial ladders. Hendon and its
surrounding patchwork of green and yellow, the lucid summer
colours of the English countryside, were laid out around them
like a gift for them and them alone. A wedding gift, if you
like.

It'd been an understated ceremony, which suited them well.
They married at St Peter's Church in Cleethorpes, while Dud
was still staying at Weelsby Old Hall. He was allowed days
out by then, as he was so much better, and in the week before
the wedding the Dobbs family welcomed him to their home
on Bradford Street. Well, Della hoped they'd welcome him
– she knew Mam would, and Cleo and Gertie and probably
the boys, Dud being in soldier's uniform and all that, which
was a source of great pride and excitement for just about any
boy you'd meet these days. But as for Pop's reaction, she
could not predict it and had worried about a potential embarrassment, about being shamed by her father's misanthropic
ways.

But the day Dud came, Pop was standing in the hall, Mam
on his arm, and Pop was almost smiling. Seeing him stood
there like an umbrella stand gave Della a start and she said,
'Oh!' Pop held out his good hand for Dud to shake it and
Della watched, mouth open. Dud shook Pop's hand with firm
yet contained enthusiasm, just right, as ever. Mam was beside
herself with pleasure, Della could see that, and was stepping
from side to side as if about to throw her arms around that
tall young man in uniform, her daughter's fiancé. Maybe they'd
thought their plain, odd girl would never marry; maybe Dud's
face just set them at ease, like he always did. Whatever the
reason, Della was bowled over with their reception.

There followed a series of congenial visits, where Mam had
gathered every ration of any worth to give them treats, such
as they were – boiled fruit cake and parkin. Afternoons were

spent at the kitchen table talking about Dud's childhood holidays, his love for beaches, for horses and aeroplanes and kites. Cleo was uncharacteristically calm around Dud, and watched him dreamily, sometimes leaning against his leg, a little smile and a cocked head revealing that she thought him the bee's knees. Gertie and Della talked of him delightedly at night and her sister thought Dud was 'peachy'. And there were solemn half hours where Dud was invited to the inner sanctum and spent closed minutes in murmuring conversation with Pop behind his study door.

After, on the walk out they took together each day, Della was voracious to know every word of what they discussed there. Dud was unnaturally reticent, but when pushed said simply, 'Oh, you know. The war.' It wasn't mentioned at any other time, by any of them. It was a shady looming thing that everyone steadfastly ignored. Gertie was permitted to mention her husband's war work, in a vague way, but no further discussion was encouraged and that was that. Dud didn't want to talk about the war either, so Della never heard what those talks were really about. She told herself it didn't matter and that the best of all possible outcomes was unfurling around her; the flower of her love for her fiancé was fragrantly scenting her family home and they all basked in it. Nothing else mattered, for that brief, halcyon time.

The wedding was just the bride and groom, Mam and Pop and Cleo. That's all they wanted from the Dobbs side, to keep it simple. Dud wore his uniform, of course, and Della threatened to wear one of her old flying suits, so infused with burnt, rotten castor oil that it stank to high heaven and wasn't allowed in the house by Mam, who went pale at the idea of this filthy thing fouling St Peter's Church. Della was only joking, or half joking, as she had refused to wear some frilly feminine thing. So they found a shop in top town that had a second-hand utilitarian outfit all in white, the jacket belted at the waist and a calf-length skirt, completed with white blouse, neckerchief and hat. She looked rather like the ghost of a girl soldier, but Dud said she was his angel.

Dud's father came to the wedding. It was good to meet him at last. She'd formed an impression of Mr Willow from his letter and Dud's accounts, a shy, serious man of great height and worldly gravitas. Yet, the man himself was surprisingly warm-hearted, in a subtle way, a bassline sweetness to Dudley's tenor. He was even taller than his son, with a square white head and humane eyes. He spoke with Pop of the theatre business as if Pop were still at the very centre of it, this natural extension of respect going down a treat with Pop, who shook Mr Willow's hand heartily after the ceremony for too long, as if tacitly thanking him for existing, for producing this son and bringing a healing joy to his house again. The only thing that was missing from the humble service was the presence of Auntie Betty. How she'd have crowed to see her Della marry that lovely boy from the beach.

There was no time for a honeymoon, as within days they were to go south to fly. Before the wedding, Dud had put in his application to the RFC, in it framing a white lie that he already knew how to fly and was to receive his licence any day now. At the same time, Della had written to Hendon, specifically to Claude Grahame-White. She had told Dud of their history, though she'd played down her own girlish feelings from the time. She knew their best chance of finding a flying school that would let her go up would be through people she'd known before the war, and the only one whose whereabouts and current activities she knew about was Claude, because she had read about him in the newspaper. He was still at Hendon, where he masterminded his aerodrome's aviation war effort himself. She'd read in the society column that he and Dotty had divorced last year and he'd just married again; this time an actress, who Midge vaguely knew and said was 'fun'.

Della's letter was brief and factual, to the point. Claude's reply was longer:

Hendon has been taken over by the RFC and is also an
Aircraft Acceptance Park for the RNAS. But we do have a
space across the road that we could possibly use for an
hour or so of civilian flying, we call it Little Hendon.
You're welcome to take up one of our training aircraft
there and show your fiancé the ropes. To be frank, if you
were teaching these cadets to fly the way you used to, we'd
have won the war by now. Come any time.

When they got there a few days later, after a crowded train journey shoved up against lots of men in uniform of one sort or another, the steward at the office at Hendon knew nothing about it. Della handed over her pilot's licence, which was scrutinised, then laid aside; the steward explained that in the early days of aviation they'd let anyone have a go, but things are a little more professional now, dearie. Then a watching lad piped up that he recognised her from the old days. He used to hang around the hangars with his dad and he remembered her flying here.

'She was good,' he said. 'She was Mr Grahame-White's pet.'

Dud glanced at Della, who blushed, but stuck her chin out. She handed the steward Claude's letter as proof, from which his beady eyes flashing up at her made her blush again, which she thought Dud noticed, which made her colour more. They were directed across to Little Hendon, the small airfield across the way, an afterthought of an airfield with cramped room for take-off and landing, and rows of Type XV trainers lined up on patchy ground sprinkled with mounds of sad-looking grass. The aerodrome they'd just left was buzzing with activity, but here a sleepier mood prevailed and some mechanics came to watch with wry smiles – the woman their boss had allowed to fly. She felt their looks burning into her back as she climbed aboard and readied herself, as they worked together to start up the aircraft; but as soon as the aeroplane inched forward she forgot them like a breath in a breeze, as she was enveloped in the beloved flow of air arcing over Dud and into her grateful face.

Now she was showing her husband the world from the air, again, for their second time. The first time they were so young still and it was night, watchful, mysterious and full of promise. Now they were children no longer, it was daytime and everything was clear and radiant, fields full of fat crops pregnant with another kind of promise. But here and there, especially skirting the airfield itself, were the stains of building work and expansion, blotted reminders of the reason they were flying at all, of what the outcome would be, of why they were here. As she circled the aerodrome, finely adjusting her path through each bumpy thermal, she saw a gang of men digging a new approach road. They learned later that these were German POWs, and that they slept in the tents they'd seen ranged in the fields beyond the site.

Beyond the main buildings she remembered from her training days, there was now a network of military huts and houses, sheds and rows of new aeroplanes. They'd built a mock-Tudor mess to house all the new arrivals and there was the new Aircraft Acceptance Park flanked by rows of linen hangars erected in front of the original wooden ones. Hendon had awoken and stretched itself out for the war, found a new purpose and thrown itself into it with gusto. Flying had nothing to do with joy, she thought, not any more.

She had landed and was taxiing up to the hangar when she caught sight of a tall man standing watching. It was Claude. Once the machine was still and quiet, she climbed out, Dud close behind. Claude strode over.

'Well, well. Della Dobbs, as I live and breathe.'

'It's Mrs Willow now,' she said, cheerfully.

They all shook hands and introductions were made.

'So, you're going in the RFC, Willow, is that right?'

'I'm waiting for my commission, sir, but I very much hope to, yes.'

'Excellent, excellent. Well, I'm sure you don't need me to tell you that you've got the best teacher here a man could want.'

'That's quite right,' said Dud, respectfully. 'I don't need you to tell me that.'

A frisson.

Claude said, 'Well, I'd love to do it myself, but I'm a businessman now more than a pilot. And all the resultant stress that entails. We have forty aircraft a week leaving my factory. And problems with government contracts and timber and whatnot. It's quite, quite mad. I envy you, Second Lieutenant Willow.'

An awkward silence. Della was looking at his haggard face and thought, *He looks old.*

Claude abruptly said it had been a pleasure, made a volte-face and left.

That night, in the lumpy hotel bed, Dud said to Della, 'Is he the one you told me about at Harrogate, then? The one you loved once?'

'I didn't think you'd remember that.'

'Well, I was mute but I wasn't deaf.' He smiled that smile of his.

'Yes, that was him. It was a just schoolgirl crush.'

'I can see why. All tall, dark and handsome. The gentleman aviator.'

'Jealous?'

'Not a bit of it. I got you, didn't I?'

'You did.'

They kissed for a while.

'Did you have other girls, before me, Dud?'

'Not really. Nothing serious.'

'Why not?'

'They couldn't hold a candle to you.'

'Oh, Dud,' she said and thought of sitting next to him on the beach that day, talking of *David Copperfield,* the quiet comfort of him, the peace of being with Dudley. 'Ditto for me.'

'Come closer, Mrs Willow . . .'

They didn't see Claude again. They went back to Little Hendon for three more lessons over the next few days, but the nights were their own and the hotel, though shabby, became the aviators' honeymoon. The lessons themselves were a challenge: how to teach your husband to fly? There was instruction to be given and inadequate time in which to give it. There was pride too. A woman teaching a man. And it was different from a wife showing her husband how she applied lipstick, or how to bake biscuits, or other traditionally female skills. She was in a man's world, a man's business, and they were watched from the ground by men. She was acutely aware of that, of Dud's nerve in not minding that, in letting his wife show him how it was done in front of those men. She wanted to make it as easy for him as possible in front of male eyes, never be seen to lord it over him; she was also wary that any corners she cut to meet that demand might prove fatal for him when he finally flew solo. So, her lessons were brisk and mostly physical, showing him in the air the moves to make, using gestures and movement. Back at the hotel, at dinner and breakfast, they talked endlessly through it, their years of aviation fandom finally proving their worth – and what a delight it was to talk about it now for real, for his own use, and not simply as a hobby. Underneath, in her mind an inky stain spread when she thought about the end result of all this knowledge: flying above the trenches of the Western Front. But she knew the more they talked, the more she showed and told him now, the more she could protect him then. He knew it too and was endlessly questioning, conferring, specifying, eager to learn. The nicest thing was the absolute trust, built up from the years of corresponding, the safe knowledge of each other's character and capabilities.

He didn't have the touch, she could see that straight away, and he knew it too. But he was astute and had that insider knowledge of the machine itself and the physics of flight. The same ilk of mechanical minds they had, she the bicycle fixer and he the radio ham. And he brought something new to the game: the grace of a horseman. His hands weren't as smooth as hers had been when she was learning, but his long upper body curved naturally into turns and dips, anticipating banks and dives, the arc of his torso and neck echoing the arc of the aeroplane's swoop. It was all about balance, she'd tell him, and he'd say so was riding. When she told him about the horizon, about keeping the wings level around a fixed central point, he'd say, 'Like midway between the horse's ears!'

He told her about his horses, the ones he'd tended at school, what he'd learned from them, riding them but also knowing them closely. He said that training horses was about training people. The horses were being themselves and it was the people who imposed their desires and their will on the animals.

Dud said, 'You can't make a horse bend to you if you don't bend yourself.'

'It's the same with the aircraft, becoming one. We've talked about this before, years ago. Do you remember?'

'Course I do.' Dud smiled. And his easy grace with people; she saw now that he must have that with horses too, and she could imagine they would trust him and want to work for him, would probably do anything for him, as most people who met Dud would.

'Gung ho blokes don't do well in an aeroplane,' she said. 'Slamming the controls this way or that and expect the thing to respond. That's the sure way to crash.'

'It's the same with horses. Brute force and whip the animal. That way never trained a horse to work with you, only fear you.'

'Yes, it's a partnership, with the horse, with the aeroplane. And it's about control, not strength. Fly with your fingertips, with your toes.'

'You know a horse could feel a fly land on their flank in a storm. They're incredibly sensitive.'

'And so are the best aeroplanes. I think the ones you'll be flying in the RFC will be a world away from that old milk horse you're training on,' she said. 'It'll go a lot faster too and your movements will become finer and finer: they'll have to, to match the speed.'

One evening, she told him that he was ready to do his first solo flight the following day. So, after dinner and before bed, Dud sat in the hotel room and closed his eyes, Della watching him. He was walking through his first solo flight in his mind. She'd told him she used to do it before a competition, those long lonely evenings in hotels on tour, and he wanted to try it too. He told her, 'When I was a boy, I'd sit on the bus sometimes and look out of the window at the fields passing by. I so wanted a horse, I'd visualise myself riding one across those fields. I'd watch myself canter and jump all the hedges in my mind. I pictured it first, so when I started riding, I'd already trained myself in my head.'

When he closed his eyes and she saw his mind working, saw his frowning face and pictured the flight he was taking in his head, her heart ached for him so plainly that she wanted to look away, overcome by the wave of love. She knew their time together was so brief, would come to an end so soon – she would not look away. She gazed at him there and breathed in the memory, his eyes closed, his mind in the skies. And all the time she knew that because she was teaching him to fly, she was probably preparing him for death, a horrible death in a fireball, or to land on his head

like Oxley. But she kept telling herself, better that than the
madness and the mud.

It was a choice in a land of no choices.

His first flight went brilliantly well, largely without a hitch,
though Little Hendon's limited room for take-off and landing
almost caused him to smash into another aeroplane that was
parked up. But he managed it, very well indeed, and they were
both euphoric afterwards. That very afternoon, a telegram
came from Dud's father. Dud had to report the next day for
an interview for his RFC application in London. There was
no time to pass the test for the pilot's licence. He'd just have
to wing it.

The morning of the interview, they were walking there and
Della said, 'Listen, you've probably already worked this one
out on your own, but when they ask you about your Hendon
training, you won't mention me, will you? You won't tell them
I taught you.'

'Well, I hadn't, uh . . . really thought—'

'You're a rotten liar, Dudley. We both know being taught
by your wife won't do you any favours.'

'Well, if you think . . .'

'I do and so do you. It's all right.'

'*You're* all right,' he said, smiling down at her, and stopped
and kissed her. 'You're a bit of all right.'

'Come on, you'll be late!'

They walked on in silence and then he said, 'We know the
truth of it. And that's what counts.'

During his interview, Della sat in a café opposite, frightened
and excited, bored and nauseous, preparing herself for a long
wait. But after only a half hour, he came out and he was
grinning.

'I'm in!'

'Blimey! They didn't mind about the licence?'

'No! I told him I'd been learning at Hendon and then he

asked me two questions: "Do you ride horses?" and then "Do you hunt?" Then he said, "Let's see you walk across the room", which I did, very well I thought. And that was that. The rest of the time was filling in forms. I have to report to Upavon in Wiltshire in three days' time for my RFC training. We've done it, darling!'

A rush of preparation followed. Dud telegrammed his father the good news and received another back that evening informing them that Mr Willow would arrange a cottage near Upavon for the newlyweds to stay in for a week while Dudley began his training, his wedding present to them. When Della heard, she was bowled over with love for the dear old chap, the kindness of it, the generosity. And her fears of separation had been put off again, at least for a week or so. So it was back home to Cleethorpes to pack, and down to Wiltshire, in a circuitous route of railway and bus stations, finally arriving early one balmy August evening. The cottage itself was hidden away behind a farm, only a ten-minute walk from the aerodrome, which they could see across the fields. The cottage was tiny, consisting downstairs of a sitting room with kitchenette, a bathroom with basin; upstairs the one room was filled with a large cushiony bed, and there was an outside lav. A meal of poached chicken, bread and boiled eggs had been left for them with a brisk note from the farmer's wife, that she'd come by tomorrow and they could order their food for the week from her. Dud was to report the following day. Ravenous after their journey, they wolfed down the food with a bottle of red wine Dud had stowed in his bag. That night was filled with lovemaking so sweet, she had to kick him out of bed the next morning in a panic. He ran down the road to the aerodrome, combing his sleepy hair back as he went.

After luxuriating in bed for a few minutes, Della stretched and took stock. She had absolutely nothing to do. She wasn't used to waiting around on her own completely without occupation. It had all seemed an admirable idea when Mr Willow organised it, but now she was here, she realised that Dud would be out all day and she would simply be waiting. Never a reader, instead she went out for a long walk that morning, in the opposite direction from the aerodrome down the road. She was drawn to it and itched to see what it was like, what aeroplanes they had there, and hopefully to see Dud fly. But she knew that on his first day in the RFC he didn't need his little wifey hanging about, making a nuisance of herself. The countryside was pretty and the day was good, but she couldn't see how she'd fill the next few days without going slightly mad.

When she returned to the cottage, she found the farmer's wife waiting for her grumpily and arranged their vittles for the week. Alone again, she sat on the bed and stared out of the window across the Wiltshire landscape, thinking of the long nights she'd spent alone in hotels on tour, around Britain and across France. But then she'd had copies of *The Aero* to read and tomorrow's flights to plan and a sense of purpose. She was a professional, back then, before the war came and took it away from her. She sighed and felt sorry for herself. Then she thought of Puck and was solemn. *I am lucky*, she told herself, *and I am grateful*. She had Dud's love to keep her company while she waited for him, and could look forward to seeing his happy face coming up the road at the end of the day, full of rousing tales about his life-saving new RFC commission and all the things he must be learning on their tip-top new aeroplanes.

It didn't quite work out that way. That evening, he tramped into the cottage looking careworn and, frankly, miserable. She was about to throw her arms around him, she'd missed him so much, but his scowling face made her shy and instead she stepped hesitantly towards him, rubbing his arm.

'Well, it's not exactly a gentleman's aviation club,' he said. 'A few of us chaps, new cadets, stood around most of the morning, swapping stories. Not a lot was going on. Then a tutor came in, said "Who's this one been flying at Hendon?" So I raised my hand and I was taken off for a flight. He's an old hand who's been flying in France since the first year of the war and he took me up for a spin in a good-looking thing, an Avro 504. But my God, Della, it was damned awful. He did all these crazy turns and dives and flew at top speed, it was horrendous. They said after he always does that, putting the fear of God into us new boys. Half an hour later I could hardly stand, my legs were shaking so badly. I felt such a rotten fool. But the others who've been there a few days said everyone's like that with him.'

'Bloody hell,' said Della. 'What an oaf.'

'Who him? Or me?'

'Him, of course!'

'Well, I think I was pretty much the oaf myself. I mean, if I can't manage one flight like that as a passenger, what good will I be to the Corps? I'll be an embarrassment or else kill myself before I've even left Wiltshire.'

The thought of this – of Dud dying now, here – was such an appalling shock. She hadn't even considered it. Why hadn't she? She must've put it out of her mind but, of course, wherever there were aeroplanes, there were accidents. And deaths. Somehow the three solid letters of the RFC gave her such confidence; she had actually felt he was safe with them, that they were professionals, the Corps, the Royal Flying Corps. What could possibly go wrong?

'One of the chaps was saying that there were two deaths last week, there at Upavon. Cadets training. I couldn't believe it. Dying in a West Country field, never even seeing France. Can you imagine?'

Della felt a wave of nausea pass through her. How could she have been so foolish? How could she have thought Dud would be safer flying than in a foxhole? They were both places of the dead. The possibility – no, the probability – of it slapped her in the face. But she knew the last thing her husband needed was for her fears to play out across her face, so she pulled herself together and affected nonchalance.

'Those lads hadn't learned to fly, I bet. They hadn't been reading *The Aero* since they were knee-high. You were an airman before you ever saw an aeroplane, Dud. You're different from them. And you won't make any schoolboy errors here. You're too knowledgeable for that.'

'I might have the theory, but I didn't expect the fear.'

'Listen, I was terrified my first flight as a passenger. And my first solo flight. But fear is good.'

Dud snorted bitterly.

'No,' she went on, 'I mean it. You need the fear. The fear makes you realise what you're actually doing. Respect for the air and respect for your aeroplane. A bit of fear is healthy. And it'll make you live longer.'

It was a sobering thought and he wasn't entirely convinced.

It was a glum night. He went off in the morning trying to appear upbeat for her benefit, but she could see in his walk that he wasn't happy. The morning stretched out like Salisbury Plain about her, and by lunchtime she had had enough and took an apple with her and walked down towards the aerodrome.

There was a stile nearby where she could perch and watch the aeroplanes come and go. She saw a couple of Sopwith Pups being tested; they were classy things, these Pups, and they went lickety-split. She realised how rapidly things had moved on since her day – even the Type XV trainer she'd flown when teaching Dud was swifter than she was used to – but these were so nifty in the air, manoeuvrable and sleek. If she had to climb in one of those right now, could she do it? Would she adapt? She was sure she would, but the thought that it worried her to think of herself flying one of them compounded her fears for her husband, as this man with a few hours of flying experience, would soon be up there in one of those speedy creatures, alone.

When he came back later, his mood was no better. Today's story concerned his new instructor.

'The chap was morose, absolutely miserable. He said, You Willow? Yes, sir. Had any instruction yet? Yes, sir, at Hendon. Well, you can do a solo then. Off you go.'

'What?' cried Della. 'Did you?'

'No, I bloody well did not. I said, I'm sorry, sir? Up you go, he shouted at me, his face a picture. Absolutely furious. His hands were shaking. There was an Avro 504 on the grass and he jabbed his finger towards it and said, "Get on with it, man." So I said, very calmly, "I'm sorry, sir but I'm not going solo. I can't fly that aeroplane. I could try that Maurice Farman over there, because it's similar to what I trained on. But not the newer aeroplane. I can't fly that aeroplane yet and I won't attempt to, not without more instruction." Well, he looked fit to explode. And he said with a sneer that I'd better go and find a flying school for girls and join it at once.'

'Did he now!'

'Yes but do you know what I said back? I said, My wife was an aviatrix before the war and I'll have you know she could fly loops round most of the chaps here.'

'Did you, darling? Did you really?'

'I did! And do you know what, he was such a moody, erratic sort of fellow, he suddenly changed his tune. He said, quite cheerfully, "What do you want to do then?" "I want another instructor," I said.'

'Good for you!' she said and kissed him. 'What happened next?'

'Well, he stalked off and that was that. I spoke to some other chaps. He has a terrible reputation as a trainer. But everyone's too afraid to say anything. We're all so glad to be there and not, you know, anywhere else. Nobody wants to rock the boat.'

'What's he got to be so angry about?' she asked.

'I was talking with a bloke from Kent called Beeson. He and I are becoming pals a bit. He's like me, not one of those really posh lot, so he can't believe his luck being here and he's awfully keen. He's a really good stamp of a lad. Anyway, Beeson said this instructor had an awful time on the Western Front. I told you his hands were shaking. Apparently, he smokes constantly and takes aspirins all the time. Sounds pretty battle-scarred to me, in his head. I wouldn't go up with him for the world.'

Della felt a pit of sickening dread in her stomach. 'You mustn't. You simply mustn't. Will you be able to get out of it?'

'I think so. He seemed to accept it. I'm hoping tomorrow I'll get a different one.'

The next day was the longest yet. She followed Dud within minutes of him leaving and sat hungry on the stile almost all day, cursing herself for forgetting to bring food or drink. Famished, when the sun was very high in the sky she eventually ran back to the cottage for something to eat, then rushed back to take up her spot. There were no crashes as far as she could see, but who knew what might have happened in the time she'd been away? When Dud returned, his face lit up to see her there on the stile and they hugged and linked arms all the way home.

'Much better today,' he told her. 'I did have a new instructor, a much nicer chap. Steadier. He was concise and friendly. He took me up in a Shorthorn, showed me how to take off and land very well. We talked a lot about the things that could go wrong, about allowing the nose to drop and such things. I've got him again tomorrow. I think it'll be all right now.'

A couple more days of this new instructor and Dudley was walking tall. Their time together at the cottage – long, hot days of waiting, of tanning her skin in the high August sun, followed by nights of passion and love – was eventually over and it was their last day together; she was due to return to Cleethorpes by train the next day and he to his billet nearby. She asked the farmer's wife for something special to eat, if that was possible,

and along with a narrowed look was given a ham and leek pie
and apple crumble, and very good they looked too. She waited
on the stile at the appointed time, eager to see the jovial face
of her love, but when she saw him striding along very fast, his
eyes down, his hands in fists, she ran to him.

'What is it?'

'Beeson's dead.'

He wouldn't talk about it at first. They walked in silence
and once back at the cottage, he flung himself on the bed
and wouldn't turn round. She waited, staring at the pie and
crumble that sat there pointlessly.

'That damned, lousy instructor. He sent Beeson solo before
he could fly the bloody aeroplane properly, just as he'd tried to
do with me. Beeson went up in a Pup and got his nose down
and couldn't pull the machine out. Smashed into the ground
and that was that. Dead. What's the bloody point of any of it?
Eighteen years old, he was. WHAT'S THE BLOODY POINT?'

They hardly slept that night. It passed in sad lovemaking
and then intense cuddles, from which they would only surface
to stare at each other and wipe away a tear. In the morning,
they were exhausted, but had to pack in haste. The farmer's
wife came early and was glad to usher them off. Dud insisted
on carrying her bag to the bus stop, even though it meant he
would be late. They held hands so hard, her hand still ached
as she sat on the bus after.

Before she got on, they kissed and held on to each other,
boys whistling at them from the back seats.

'Write to me, won't you?' was the last thing she said.

'Course I will. I always will,' said Dud.

And the bus driver lurched off, jolting Della sideways so
that she fell into a seat and the boys snickered at her. She
stared from the window at her husband, tall and slim, arm
raised in a crooked wave, until the brow of the hill took him,
and he was gone.

20

10th September 1917

No. 60 Squadron
Royal Flying Corps
British Expeditionary Force

Dearest Della,
    Well, here I am, back on the continent. I arrived here
at ▆▆▆▆▆▆▆▆▆▆ *last night. On landing I was put*
on a tender and had a ride of several hours through the
rain, worse luck. As the night's weather was a bit wild,
there was no flying first thing, so I had time to accustom
myself to my new surroundings. This place seems pretty
good to me, but the squadron haven't been here long and
all moan because their last base was much better appar-
ently, at a farm with home comforts, whereas this is all
rough and ready. It's certainly a work-in-progress, as
this morning I saw a group of Chinese workmen in
padded blue uniforms laying wooden slatted walks
between all the huts and hangars and sandbagging
everywhere. The mess is good and there is a church hut
that will soon be showing movies. The fellows here seem
very good men and yet many are tired out, of course,
though there are a few of us new boys just arrived to
liven things up.
    I met our flight commander, Capt Gregory, who I've
heard is a great Hun Strafer. He told me, once I've had

more practice, that all briefings are posted on the blackboard in the hangar and it's my duty at all times to keep an eye on these. By mid-morning, the weather had cleared and so they let me have a first go on my machine. We have new ones here that are absolutely topping: a ▮▮▮▮▮ scout. You'd be in a perfect ecstasy if you saw one. It climbed extremely quickly and flew level at an astounding speed. I did some machine-gun practice, where one must dive at a target on the ground and fire at it. At the perimeter of the drome there's a mock German machine pegged down in a field, with black markings of the cross which you see on all German machines. I got an awful fright when I did my first dive and opened fire as I suddenly saw a chap run away for dear life from the thing. He had been standing nearby in dark clothes and I hadn't spotted him. Well, I felt bloody about it and thought I'd be in for it, but afterwards they reprimanded him and signs have now been put up around the field warning people not to go near it. It's because the Sqn has just moved here and everyone's at sixes and sevens, it hadn't been done yet. But still, my first near miss and just imagine what an inauspicious first flight that would've been if I'd killed one of our own. I shudder to think of it . . .

Oh, I almost forgot to mention a super thing: I've met up with an old friend of yours and someone I've met once before too, in a Waltham airfield one magical night, do you remember? It's Jim Porter, your old ground crew chap for your round-Britain tour. Apparently his brother Ronnie is still working ground crew, at an airfield in Dover. His eyesight was too bad to go and fight, lucky devil, so he's serving the war effort looking after RFC aeroplanes. Jim got the flying bug after your tour, apparently, learned to fly. And you'll never guess — that two-

seater Blackburn you flew me in? – *Jim and Ronnie bought it and keep it in a hangar. It's gathering dust there now! How fun it would be to see it again, one day, after this war is over. Jim said it's waiting for you to give it a spin! (Though of course the old Blackburn will be obsolete after the technology of war is finished with the aeroplane. But Jim said it'll always be a first-class flyer, the Blackburn, perfectly balanced.) Jim joined the RFC about a year and a half ago. He's a beanpole like me and we've sort of palled up today and I think we'll get on well. Though he's a quiet sort, he really is a good chap and a topping pilot. He asked after you and looked at me very seriously when I told him all about everything you'd done since he saw you last. Between you and me and the flypaper, I think he might be sweet on you! Well, who can blame him?*

When I was in that tender coming over here in the rain I thought of your tears when we said goodbye in that country road in Wiltshire and how I kissed them from your cheeks. It thrilled me, darling, to think of your precious tears. I will treasure that memory forever, that you should cry for me. I am the luckiest man alive.

Please send your news soon, of your mechanical days fixing engines, of your Mam and Pop, of Gertie and the boys, and what naughty tricks dear Cleo is up to. I long to hear all of it.

I will write again soon, when I have more to tell.

All my love,

Dud.

P.S. Could you send me another bath towel and khaki shirt, please, darling? To think I took such trouble to keep down my kit, when travelling was so easy I could have brought twice as much. We live and learn.

18ᵗʰ September 1917

No. 60 Sqn
R.F.C.
B.E.F.

Darling wife,
    Thank you for the things you sent, gratefully received. I was so happy also to receive your letter this week. You may think your daily details are dull but to me every moment of the Dobbs household is more thrilling than the latest bestseller. I have enclosed a photograph of myself in uniform with a message on the back for you. I hope you approve, though I think I look rather long-faced. But then, I suppose I always did. Heaven knows what you see in old horse-face, a pretty darling like you.
    I have some news! I've had quite a few training flights this week and was starting to think I'd never get up on a proper patrol. Then today, after lunch, I thought I might just visit the hangar again to see whether we were on any operations and imagine my shock when I saw my name on the board for a briefing at 2pm. The next thing I knew, we were on our way to our aeroplanes and Capt Gregory was saying that if we're shot at from the ground, we shouldn't disperse but follow his jinking. Then we were up, flying in a triangular formation to do my first line patrol. We worked down on our side of the line, crossed it at 12,000 feet and worked back north about 8 miles the other side. We saw 4 Huns but they kept a long way clear of us and we were 'Archied' much of the time. You must be wondering what that means. Well, I'm learning quite a few new words here, some of which I'd never repeat to my wife (as worldly as you are, darling). There are quite a few words for our aeroplanes, the most common I've heard is 'bus' (although, to be in with the crowd, I used this in conversation the

*other day and was quite scolded by a superior who told
me to use our aircraft's proper names and on no account
were these beautiful machines a 'gunbus' or 'bus' or
anything of the sort! Some of these RFC officers are quite
snooty, I tell you.) Anyway, Archie is RFC slang for
anti-aircraft fire, and of course, it's no joke if it hits you.
However, it's often out of range, so with any luck, one can
keep clear of it. When the Archie bursts come reasonably
near, one can hear them and the noise is strange, like a
kind of Whoof! Then a Blupp! Something like that! I saw
a good deal of the front line though most of the time I was
worried about trying to keep my place in formation. Our
Capt led our patrol and I closely hung on his tail, as I
have tremendous confidence in him. I did try to note
various towns and villages in the area we covered.
Afterwards, Gregory told me I had flown 'very well'.
That'll do for me. Later, I was spoken to by the Major,
who asked me how I was getting on. I said I was fine and
he said he had good reports of me, especially since I'd been
taught to fly so well before I arrived. So, again, I have you
to thank for being ahead of the game, more than the other
new chaps. I am a most fortunate fellow.*

*I am sure I shall have more exciting news to report
soon, once I start going on daily patrols. Despite the
obvious risks, I must say it is such a privilege to feel a
part of this air war at last and be doing my bit. I've been
out of the game so long, I was starting to feel like a spare
part. Now I really feel I can make you proud of your
husband.*

*I think of you often, dear one. When I'm flying, when
I'm not flying, when I'm alone, when I'm in company . . .
all the bally time!*

Much love to you,
Dud

30th September 1917

No. 60 Sqn
R.F.C.
B.E.F.

My wife — dearest,
   Things have livened up here considerably, due to the
fine weather. Never in all my life has the weather been so
crucial to each and every man around me. I understand
how it must have been for you now, when you were flying
every day and needed to constantly watch the skies. We
have had a spell of perfect sunshine every day this week
and thus there have been more or less constant missions
from dawn till dusk, the first leaving at 6.03 and the last
at 17.45. I'm quite the veteran, with hours of daily flying
under my belt now (all rather exhausting and leaving one
rather wishing for bad weather). So, it was inevitable that
at last I should engage my first Huns.
   It happened yesterday. We had been out and seen none,
which was frustrating as messages were coming in from
infantry and artillery that they were around and about in
their hundreds. Before we went up in the afternoon, I
prepared my cockpit thoroughly, checking my supplies and
gear — including a 2 ½ lb hammer safe in its leather socket
(remember that hammer, as it becomes important later). It
was a blue-sky day with a heat haze at around 3,000 feet.
Lifting above it gave us the most splendid view of its
extraordinary shimmering liquid surface. The incredible
things one sees when flying, even in war, never cease to
amaze me, as I'm sure you felt too in your day, my darling
flyer. We crossed the lines at around 8,000 feet and climbed
steadily, flying all alone for about half an hour.
   All of a sudden, Gregory whipped round and went into
a dive. He must have seen something, though I hadn't

spotted it yet. When you're on a patrol like this and your leader dives, the other scouts have to search the sky above and behind for other Huns before following. Sometimes the Huns like to plant a couple below you while two more wait above and dive on you when your attention is elsewhere. But there were only these two, camouflaged in a sort of dappled brown, almost invisible against the pattern of woods and fields below.

I saw my compatriot Drewery's tracer fire begin and I lined up my Hun and pressed my lever to fire on it. At once, the Huns swung east. We dived towards them and I could hear the wires shrieking. Again, I was aiming to fire, I pressed the trigger and – damn! My gun jammed! Now, remember that hammer I told you about earlier? I grabbed it from its socket and hit the cocking handle hard. It wouldn't budge. I whacked it again, perhaps ten more times with all the force I could, all the while trying to fly straight and keep out of the Hun tracer fire. At long last, after a few more desperate hits the damned round finally went in and I pressed the trigger and I was back in business.

But by this time, the Huns had long gone and my formation had disappeared too. I was all alone up there. I had a while left of my patrol, so I decided to look for another Line Patrol and join it. But I could find none and in the end, on my way home I took a quick tour of the area, testing myself on the landmarks I was learning in our sector. On the way, I saw the ruins of a great town, and as I circled I thought of the ruined English abbeys of the Reformation and how we too are making a new world with this war and one day tourists might wander through these ruins as we do now, thinking of the folly of the past.

So, my first proper engagement with the Germans was a damp squib, as I lost my patrol trying to get my blasted gun going. That very night, Jim Porter went out on a spectacular bombing run alone and destroyed a shed full of

*Hun aeroplanes, returning in one piece with only minor
damage to his aeroplane, and was the toast of the
squadron. I know I shouldn't be jealous, that we're all in it
together, but I must admit I was sick with envy and I
daresay you think me a fine fool. After all, I have
completed many patrols and got back safely, without
damage or loss, and that, of course, is the main thing. The
sad truth is we have lost some men this week, through
injuries or landing on the German side and being taken
prisoner, through engine failure and crash landings,
another having his guns fail like I did but this resulted in
him being shot down and captured. They say our gain and
loss ratio for the week was good. But there have also been
some deaths of fellows in our squadron, one very close to
home and quite upsetting, but I'm sure you don't want to
hear about all that.*

*I think of you always, in the air and on the ground.
When I went into battle against that Hun I heard your
voice in my ear, calming me down with your fond words. I
think of our sweet nights in the Hendon hotel and our
heavenly cottage in Wiltshire and relive them in my mind.
I am loving you just all of the time.*

All yours,
Dud

When the first letter from France arrived and Mam handed
it to Della after a long day at the garage, she took it wordlessly upstairs, sat on her bed with the door closed and read
it very fast. Then she went back to the beginning and read it
again, twice more, then folded it up and held it to her chest
for a minute or two, next to her heart. She put it away in a
special drawer and closed it, thinking of it sitting in the dark
drawer, his writing shadowed and secret, hidden and safe until
the next time she took it out to read. Afterwards, she went
down and described its contents to Mam and Gertie (the

facts of it, not the endearments) and Mam passed this information on to Pop, and Gertie delivered a jaunty expurgated version for the boys and Cleo.

When the second and third letters came, she found herself playing out the exact same routine, as if only the solemn ritual of it would be enough to mark the occasion. Dud's letters and the winning presence of him that rose from them like a friendly spirit gladdened the Dobbses home, a house that yet again was mourning the lack of a young man. This time, the fear was keener, sharpened by the cruel loss of the first, as a mother who has miscarried once lives through the next pregnancy in fear, so the house, pregnant with waiting for news, throbbed with anxiety. The appearance of a letter was like a baby's kick: he's still there, it told them. He's still alive and kicking.

After reading all three letters several times, it occurred to Della that there was something about Dud's tone that wasn't quite right, wasn't quite him. Were they a little too cheerful? Or it could simply be that he was genuinely having a good time? She read the letters over again and couldn't shake the feeling that he was hiding something from her, glossing over the truth. He would do that, to protect her, she thought. That's how Dud was. It was how Puck was, with Mam and Pop. She thought of Puck's secret letters to her and found them again where she'd hidden them beneath all of Dud's childhood letters in a shoebox. She sat on her bed, her door closed. She held them, bound and closed as they were, and considered them. The door opened and it was Gertie in full flight, looking for cotton or something, some sewing in her left hand.

'Letters from Dud?' she said.

'No.'

Della told Gertie, the first time she'd ever spoken about Puck's secret letters, how he'd asked her to keep them secret. She'd not even told Dud – couldn't bear to before he went to war, and it didn't seem right after what he'd been through. Why bring it all back up? Now, on a whim, she chose Gertie to tell. Her elder sister sat beside her on the bed, put down her sewing.

'Don't you want to read them?' said Della.

Gertie sighed and thought a while. 'No, I don't think I do.'

'Really?'

'Really. Not now.'

'Did I do the right thing, keeping them secret?'

'It's what Puck asked you to do. So, yes, I believe you did.'

'Do you think perhaps we should give them to Mam and Pop?'

Gertie turned her head sharply and snapped, 'No. Absolutely not.'

'Really?'

'Really. They've suffered enough.'

Della felt the weight of the letters on her lap, in her hands. She studied the familiar slope of Puck's hand. She thought about Dud's letters from France, how she read and reread them, analysed the shape of the letters, fingered the paper and folded and refolded them, running her fingers along the creases in the same place his fingers had touched to fold them the first time. Maybe it was wrong to have kept that from Mam and Pop, by keeping Puck's secret letters a secret all this time.

She said, 'I think I'd want to know, Gert, if I were them. I think I'd want every last bit of . . . him.'

'For all they know, Puck was having a ripping time over there and died bravely doing his duty, cheerfully and gladly, as was his way. That's how they remember him now. As a mother, I could say rationally, yes, I'd want to know every moment my boys went through and honour those moments by knowing about them, by reliving them. But you've done that for him, dear. You took that burden and carried it for Mam and Pop. I'm glad you've shared it with me. We can carry it together. But's let not load it onto them. Puck would hate that.'

She thought about Dud's cheery letters, wondered if it
were simply his joy at not being in the trenches, being
instead miles above them. Or if it were his shame at admit-
ting fear or weakness to his wife, particularly a wife such
as her, who'd been an early champion of the very thing
with which he now spent his days risking his life. How easy
would it be for a man to admit to such a wife that he was
terrified – nervous even – of climbing into the machine
and facing that possibility of death every single flight, especially after that same wife had taught him to fly in the first
place? But she wanted to erase all that, wanted to be the
one person in the world he could talk to openly, admit
anything to, share everything with. She'd have to tell him,
make it clear.

The next time she wrote to Dud, she added a postscript:

*I want you to tell me whatever the censor will allow. If
you feel lousy, tell me how lousy you feel. If you're
scared or angry or miserable, tell me it all. I won't show
it to anybody. I know you want to protect me. But don't
forget I'm an aviator too and us pilots, we know about
fear and we know about death. If a death has upset you,
I want you to feel you can describe it to me, if that is
what would help you. Whatever you're seeing and feeling
and thinking out there, please be assured: I can take it.
It's the very least I can do. And besides, I've done it
before. I never told you this, but Puck wrote to me
during his time in France and they were secret, honest
letters written only to me, sharing his darkest hours. I'm
glad he did it, glad that I could do that one small thing
for him. I want to do the same for you, if you'll let me. I
don't know how much you RFC chaps talk to each
other. But through your letters, you can always talk to
me, my love.*

14ᵗʰ October 1917

No. 60 Sqn
R.F.C.
B.E.F.

Darlingest,
 *You know me so well. You're right that my previous
letters were putting a sheen on things. Well, you say you
never mind me having a good moan, so prepare yourself
for a champion one. My subject for today's sermon is on
the reliability of our great and glorious aircraft, the* ████.
 *We have these French engines that really do go crock
on us. Far too often, we return from patrol blinded with
oil. Everything leaks – the petrol pipes and the radiators.
There are so many rubber joints in the oiling system, and
the castor oil gets so thin when it's hot, of course, that the
joints will always leak oil and thus we run out. I'm often
landing at nearby squadrons on my return to top up
with oil. Other than that, I've had the carburettor choked
or the gears are wrecked. Sometimes the propeller will fail
because the gears have seized up which burns the
propeller bosses or the bosses themselves work loose
because of the shaft's faulty grinding. Many of our
patrols end up with forced landings in ploughed fields,
and we're bally lucky when it's this side of the lines and
not theirs. And the latest thing to annoy me is burnt
hands, the reason being that the exhaust pipes run alongside the cockpit, so you can feel the heat from them as
you're taxiing particularly. And because I'm so tall, I've
had my cockpit cut down to give me more room, hence
when one is in a hurry to disembark, one puts their
hands down on each side and plonks them straight on to
the exhaust pipes and burns them. Just another quirk of
this aeroplane that drives me up the wall.*

Don't get me wrong: it's a lovely flyer – you'd be in heaven to fly it, darling. It flies really well at all speeds and it's easy to fly, so important when you have other things to worry about, like a Hun on your tail. They have these new engines that aren't rotary like the ones we're used to, but inline, liquid-cooled. All the talk in the mess is of the relative merits of the old Nieuports and this one. Without a rotary engine cooled by the air, it needs its own coolant and a radiator, and we must control shutters on the front of the radiator to keep the temperature under control. Well, that's one thing to worry about and there are extra dials too. Some of the old hands still don't like to use the new aeroplanes and wax lyrical about their old Nieuports and how they could turn them on a sixpence using the old ways, but let's face it: it was all right turning one way but never the other, because of the peculiarities of the old engine. This one's manoeuvrability is spot on and we can finally keep up with a diving Hun in his Albatros, and our wings won't come off in a steep dive like the Albatros's might. In a group we call them the Albertri! They are very good aeroplanes, squat and very nippy, but structurally our new ones are better.

But it has so many teething problems, despite our super-human efforts and that of our ground crews to manage them, that we feel utterly undermined at every turn, and very insecure about flying the damn things and getting home in one piece, Huns or none. The thing is, one knows that new aeroplanes are being designed so quickly to suit the war, that the war itself is driving our science upwards to great new heights, but there's no time for testing or experiment, and the guinea pig of each new design quirk is the RFC pilot fighting for his life over the Western Front, paying for design faults with his very life.

Well, rant over for today. Apart from the fact that the

castor oil I've ingested is giving me the runs. You wanted
to share everything, darling, so now you know. I'm so
looking forward to hearing about the state of your bowels
whenever it is I at last get to see you, darling. After all, we
should share everything, don't you think? (I hope you can
detect the heavy hint of sarcasm in my tone, dearest.)

   You may regret asking me to open up if this string
of complaint is what you get. But, with your permission, I
will write more honestly of my life here, as things
arise, and hope you can forgive me if I ever moan too much.

   Yours grumpily but with all my love,
   Dud

21ˢᵗ October 1917

No. 60 Sqn
R.F.C.
B.E.F.

Dearest One,

   If you are sure you don't mind, it would help me to get
some more things off my chest. It's not just the aircraft
that vex one, but there is more to tell, much more.

   It is difficult here, very hard in some ways. But there is
an overwhelming feeling that one must be stoical and
endure and it wouldn't do to grumble. And all the time I
am continually grateful that I'm not in the trenches. If we
compare the two wars – the trench war with the war in
the air – I'd say the air war is in credit by a long chalk. I
am able to get a good night's sleep in a decent bed (despite
the rasping snores of my room-mate Calcraft, but I'm so
tired I can even sleep through that). The food is good and
we can sit and eat like civilised gentlemen. Our only duties
are flying and outside of this our time is our own. We play
chess and talk, one chap plays the violin, there is a piano

and cards, books to read, letters to write and one Capt has a gramophone and records he lends out on occasion. We also have a number of dogs that cheer the place up no end, and we keep six pigs and chickens too, so there is no shortage of eggs about the mess. Calcraft and I often go into the village and visit the estaminet – a small café – and have a glass of wine or some of this tasty French coffee. And best of all, the trench stench is gone from our nostrils, something that still haunts me. In the trenches, you never knew when death was coming, as you faced it every second. Here, at least, you know that between flights, you are more or less completely safe (apart from bombing runs, but these are not common). So, one can count down the hours until a flight and know that in these hours at least, you will be alive.

But in the early hours of the morning, before your man comes in to wake you, you lie staring into the darkness – knowing that silently your room-mate is as wide awake with fear as you are – listening to the boom-boom of the guns and dreading that dawn patrol that approaches steadily as the clock ticks onwards. The only reprieve is bad weather. There is nothing like bad weather to lift the spirits. The most marvellous thing is for your man to come in and wake you, tell you there won't be any flying this morning, sir, and let you sink back into blissful sleep. On those days, few as they are, he knows not to wake us again till 9.30, after which we all roll up for breakfast in a motley collection of pyjama bottoms, flying boots and woolly scarves. These bad weather days are called 'dud' days, would you believe it! And they certainly are, the very best of days for your old Dud. They are our greatest joy.

Having said that, despite the atrocious weather, we are sometimes still sent up on operations, and it's no fun trying to fly with clouds no higher than 400 feet and the wind getting up. But, more than the odd bad flight, it's the strain of the constant daily flying and at such heights, it's the cold that gets to you and the pain of warming back up. And the length of the flights, two hours or more on patrol at times, plagued by the worry that your aeroplane will fail you. Death in the trenches may take you by surprise, but in the air you can see death coming to you, if your machine catches the dreaded fire. You can either stay in the bus or jump, but either way, death has your number. I'm not sure which is worse, to be frank, knowing or not knowing when death will come for you.

And all the while you fly, there is the possibility of being attacked by a Hun aeroplane, of dogfights and flying for your life, to kill or be killed. Yes, I've killed in the air now. I killed in the trenches too. It never gets easier. Despite the fact that we are enemies, and that killing is my duty, there is a fear that one is doing wrong, even with permission to kill, as in war. On patrol, I look down on the trenches from the air. It's like a colossal boy gazing down at his toy soldiers. One can see the tiny men running forward and jumping into the Hun trenches and running down the communication trenches. I know I was down there once, struggling in the mud, but I can't quite fathom it. From up here, the worst thing is that one can see beyond that strip of mud where pockets of men fight to the death for a patch of earth, for their next objective 30 yards away, and one can see the next objective and the next, 50 or 75 miles beyond. And one realises the undeniable truth, that the entire war is a huge and pointless waste of life fought to secure a strip of earth that looks as thin as a matchstick from the sky. If only all the kings and prime ministers of this war could be taken on an aerial tour of the front line and see the utter futility of it, surely the war would be over in a day. It's worse to be down there in it, but to fly above it and see it in all its folly, is a horrible truth to carry.

Sometimes I wonder if I'm not granted leave soon, I will start to lose my nerve. I get the shakes a little after flying as it is, though I do believe this is exhaustion instead of anything to fret about.

But one reason I didn't want to go on about all this is that you must understand how very grateful I am to be up here instead of down there. In every way a person can, I feel you have saved me, darling wife, from the madness I was encased in at that hospital, from the trenches to the air, and your love itself has given me hope and life. It is a miracle to me and it was unworthy to make complaint when one has been so fortunate.

I send you all my love.
Dud

6th November 1917

No. 60 Sqn
R.F.C.
B.E.F.

My dearest darling Della!

Capital news! They tell me I will be able to come <u>home on leave</u> at the end of this month or else early December! I will be seeing you – very soon, my darling! I will take no risks and pray to the weather gods to bring us storms and hail until that day, so that I may stay in my bed each morning and dream of you. Please don't worry yourself too much until that wondrous day, my love, as I will take extra care in the air at all times, especially now I have such a goal to aim for, as to hold you in my arms again and kiss you on the mouth. Oh, how sweet the remembrance. I've gone all poetical. Soon, sweetheart, soon . . .

21

Della woke slowly, with a pain in her leg, hearing the chatter of the seagulls, the sound of the sea. The warmth of him against her, the weight of his leg on her leg, his breathing. It was a joy to do any small favour for him, to lie with him and let him sleep, when he had had such troubled sleep the last two nights. Her leg ached with the weight of him, such long legs, muscled and so heavy, crushing her own, but she dared not shift even an inch, so that he would not wake and would not be disturbed.

The first night he had woken in a sweat and cried out. The next night she lay awake beside him, listening to him thinking. Every now and again she would stroke his hair and whisper his name, hoping he would be asleep and wouldn't reply, but each time he would say, 'Still here,' and she'd know that sleep left him abandoned. Mam suggested Veronal – something Pop used to take after his accident to help him sleep. But Dud said no, he didn't want any chemicals. He wanted to stay focused and clear. He'd need to for flying and didn't want to become addicted to anything. Now, at dawn, he was at last asleep and Della knew she would not move her aching leg unless a bomb went off, so grateful was she that her husband had some peace at last this night.

To see him again was so moving; they had said very little at the railway station, walked almost in silence up the Kingsway to home, clutching arms so tightly and stopping more than once to hug, the December winds whipping up from the beach and slapping them on the backs, threatening to lift her hat and his cap and make off with them on the breeze. He looked about ten years older. Dark rings beneath the staring eyes and that twinkle almost gone. He was thin too. All the diarrhoea, she supposed. It was wrong, all wrong, what the war did to bodies. An infernal machine, that chewed them up in battle or else took them apart slowly, faculty by faculty, ending with the mind.

Mam and Pop and Gertie and everyone was shocked by his appearance. Cleo, the seven-year-old diplomat, blurted out, 'What's wrong with you?' when Dud came in, trying to smile.

'Bad egg sandwich on the train,' he said, right off the bat, and she giggled, liking the idea of a naughty egg and what mischief it got up to.

'Such a handsome uniform,' said Mam, kindly, and it was, though Dud looked dwarfed by it, he'd lost so much weight.

They all had dinner together that evening and everyone wanted to know his news, what it was like in the Royal Flying Corps and stories of the aces. The boys in particular quizzed him quite brazenly about numbers of kills, before Gertie put a stop to it. It was obvious, to the adults at least, that Dud was shattered and making a tremendous effort just to stay upright. Food was wolfed down and Mam leaned across to say wouldn't he rather go and have a rest upstairs, and he did, the family watching him go in silence. They cleared up in silence as well, apart from the clamour of three boys and Cleo engaging in dogfights up and down the hallway. They'd been told to hush, to let Dud sleep, but with sparse success. Their mother was sleeping in with them, so the newlyweds could have their privacy, and that kept them quiet at night. Nobody had heart enough to shush them during the day. They brought such rambunctious joy to the house and wasn't it needed? There was an ever-present fear of silence in that house still, and Dud's haunted appearance had reawakened that sleeping spectre and let its icy presence sidle in once more.

Della went up to be with Dud. They did make love that night, a sad, exhausted love that ended with him fast asleep on his tummy within seconds and her awake for a while, listening to him breathe, her cheek laid on his shoulder, her arm across his back. A recollection came of Betty talking about the love of her life, Truman Perry, that he'd put his arms around her and the whole world would fall away. She understood her great-aunt now, knew it deeply from the inside. Her love for Dud was so total, so overflowing with a desperate aching, her pity for him and fury at the war mingled with the intense desire for this flesh, this body beside her. She held on to it territorially, daring the war to take it from her, frightening herself with her taunt, crossing her fingers and wishing it away superstitiously. How sad Betty would be to see Dud now: *What a waste*, she'd say. That lovely boy, all but gone.

But Della wasn't giving in to it, wouldn't let it beat them. The next day she got Dud out of the house and persuaded him to come on the bus with her out to Brigsley. They got out at the village and walked up beside a wood, shadowy and whispering, until it opened out into fields. Here and there, a winter tree stood stark against the cold blue sky, the hedgerows twiggy and bare, the fields flat and lonesome. But the wind in their hair and the sight of a robin hopping on the rugged mud path before them, and then a sparrowhawk way above, circling, took them out of themselves and Dud started to talk.

Once he started, she couldn't stop him, even if she'd wanted to, and how she loved it. To hear that voice she'd read in his letters, chatty, frightened and sad at times, at others cheery and even peaceful, as if his face were the sky on a windy day, white and dark clouds scudding across it in turn. She knew the Brigsley walk would do the trick. There was something about these vast Lincolnshire skyscapes that opened the mind.

Della asked him about his aeroplanes.

'They're called SE5s,' he said. 'Oh Del, they are exceptional, despite the niggles. So quick and robust too.'

'How many ailerons does it have?'

'Oh, four, one on each wing of course, and so a really good rate of roll.'

'How does the engine help with turning?'

'Well, it's an inline engine, cooled not by air like the old rotary engines, but by a radiator one must remember to manipulate to cool it down. You know how the rotaries would turn very well in the direction of the propeller but you'd have to fight it round the other way? Well, these engines let you turn either way freely.'

'Sounds like heaven!' cried Della. The new breed of aeroplane was beyond a pre-war pilot's wildest desires. She was almost envious of him.

'Oh, it is! Easy to fly, easy to land. Powerful, fast and very manoeuvrable. Well-armed. They dive like the very devil. Everything that you want in a fighter.'

And there it was, the point of it all. It shut them up for a while, that stab of memory from the war. The sparrowhawk was still wheeling about up there, a war bird of its own sort, from a sparrow's point of view.

He felt in his tunic pocket and found his RFC war diary, filled with advice for the airman and blue line drawings of pertinent items, such as a flag or a knot and more exotic things like a Collision Mat or a Wonderful Sikh Weapon. It had a short pencil attached, which he used to make a sketch of an SE5 for Della, showing her the aggressive, angular look of it. Perhaps that snobby officer was right: it was wrong to call such an impressive aircraft a 'bus'.

'It does look fine.'

'You'd look fine in it, darling. How well you'd fly one. Should've been you, really. Though I wouldn't wish aerial combat on my worst enemy, not even Fritz.'

'How does it work though, Dud? Is it all done in a kind of panic, just flying around randomly? I'd imagine not. I'd imagine there are techniques and strategy.'

'Yes, of course. It may feel random at first, but you listen to the more seasoned chaps and then you learn by doing. No amount of theory can prepare you for combat. It's a thing that must be experienced. You have to know all the capabilities of your own aircraft and your enemy's too – who's faster on the straight and in a dive, who can turn more tightly. Speed is the most important thing. Not only in a dive or a chase. If you're faster, you can simply retire if needs be and the fellow can't catch you. There's skill and experience. They make a difference. But mostly it's about surprise. Surprise is the one thing you need for the best chance of getting a kill. Most of your kills are won in the very first pass. Coming from above, coming out of the sun. And it helps if there are a few of you. Flying in crowds is much the best way. Some chaps have a lone wolf style and fly around looking for trouble on their own. They like it that way. Some build up quite a record of kills. But they don't last long. It's so bloody dangerous, flying around out there alone. It's almost suicide.'

There was that raincloud again, passing across his features.

'You have no idea how utterly courageous you are, have you?' she marvelled.

'Oh, stuff and nonsense,' he said, and he wasn't being modest. He was genuinely annoyed. 'I'm sorry, darling, but you can't understand bravery till you've seen it, really seen it in other chaps you know, diving into hopeless fights or back in the trenches, chaps like stretcher bearers in no-man's-land. That's true bravery and I don't have it. I'm always found wanting. I hate myself for it.'

'You are very hard on yourself. Too hard.'

'Not hard enough. Not by a long chalk.'

'Not true. Nobody asked for this war, nobody like us, ordinary folk. Just fighting, staying alive, takes every ounce of bravery a person could have.'

'No!' he shouted, then stood apart from her. 'You don't—' then he visibly sought to contain himself.

'Shout if you like. Shout your head off.'

But he wouldn't. 'I'm awfully sorry, darling. But you don't understand at all. I can't explain it. Not really. It's about guilt, I suppose. The guilt of being alive when so many others are dead.'

They stood and waited for that truth to sink in, Dud rubbing a dry patch on his hand too hard.

'Come on, love,' she said and took his arm, strolling on to turn down another path beside a field that lay north-easterly towards Waltham. They could see the white sails of the windmill above the horizon, something to aim for.

'Do you remember that windmill?' she asked, pointing.

'From our first flight? Is that really the one?'

'That's it.'

They walked on, watching it reveal itself brick by brick over the curvature of the earth.

'*Very old are we men,*' said Dud. 'Walter de la Mare.'

Always a bookish chap, thought Della, smiling. 'Do you read when you're not flying?'

'Not much.'

'Don't you have *Copperfield* with you out there?'

'No and I just don't find I'm able to read. One's mind is so tense with concentration. So . . . taut. When you're resting, at times one can hardly string a sentence together. Even talk becomes impossible. One just wants the mind to go blank. One just wants . . . peace. I say, are there any horses around here?'

'That's where we're going, silly. There's a farm just over the brow of this hill and they have two old Shire horses. Or at least, they did the last time I walked here.'

'Well, they might have gone to the war. Let's hurry up and find out. You are brilliant, Della. You do know me. Better than anyone.'

The field sloped down and they broke into a trot, then a gallop, pushing at each other and laughing. His first laugh since he had arrived. Colour in his cheeks. When they got there, no horses could be found but Dud waved it away. It was the thought that counted, he said, and hugged her, kissed her lightly, then passionately. And with nothing or nobody about to see, not even a horse or a sparrowhawk, they lay down at the edge of the field beside the hedgerow and made feverish, prickly love and he shouted his pleasure for all the natural world to hear, and ignore.

That night was their second and he'd not slept. She foolishly thought she'd cracked it on that walk, but his moods were fleeting and unpredictable. The next few days passed in walks and talks, mostly about flying, when he wanted to.

One night lying in bed, she said, 'Isn't there a way you could do other things in the air, other than fighting? Other . . . missions?'

'I have. I mean, there's reconnaissance. And spy drops.'

'Ooh, what's that?'

'It's not exciting. Just worrying. You have to go at night, over the lines, taking a two-seater. Then you have to find the right field in the dark, drop him off and find your way home again. It's awfully nerve-wracking. One time the bastard wouldn't get out, got spooked by some Archie and wouldn't bloody go. Nothing to do but go back with him. I was furious. I heard of another who turned their gun on the airman. A double agent. Would you believe it?'

'Blimey!' How many stupid ways there were to die in a war. 'But it must be preferable to all that diving about, surely. It strikes me it's the combat that's cracking you up.'

'I think it's flying, full stop, to be honest.'

'Really? But you always loved aeroplanes so much.'

Dud grimaced and turned away. 'Sorry to disappoint you,' he muttered, not grudgingly. Sadly.

'Not a disappointment at all,' she said, matter of factly. Then softer, 'Flying has been spoiled for you.'

'Yes,' he said and turned to look at her. 'That's it.'

He stared at her. She could see the whites of his eyes, reflecting the moonlight seeping in from outside.

'I can't get something out of my head.'

He was staring desperately, so frightened.

She whispered, 'Tell me.'

'It happened last month and I've been dreaming about it. One of our men died close by and it simply won't leave me. He was on his way back from a patrol, when suddenly his aircraft nosedived onto the aerodrome and burst into flames. I was there and some of us ran to the site to get him out, but his ammunition began to explode which drove us all back. We couldn't reach him and soon he was burnt to death.

'I saw his body in that inferno, saw the black form of it inside the red and the orange . . . *hell* and there was nothing I could do but stand and watch it happen. I think of that black body always, all the time, the silhouette of it's imprinted in my brain, as one sees the window frame on a bright day after closing your eyes – there, stark in my memory. Like a bruise that won't heal.

'I dream of it over and over, sometimes standing and watching the horror and, worse, sometimes I am him and my machine is engulfed in flames. Every time I fly now, I wonder if it will be me there, ending in fiery death. There are lots of ways to die in the air, of course, but that is the one that eats away at me, day after day. I suppose one might call it a morbid fascination.

'I have heard of one case where the pilot managed to land and escape from his burning aeroplane and also another case where a pilot put his flaming aeroplane into a dive and the fire was blown out. I hold onto these like . . . prayers. But I know they're extremely rare and therefore pointless to waste time thinking about.'

Della willed herself not to cry. If he upset her, if he saw he was, he'd stop. But maybe he should stop. Did it help, all this? Could anything help? 'Dud—' she began.

'No, you see, I must finish. What I must tell you. You see, I take a revolver up with me every time I fly. Not to shoot at the Hun, as I have my Vickers for that. But if fire breaks out, I will blow my own head off.'

After he'd gone – first to spend a day with his father in Bradford, then straight down again to London and onto the boat train – she had no time to be lonely, as Gertie came bustling in and moved her toiletries back in to Della's room, their shared room as it had become.

'Sorry you've lost your fellow, dear, but I'm not sorry to be back in here away from my little terrors. They've been driving me up the wall. Clambering all over me in the night. Who knew boys needed so many cuddles? I would quite like to have my body back. It's exhausting being with needy children all day and all night. Back to the awful baby days. You'll see. Darling, what's wrong? Oh, darling!'

Della was crying and didn't know how to stop. She could have cried a whole sea, all the way to France.

Over the winter, Dud wrote less often than before, shorter letters, few and far between. Their tone was different too, less confessional, more about the goings-on in the mess than his flying or his fears. He talked about the cold, how even a face smothered with Vaseline couldn't stop his nose from freezing at high altitudes. Trying to warm up on the ground was a painful procedure, involving the drinking of hot milk and rum, an unnatural concoction. These young men were being treated as malfunctioning machines, with fuel being rammed into them to make them work harder.

Della could have told him again to tell her everything, but she had lost faith in the talking cure and wondered if it simply made things worse. If he wanted to write those things to her, he would, as he knew he could. He was choosing not to, and that must be his choice, she decided. But she missed being his confidante, and she missed his company and his body from those days and nights they'd shared. Most of all she missed the old Dud, the boy from the beach. She feared he might be lost forever, lost in every sense of the word, body and mind.

It occurred to her that her existence in the Dobbs household was all about life and living. Despite Pop's dolour, which was anyway lessening as his reasons to be joyful increased, the house was filled with activity and chatter, a busy hive of compatriots making noise and effort to drive their lives forward, however young they might be. Indeed, the younger ones were usually the noisiest about it. But in Dud's world, his band of brothers were engaged in the business of death, dealing in it and with it, doling it out and coming home to it. Some titanic, invisible hand had deemed it so. Not God, not that – she didn't know if she believed any more, or more accurately that she wanted to believe in the God of her childhood. But the indifferent hand of history, picking up lives and replacing them in new terrible corners of the earth, brushing things aside and knocking over the pieces, random, uncaring, unseen. It all seemed so set and impossible to shift. It all seemed so unfair. Such was war.

In March, Dud's situation was unsettled further by a move of aerodrome. The new site was much nearer to the front line and came under shellfire every day. Behind the hangars was a graveyard, which one day, Dud wrote to her, was hit by two heavy shells, and stony lumps of gravestones fell around the airfield. Della worried intensely about the effect this shelling would have on him, on his rattled nerves, on his mind. Death was coming closer to him and she was more fearful now than she had ever been.

It was early spring and as life began to assert itself all around her in Cleethorpes, bulbs pushing through the soil, she received another letter from Dud. He was not immune to the time of year himself, though for him and his friends, all life was ever present with death, the two – separated in the proverbial lifespan by three score years and ten – were entangled in a terrible dance, graceful in their aeroplanes cutting through the spring skies of France, but a waltz of death all the same.

21st March 1918

No. 60 Sqn
R.F.C.
B.E.F.

My wonderful wife,
   Calcraft is dead. His aeroplane engine malfunctioned and he crashed into a field. No fire, no enemy, just an accident. I do miss him awfully. When one of us had a bad war-dream, we'd talk the other one round. Now I'm alone at night it's really rather bleak. I don't know who I'll share with next, but they won't have that understanding that Calcraft and I built up these past months lying awake in the early hours, as we did so many days. Sometimes we would call out to each other, and light a candle, stare at the flame and talk a while and banish some of our anxieties. I don't think I could trust another chap in that way, not again.
   Jim Porter also had a very close shave the other day and it really got me thinking. Since Calcraft went, he is the only chap around here I feel comfortable with. The other chaps are all fine, though some are a bit snobbish (remember the one who told me off for calling my machine a bus?) and others are just drunks in pilot's clothing. To be fair, they drink to ease their stress, but it makes for poor conversation.
   You see, I am getting to feel so sorry for the chaps I have killed. I am beginning to feel quite the murderer. I'm starting to shake every time I walk to my aircraft. I get these awful spasms of wind-up and then I believe I'm all in. I have to dig my fingernails into my palms in order to stop it, and

surprisingly, this works. But for how much longer, who can tell. Darling, every time I write such things to you I curse myself for my weakness, not only in having these faults but in burdening you with the knowledge of them. But now Calcraft is gone, I am so terribly lonely. I can talk to Jim but not of these things. Though he is a sterling chap I just can't bring myself to admit my failings to him. Perhaps it's his envy of me as your husband – yes, I'm afraid that's become quite obvious to me, the way he talks of you. And I am so very proud that you chose me and, call me an old fool, I cannot quite bear to admit to Jim that the man who married the marvellous you is a shivering wreck, or going that way. So, I've decided I mustn't funk it and it's not all up with me. I simply need to pull myself together. If Jim can do it, so can I.

I've got a bad cough these days and feeling really rather sorry for myself. My old chesty trouble seems to be back and there are headaches. I know I must go to the doctor and get it looked at, but lots of the fellows here have similar things and we can't all go off sick at once. I will get it checked soon though, my darling. Don't worry.

One thing I'm doing to relieve the strain is spending time with the animals here, helping to feed the pigs and chickens. Some of the dogs are owned by officers who are proprietorial about them, but there are some that are more like squadron dogs and I play with them when I can, throwing a ball or a stick or simply sitting with them and watching them breathe. It is a comfort to feel a dog's warm chin rest on one's leg, I have found. It puts me in mind of the time I once spent in the company of horses. Oh, how I'd love to be with them again. The simplicity of that life. If I get out of this bloody awful mess, darling, I have promised myself I will work with horses one day. It will be my reward for this hell. In the meantime, I'd like to start a patch of garden, with spring on its way. To see new life come from the mud here would bring me great peace, I feel,

*something sorely needed. Perhaps you could send me some
seeds, my love – some mustard and cress, some flower seeds,
something like sweet peas or anything else that won't take
too long to grow. They must grow quickly, you see. I don't
think I need to explain why.*

*I think perhaps it was selfish of me to marry you, after
you'd lost your brother to the war. And now of course it
may happen again and it's my selfishness that has put you
in that position. I am sorry, my darling. But I'd be a liar
if I said I regretted it.*

You own all of my love, every scrap.

Your fondest husband, as long as I live.

Dud

One morning soon after receiving that letter, Della was about
to head off to work when she found Mam having a soundless
cry in the alleyway next to her pushbike. She was hiding her
sorrow from the house's ears, Pop's, but the children's too, and
when asked, she told Della that Puck's two-year anniversary
had passed with no comment. Della felt awful she'd not realised
it herself, so caught up in her own woes was she. Had anyone
else noticed? It seemed not, and because nobody had mentioned
it in the days before, Mam had been more upset that it had
been so forgotten, that Puck had passed uneventfully from this
world and all was dust, with no one to even commemorate the
day of his passing.

'I'm sorry, Mam.'

'You have your own worries, love. Don't fuss yourself. Get
to work.'

On her bicycle ride to the garage, she gazed across the flat
shining sands, the sea far out and unreachable, and thought of
Puck's lost body out there on the continent somewhere, never
to be found, lost in the chaos of the war. If they'd had a grave,
a memorial here, they could go and stand by it every year, and
have a place to direct their mourning. Package it into that one

day and in that way make it manageable, boxed and not liable to spill messily all over their everyday lives. But for all the boys reaped in great swathes across Europe and beyond, there were no bodies, no funerals, no memorials. This was wrong, wrong, wrong. When her parents were growing up, their England was Victorian and treated death with majestic reverence, the black plumes and mutes and solemn rituals according death a privileged place in their lives. But now, in 1918, with the numbers of dead English boys in the tens of thousands – could it be hundreds of thousands by now? – there was no choice, no place for so many bones. They lived on only in the memory of those who knew them. England had not had time to find enough stones to mark their passing.

She arrived at her work at the garage flushed and tearful. Her employer Mrs Lancaster was used to it, sometimes gave Della a hug when she found her reading a letter from Dud or suchlike. Her son and husband were still away, still alive, but she knew the waiting game herself, all too well. She brought Della a cup of tea as usual and Della was cack-handed that morning and dropped it, watched it smash into pieces on the concrete floor of the workshop and apologised over and over, called herself a bloody fool, which shocked Mrs Lancaster and Della felt compelled to apologise again. While more tea in another cup was being fetched, a knock on the workshop door made Della look up and squint; the spring light poured into the garage and the figure in the light was silhouetted and difficult to make out. Tall, very tall and upright. Della stepped forward hurriedly and almost cried out. But it wasn't Dud, though it looked very like him. It was Mr Willow, Dud's father. And his face was the very picture of despondency.

'Hello, Della,' he said benignly.

'Tell me,' she croaked, her voice lost in its terror. 'Is it . . . ? Tell me.'

'Dudley is missing, my dear. I received a telegram from the War Office. Missing in action.'

22

'After all, many airmen have gone missing and afterwards have been reported prisoners of war. I'd imagine it happens a lot with airmen.'

Mr Willow looked altogether too tall in the Dobbses kitchen. Everyone in their family was medium to small and the Willows were, well, they were willowy. Della had walked home with him; Mrs Lancaster had given her leave to have a half-day. That woman had been so understanding, what with Della's leave when Dud was in Harrogate, and their hastily arranged Wiltshire honeymoon. She was fond of Della and under-standing. After all, she had her own two men away, and so there was a mutual, unspoken bond over that.

The walk from the garage home with Mr Willow was achingly long and once the scant details of Dud's situation were interrogated, there was absolutely nothing else to say. All he could tell her was that a telegram had arrived from the War Office informing him that Dud was missing in action. He told her he'd be travelling down to London the following week to visit the War Office and see if he could gather any more information, which he'd certainly relay to her, if anything was discovered. She had so much she could have told him, about Dud's state of mind, but could not frame a way of saying it that wasn't hopelessly bleak. And what good would that do?

Once in the Dobbs household, after the initial shock at seeing the tall Willow man in their front room and hearing the alarming news, nobody knew what to say, least of all Della.

'Would you like more tea, Mr Willow? Yours has gone stone cold,' said Mam, taking his cup.

'No, thank you, Mrs Dobbs. I really must be on my way. My train leaves soon. I just wanted to bring the news myself and of course, I will be in touch with any further information as and when it comes.'

Della saw him to the door.

'Thank you for coming such a way,' she said as she handed him his hat.

'You're most welcome. It didn't seem right to send a telegram with news . . . like this.'

'I'm glad you didn't.'

'Keep your pecker up, my dear. Things may not be as desolate as they seem.'

Desolate, thought Della. *A lovely word for a terrible thing. I can see where Dud gets his poetical leanings from.* Oh, Dud . . . It began to sink in. She watched Mr Willow stride off down the Kingsway, buffeted on his right wide by the wind whipping in from the beach. He held on to his hat and strode resolutely on, weathering it. A man whose wife died in childbirth, whose only son was missing in action in surely the worst war in history, where countless other sons had gone before him. What would she do if Dud were gone, really gone? Would she keep in touch with Mr Willow? She would if there were a child. A child. If only there were a child. But the curse had come since Dud's leave, the curse had come every month after they'd been together. Was there something wrong with one of them, or was it simply that the time wasn't right? Mam said upset and worry stopped a baby sometimes. And they'd certainly had their fair share. But oh, if only there were a child in her belly to keep her company. A part of Dudley Willow to cherish.

Everyone kept smiling at her after that, or shrugging shoulders, or sighing. The house was on tenterhooks – on the edge of the abyss, to be precise. Thank heavens for those noisy children; yet even the boys were subdued. With forethought, it probably should've been kept from them, but they saw Mr Willow come and overheard everything. The house wasn't big enough for private conferences. Cleo was the most outwardly upset to begin with, but then she set her mind to be cheerful and thereafter was a champion of optimism.

'He's on the run and being helped by milkmaids,' she announced.

Della lay awake that night, thinking of French milkmaids. Wouldn't it be nice if that were true? But the reality must be considerably different. She worried it was more than the simple 'Missing in Action' label suggested. She fretted that he'd lost his nerve when flying and crashed and died, that he'd just not been found yet. Or that he'd killed himself, flown his aeroplane down in an arc to the ground, to end it all. Even without the terrible strain he'd been under, as a pilot she knew that need, that wish for it all to be over, the mental stress of controlling an aircraft and the desire for peace. Or had he given himself over to the Germans, to escape the infernal round of patrols? Or gone AWOL? She imagined he might do almost anything that would allow him to escape, anything to end it. She felt responsible, that she hadn't helped him enough when he was on leave, hadn't said the right thing then or written the right thing since he went back. His letters had been more distant, and she blamed herself for that, and she blamed herself for pushing him into the RFC to begin with. (Underneath, she knew there was no choice, but somehow it felt more active to blame herself than blame the nameless, shapeless war machine. If she blamed herself, perhaps there was something that could be done. Nobody engaged with the war machine and came out of it well.)

A day passed, going to work, coming home, not talking about it. She felt numbed by it. She hadn't even cried about it. Somehow her emotions had become entirely disengaged, but her mind was firing on all cylinders, randomly and fever-ishly at all hours. It was as if it were trying to find a solution to a puzzle. But after all, what difference did it make what she thought or imagined? She couldn't solve it. She was stuck here in Cleethorpes, hundreds of miles away, a wife, a woman and just another of the countless females receiving bad news about their men. There were women in the town who'd had telegrams or letters about their menfolk missing in action back at the very beginning of the war, back in 1914, and still, four years later, nothing. Missing in action meant they couldn't find the body, that's all, or there was no body left to find. But there were stories in the newspa-pers, stories of men turning up out of nowhere, hiding in occupied territory then finding their way home one way or another. Indeed, she had read an article earlier in the war about her old friend Hilda Hewlett's son, also in the RFC, who had gone missing in France but managed to find his way home, to everyone's astonishment and delight. Miracles did happen. If you had nothing else to clutch on to, a miracle would have to do.

Two days after the news, they were having lunch at the kitchen table, potted cheese on toast, a dubious ration-beating concoc-tion of cheese crumbs, margarine and mustard, cooked up and spread on crackers. It was all right, better anyway than the fish sausages they'd tried to make the week before. A knock on the front door and Cleo went, her favourite thing. She always liked to make conversation with visitors and ask them personal questions.

They heard Cleo open up the door and gabble on for a while, then she called down the hallway: 'It's a man called Jim Potter and he wants to see Della.'

'Who on earth is Jim Potter?' said Mam.

'What? Can you speak up?' Cleo's strident voice was saying.

'Not Potter,' said Della, throwing down the grim cheesy

toast and rushing out of the kitchen door. There was a tall blond chap in RFC uniform standing by the coat rack, stooping slightly to allow the child to interrogate him about his name.

Cleo said, 'He's very shy and he ought to speak up. He said it's Porter, not Potter. Jim Porter.'

Della said snappishly, 'That's enough, Cleo. Back to the kitchen with you.'

'Oh, yes madam. Whatever it is you say, madam, don't you know,' simpered Cleo and minced off down the hall. That child.

Della held out her hand and Jim took it. They held on to each other's hands, there in the hall, in lieu of hugging. He looked even taller now than he used to; something about his gait, more confident and upright than it used to be. Flying Corps life clearly suited him. There were patches beneath his grey eyes though and he had a strained look, but he had filled out well since she last saw him and had become more himself, somehow. This was the man who had carried her from her crash that day in Lincoln, who had stroked her hair when she drifted in and out of consciousness, who'd prepared her aeroplane and always supported her, rooted for her and praised her, all those years ago. In recent months, he had been with her husband and helped him too, been company for him and provided some comfort, a reminder of better days. She decided to risk embarrassment, and reached up and kissed him on the cheek.

'Jim, it's so good to see you.'

'Hello, Della,' he said, smiling shyly and blushing keenly from the kiss.

'What can you be doing here?' she asked, then, without thinking, ploughed onwards, 'Is there news? Do you have news of Dudley?'

She did briefly consider that he'd come a long way to be standing here in her hallway – she hadn't even got him out of it yet and into the front room, and already she was firing

questions at him. Mam appeared behind her and, after introductions, took it all in hand and prepared tea while Della
took Jim to sit down on the settee. But she couldn't wait for
tea or politeness, and as soon as they were seated, she began
again.

'Is there news, Jim? Please tell me.'

'No news, I'm sorry.'

'Oh,' she whispered, crestfallen.

'But I did come to tell you some things.'

'What things?'

Mam came in with the tea. 'I'll leave you two to it. You
have lots to talk about, I can tell,' she said, then went out,
shutting the door behind her.

'Your family are super,' Jim said. 'Dud told me how super
they are and he wasn't exaggerating.'

'Thank you.' She smiled, but there was a job to be done
here and he was hedging. 'Please, Jim, is it bad news? Please
don't hesitate. You must tell me.'

'Not at all, Della. Don't worry yourself. Just after Dud went
missing, I had some leave and I was going to Dover to see
Ronnie. He's working ground crew at an airfield there. But I
stepped off the boat and found myself going straight to the
railway station and finding my way up here to you. I'll go
back to see Ronnie tomorrow, but I felt I must come and tell
you something. I could get into trouble for what I'm about
to tell you, but honestly, this'll be my fourth year in this
blasted war, and I really don't care any more. I just wanted
to come and see you and tell you what I know. He's a smashing
bloke, Dud. And he's your husband. That's all the reason I
need. So, I've come to tell you some things you ought to
know, about Dud and what's happened.'

Della was quite overcome with gratitude. 'Thank you, Jim,
dear Jim. Now, do start at the beginning and tell me everything.'

'Well, first of all, I bet you anything he's still alive.'

'Oh!' she cried and broke down into sobs. To hear those words spoken aloud, with such confidence, and from an RFC man too – they were like manna from heaven.

'There, there,' Jim said and timidly patted her shoulder, rubbed it a little.

'It's all right, I'm sorry. I'm all right. Why, Jim? Why do you think that?'

'Because of what he was doing. A spy drop. Do you know what that is?'

'I do! He told me all about them. Oh, no! Do you think the spy turned double agent and shot him?'

'Unlikely. This Frenchman was known about and not a bad egg, by all accounts. No, I believe he had engine trouble and had to ditch the aeroplane. It was playing up that day, but the men had a look at it and fixed it, so they say. But it could've let him down.'

'He could've crashed, then. Been injured or killed.'

'Possible. But it was a low-level flight, a quick turnaround. I think it's much more likely he got it down. He's such a topping flyer.'

'Is he, Jim? He always puts himself down.'

'Oh blimey, yes, he was one of the best. Brilliant at land-ings. Just before he first came, we moved to a new base and everyone complained about the limited landing area, but he managed it first time, no problem. I really think he could've got it down, then ditched the aeroplane, burnt it out and gone on the run.'

'What would that involve, going on the run? What would he be trying to do?'

'Evade capture for a start. We'd have heard by now if he'd been captured straight away, on landing. He'd be making his way back over the lines if he could, but I've heard of some going through Belgium and on to the Netherlands, coming back to Blighty that way.'

Could he manage it, she thought, *the state he was in?*

'I suppose it's very dangerous, terribly dangerous? Being on the run?'

'It has its dangers, of course. But many French are willing to help. We had one bloke in our squadron, went on the run in France and every time he needed help, he'd go up to a likely-looking French person and say, I'm an English pilot. Will you help me? And they always did. I think Dud would do very well.'

'Do you?'

'Oh, yes. He's so resourceful. You should see his cockpit: so well organised, everything in its right place. Hammer here, map there, chocolate in case he gets hungry. Well prepared. Always thinking up improvements to the way we did things, in combat, tinkering with the engines, even in the mess, or with the chickens. He started a patch of garden, got that all set up nicely. He's such a handy bloke to have about. And he never shows fear. Really bloody brave.'

Della was completely overcome. To hear one of his closest comrades talking about him in such glowing terms – yes, this was the Dud she once knew, the Dud from his younger days, full of optimism and gladness. She thought he'd been lost, that man.

'But when he was on leave . . . oh, my. In his letters. He was cracking up. His state of mind was really bad. Did you know he'd been treated for shell shock?'

'Yes, I did. I heard that.' Jim looked softly at her. 'Look, I know he was struggling, badly. His room-mate's death hit him very hard. But he held himself together for the Corps. And people admired him for it. Everybody liked him, Del. He was always concerned about others, looking out for them. The mood was just rotten after he didn't come home. He always made everyone feel . . . so peaceful, you know? The blokes just loved him, to a man.'

Della marvelled at the description of her husband. She had suspected all this, knew that this was the real Dud, that the

one she saw on leave was the ghost Dud from the convalescent hospital. How clever he'd been to hide it from all the
men, how strong of him. She alone had the privilege of seeing
the ghost Dud, of the insight into that haunted mind, but at
war, with his comrades around him, he'd worked so hard to
present himself properly and keep their morale up as well as
his own. How proud she was of him, how filled with it she
was; it straightened her back, broadened her shoulders.

'I can't tell you, Jim, I can't . . . how happy it makes me
to hear that. But, he was desperate when I saw him. I thought
at one point— well, I imagined some terrible things. That he
might even end it all. He had terrible nightmares. He'd lost
so much weight. And he wrote that he had an awful cough.'

'Yes, he did. That's true, it was a hacking cough. He said
he was going to get it looked at, but he didn't get round to
it. It didn't sound good. Someone else was going to do the
spy drop but couldn't, so he volunteered. I'm not saying he
was the picture of health. None of us pilots are. We're all
wrecks in one way or another. But I am saying that, of all the
airmen I know, if anyone was going to land a dodgy aeroplane,
escape and go on the run, it'd be Dud Willow.'

Della was deep in thought. So, he might be out there, in
France on the enemy's side of the line, sleeping rough, not
eating. With that awful cough, with his fragile state of mind.
She welcomed Jim's optimism, and the idea that he hadn't
necessarily been killed, the news that he was engaged in a spy
drop, not on a deadly patrol or dogfight, was miraculous. But
after the euphoria of that had dulled, she began to seriously
worry about his ability to get by, with his twin handicaps of
ill health and an exhausted mind. Could he really make it
through France, to Belgium, Holland and home? He would
need help, a lot of it. And if he were captured, would he be
treated well? How long would he last in a prison camp with
that cough? Someone needed to go there and find him, get
him and bring him back.

'What happens to men on the run? Does anyone go looking for them?'

'Oh, no. Never. We couldn't spare a man for that.'

'There's no way one of your chaps could do another spy drop in that area, have a scout around for him?'

Jim snorted, then looked down. 'It doesn't work that way, love. Once a man's across the lines, he's on his own.'

'Did you know where he was heading for that spy drop?'

'Yes, I do. I know where he was going. I was at the same briefing. It was a field south-west of Douai.'

'So you know what route he'd take, where he could've come down.'

'Yes, but there's no way of getting to him.'

'Is flying the only way to get across the line? Is that why they get pilots to drop spies?'

'Well, yes, of course. But we can't fly about looking for someone.'

'Not you, Jim. But someone could.'

Jim sighed, on his face a pained yet patient expression. 'No, Della, they really couldn't. They'd be Archied, anyway. Or shot down by a Hun aeroplane. The RFC would never allow it.'

I'm not in the RFC, she thought, slyly. And she knew Douai too, of course. It was where Jérôme had died.

Jim stayed for an early tea and charmed the Dobbs family, who perked right up at his tentative good news of Dud. Laughter and smiles around the table again, at long last, chatter and banter. Even Pop graced the table with his presence and was discreetly impressed by Jim, Della could tell. While they were busy, she excused herself for a minute and rushed up to her room. She used the chatter downstairs to mask the noise of finding her old carpet bag, expeditiously packing it with her overalls, long johns, a thick winter coat, a woolly winter scarf and a change of clothes; her compass, her old

French maps and dictionary from her touring days; her helmet and goggles; and plenty of cash. She sneaked downstairs to hide it in the hall closet, where the winter boots were kept and where no one usually went at this time of year. That evening, when tea was done, Jim gave his thanks and said his farewells; he was planning to stay in a local guest house, where he'd left his kit. Della walked him there and when she said goodnight, she added, 'What time's your train south tomorrow, Jim? I'll come and see you off.'

She couldn't tell her family what she was doing before she did it. They wouldn't let her out of the door. And even if they did, she wouldn't put it past one of them – Mam out of desperation, Pop out of duty or Gertie out of general busybodyness – to inform the authorities to stop her. In bed, under the pretence of writing to Dud, she wrote two letters, one to the family and one to Mrs Lancaster, apologising for her truancy from the garage but explaining that it really couldn't be helped. She was going to find her husband.

23

She'd been awake half the night, making plans mentally, thinking of other things she'd need. She'd have to get them in Dover, couldn't carry them all on the train anyway. Her mind scrolled madly through lists of possibilities, eventualities, risks and debates. Some would say it was madness. She considered this, the feverish way her mind had been playing out different scenarios these past days, never at rest, never slowing down. But now, she saw this as a good omen, that her mind was preparing itself for action, that somehow her subconscious had known what it would be called upon to do and had begun its workings, cranked itself up in good time and now was working at full throttle. Perhaps it was madness, but better that than days, weeks, months – years? Who knew how long this bloody war would drag on? – of waiting and hoping and trusting in – what? She didn't trust life in general. The movement of history would offer nothing to a lone lost pilot with a patch of pneumonia – who knew it wasn't? – in his lung. So, she would have to do it.

She'd go and see Ronnie, persuade him to help her and take that two-seater Blackburn of theirs (good old Dud, mentioning it in his first letter. He'd known she'd want to hear about it, a memory from better days). If she could get the Blackburn over the Channel (well, if Blériot had done it in his awful crate of an aeroplane nearly ten years ago, she could do it too). If she could use a compass and maps, her own memories and Jim's knowledge to navigate her way to Dud's landing site, flying over the lines, and land it in a field.

If she dressed up in civilian clothes, looked like a local, acted like a local. Blended in. Asked around. People talk. He'd have had help, from someone, at some point. She could find him, if she could get to France and get over the front line. She could find him, put him in that beautiful Blackburn and bring him back home. Oh God, it was madness, utter folly. But there was a worse kind of madness, the slow, grinding insanity of waiting and grief. And that she could not bear. She hated to live in her head, always wanted to use her hands to get herself out of trouble. And now she could do something, really do something for Dud at last. She was no good to him listening, writing, even mourning. But she could fly to him and get him home. She could try. The alternative was waiting to hear of his death. Oh God, she'd rather die than that, rather die than live life without her Dud. Rather die trying to save his. Now she was glad she didn't have his child inside her. Nothing to lose.

By the morning, her mind was set. She had not slept and instead had watched the sky lighten. She stole from her sister's side, snoring in their bed, and silently wished her goodbye. She sneaked down the stairs and stealthily removed her bag from the closet and slipped on her coat and hat. She left the letters on the kitchen table, unbolted and unlocked the back door as soundlessly as she could and pulled it to. Her keenest regret was Cleo and Mam, that she had not said goodbye, that the little one would rage and cry and feel abandoned by her adored big sister, and that Mam would understand only too well and love her for it, but might be broken without her Della. It was a risk Della had to take. Mam had Gertie and Pop, and Cleo to look after and the boys to cheer her. Della had to look for her own life, and he was out there, alone and in mortal danger. She couldn't help him in combat, but in the civilian world, all was fair in love and war, and she was going to France to find her husband. She'd spent this war so far waiting, with all the other women. Not any more.

But first she had to wait for Cleethorpes to wake up. She hung around in a park near Jim's guest house till a more sociable hour, then turned up on his doorstep – having to persuade the fierce landlady to fetch him – and, when he came to the door, he found her there with her carpet bag and a grin.

Jim narrowed his eyes at her. 'What's the bag for?'

'I'm coming with you to visit Ronnie.'

'Need a holiday?'

'Something like that.'

They didn't talk much on the train at first. Increasingly awkward, Jim found a newspaper and read it for a while, then folded it up with a flounce and flung it down.

'What's going on, Della?'

'I don't know what you mean.' But she was smiling. She couldn't help it. Neither could he, but he was worried too.

'You're up to something. What is it? I'll . . . well, I'll detrain at the next stop if you don't tell me.'

She'd thought about going all that way with Jim, then springing it on them both in Dover. After all, she didn't want Jim trying to stop her, in some act of misguided chivalry. But he'd rumbled her and it was best to come clean.

'I need to see Ronnie. He's going to get me your Blackburn. I'm going to fly it to France and find Dud and bring him home.'

It sounded reasonable, when you said it like that.

'No, you're bloody not!'

'Yes, Jim, I bloody am.'

Across the green stretch of wind-whipped land beyond the aerodrome, you could see the squat dependable form of Dover Castle rising above the cliffs, with the sun setting behind it. The array of hangars and huts where Ronnie worked at Swingate Down kept fledgling RFC pilots busy with Avro 504Ks and Sopwith Pups, where, Della thought, the poor chaps would be struggling to take off, let alone fly right on top of the hills here, with the clouds almost sitting on the ridged ground and the wind blowing like hell.

When they saw Ronnie, he was in front of a hangar, scolding some minion and throwing his weight around. Jim called him over and he turned, his face lighting up at the sight of his brother – in one piece, returned from France alive, this time at least (apart from the pilots themselves, nobody knew better than ground crew the deadly price of flying) – and then his eyes changing, his face tense with surprise as his gaze fixed on Della and he watched them walk towards him.

'Bloody hell, it's the girl wonder!' he said and guffawed, and without pausing to think, Della opened her arms and they were hugging and laughing. Ronnie recovered enough to notice the two bags Jim had been carrying – his kitbag and her carpet bag – and frown. 'You two getting married or something?'

'I'm already married!' She laughed. 'That's why I'm here.'

More frowns and Jim shrugged, then Ronnie agreed to meet them in a while at a village pub down the road for a pint and something for supper. He came sooner than they had expected, clearly eager to quench his curiosity, and, once supping an ale, he demanded she tell him what the hell was going on.

'I want to go and find Dud. I want to fly over there and get him back.'

'You what?'

'You heard me.'

'You stupid cow! What're you going on about?'

'I mean it, Ronnie. He's out there alone, on the German side of the line. He's not safe.'

'He's in the RFC, for God's sake. That's his business. He'll be taken prisoner or he'll find his way back to our side. He's a likely fellow. He'll be all right.'

Jim piped up, 'Just what I said.'

'He might be injured,' answered Della. 'And he was losing

his nerve. He was having nightmares and headaches. He was certainly ill, with a hacking cough. Jim said so and Dud told me in his last letter.'

'What, are you a nurse now? A bloody doctor? You're talking nonsense.'

'Look, he had influenza. And shell shock. He was very ill. But they were going to send him back to the trenches. It was my idea to teach him to fly. It's my fault he's there now.'

'Don't be stupid. It's the war. It's the war's fault, not yours. You're not responsible for him.'

'He's my husband. Of course I'm responsible for him. I love him.'

'And he loves you, I take it? Then the last thing he'd ever want is you going on some damned fool jaunt across the Channel in wartime.'

Jim again: 'I said that! He'd be mad as hell.'

And Ronnie added, 'Don't you realise that all civil flying has been banned?'

'I know that.'

'And even if you were idiot enough to try it, you might be shot at when you get to France?'

'We all know that Archie's a bit hit-and-miss.'

Jim laughed, a hollow laugh. 'Easy to say,' he muttered.

'So,' Ronnie went on, tapping his blackened index finger on the beer-stained table at each salient point, 'say by some miracle you get over the Channel in one piece without going in the drink and you get past Archie without being shot down and say you land without detection across enemy lines and you could actually navigate yourself to the place Jim told you about—'

'I know that area. I've flown there. Won a prize in 1913, the Douai to Arras Cup.'

Ronnie stared at his pint glass, thinking.

'You see?' Della went on. 'It's not impossible. You're changing your mind.' She smiled.

'No, I'm bloody not. Look, I know what you're like. Since the RFC wouldn't take women, you're thinking, Bugger them. I'll show 'em. But this is dangerous, Del. Is it worth it, just to show them?'

'It's not for them. It's for Dud.'

Ronnie raised his voice and blurted, 'You're talking like a lunatic because you're blinded by love for that beanpole husband of yours!'

People looked up and the pub went quiet. The three around the table fell silent too and Ronnie drained his pint, sighed and rubbed his eyes. His voice softened. 'Look, love. Just trying to talk you out of it. This is bloody risky. Not just injury, but worse. Drowning, probably. And then you're dead. *Dead*, Della. Are you ready for that?'

'If I were a man, flying off to rescue his wife, you wouldn't question it.'

That shut him up. An aggrieved look from Jim, followed by another long sigh from Ronnie. Their food arrived, three plates of ploughman's, minus the ham, with extra bread. Rations made for a miserable pub supper these days. They fell to eating, no talking.

After a while, Ronnie threw down his fork and said, 'Bloody hell, you're going to do it, aren't you?'

'Yes.'

'With or without my help.'

A blank look from Della.

'Of course, you are, you bloody fool of a woman . . .' He slapped his hand on the table, huffed and puffed and then stopped, a flicker of something in his eyes. He half-whispered, 'But it'd be quite a coup if you bring it off . . .'

'I don't care about that.'

'Yes, but, just think! An Englishwoman in a Blackburn, crossing the Channel!'

'Ron!' scolded Jim.

But Ronnie was warming to the whole escapade. 'Shame

we can't tell anyone about it – ever. But it would be quite something, eh!'

Jim shook his head, but Ronnie had made up his mind. And Ronnie was the older and always the more decisive brother. Della knew that Jim wouldn't want her to risk her life or anything like it for very particular reasons best known to himself. Well, there was nothing to be done about that.

They talked all evening. The more they discussed, the more problems were revealed. First, the Blackburn:

'Its engine was requisitioned at the beginning of the war. I'd have to fit another one. I can lay my hands on one, but it'll take some tweaking.'

'Tweak it, then,' said Della and grinned.

'Tweak it, she says! I'll have to work at night.'

'Work at—'

'Yes, yes, work at night then,' he parroted.

'I can help you,' she said. 'I'm a good mechanic. That's been my war job.'

'I know, I know. You're a genius at everything.'

And would the Blackburn – old and, some would say, obsolete – make it to France?

'Absolutely,' Ronnie assured them. 'It's a fifty-horsepower engine and a twelve-gallon fuel tank. The engine will burn, oh, not much over five gallons an hour. So, say you're looking at about two hours flying to France with, say about thirty minutes' reserve? Well, then you've enough fuel for 120 miles in no wind.'

Next, the fuel and oil. She'd have enough to get there, but what about coming back?

Jim said, 'There won't be any castor oil to be found on the streets of France. Or in the farmhouses or wherever. You'll have to take it with you. Same goes for fuel.'

'The Blackburn's a two-seater,' said Della. 'I can put spare oil and fuel in cans in the passenger seat.'

'You won't need both,' said Ronnie. 'You'll need more fuel,

yeah. But she's got four and a half gals of oil. That'll fly her
for, oh, I should say, about seven hours? More than enough
for the trip there and back.'

'What about weight?' added Jim. 'Della's a tiny thing. But
she'll need clothes and supplies and now extra fuel. Maybe
some tools to fix it and a few spare parts, if it breaks down
in France.'

'True. You'll have to be careful with weight. Take your fuel,
obviously. After that, no more than the weight of a passenger,
in total. As for the way back . . .'

Everyone paused and the three separate minds all pictured
the possibility that it was very likely there would be no journey
back, that the whole thing was pie in the sky and highly
dangerous. But if you're going to do a thing anyway, there's
not much point in dwelling on that.

Ronnie continued, '. . . you'll have to leave some things
behind, as you'll have your passenger's weight to carry.
Unless—'

'There's no unless,' said Della, firmly. She was trying very
hard to be resolute. The whole scheme had enlivened her – a
chance to act after years of inaction – yet as the details piled
up like bills to pay, she began to feel her resolve shaking.
What did she imagine would happen, if she could not find
Dud? The longer she searched, the more likely her aeroplane
would be found and either burnt or taken. Well, then she'd
stay in France – or Belgium or wherever he'd wandered – until
she found him, or found out what had happened to him. After
that stretched a blank that she did not care to imagine.

'Don't forget your funnel,' said Jim and, after a pause, they
all fell about laughing.

That night, Ronnie found digs for Della at a guest house on
the same road as the pub, while his brother went home with
him to sleep on the settee. Della sat up, sleepless, into the
early hours, with a pen and notebook she'd packed, using her

French dictionary to list every phrase she could think of that she might need. She'd learned some when she was there touring those few years back, but her French was rusty without use. Writing it down helped it to begin to flow again in her mind. She imagined herself talking to French people, asking for help. 'Have you seen this man?' she would say, and show them the photograph of Dud she'd brought with her. 'He is an English pilot who crashed near here. He is my husband.' *My husband*, she thought, and touched the long face on the photograph, the good-hearted smile, the pilot's uniform, the loving eyes. *To my Beloved, with every little bit of my love*, he had written in pencil on the back. *Oh, my Beloved*, she thought, and closed her eyes, willing the hours to fly by until she was up in the air and heading his way.

The next day was Saturday and Ronnie had the day off, so together they met her at the guest house and Ronnie drove them to the hangar where the Blackburn had been mothballed. It was another Dover airfield called Whitfield, in an emerald-green field the locals called the meadow. The aeroplane was housed in a black painted hangar, over which a huge horse chestnut spread its branches protectively.

'You knew Gustav Hamel from your Hendon days, didn't you, Della?' said Ronnie, holding open the truck door for her.

'I did. Outstanding pilot. He went missing, of course. Just before the war.'

'Well, he flew from here in those days, many a time.' They walked across the plush green grass to the hangar, pausing to look out at the view. It was a prime site for an airfield, protected and bounded by trees and bushes, yet with glorious views out across the sea and the curve of the Kent headland. 'And that's not all. This is the very spot where the first woman to fly over the English Channel started her flight.'

'Harriet Quimby flew from here?' gasped Della.

'She did. In her purple flying suit. Fog and cloud and a

good eye for a compass. If Harriet Quimby could do it, so can you.'

Della was delighted at the thought. She'd read about Quimby's exploits in those early days when Dud used to send her *The Aero*. Any mention of an aviatrix was pounced upon then by Della and her aunt, of course, and they read avidly of anything Quimby did. She was glamorous and adored for her flying exploits – and particularly her purple flying suits – but she was also a damn good flyer. She came to a bad end, dying on a beach, but that was no reflection on her skills, or on Hamel's either. On any of the genuinely gifted pilots who'd given their lives to aviation over the years.

'She landed on her head in the mud flats, you know,' said Della.

Jim said, 'But she wasn't as good a pilot as you.'

Ronnie produced a key and opened up the padlock on the hangar door. The interior was dim and dust-ridden, with bits and pieces of aircraft lying on benches and on the floor all around. But there, near the back, was her old friend the two-seater Blackburn, grubby, though the white sides showed through the grime. She went to it and reached out, laid a flat hand on its flank and patted it.

'Hello, old girl.'

They worked all day on the engine, on gathering supplies, on preparation. Ronnie was at work the next day, which Jim and Della spent at Whitfield on final tinkerings and also, sitting in the sunshine outside the hangar, going over Della's map of northern France, where she pencilled out the route and the landing spot that Dud had been aiming for. Jim was a mine of information about the area: where he'd come across anti-aircraft guns before; where heavily armed emplacements were; that is, what to avoid and which route precisely to fly and at what height to get to the right spot.

Jim also gave her a gift.

'RFC-issue goggles. You've got your old ones, I know, but

these are better. And you can keep your other pair as a spare. Look.' They were made of a good, strong leather with fur on the back, and a piece of leather coming down that fitted over the nose and cheeks. 'Wear that with a scarf across your mouth and chin and it'll give your face more protection. You'll need it with that rotary engine chucking oil at you all the way. They're comfortable too.' Jim handed them over and sniffed.

Della inspected them. 'Thank you, Jim. And thank you for all this. For everything. Most of all, for telling me about Dud. You didn't have to do that. I hope you don't get into trouble.'

Jim sighed. 'I'll probably be dead before that happens.'

Della looked away from him, out across the leaf-green meadow, bordered by clumps of snowdrops in the green that had just lost their white flowers.

'Don't,' she whispered.

'Don't what?'

'Don't say that.'

'It's probably true,' he said mournfully. 'Why not be honest? If I'm going to die, I might as well be honest. I might as well say the truth, that my life might be over very soon, that I don't want you to go on this stupid, dangerous thing you're doing . . . and that I've always loved you.' Della looked at him but he wasn't looking at her. Instead, he was inspecting his bootlaces. 'Dud'd kill me for that.'

'No, he wouldn't. He knew.'

Jim looked up. 'Did he?'

'Oh, yes. He liked you for it.'

'He's a good bloke, Dud.'

'He's the best.'

Jim nodded and together they sat and stared out at the white cliffs, the grey Channel twinkling in the spring sunshine, thinking very different thoughts.

Ronnie came by that evening with a fistful of francs he'd borrowed from an airman pal who'd just returned on leave. Jim had some more, so she had a good haul, to be used in emergencies

if she had to go on the run. She had her overalls and layers for
flying, her old goggles and flying helmet and a thick coat, gloves
and woolly scarf. It was early spring and she knew it'd be bitterly
cold, but it was all she could muster at this short notice. If only
she had a custom-made full-length flying coat of fur like Melli
Beese's! But there was no time for that. In her carpet bag she
had a change of more feminine clothes for blending in with the
locals on the ground, including a dowdy scarf from Ronnie's
wife to cover her fashionably shingled haircut: Ronnie added,
'Mrs Ron says, French farmers' wives don't have boys' hairdos.'
Della had brought her bag with her from the guest house,
packing it carefully over and again to make it all fit – clothes,
tools, a few spare parts, maps and other essentials – leaving
space for food and drink, and a neat handbag, inside which
was her purse stuffed with money from two nations.

The weather was good that evening, calm and clear, so clear
they could just make out the French coast outlined dimly
across the Channel. It didn't look far. Not so very far.

'If it's like this at first light, I'm going,' she said.

The brothers were staring out to sea, as if by staring at the
French coast they could will it closer for her. Nobody spoke.
They'd agreed that she'd sleep in the hangar that night, and
Ronnie had disappeared off home to fetch her blankets. He
brought back food made by his wife, charitably using their
rations to make her a portion of apple pie – 'Mrs Ron says,
a taste of England for you,' Ronnie told her. He frowned as
he said it and had to turn away. Jim was morose. Della noticed
there were several blankets on the pile Ronnie had brought,
and so it was that the brothers stayed with her that night and
they all bedded down near each other, close to a wing of the
now-prepared Blackburn, its white flanks cleaned, its silver
panels gleaming, the engine tweaked and tuned and ready to
go. It didn't need to be so clean to fly all right, but it was
obvious that this was a labour of love for Ronnie and he had

polished it till it shone. It was a handsome aeroplane that would have to prove its worth the next day, and keep her safe above the waves. Della thought about learning to fly on that super Blackburn above Filey, about Oxley and the valuable lessons he had taught her, even his death, which showed her that a calm, safe pilot wins the day. Taking this aeroplane now felt like a tribute to him and to those early days of hope. Given the choice of any aircraft for this dangerous mission, she'd have chosen a Blackburn.

She knew she should sleep, rest for the day ahead of her, but she could not. The last day of March melted into the first day of April, and Della was awake long past midnight and then slept fitfully for only two or three hours. Before dawn, she was up again and putting her bag and the petrol can, her map, her old goggles and rags for wiping them clean – and yes, her funnel – in the cockpit and on the passenger seat floor. In her pocket, she stowed the spare wires carried by all rotary engine pilots, just in case anything came loose in the engine. The men groaned and shuffled in their sleep as she got ready. When she stepped outside to check for the umpteenth time that the weather still held, she strained her eyes at the horizon to look for that very first glow that meant she could go. It wasn't there yet, but a few minutes later she came out again and there, at the curve of the earth's surface, was a distinct line of pale blue. That was all she needed.

'Ronnie . . . Jim.' She tapped each on the arm with her toecap. They awoke, looking almost like twins, their confused waking expressions the same. Jim, used to early starts and a battle-ready stance, leapt up, while Ronnie crawled up, holding his back and moaning.

'Bloody woman, bloody hare-brained schemes.'

Della smiled. Jim handed her Mrs Ron's apple pie. 'You must eat,' he said. 'Eat all of it. Keep your strength up.'

'Thanks Jim,' she said and bolted it, eager to get into the aeroplane and get going. Once she'd shoved it all in (it was delicious and made her think of Mam), she was ready. There was nothing left to do, nothing left to stay for.

'Right,' she said and looked at the Blackburn, looked back at her two dear friends.

By the time they had it outside, the line on the horizon was a strip and Della was champing at the bit to get going. She climbed in and readied herself, compass all set, goggles on, facing the Channel and trying to breathe steadily.

'Bloody proud of you, Del,' said Ronnie. Jim couldn't speak, she could see that. He was choked up, so she didn't ask him any last-minute advice. It was all sorted out anyway. She just needed to do this damn thing now.

The brothers got her going, pulled the chocks away and she sped forward across the fine, smooth ground. She was too occupied to turn, yet wished she could have seen their faces one last time before she left English soil. Rising above those white cliffs, she circled over Dover Castle, which faced outwards as if pointing the way clearly to Calais, and she turned her aeroplane due east. She wanted to get as high as she could pronto, to avoid any trigger-happy anti-aircraft gunners at Dover below. But luck was on her side and nobody fired at her, and very soon she was away over the water and free.

Ahead she spotted France, although it might be just the cloud hugging the coast that she could see. The sea rolled beneath her and she left her country far behind. No turning back, no second thoughts. A memory came to her of Claude, at their first meeting, pontificating that a woman could be a pilot if she would 'stick to aerodrome flying and not attempt the rigours of cross-country'. Well, what about this now? Flying across the sea, not even the land! A moment of pride shot through with panic. What the hell was she doing? She said out loud, for the second time in her life, 'You've fucking done it now.'

24

'I'm not going to die here,' she said.

There'd been patches of thick fog over the Channel that morning, a scrap here and there of blue-sky clarity but otherwise a freezing soup of white. Navigation had been a matter of skill, luck and faith, and constant attention to the compass.

She spoke again: 'I've got the touch.'

They always said that about her, *She's got the touch.* She can feel yaw in her bones, knows where the air is coming from and how it'll lift or drop. She can step into an aeroplane and strap it on and fly.

'Not far now,' she told herself. But the cold was petrifying her. Every muscle felt encased in ice. The rush of freezing air from the propeller wash was like an assault. The oil sprits in her face had ruined Jim's goggles and she was onto her second pair. The rag she'd used to try to wipe them had been flung away out of her hand by a gust of wind. The chin strap on her helmet was a bit too long for her small head, and all the way it had flapped in her face and every effort she made to tuck it away was foiled by the spiteful wind that freed it to slap her cheeks over and over, bruising her skin. What with that and the cold, the tiredness, the oil in her eyes and the strain of keeping sane, she was ready to give up. She simply had to keep her pecker up, or she'd be all in. If Dud could do it every day for weeks with Huns on his tail, she could do two hours of flying this once for him.

'Not far now,' she told herself, as if comforting a child. 'The sea's behind us.'

The land scrolled beneath like a toy farm, glowing squares of light here and there marking life and habitation, hearth and home. There was fog here too, in infrequent patches, so the landmarks she'd prepared herself for were difficult to spot. She checked her compass for the thousandth time; then, once the fog had begun to clear, she checked her position and found she was too far west. She adjusted her direction and headed east, looking out for a crossroads of two waterways that would signal that Douai was close by. At last she spotted it, the canal gleaming in the dull light, and then she knew it was only a few miles to go to her landing spot.

But then, she smelt fuel. Stronger, keener. The stink of fuel was filling her nostrils. Then sputtering, then the engine stopped. Failed utterly. The horror of it froze her. She had to think like wildfire. It must be a fuel leak. That's why she could smell it. She shut off the valve to prevent a fire. *God, no, please, not a fire.* Within a second, the aeroplane was pitching forwards, its power gone. Her hands gripped the stick. Terror took hold and the animal part of her mind longed for the ground to come, for the impact and the destruction, for it all to be over. The exertion necessary to fly, to concentrate, to save yourself, was exhausting. At least death would mean rest.

'Must keep the nose down. Must land,' she said, her voice high and shrill against the silence of no engine, shocking her out of her stupefaction. With no power, the aeroplane was gliding, decelerating, its destination inexorably down to earth. If she didn't keep the nose down to keep up the speed, it'd fall from the air. She grasped the stick and eased her feet on the rudder bar to bank into position for landing.

'Don't get slow. Don't stall,' she said.

Seeing a field to the right beckoning with its flat acres of mud, she pitched the nose down and hoped to heaven the undercarriage wouldn't smash into that line of poplars edging the field. As she struggled to maintain control, her machine pitched forwards, the wires screaming and the ground hurling itself at her face, and the thought leapt into her mind that she had failed him, by crashing, by abandoning him to his fate, by dying.

As the ground rushed towards her, she saw gaping puddles in the muddy, saturated earth. How the hell she'd get her aeroplane down safely was beyond her. All became instinct. Knowing she was seconds away from impact and seeing a huge waterlogged pothole to her left, she tried at the last moment to lift the nose, to see the flare of the ground open up for a safe landing. Then she threw the stick to the right to land on one wheel and came crunching down heavy; her right arm whacked against the side with the impact and she felt a searing pain in her right wrist. She rolled along briefly in the quagmire, the wet mud spraying up all around as the aeroplane careered through it. And then it stopped. She'd done it. She was down and safe and the aeroplane was in one piece. She went to lift her right hand to pat her aircraft, to say thank you to it for getting her there safely, but her wrist hurt so much she daren't move it.

With her left hand, she took off her goggles and stowed them away in the cockpit. Then, with some difficulty, she climbed out to look. Now, where was this fuel leak? She was about to open the access panel to check the fuel pipe when she recalled that she was in France, in occupied France, over the lines, in German territory. She could be discovered by the enemy and taken. She was at war now and must stop acting like a tourist on a pleasure flight. These Germans were not friendly. She thought of Melli Beese, her German aviatrix friend, and her fearful French husband who'd accurately predicted the war. Where were they now? *Concentrate*, she cautioned herself. Her right wrist was aching awfully and getting worse. *I'll check the fuel pipe later*, she thought.

She looked about and got her bearings. The aeroplane had come down in a farmer's field, bounded on all sides by more fields. This one was surrounded by thick rows of tall trees, which luckily gave her and her downed aeroplane some coverage if anyone had been looking across the landscape. There was nobody around, no roads nearby as far as she could see. It seemed that no Germans had spotted her aeroplane coming in nearby; surely they'd have been here by now. She was only just across the line, so if she'd been seen before now, it would have been by allies. Some of them might turn up, but that would be all right, though complicated. Ideally she'd have wanted to taxi the aeroplane to a place beneath the trees, to give it more coverage, but that wasn't going to happen. She knew she had to get her things and get moving.

She was light-headed with fear, exhaustion and the pain radiating from her wrist, as well as exhilaration that she'd made it across the water without going 'in the drink', as Ronnie had put it. How proud he'd be! And she'd landed despite engine failure and not ripped out the undercarriage. And the aeroplane was fixable and intact, and with any luck and a bit of tinkering, she could fly it out of here – if it didn't get found by the enemy first, that was.

'Bloody good job, girl,' she said aloud, then winced at the pain in her arm, worsening still. She couldn't use the arm – that might be a problem, a big problem. *Don't think about that now. Get your stuff.* She pulled herself up with her left arm and climbed back into the cockpit, where she hauled her bag over her left shoulder and grabbed the fuel can from the passenger seat. She had a plan to hide it among the trees; anyone finding the aeroplane before she'd had a chance to move it would probably take that as a useful prize first. With difficulty, trying to protect her sore right arm, she managed to jump down and not drop her bag in the mud, though she did drop the can, which promptly got splattered in wet mud. Never mind. She crossed the field and got to the safety of the trees, and felt better. She put the bag and can down. Her arm was really painful. She held it up and charily pushed her coat sleeve upwards to look at the wrist. Swollen, definitely swollen. Sprained? Or fractured? Broken?

'Damn. Damn!' she scolded herself. 'Careless. Careless!'

But there was no point in dwelling on that now. She retrieved her map and spread it out on top of her bag to keep the map clean. She was two miles or so from Dud's landing site. She was very satisfied with her navigation. Despite the fog and the forced landing, she wasn't far off her target. She hid the fuel can in some undergrowth beneath a tree, counted which number it was in the line of trees and scribbled that down on the edge of the map, just in case she forgot where it'd been hidden in the days (or weeks?) before she might get back to it. She put the bag on her left shoulder, tried to ignore her pain and tramped onwards, using the map and her compass to keep checking her position, trying to skirt the fields and stay beneath the trees. She was starting to shake and a clammy sweat was blooming along her thighs and around her neck, probably the shock of hurting her wrist as well as the strangeness of her situation. Yet she had rarely felt so alive; only when flying.

Still no people about. A farmhouse was visible in the distance and she was heading towards it. Dud's landing site was near to it, two fields along. She went a slightly long way round to avoid it. The French were of course her allies, but she didn't want any more complications just yet, not before she found where Dud had been aiming for. And then she was nearly there, the next field along and she scanned the ground beyond for signs. No aeroplane neatly sitting there, though she hadn't expected that as such. As she got closer, she saw there was something there, or the remains of something, at any rate. Closer still, she saw the blackened patch of ground and broken carcass of what was once an aeroplane. Her heart lurched. She dropped her bag and ran to the ruin, her arm painful as it bumped against her side. The aircraft had burnt up all right, the fragile body devoured by fire, only the twisted charred bones of it left. Bits and pieces were scattered around, perhaps from the impact or maybe locals had been messing about with it, taking bits away to use as parts or else souvenirs. Her eyes filled at the sight and, suddenly, the constant pain, her tiredness and the fraught last few hours hit her and she sank down in the mud and began to cry. Was this Dud's aeroplane? And had Dud's greatest fear – fire – destroyed it, and him? What had become of him? There was no sign of a body or bodies. Had they been taken away? But then she remembered what Jim had said: Dud might've landed the aeroplane, ditched it, burnt it up and gone on the run. Oh, thank heavens, yes. That's what could have occurred here. She sobbed with relief.

Then, voices. She stopped sobbing, was absolutely silent. Looked around. Behind her, coming from the trees at the edge of the field, were two small figures. Children. Two girls, holding hands, stepping assuredly with large rubber boots on, walking with confidence beyond their years, crossing the field as if it were theirs; it probably was. One pointed at her and they broke into a run, wide-eyed and delighted to find a curious stranger sitting in their field, covered in mud, with tear tracks down her grubby face.

The girls stopped nearby, wary. They were dressed in simple frocks with identical grey woollen coats and long creamy-coloured scarves, home-knitted perhaps. Then one, the taller, probably the older and braver one, started forwards and peered at Della. Then a few more squelchy steps and they were standing quite near, staring at her.

'*Bonjour*,' said Della. Now was the time to dredge up that French.

'*Bonjour*,' they chorused. The older one said, '*Pourquoi êtes-vous triste?*'

Triste? Sad?

'*Bonjour. Je suis anglaise. Je cherche mon mari.*'

'*Votre mari?*' asked the older girl. They turned to each other and gaped, then broke out into a peal of giggles. They reminded her of Cleo.

The younger one piped up now, finding her voice, '*Vous êtes une femme?*' she asked, incredulous.

Of course, Della realised, she would look a fright. With her helmet on and short hair beneath it, with her overalls and heavy coat and boots on, she'd look like a man, a very muddy, oily man, not like any woman they'd ever seen.

'*Oui, oui! Je suis une femme! Je suis une femme qui vole. Une femme pilote.*'

'Oooh,' they both crooned and their chocolate eyes widened as they drank her in, this exotic creature who'd landed in their field, fallen from the sky.

Della smiled at them, then winced, her arm throbbing.

'*Vous êtes blessée?*' asked the older girl. Della didn't understand.

The other sister pointed at Della's arm. '*Mal?*'

Della nodded and passed a hesitant hand over her sore wrist.

'*S'il vous plaît venez avec nous. Notre mère va vous aider. Allons-y.*'

Della stood up and looked down at the girls, who pointed over to the farmhouse she had seen earlier. They began to walk off and she followed them, scanning the surroundings for signs of other life, but seeing none but a trio of rabbits hopping about at the edge of the field.

They came near to the house; it looked a tumbledown place, with a hole in a barn roof, but there was a very neat vegetable patch with tiny seedlings in straight rows and a pen with some crooning chickens pecking around inside. They must have had little extra to do repairs, but the place itself was tidy and well looked after. A French family doing their best, was the impression Della had. The girls ran ahead, through the porch, and flung open the front door, shouting over and over, '*Une femme pilote!*', though Della was sure she heard one say, '*Encore un pilote!*' *Encore* means another? '*Anglaise!*' she heard another shout. They had run into the kitchen as Della waited outside, and she could see their figures passing a kitchen window, pointing out at her and babbling on. Then a woman's white face appeared at the window, wide-eyed, and disappeared.

Out of the front door came their mother, thin and worried-looking, wiping her hands on her apron, then frowning at the muddy man-woman standing before her.

'You are English?' she said.

'Yes! You speak English!'

'Some,' said the woman, looking Della up and down. 'Come. Come in. No. Wait.' She pointed to Della's dirty boots and shook her head. Della managed to slide one boot off with the other toe, but her right boot eluded her; with her bad hand useless for boot removal, she struggled. The woman tutted and bent down, pulled off the boot and went inside, gesturing for Della to follow.

The kitchen was warm and cluttered and very welcome. The girls fussed over Della, the mother was taciturn. They pulled out a wooden kitchen chair for her and made her sit down. Della was still shaking. The girls were telling their mother about her arm. With no words, the woman carefully looked at the wrist, dabbed it with her fingertips and shook her head. She poured out hot water from a kettle into a bowl and added some colder water. She motioned to Della's clothes, then said, 'Coat take off.' Della managed to slip her left arm out of her heavy flying coat, but she struggled with the right and the woman helped her. She wet a cloth and cleaned Della's muddy hands and lower arms, then cleaned her face. Della sat and let her do it. It was so calming to be washed, even with the girls chattering away a mile a minute about who knows what and giggling every so often. The woman took her time and when it was done, Della realised she wasn't shaking any more. The woman started shaking her head, then said, 'No good. Too much dirt. You need bath later.' She passed Della a hand towel to dry her skin, but the oil that clung to it blackened the towel and ruined it.

'I'm sorry,' said Della, grimacing.

The woman left the room and came back with an old sheet. She tore a strip from it and wrapped it firmly around the wrist, at which Della took a sharp intake of breath and the girls warned their mother to take care, which she ignored. Then she tore a larger strip off and tied it around Della's neck, to make a sling. What a relief it was to rest that arm.

'*Merci beaucoup*,' said Della.

The woman left again, this time returning with a paper bag, inside which was a handful of white powder. She poured some of it into a glass and added water, stirred it round and handed it to Della.

'Drink,' she said.

Della guessed it was a painkiller and drank down the bitter brew. The woman watched her do it, arms folded across her thin chest, then gestured to the arm and said, 'I think not broken. I don't know English word. Hurt inside, but not broken bone.'

Sprained, thought Della. Thank goodness for that.

Next, the woman produced hot coffee and bread, cheese and hard-boiled eggs. Della gobbled the food down. Still the woman had not talked to her more than was absolutely necessary, though the girls had talked enough for all of them.

After Della had finished and the plates had been cleared away, the woman poured more coffee for them both and sat down opposite her, unsmiling yet eyeing her curiously. As Della looked at her face, she saw she was older than she had at first appeared. There were grey hairs in her fringe amid the brown curls and she had deep lines on her forehead. She had soft, blue eyes that looked sad and tired. The girls must have had their big brown eyes from their father.

'Why you here?' she asked curtly.

Della thought to herself that the French must have seen their fair share of trouble and wanted no more. It was good of this woman to help at all and Della couldn't blame her for being suspicious.

'I've come from England, over the sea, in an aeroplane. I am a pilot.'

The woman's eyebrows rose up. The girls were bothering her, presumably asking her to tell them what the lady was talking about. The woman lost her patience and scolded them, sent them away; they went immediately, good girls that they were, but grumbled as they shuffled out, again holding hands. Then she called after them, gave them a direction, something about their father. The girls assented with glee and ran out into the backyard.

The woman turned her attention back to Della. 'And? Why? Why come in aeroplane?'

'I'm looking for my husband. He is a pilot. With the British. His aeroplane came down near here. I've come to help him get home.'

Della was about to reach into her right hip pocket when she remembered that her arm was bound and she could not. She stood up and gestured to the woman – 'My pocket, please. A photograph.' The woman stared suspiciously at the pocket, then stood and bent down to it, looking carefully, then reached in and pulled something out. She stepped back and surveyed the photograph, then lifted her eyes to Della and smiled. It changed her whole face. She looked years younger.

'Yes,' she said. 'I know him.'

Della hopes leapt in her breast. 'You do?'

'Yes. We helped him. French man came to us, said British pilot fly him here. Need clothes. My husband went to him in field. Aeroplane broken. They burn aeroplane. Keep it from Germans. Burn uniform too.'

Jim was right! thought Della. They wouldn't leave an aeroplane for the Germans to find and use, or learn from about the latest RFC developments in aircraft design. They would burn it. And of course, there were no charred body parts there. A wave of joy swept over her and she almost wept with it. The woman leaned over the table and touched her arm.

'He was not hurt. No bones broken too.'

'Oh, thank you. Thank you!' said Della. 'Where is he?'

The woman's face fell serious again. 'Your husband not hurt in aeroplane. But not well. Ill. Bad . . .' She was searching for the right word, but made the sound instead.

'A bad cough,' said Della.

'Yes, cough. Very bad cough.'

'Where is he now?'

'I explain. He come here, bad cough. We help. Give him bed. Rest. Food. This.' She pointed to the drained glass Della had taken.

'Medicine,' said Della.

'Yes, medicine. He rest here. Days. Cough no better. But my husband say must move on. He say yes. Your husband say yes, he agree, move on. Wants go to *Belgique*. And go north after. *Les Pays-Bas*,' the woman said, pointing upwards.

The Netherlands? wondered Della. 'When did he go?'

'Yesterday.'

'Only yesterday?' Della cried. She had a fighting chance, he was so close! Perhaps he had even sat in this very chair, only yesterday.

'Yesterday he go to Douai. Town near here. Friends. Stay their house. Go to train soon, train to *Belgique*. You hurry. My husband coming now. He take you friends' house. Drink, drink your coffee.'

The woman stood and went out to meet her husband. Della looked around the kitchen, the simplicity of it, the bric-a-brac of family life. She thought of Mam and Cleo, mourning her impulsive disappearance. She had not written to them since leaving on the train, had barely thought of them. It was selfish, she knew that. She regretted it. They would be so terribly worried. But she had other problems now and they would have to understand. Something told her Mam would.

In came the woman, flanked by her daughters and followed by a man. Muddy clothes and a ripe, country smell told her this was the husband, a farmer. He spoke to his wife in a guttural speedy French, none of which Della could catch. They discussed her for a while as she finished her coffee and watched them expectantly. The woman was pointing at Della. She turned to her.

'Bath now. And your clothes. You must change.'

'I have women's clothes in my bag.'

'Good. Come with me.'

Della smiled at the man. He was frowning at her but he managed a tilt of his mouth beneath the thick greying moustache. These were serious times, but still people could manage a smile, however small.

The woman took her into a pantry behind the kitchen. There was a fire in there and a tin bath set before it. Della sat in a chair nearby while the woman heated up kettles of water in the kitchen, carried them in and poured them into the bath. Della offered to help, but the woman just shook her head and carried on. Sitting on the chair staring at the fire, watching the woman prepare her bath, was so relaxing and comforting that Della slipped into a welcome nap. The woman woke her with a gentle shove and handed her a lump of grey soap, gesturing to the bath, then went out and shut the pantry door. Della, with some difficulty, removed her sling, bandage, and her clothes, folding up the latter as neatly as she could and placing them in a corner, away from all food and anything but floor; her flying clothes were sticky with oil and she hated the thought of staining this woman's clean house. She stepped into the warm water. It was only a few inches deep, but it was heaven. She scrubbed everywhere she could, then found a bath towel, rough yet large enough to wrap herself in, and stepped out and dried herself off. Every movement sent waves of pain up her arm from the wrist. A knock came on the door and the woman's head popped round. She had brought Della's bag, which she put down on the floor. She was about to edge out and close the door behind her, but Della said, 'My arm. I might need your help.'

The woman understood; she shut the door before coming over, then opened Della's bag and took out her civilian clothes – a long woollen skirt, blouse, waistcoat and jacket – and laid them out on the back of the chair. Della's change of clothes was not too smart, not too shabby; something that wouldn't draw attention either way. She found her hairbrush and tried to tidy up her damp hair. Thank heavens for this short bob hairdo; how inconvenient long hair would've been at a time like this. Della retrieved Mrs Ron's cotton scarf to tie around her hair and took out her handbag with its purse full of francs. She also took Dud's photo and put it into the jacket's left-hand pocket, so she could get it out easily herself. Now the awkward part. The woman, with great gentleness, helped Della dress and replace the sling, and tied the scarf around her head. She took a step back and said, 'Very good. You leave bag. I wash your pilot clothes. When you come back for aeroplane, all clean.'

'Thank you,' said Della. 'Thank you for everything.'

The woman smiled and shrugged, motioned Della to the door. When they came out, the husband was standing in the hallway waiting solemnly. The girls had lost interest and were playing hopscotch or something similar outside. The farmer looked up at her; his surprise at the transformation from scruffy pilot to young woman showed clearly on his face. He chortled and made some ironical comment in French that eluded Della. She guessed he spoke no English.

Della turned to the woman. 'Please, can I ask about my aeroplane? Can your husband take it, put it somewhere? Hide it?'

'Ah, yes. Uh, wait,' said the woman. She spoke to her husband. They had a few words, some doubts, some head-shaking, some pointing. 'Yes,' the woman said to Della. 'He can pull with horse, big work horse. Pull into barn.'

'That's good. I can show you on my map, where it is.'

She fetched it from her bag and spread it out on the kitchen table, pointing out the field to the farmer. He said something to his wife – about a rope? – and they discussed it briefly.

The woman turned to Della and said, 'He do later. Take you now. To Douai.'

Della followed them out into the yard where the girls were still hopping about. They came running up to Della, and their mother told them the lady was going now. The younger one's face fell and she looked about to cry, while the older one threw her arms around Della, just avoiding crushing her poor right arm in the process.

'*Vous-allez voler à la lune?*' asked the serious little face. *Are you going to fly to the moon?*

'*Non, ma petite,*' said Della, smiling. '*Je vais trouver mon mari.*'

The girls looked most disappointed; obviously the moon was much more interesting than a husband.

'Goodbye,' said the woman, holding out her right hand to Della's left, so they could briefly clasp hands. 'If no luck, come back here.'

'Thank you so much,' said Della. Then she realised that through all the business of meeting this family and receiving their help, no personal details had been swapped, not even their names. Before turning towards the husband and his truck, into which he was climbing, she said to the woman, 'My name is Della. What's yours?'

She pointed to her family in turn. 'Louisa. Ricard. Mimi and Gabrielle. Good luck, Della.'

Della was right in supposing Ricard did not speak English. He was inscrutable behind that slate-grey moustache. His daughters' dark eyes were his, and now and again he'd turn them on her edgily. *It's so good of them to do this*, Della thought. To help Dud and now her. And she guessed there would be nameless danger to them and their family if they were caught. But perhaps it was one in the eye for their so-called conquerors, and they looked forward to the day when the British and their allies might chuck the Germans out.

It was mid-morning and the town of Douai was busy with market day. It was a pretty place, with smart buildings of light stone facing a waterway that cut serenely through the town. Ricard made his way through the traffic of horses and carts, wagons and omnibuses, and here and there pairs or groups of German soldiers, in a truck or on the street, walking in groups or riding horses lazily down the streets in pairs. Della tried not to look, but couldn't resist staring at these exotic creatures, real life Huns. In England, they were a thing of legend, only seen in POW uniforms building roads or such-like. Here they were in their element, in full uniform, the satisfied interlopers on occupied territory, with high collars and caps perched conceitedly on their heads. She looked away though, not wanting to attract any attention from such as them.

Ricard turned down a side street and pulled up outside a row of shops, a grocer, a baker and so forth, ending with a blacksmith's forge. He got down from the truck and Della followed him around the back of a furniture shop. She found herself in a yard cluttered with old bits of chairs and tables and armoires and an ottoman. Ricard knocked on the back door and they waited. It took a while, but eventually there was movement within and the door opened. A man, older than Ricard with salt and pepper hair and round glasses, stepped aside to let Ricard in, then he spotted Della and said something urgent in French, standing in the doorway so she couldn't pass. Ricard answered gruffly – Della still couldn't penetrate his accent – and the man peered at Della's arm in the sling, then at her face. She smiled nervously, clutching at her handbag in her left hand. She didn't know who this man was or what part he played but she hoped he could lead her to Dud, so she was desperate to please him.

'*Bonjour monsieur*,' she said and smiled again, too wide.

More discussion between the men and finally the older one stepped back and Della was allowed passage into the house.

They went into a workshop suffused with the scents of sawdust and varnish.

Ricard and the man were talking again, the man pointing upwards and shaking his head.

'*Excusez-moi,*' Della said, losing patience. '*Avez-vous vu mon mari?*' She put down her handbag on a bench, retrieved Dud's photo from her pocket and passed it to the man.

'*Oui, oui,*' said the man irritably. '*Il était là. Mais il est parti.*'

'*Párti?*'

'*Oui, ce matin. Il est parti. Disparu.*'

Disappeared? Has Dud disappeared?

'*Disparu?*'

The man said something like 'Gah!' or some such French sign of exasperation and rolled his eyes. Then he spoke louder, as if she were hard of hearing, not merely a bad speaker of his language.

'*Il est allé à la gare. La gare. Ce matin. La gare?*' Then he started puffing and whistling. Della stared at him dumbfounded.

Ricard started to chuckle and Della cursed her basic French. He added, '*Chemin de fer.*' Then he crooned, 'Choo-oo, choo-oo.'

The railway station! '*Ah, oui! La gare!*' she cried and the men clapped each other on the back, laughing with relief. But he might have boarded the train and gone by now. She tried to think of verbs and tenses in her head, but nothing came, so she said it the simplest way she could. 'Destination? Terminus?'

'*Lille. Et puis l'omnibus à Tournai. Et après à Bruges,*' said the older man.

So, Dud would have needed the train to Lille. She had to get to that railway station as soon as she could.

'*Ricard, s'il vous plaît. Vite! A la gare. Tout de suite!*' All politeness had gone out of the window. She had to get to the railway station now.

'*Bien, bien,*' muttered Ricard and swapped obscure quips with the other man before ushering Della out of the back door into the yard.

She turned back to the door to see the man standing on the doorstep, watching her go.

'*Merci beaucoup,*' she said.

'*Je vous en prie,*' he answered, very courteously, a crooked smile on his face. '*Bonne chance!*'

Ricard held the truck door open for Della. She climbed in and they made their way through the infuriatingly slow market traffic to the railway station. Ricard was trying to explain something to her about the railway line, but she couldn't understand much. It was something to do with the line being bombed. It sounded as if Dud would have had to get the train a short way and thereafter take a bus, or walk, or find some other way to get to Belgium. At least, she thought that's what Ricard was saying. His voice was so deep, his accent so thick, she had to guess much of it, but she said '*Oui*' a lot and they got by.

He drew up outside the station building and got out, coming to open the door for her. He spoke at length again, pointed back in the direction they came. She guessed he was saying that if she needed to come back she should go to the furniture man's house, and he would get her to their farm. He said something about her aeroplane. He was assuming she understood every word. If only she could. But she was desperate to get into the railway station and she took his hand with her left and squeezed it.

'*Merci beaucoup, Ricard,*' she said and he looked at her hand holding his with something akin to shock, then patted it. A kind though guarded man, she thought.

She turned and ran through the archway into the station before remembering her decorum and slowing down, so as not to attract attention. Her arm in a sling was sign enough of her oddity and she reminded herself to blend in more.

There were plenty of people milling around. As she went out onto the platform, she was horrified to see on the opposite platform, across the tracks, a throng of German troops, lolling about all over the place. She felt sick, but knew she had to hold herself together and act as normally as possible. There was someone in a peaked cap, not military. It must be the guard. She approached him and asked, as simply as she could, to avoid speaking French, to avoid being rumbled as English: '*Lille?*'

'*Il est parti il y a dix minutes, mademoiselle. Le prochain train est en deux heures.*'

'*Merci.*' She walked down the platform, hiding her forlorn disappointment. It was gone lunchtime and the furniture man said Dud had gone that morning. He had surely caught a train and gone hours ago. So, the last train to Lille left ten minutes ago and the next was in two hours. There was nothing she could do but wait for it. And when she got to Lille? She'd have to follow the route the furniture man had relayed: from Lille to Tournai, then Bruges. And Dud was hours ahead of her. So where would he be by now? If by some chance he'd been delayed at a station on the way, she might spot him. There was that chance. She recalled what Jim had said, that another RFC pilot had asked the French to help and they always had. She could ask a guard at Tournai, once they were away from all these German soldiers,'Have you seen this man?' The alternative was going back to the farmhouse and then going home alone. Never. There was no other choice. Onwards, to Lille.

She went back to the ticket office and mutely paid for the journey to Lille. Back on the platform, she sat down on a bench. Spread out before her, all along the opposite platform, was the mass of troops. They wore rumpled greenish-grey uniforms with a row of dull metal buttons down the front, rounded collars and helmets, puttees or brown boots; attached to their belts and shoulder straps were a collection of war necessities, rifle, water bottle, spade. Many had thick moustaches just like an Englishman and others had shaved their beards to look like the beard of a tidy goat. Lolling around in a very unmartial fashion, they looked, frankly, exhausted. Some were talking, many were smoking cigarettes and flicking the butts onto the railway line. The sound of their language hacked through the spring air. Harsh it was, and blunt. Nothing like the soft tones of Melli Beese and her compatriots at her airfield in 1913. The melody and lilt of that German was nowhere to be heard here, only the hard-edged blocks of soldierese. She suspected a foreigner listening to a bunch of British soldiers would hear the same kind of thing, though. The nature of the beast.

Watching them drew their interest to her, so she looked away. A look-see confirmed that two were still staring and commenting on her, appraising her. Her palms felt clammy and she swallowed to try to clear the lump in her throat. The French people waiting on her side were nervous too, muttering and deliberately looking away from the opposite side. A yappy dog was barking furiously along her platform, and somewhere beyond someone was coughing. Some of the soldiers, with nothing else to do, were mocking them, aping the sounds of the yappy dog and the coughing, like bored, cruel children.

The guard came back from some errand and began to stroll up the platform in her direction. She wondered if she should ask him if there had been a man fitting Dud's description on the last train to Lille, but she couldn't get the French vocab right in her head; she feared she'd come across as obviously English and she couldn't trust the guard not to comment on it and draw attention to herself.

The two interested soldiers were still staring at her, now whistling a folk tune together as if it were a peculiar serenade. She stood up slowly and walked further down the platform. Then a German voice called out. She looked round, everyone did. A soldier was calling to her, *Fräulein! Fräulein!* The other was saying something rude about her arm in its sling; she was sure of this as others around him were laughing and nudging each other, looking in her direction, making strange hand gestures. Her face turned beetroot. What would they do? What should she do? She didn't have long to wonder, as the sound of a train puffing into the station on the opposite platform gave her the answer: the train to Paris, as the guard's call confirmed. Thank God. The rabble of soldiers shuffled forward, some getting to their feet, picking up discarded bags and other clutter and shoving to get to the train. Her two admirers lost interest immediately, thinking of their seats, a bit of warmth and sleep, perhaps. Not one French passenger shared the platform with them, so they'd have the train to themselves.

Her relief drained through her and she sat down again on another bench, closer to the sounds of the yapping dog and the coughing. She looked down the platform to see where the sounds were coming from. But she could not see the dog or whoever was coughing, poor sod, only some wooden huts. Perhaps they were behind those. As the Paris train continued to fill with soldiers, their German complaints and chatter filling the air, something compelled her to stand and stroll speculatively down the platform. She walked towards the huts, four of them, each with a man-sized gap between. After the first was a couple kissing. After the next was a woman with the yappy dog, which was straining at its lead, barking its French head off at the enemy boarding the train opposite while its owner leaned against the side of the hut, reading a newspaper. From after the third hut came the sound of the coughing man, a tall figure bent double with his affliction, dressed in grey trousers and a jacket clearly too short for his long arms and legs; his socks and white wrists were exposed as he crouched down, trying to contain himself, gasping. He stood up, recovered himself and looked at her.

25

Her husband was staring at her, recovering from his coughing fit; his mouth gaped, then turned into a smile. She took the steps towards him in a tumble and then they were pressed together, kissing each other's faces and hair and holding on for dear life. The Germans were leaning out of the train window, shouting at them. Whooping and laughing. Drawing attention. Della looked cautiously round and saw one making an obscene gesture, before she turned her face back and buried it again into Dud's shoulder. The noise of the Paris train departing covered their whisperings and tears, their joy and relief. It was an awkward embrace, due to her strapped arm, but the intensity was overwhelming. She nearly fell with the weight of him leaning into her, his height enveloping her, his love and hers flooding through them both.

'Darling,' he murmured over and over as he pressed his cheek into her hair. 'Are you here? Are you real?' He had stopped coughing altogether, as if the touch of his wife had cured him.

She whispered. She didn't want the locals to hear them conversing in English. 'Don't speak.' The soldiers were gone, but who knew which of the French you could trust? They couldn't all be loyal, not every single one. And now she'd found him, she wasn't going to take the slightest chance.

But he wasn't so cautious. He asked her, whispering hoarsely into her ear, 'How are you here? How on earth did you get here?'

'I flew, of course. Now, shush. We must get out of here.'

They pulled themselves together and Della surfaced to survey the platform, noticed the guard watching them curiously from the other end. Dud looked at her strapped arm and nodded at it, concerned. She nodded back, reassuringly. She kissed him on the cheek and he coughed again. Not cured then, of course not. But improved. They turned and walked to the entrance. One glance told her the guard had lost interest. Just another emotional wartime couple at a railway station. There must be thousands of those, all over Europe. She reached up and said into his ear, 'Back to the furniture shop.'

They walked without speaking, Dud beside the road, flanking her from it, protecting her in the only way he could. Her left hand was in his right, entwining, clutching and speaking their own manual language. It was a sunny day, the town bustling with market traffic and goodwill. When they found the street and passed the forge, the blacksmith's fire glowed at them and Della felt a blast of heat. As they arrived at the shop, she saw that Ricard's truck was parked outside; he must not have gone home yet, must have gone back to his friend the furniture maker. He would be able to bring them back to the farm, she guessed. The world helped them, or that's how it felt to Della, walking through Douai with her beloved. They squeezed hands again as they went around the back. A knock on the door brought the same man, who smiled at Dud like an old friend and let them in to find Ricard still there.

Della prepared herself for some excruciating back and forth in her bad French, but Dud cleared his throat and launched into a long string of French, shaking hands with both men and laughing, as if they'd all known each other since childhood – indeed, as if Dud had been born next door to them.

She stared at him and he grinned. 'Schoolboy French,' he said, modestly.

The men all talked away – well, mostly Dud and the furniture man, who Della now learned was called Xavier.

He was surprisingly chatty now he had someone to really talk to, while Ricard was happy to listen and add the odd pithy remark. Dud was explaining what had happened at the station, she caught that much. She tried to keep up, but mainly she was content to marvel at this talent of her husband's, another that he hadn't fully revealed to her before, another testament to his modesty. Then he said something about her, put his arm around her and said, '*Elle est un merveilleux pilote! Le meilleur!*' She understood that. Oh, to get out of this stuffy workshop and be alone with him, so they could talk at last, in their own tongue; to be alone with him. She was greedy for him and had run out of patience. But she was too happy to break the cheerful mood, and waited for the men to finish chatting. She basked in Dud's voice – husky and punctuated by his recurring cough but mellifluous and charming speaking in French.

Before long, Ricard suggested they go. Della was pleased. Lots of *merci beaucoup* and hand-shaking with Xavier and they were finally out of there and into Ricard's truck, Della and Dud shoved up on the bench seat beside Ricard, Dud in the middle so her bad arm wasn't squashed against him. Ricard was not a talker; he seemed content to drive and at last, Della and Dud could speak.

Dud began with the thing he was clearly most worried about. 'How is your arm, darling? What happened to it? Is it serious?'

She explained and gave an account of her Channel crossing and the crash landing, of Ronnie's marvellous Blackburn, and Jim's visit before that, of the telegram from the War Office that began it all. Dud listened incredulously, but beaming with pride.

'My wife, my wonderful wife,' he said in awe. 'I should be angry with you, for risking yourself like that. I am angry with you, furious. But bloody hell, Del, I'm so proud too! And I cannot believe you'd do such a thing for me.'

Della hesitated, embarrassed, glancing at Ricard, but then she remembered he couldn't speak English.

'I'd do anything for you, darling.'

He kissed her on the mouth. He clearly didn't care about Ricard's presence. After all, who cares really? It was war and the times were extraordinary. She kissed him back and was lost for a while. Oh, that moment, when he had stood up and she could see that it was him, his lovely face, his astonished eyes. He had looked wraithlike, but the second he'd realised she was really there, the smile that had spread across his face was thoroughly beautiful.

'Why were you still at the station?' she asked. 'Why hadn't you got the train to Lille?'

'There were too many Hun around. Not just that lot going to Paris, but another crowd of them going to Lille, before you arrived. I couldn't risk it, being stuck on the train with them. So I hung around for the next one, hoping they'd have all gone by then.'

'If they hadn't been there, I'd've missed you!'

'Thank God for the bloody Hun!' Dud cried, then coughed, then laughed, then coughed again.

'It's bad, isn't it?' she said.

'Yes, pretty awful.' He sighed.

Ricard was turning into the lane that led to his farm.

'We're going to get you home,' she said to Dud, and reaching over with her good hand, she patted his leg and listened to him coughing again. Hearing it was distressing, but she was relieved he wasn't worse than he was. After all, with her arm in a sling, it'd be Dud flying them back to England.

There were more cheerful reunions inside the farmhouse, with the family's regard for Dud shining through clearly. Everyone was delighted with Della for finding him. There was an overwhelming glow of goodwill radiating from every member of the house, that these two English people had found each other. There was talk and more hand-shaking, and the girls jumped up and down at Dud, the tall Englishman who chucked their chins and made them giggle. Then he started coughing and couldn't stop. Della rubbed his back.

'Too much talking,' she said. 'Too much excitement.'

Louisa said, 'Come upstairs. We have a room, a bed. Small but you can share. He needs rest.'

They followed her up the steep, uneven wooden staircase to a simple yet immaculate guest room at the top.

'I bring medicine. Bed for him.'

Dud lay down on the bed, his arm flung across his brow, clearly shattered. Della heard the sound of a horse neighing below the window and the clucking of hens rose up from the yard. She realised how exhausted she was herself and sank down onto a carved wooden chair beside the bed, reaching across to hold his other hand. Louisa brought more of her white powder dissolved in water, which Dud downed sleepily in one. Louisa returned soon after to fetch the glass and gave Dud a new, steaming concoction. It smelt of apples and something alcoholic, and had a teaspoon of honey resting across the top, which she stirred in before putting the mug on the bedside table.

'Drink slowly,' she advised, miming a sip, and went to leave the room, taking the spoon with her and giving it a quick lick as she went.

Della called out, 'My aeroplane! It's still in the field. Can I go with Ricard and—'

'Shush, shush,' replied Louisa. 'Ricard has gone. You stay, rest. He will find it.'

'Oh, thank you,' she said and Louisa shut the door behind her.

Della looked back to see Dud unmoving, eyes closed, his chest rising and falling with a faint wheeze. She touched the mug but it was too hot to drink just yet, so she left it on the bedside table and sat watching Dud while he drifted into sleep, squeezing his hand as he did so, until he was far gone and his clammy hand went limp. Della watched him sleep and worried. She heard the chickens clucking alarmingly outside and looked out through the window to the yard. There, Louisa took a bird from the pen and in one swift, sure movement wrung its neck.

Della realised how stiff her arm was. She removed the sling and stretched out her arm, biting her lip to stop herself yelping at the pain. She curled up beside Dud on the narrow bed. But sleep did not come easily, as she found her body could not fully relax, her wrist aching and making it impossible to get into a comfortable position. But mostly she was kept awake by anxiety, fearful of Dud's condition, exhausted yet still operating on fight or flight energy coursing through her blood.

At some point the rustic cooking scent of chicken soup or stew from some delectable French recipe wafted up the stairs and wrapped them in comfort. Memories of Mam's pies and Puck's dead rabbits unfurled in her mind and sleep finally came, bringing with it dreams of home and family, tinged with anxiety; dreams of the pier burning down, the flames eating the sky and the sound of crackling wood and timber collapsing. She woke with a shock.

Louisa stood beside the bed, looking at the hot drink Dud hadn't drunk, now cold, clucking with disapproval. 'This is very good for his cough. Settle it. Must drink. I make more later,' she said. 'Come and eat now.'

Dud stirred and Della kissed him awake. They rubbed their eyes and helped each other up, he with his bad chest and she with her bad arm. 'We're quite a pair,' he said, smiling sadly.

Louisa had cooked up the chicken with onions, potatoes and pearl barley into a thick broth, nourishing and delicious. They all ate at the table, Della watching with some envy as Dud talked in French to the girls, teasing them gently. As promised, Louisa gave Dud more of the hot drink and he sipped it, remarking how soothing it was. His cough did ease, almost immediately.

'Thank you so much,' said Della to Louisa. And she tried to help her clear up, but Louisa wouldn't hear of it, even seemed offended, and said they should go back and get a good night's sleep now.

'But we should talk and make plans,' said Della to Louisa and Dud agreed, adding, 'The longer we're here, the more danger there is for you and your family.'

Louisa regarded her daughters, sitting on a rug on the floor beside the fire, playing with a rag doll. 'We will talk in morning. Don't worry. Sleep now. Rest. Goodnight.'

In the morning, after a wash and a filling eggy breakfast, Dud, Della and Louisa drank coffee around the table and talked.

'As I see it,' said Dud, 'we have two choices. Go on to Belgium and Holland and get back to England that way, or try to fix the aeroplane and fly it back across the Channel.'

'We could fly you across the line and land in our territory. Then you could go back to your squadron,' said Della. But she said it only because she thought it was their duty, not because she wanted it herself. She knew that she'd have to find her own way home by alternative transport; this wasn't too onerous an idea, but a worse one was that her ill husband, her beloved, would be back with his squadron, back on the front line. And she loathed the thought of that.

'No, that's not advisable,' answered Dud. 'We may well be shot down or even attacked by RFC pilots if we try to land on our side. And also you'd be in a lot of trouble, my darling, as a civilian flying illegally in wartime. You may even be arrested. I'm not risking that.'

Della shook her head. 'I don't think there is a choice then. You're too ill to be tramping through Europe. We must try to get the aeroplane home.'

Louisa said, 'I agree with her. Too ill. You are bad here, resting. But in cold, out there, for maybe weeks. It will kill you.'

That sobering thought silenced them, allowing the sound of the girls singing a nursery rhyme outside to drift into the kitchen.

'The only thing is, Dud, because of my arm, you'd need to fly the Blackburn. Do you feel well enough for that?'

'Absolutely, absolutely,' said Dud, unconvincingly; but then, there was no safe alternative and it was better to be positive than not. 'The aeroplane it is. What's up with it?'

'I think it's a fuel leak. We'd need to check, but I suspect the pipe is split.'

'Let's go and have a look then.'

They went to the barn with the hole in its roof, where the Blackburn had been towed by Ricard the day before when they'd been sleeping.

Dud knew his SE5 well, of course, but the Blackburn was Della's territory. Yet with her right arm still in its sling, they had to work as a team, something they were well suited to. Della instructed him and he followed her, no questions, no pride, no argument.

'There's the access panel. Open that up and let's see that fuel pipe.'

It was a little square door beneath the right wing. What she didn't want to see was a split in the pipe. If there was one, they'd have to improvise a repair; they'd need to find rubber tubing and some sort of clip to hold it on. Or perhaps it could be secured with wire; but whether or not it'd last across the Channel was the question. What she'd rather see was a simple connection problem. Dud opened the panel and she crossed the fingers of her left hand, held her breath and peered inside.

'Thank God for that,' she said.

'I see it,' said Dudley. 'That large nut there.'

'That's it. It's the fitting for the fine adjustment valve. It just needs screwing back on to connect the valve to the carburettor. Then we're back in business. I'll get my tools. They're in my bag.'

As she stood up to leave the barn, Dud called, 'But what about fuel? You'll have lost quite a bit with that leak. There won't be enough.'

'Fancy a walk with the girls?' she replied, smiling. After Dud screwed the connection back on, they took the girls on a stroll across the fields to the place where she'd landed. There, beneath the seventh tree along, Della asked Dud to tell the girls there was treasure. They scrabbled around and found the petrol can, still intact. A little cheer went up and the girls fought over who would carry the treasure back to the farm, getting their hands and skirts filthy in the process, for which Della reminded herself she must apologise to their mother when they got back. The can would be far too heavy for the girls to carry anyway, which Dud told them; then he made them giggle as he made a great show of hauling it up as if it were the weight of an elephant. It was a warm spring day, the second of April, and there were clumps of purple hellebores and tiny jonquils in the woodland patches they walked by. Here in the French countryside there seemed to be no war, but the night before she had been woken by the distant boom-boom of guns on the front line and that morning they'd heard the whine of a flock of German aeroplanes nearby, perhaps going on patrol. Other than that, the fields and flowers and even these girls were unaffected by the horrors of what was going on in the trenches only a few miles away. It felt impossible that not far across this rolling countryside was the place where thousands of men were blowing each other to pieces, the site of Puck's death and of who knew what had happened to Dud in that trench that sent him mad.

'It's so quiet here,' said Della as they walked.

'Not for long, I bet.'

'Why do you say that?'

'If the Germans retreat, which we hope they will soon, of course, this whole area and Douai itself will be in their direct path. I fear they'll sack it as they go. There won't be much left if they do.'

Della was horrified. What about Louisa and Ricard, the girls? And Xavier and his furniture?

'Do they know, our friends?'

'Yes, of course. But there isn't anything they can do. They just have to wait and see.'

They walked the rest of the way in silence, watching the girls ahead frolicking. Della couldn't stop thinking of what might happen to them, and it made her feel desperate to leave as soon as they could, yet horribly guilty for leaving these good people to their fate. But what choice did they have? Two English pilots with an illegally flown aeroplane, a bad chest and a sprained wrist? No good to anyone – hardly even to themselves.

The weather was still and fine, and if it held, they decided, they must try to fly home the very next day. There was no advantage to staying; Della's wrist might improve but it would take days before it'd be strong enough to fly with, and Dud's cough may well worsen in that time. And, of course, the longer they stayed at the farm, the more danger they put the family in if they were caught. This family's future was uncertain enough as it was. Della and Dud wanted to spare them what trouble they could, when they could. They told Louisa and she agreed, making them a parcel of food to take and helping Della lay out her flying clothes, which she'd cleaned so well the day before. *In another life we could have been friends*, thought Della, and yet she didn't know how to convey this to Louisa, with her tired face and thin arms, always on the move, always busy around the house and with the girls. Maybe she felt that way too, or maybe she was too tired, too worried to care about friendship.

Della and Dud spent the afternoon preparing the Blackburn, checking the oil level, filling the fuel tank, scanning every inch of linen and wire, tightening all the nuts, just in case. They packed what they could into the cockpit and passenger seat.

With no uniform or other insulating clothes to fly in, Ricard gave Dud some long johns (too short but better than nothing), a thick winter coat and scarf, a pair of leather gloves (his best ones, Louisa said); and they had the two pairs of goggles, one each, newly polished up by the girls. That would have to do. By the evening they were worn out and so went to bed early. They felt well enough to enjoy their bed together and make love, a careful, tender love to protect Della's arm. Afterwards, they lay in bed talking about things. Della was nervous yet excited about the prospect of flying home. After all, the Blackburn – any aircraft – was her element, one that had been absent from her life for so long that she was eager for any excuse to climb back in. She went over the navigation and some of the landmarks they'd see, then talked Dud through the idiosyncrasies of the Blackburn and how it responded in different conditions, while Dud lay listening, staring at the ceiling.

'You all right?' she asked, after a pause.

He sighed, then looked at her, his eyes wide, studying her face. She knew that look and it frightened her. She'd seen it in the hospital.

'You shouldn't be here,' he said and looked away.

'Course I should. Don't you want me here?'

'No. I don't. I want you safe in your mam's house in Cleethorpes. You shouldn't be here in danger, surrounded by the whole German army.'

'Well, I am,' said Della, kissing his shoulder. 'And there's nothing you can—'

'I'm not joking,' he said sternly. She sat up, naked, staring at him. He coughed, then cursed, 'Fucking chest, weak chest.'

She reached out to touch him. 'We just need to get you—'

'We?' he said. '*We* shouldn't be doing anything. I should be back with my squadron and you should be in England. This is all wrong. And it's all because of me, because of my weakness.'

'That's nonsense.'

'No it's not! It's not the natural order of things. Wives shouldn't be rescuing husbands. If I'd been stronger, you'd never have thought of coming here. You wouldn't have felt you needed to.'

'It's not your fault.'

'Of course it is. Who else's?'

'The war's.' She remembered Ronnie's words to her. 'The war is responsible.' She thought of Melli Beese and her friends, her family. They couldn't be all bad, all enemy Huns. 'I don't even blame the Germans, not all of them. If anyone, I blame the leaders who brought us into this, who made this war. The war is to blame, for Puck's death. For nearly killing you, for your cough, for what put you in hospital, for everything that's happened to you in the air, in that trench.'

Dud's hands went to his eyes and he groaned, rubbing his eyes and hiding his face from her.

'I'm sorry, darling,' she said. 'I didn't mean to—'

'There was this pal of mine,' said Dud behind his hands, almost under his breath. She leaned closer. 'We'd done some sniper training together when I was first out there. He was Canadian. A horseman. We used to talk about horses – whenever we could, we'd get together and talk about horses. He knew all about them. Whenever he could, he'd go out to his cousin's farm on the prairies back home in Canada and work with their horses. He had this method of training he told me about. No whips, no cruelty, nothing medieval. All through trust and gentleness, getting the horses to feel no fear and want to ride with you and bond with you. One of the things we hated most about war: all the dead horses. He was the most peaceful soul I ever met. His name was MacNeill. Matthew MacNeill. One morning, early, just past dawn, the KOYLI and others were advancing. We'd captured a German trench. I ran down it and so did he. We bumped into each other and laughed. We couldn't believe it. We'd both got separated from the rest of our lads and then—'

Dud stopped to clear his throat, swallowed it down and sighed deeply. 'A shell came whistling over. He pushed me down and threw himself on top of me. It blew his legs off. He lay in my lap for a long time. I don't know how long. We were cut off from the others, so we were all alone there. I stayed with him while he died, slowly. Terrible sounds he made, over and over, with every breath. The most terrible sounds I'd ever heard. I've heard rabbits screaming when they've been shot. I've heard dying birds in my garden tortured by our cat. I've heard men call out in no-man's-land begging to be finished off. But I'd never heard a sound like this in my life. I can't even describe it. It was . . . blackness. Hollow. Like all the pain in the world had been squeezed down into one awful cry and let loose one breath at a time. I listened to him till he died. I couldn't even speak. I couldn't speak to him when he was dying. I'd lost my voice. Something took it away. I couldn't tell him it was all right, that I was there, that his friend was there. I couldn't ask him if he wanted to give a message to his family, his girl. I couldn't talk to him about his horses. I couldn't give him that peace. I crawled away from him and hid around the corner. I couldn't bear to look at him. I left him alone, all alone. I let him down. I let him down.'

Dud was crying behind his hands, the tears seeping out between his fingers, his nose wreathed in snot. He turned over to hide his face and coughed up phlegm and wiped it on the pillowcase. All the time, Della watched him and wanted to touch him, but felt it was very important he should not be disturbed, not be stopped or distracted in any way.

'I'm sorry, darling,' he said, looking at the grey smear on the bedding, turning the pillow over to hide it. She took this as a cue to touch him and he gathered her into him, taking delicate care over her arm and ensuring she could lie against him comfortably. They lay like that for a time.

Then she said, 'I'm so glad you told me.'

'Me too,' he whispered and clutched her tighter.

'Can I say something now?'

'Yes, of course,' he said and kissed her hair.

She extricated herself and sat up, looking down on him.

'You said it wasn't the natural order of things, for me to be here looking for you. Well, I say, there's nothing natural about war. It's the most unnatural thing there is. But then, what is natural anyway? Fish swim and birds fly. And now people fly. Betty told me the Wright brothers were mocked for trying it, that it wasn't natural, that if God had meant men to fly He'd have given them wings. But we made our own. And then it wasn't just men who could fly, but women too. I've lost count of how many times I've been told a woman can't fly, that it's not *natural* for her to do it. I say, the whole business of flying is unnatural, it's madness really, when you think of it. What did you say to me, all those years ago? It's preposterous? You're right. So is this war and everything it does to people. One day it'll end and the madness will end too. I say we decide what's natural, what isn't. In a world gone mad, we make our own sense of it. We're a partnership, you and me. Through thick and thin, for richer or poorer, in sickness and in health, and all that. You love me, I love you. You help me, I help you. We're equal and we always were and always will be.'

Dud was watching her with great seriousness.

'I'm so lucky to have you,' he said, touching her face.

'And I'm so lucky too. Listen, remember what you told me, how you used to talk to Calcraft at night? You'd lie awake worrying, then call out to each other in the darkness and light a candle. And then dawn would come. A new day. Well, that's what we have, you and me. I've felt very alone at times in my life. I've lain awake at night wrapped in myself, watched my sisters go off and make a life, and hurt inside at my loneliness. And I know you feel the same way. I know you've felt very alone in your life.'

She thought of the boy on the beach, on holiday, wandering about on his own. His mother dying to give him life. His tall, serious father, kind but no companion. That clever, thoughtful boy reading *The Aero*, tending the horses, planting sweet peas, alone.

'I'd always felt different,' she went on, 'always the odd one out. The disappointment. Flying helped, gave me a purpose. But I was still alone inside. When I found you, that loneliness disappeared for the first time in my life. I wasn't going to give that up. I wasn't going to lose you. I'd do anything to keep it. I know you would too. And we've found each other now. We can be each other's candle in the darkness.'

Hark at me, she thought. *Making speeches. Who'd have thought it?* But love made her eloquent, Dudley Willow brought it out in her, brought out the best in her.

'You're not daft,' he said and smiled that nice smile of his. Dud was back, from the brink. She snuggled back down beside him and, wrapped in each other, there were no more words. They slept till the cock's crow woke them at dawn.

It was time to go. Ricard had taken the Blackburn to one of his fields. With no rain for the past two days, the mud had dried up. It wasn't ideal for taking off, but it was flat enough and dry enough to make a go of it. It wasn't a huge field and Della was worried there wouldn't be enough room to get into the air before the trees that bounded it at the far end, but Dud looked at it once and said it'd be fine, that he was rather good at take-offs.

When Della and Dud were all dressed up in suitable clothes and ready to go, they stood at the porch, unwilling to muddy Louisa's clean floors with their mucky boots, and said farewell to the girls, who cried their hearts out. Della turned to Louisa and pressed into her hand the wad of francs she'd been given for the trip and not yet used up. Louisa shook her head fiercely – no, she wouldn't take it – but Della insisted, pressing

harder and saying, 'I won't need it. You will. Please, please
take it.' She wanted to add *And go, go away from here and find
a safe place, away from the German retreat, if it comes.* But there
was no use. These good people had their home and their land,
their farm, their family. They would make the decision when
the time came. Perhaps the money would help them.

They left Louisa and the girls behind and walked with
Ricard to the field. Dud and Ricard were talking. From Dud's
arm movements and her basic French, Della surmised that
her husband was giving instructions on how they needed
Ricard to hang on to the back of the machine once they'd
got it going. Dud gave him a firm handshake, then he coughed
into his hand and apologised, coughing again. His chest was
bad in this cold air. Della feared how it would be after two
hours flying in the freezing thin air up there. Well, the alternative was weeks or months on the run. There was no alternative. So, they'd better get on with it.

Della climbed aboard, into the front seat. Dud primed the
engine and swung the prop to get her started, while Ricard
stood behind holding on. Dud clambered into the seat behind
Della and lifted his arm, then dropped it and Ricard did just
as he'd been told and let go. Then they were bumping along
the rutted field and heading for the trees that edged it, Della
gasping as Dud pulled up just in time to swoop above them
and head up gradually above the fields to the free sky. *He
really is brilliant at take-offs,* she thought. She tried to look
back to wave at Ricard but could see no sign of him. *Goodbye.*

They headed north-west and she prayed they'd come across
no patrols. They both knew that their biggest danger was not
the aeroplane itself going wrong, or the weather turning against
them, but coming up against another aeroplane, of whatever
nationality; without any markings or roundels on the Blackburn,
they would be a target for any gun. And any aircraft that
spotted them could outrun them in a second, with this old
bird flying at 60 mph max and some these days flying at three

times that speed. Della scoured the skies all round for a sight of one, at the same time pointing out the direction Dud should fly in according to her navigation. She was so busy searching for other aircraft, she didn't notice the *Whoof!* and *Blupp!* until she saw a puff of what looked like cloud appear close beneath their left wing. Archie! Good God, they were being shot at.

'Fucking hell!' she shouted and swivelled round to gape at Dud, who swiftly wrenched the wheel and rolled over to the right. 'It's not made for it!' she screamed at him uselessly behind her scarf, her voice lost in the roar of wind and engine. He was used to his state-of-the-art SE5, not this old thing. But the Blackburn held true and Dud handled her serenely, bringing her higher, out of reach of the anti-aircraft fire – probably one of their own shooting at them – until they were flying safely at a height where no one on the ground had a hope of reaching them. Of course, that made it even colder and when she turned round to look at him from time to time, and though most of his face was wrapped in Ricard's scarf, she could tell he was coughing; she saw his body shudder with it.

She was too busy map-reading, checking on Dud and worrying about enemies of the sky to do more than take a brief survey of the great scar of the Western Front gashed across the landscape below them as they passed. It impressed itself on her deeply though; it seemed to cut through her own sense of history – something was happening here that would be remembered forever, if not by people, then by the land itself; forever marked in the height of crops, if life ever came back to this wasteland. Pilots would know it, even if those on the ground came to forget the dead of this great war.

Now they were high up and scot-free, flying north-west towards Calais. Below them, Della looked at the land. She'd not seen much on her way in, due to the fog patches and spending much of her time studying the compass and looking for the canal near Douai. Here there lay green countryside broken by village after village in ruins, miles and miles of them. Here was the brunt of the bombardments, the cost of war on the ground: the homes and town halls and shops and churches reduced to the rubble that had built them, like towns of sandcastles, shored up with pebbles, kicked and trodden underfoot by a great beach bully. Streets and streets of trampled buildings, only a frontage here or there left standing, its windows blank and empty, affording no view outside but ruin and no room inside, only air where a room once stood.

Will they rebuild all this, thought Della, *or leave it as a monument to the millions of dead buried in the mud all over Europe?* Somewhere in all that were Puck's bones. She nodded to them, to her brother, wherever he was. Ahead lay Calais, and the welcoming sea.

Flying over water was disorientating and deadly dull. Della had to keep her wits about her to navigate them straight and true to Dover. No fog today, thank heavens, but there was a bit of wind, which buffeted the Blackburn from side to side. Della tried to stop herself looking back at Dud all the time, every time something threatened them, in case he thought she had no faith in him. But it wasn't that. She just wanted the sight of him, as a gift to cheer her, keep her going. Behind his goggles and scarf, she could not see his lovely smile. But something in the way he held his head told her that when she did look round at him, he always smiled at her.

They made excellent time. By the time the good people of Dover were rousing themselves to go back to work after the Easter celebrations this day, the third of April 1918, Della and Dudley Willow were flying over the white cliffs, circling neatly over the castle, and coming into land on the meadow at Whitfield. Against all the bloody odds. England. Home.

EPILOGUE

1922

The wide blue skies of the Saskatchewan prairies reminded her of home. From the ground, the green and yellow acres – prairie grass and rapeseed crops – spread flatly out like an augmented version of Lincolnshire, the land rising and falling like the Wolds but so much larger and grander, infinitely more room to stretch your wings. From the air, everything is flattened and, if she squinted, she could imagine herself over the Lincolnshire plains – if you took her home county and cubed it, added forests and lakes and sand dunes, but left it land-locked. She missed the sea, that was true. But Canada won hands down for space. The littleness of England – its condensed wildernesses, its cramped, friendly towns and pocket villages – was exploded here and mile upon mile of open country lay ahead for the pilot or horse rider alike, for her and for Dud. They'd made their plans in a spirit of post-war optimism: for him, it meant a place to train horses in peace and room to breathe. For her, it meant great stretches of space between homesteads begging for an efficient way to get their letters and packages from one marooned place to another: airmail.

Canada was going to be the heaven they sought after the hell of the Great War. Dud's reward for the mud and blood, the dead horses and flaming aircraft. Della's dream, of flying for a living, of freedom yet a way to be useful, to earn a living in the air and provide for her family, her new fledgling family. The seeds of it were sown by a conversation on Cleethorpes beach on Armistice Day in 1918 (they avoided the street celebrations; it just felt plain wrong), looking out at the restless sea. They were talking of Dud's Canadian friend, Matthew MacNeill.

Dud said, 'I must write to his parents. I wanted to, back then, but I was in no fit state. He told me they lived in Saskatoon, Saskatchewan.'

'Saskatoon, Saskat . . .'

'Saskatchewan.'

Della tasted the words like a rich new flavour. 'Saskatchewan.'

'I must write and tell them I knew him. I won't tell them . . . everything, but I can say what a great chap he was, what a good friend.'

'That'd be nice,' she said. 'It helped us when Puck died, to hear from his CO. Mam read that letter a thousand times.'

She imagined the young Canadian's parents opening the letter all the way from England and wondering what it could be, all these years later, after the loss of their son a world away in France. She tried to imagine their Canadian house, their street, the city beyond, the land beyond that.

'I wonder what it's like,' she said, 'in Saskatoon, Saskatchewan, Canada.'

'Good horse country,' said Dud, 'so MacNeill told me. Prairies. Grass. Lots of sky.'

They found the address from the War Office and Dud sent his letter. The reply was gracious and thankful, ending with an invitation. Possibilities unfurled from that simple phrase: 'Come see us.' A hand held out across the Atlantic to the dark-grey English days of winter stretching into 1919, uncertain, hard, cold and depressing. The aftermath of war was worse for many, they knew that – they had heard from Ronnie that Jim was killed in the last weeks of war, his aeroplane catching fire over Belgium somewhere, his body not found. How she wept when she heard, cried in a way she'd never managed for Puck. It was the loss of both of them, the near loss of Dud; it just all spilled over in one great bout of weeping that wouldn't stop. They heard too that when the Germans retreated past Douai the town was sacked and burnt to the ground, utterly ruined. Heaven knows what happened to Louisa and her family, to Xavier's shop, except the horrible thought that tables and chairs burn well. They wrote a letter to the town mayor, praising their helpers during the occupation, but reply never came. Perhaps there was no town hall left to receive it. Flying past it all those months before, Della had noted what a pretty town it was, full of civic pride, reflected in the blue-grey waters of the river Scarpe. Now it was rubble. The ashes of the fires must have drifted down to settle on the waters. The guilt of the survivor took hold of her at times like that, as she remembered the flight away from the ruins of Europe. The liberty of being able to leave the land and cross the sea, the miracle of flight – but it wasn't sheer luck of course; both she and Dud had earnt their flying stripes in their own ways and so their escape wasn't a gift from above, rather a reward – served admittedly with a dose of good fortune – for all their hard work through those years of flying. Landing in Dover and clambering out of the aeroplane, Dud had crouched down and actually kissed the green dewy grass of Whitfield meadow and said he never wanted to set foot in an aeroplane again as long as he lived. Della felt the opposite, patting the prop of her beloved Blackburn after Dud had helped her climb out; she felt the trusty aeroplane had rekindled her love for the air and when this war was done, she'd do whatever it took to get back up there.

They were both ill, those days after the escape, and for safety's sake, they had to split up and approach in different ways to get the medical help they needed. Dud had to go to report in at the nearest RFC airfield, which happened to be Ronnie's at Swingate Down. Della wished she could have seen Ronnie's face when her beanpole husband turned up in his ill-fitting French farmer's gear. They concocted a story that he'd got to Belgium by train and omnibus, thereafter crossing the Channel in a friendly Belgian fishing boat (this was stolen from the story of Hilda's Hewlett's son and his Dutch trawler). The missing did return, from time to time. Via boat, or train, or on foot, pilgrims from war, or secretly, by aeroplane . . . Not only Dud, but Jim and Ronnie and she herself would be in a great deal of bother with the authorities if their method of escape had been discovered and confirmed. Court martial at the least, and who knew what else? So, a story was told and believed, and four friends kept quiet and locked away the Blackburn again, its flanks caked in French mud and sea spray. Ronnie did come to see her later, as she went straight from Whitfield to a hospital to have her arm checked, to find that it was fractured, not sprained. They kept her in for a few days for observation, exhausted and run-down as she was, feverish too from an infection. She heard from Ronnie that Dud had been sent to a military hospital outside Dover. She was weak when he came, so he was calm with her, but nothing could hide his delight that she'd done it, flown the Channel in his Blackburn, the girl wonder. It made his eyes shine.

Telegrams were swapped and Mam came to look after her, visiting her bedside with awful news. Dud had pneumonia. They said he would not last the week out. She begged her doctor to let her go, but was refused. So Mam came and took her, brooking no argument, and they turned up at the military hospital, Della's arm in a pot, unwieldy but good for pushing through gatekeepers and nurses barring corridors, which they did to find Dud's bed empty. The nurse said that patient had died. Della looked at Mam, then a veil came down and she passed out. She woke on another bed, surrounded by soldiers sitting up in their own beds watching her with great interest and Mam stroking her hair, like she had on childhood sick days, smiling down at her.

'Dud's alive,' said Mam urgently. 'It was a mistake. They sent us to the wrong bed.'

'You sure?' Della muttered, her throat dry.

'Sure. I've seen him. He's ill but stable. They think he'll make it.'

'Good grief,' moaned Della and thought, *I can't take much more of this lark*. War had this habit of plateau and abyss, stretches of boredom or joy where everything was peachy and fine, then the floor opened and swallowed you up with all your hopes and closed over your head afterwards, leaving you falling in the darkness. It was like a monumental board game played by a bunch of cold-hearted gods, who cheered the snakes and booed at the ladders. For the tiny human counters caught up in it, lives were arbitrarily preserved or destroyed, burnt or buried, blown up or saved in an aeroplane, sailing through the air towards home.

Dud never had to strap on a war aeroplane again, at any rate. After recovering from the pneumonia, he was allowed to stay in England, sent to the Northern Command Depot near Ripon. It was a halfway house, for those too well for convalescent hospital but too ill for active service. It was all quite clubby, with football matches and gardening, musical concerts and vaulting horses, while Dud was billeted in a local house, as all the officers were. It all seemed a bit silly though, to Della. Why didn't they just let the poor bastards go home? They'd done their bit.

Della went back to Cleethorpes with Mam and work at the garage. She and Dud missed each other and visited each other when they could, but at least he was safe, would always be safe. They wouldn't send him anywhere now, not with his lungs, however long the blasted war lasted. But they didn't have long to wait – by November it was all over. The Lancaster men came home and took over the garage, so Della was out of a job. Gertie and the boys went back to Hull and Della resumed her role as Mam's helper. Dud came back to live in the Dobbs house and got work as a conductor on the omnibus. He liked it, the freedom and sociability of it. He wasn't shy, like Della. He liked talking to people and riding around the town, especially the seafront. He liked the movement of it, not being in control and the mindlessness of it. He didn't have to think or concentrate. But it wasn't right for him, wouldn't be for long. There was something about being in the town that depressed him. It was the drabness of it all, how hard it was getting by, how worn down everyone was. And what had they to stay for? The streets empty of able-bodied men, war-wounded everywhere selling bits and bobs or begging. It was a disgrace. It was not victorious.

What had they won, after all? Europe was ruined. It was bound to be much worse in Germany of course, and the shambles of France and Belgium. At least they'd never been occupied here in England. But nobody was benefitting from peace. Who'd won the war and who'd lost was irrelevant. Della thought of those four years like a great storm that might come upon you in your aeroplane, wrecking every flying, free thing in the sky, then passing on, leaving broken wood and kindling in its wake, buried deep in the blood-soaked mud. Nobody could beat a storm. It moved of its own volition and didn't take sides. It crushed you like a kite caught in a tempest, a kite without a string.

And the end of war didn't mean the end of suffering, for Dud at least. There were headaches and nightmares, crying out at night, waking in a terrible sweat. Della holding him and stroking his forehead in the hours before dawn, listening to the seagulls waking up the day. The days and nights were filled with waiting, but for what? When the letter came back from the Canadians, it was the day before Della's birthday. At least there were eggs for a decent cake. Soon after, another letter arrived, from the family solicitor. Auntie Betty's house was to be released to Della, as she had at last turned twenty-five. There was a family renting it with three children under five. They'd been there for years, the arrangements adminis-tered by an agent. Of course, Della and Dudley could take up residence, Dud working on the buses, Della doing . . .

something. They'd have to ask the family to leave. Della and Dud talked about it.

'What shall we do?' she said. 'What about this family, living there?'

'What do you want to do?' Dud asked carefully. 'It is your house, after all. Your legacy from dear old Betty.'

'It seems wrong to turn them out, poor sods.'

'We could sell the house. And buy you an aeroplane.'

'Oh, Dud, you're good to me. But what would I do with it? Who's got any money around here these days to have flying lessons? It's hopeless. And they won't let a woman near it, near anything. All the women are being sacked from their war work. They did their bit and now they can toddle off back home, thank you very much. I can't make a living, flying in England.'

The letter from the Canadians sat on the dresser beside them. That night, Dud's nightmare was worse than ever; he screamed the house down about dead horses, dead horses. Cleo cried. Nobody complained – how could they? Della sat awake in her childhood home, trying to soothe her war-wounded husband back to sleep, listening to the sea and looking at the Canadian letter on the side there. She'd miss the sea. She'd miss Mam and Cleo very much, even Pop to some degree. But there was nothing to stay for, not any more. She was sorry for the family in Betty's house, but she couldn't be responsible for everyone. She sold the house and they used the money to buy passage on a ship to Canada, the rest of the money safely put away in the bank, waiting, along with a generous (and secret) loan from Mam, who wanted to help set them up and wouldn't take no for an answer. They had no firm plans for what to do when they got there, except to take the train to Saskatoon, visit Matthew MacNeill's parents, and pay their respects to their son.

In the week before they were due to leave, an aeroplane appeared on Cleethorpes beach. Some local likely lad had bought an old two-seater Sopwith 1½ Strutter – God knows where he'd got it from. It was unused since the war and he'd painted it up, offering joyrides off the beach for a fee. Della went over and watched. She went up to the bloke and told him about herself, showed him her flying certificate. He let her take it up and praised her when she came down. It was much faster than anything she was used to, and she revelled in the speed and whooped with joy going full pelt down the coast. Over land she sped over thermals; it was far less bumpy than a slower aeroplane. It banked more steeply, the horizon tipping at an alarming angle that took a bit of getting used to. So, the war had driven the aeroplane to this zenith; it was deadly competition that had caused this evolution. She felt fortunate to be flying it in peacetime. And how gratifying it was to soar over Cleethorpes again, watching her town raise its head and wave to her, Meggie Magpie, the pre-war flying sensation, grown up now.

She had felt weary of life, but flying, she felt more alive than she had for months. That settled it for her. Whatever happened in Canada, she'd be buying an aeroplane. She'd make it work for her. And she'd buy a horse for Dud. They could live in a shoebox for all she cared, but she must fly and Dud must ride. It was the only way they'd be happy.

There was one day to go before they were to get the train to Liverpool for the ship to Canada. Della spent as much as possible of the time left with Mam, pottering about in the kitchen together, chattering, reminiscing. Mam would wipe a tear away now and again.

'Will you come over and visit, Mam? Don't let Pop stop you.'

'When you start having babies. Then I'll come,' said Mam, bleary-eyed and brave-faced.

Della felt a cold wash of anxiety prickle her skin. 'No babies, Mam. There won't be babies. All this time and no babies yet.

There must be something wrong with us. With me. Or Dud. Don't be sad about it.'

Mam took her daughter's face in her hands. 'I don't believe that, love. I think it'll come right for you there. Remember what I told you. It's sickness and sadness can stop a baby coming. Out there, in that big old country, there's no memories to get away from, no memories at all. It's all fresh and clean. You'll be happy, you two, and you'll have babies, you'll see.'

'Oh Mam,' she said and they hugged sadly and held on for minutes, till Cleo came in and elbowed between them.

Della had also been spending as much time as she could with Cleo, comforting her, telling her how she could come and see them when she was older, that there'd always be a bed and a warm welcome for her with them.

Cleo said, 'But who'll stand up to Pop when you're gone?'

Della was amazed. 'Why, you, of course, Cleo. You were always the one who stood up to him. Not me.'

'But I learned to be brave from you,' said her little sister and sobbed into her lap.

Before she left, Della went in to see Pop in his study. Still writing plays nobody read, he looked older than ever.

He said, 'What are you dressed like that for?'

'Come with me, Pop. One last thing before I go. Will you?'

'Come where? You know I don't like to.'

'Just trust me for once,' she said and held the door open for him. 'Put on your coat and scarf.' They went out of the front door, crossed the Kingsway and the prom, then stopped at the top of the steps down to the beach. The Sopwith was waiting for them there. She'd arranged it with the amiable owner the day before. Pop's first flight.

'Oh no, I don't think so,' said Pop, turning awkwardly on his bad leg and about to make his escape along the promenade back home.

'Please, Pop. Do this one thing for me. First and last thing I'll ever ask of you.'

He wasn't keen, but he did it. Once they got up there, she watched him carefully to see what he thought of it. He was stiff as a board for the first few minutes, but after a time his left arm shot up at an angle, diagonal against the sky, fingers reaching cloud-ward. If it hadn't been for his withered arm, she guessed he'd have lifted both, an embracing salute to the beauty of the air. It was the only movement he made the whole trip. Afterwards, he was breathless and speechless, but he did pat her on the shoulder and, through the short breaths, he said, 'Good girl. Good girl.' It was the nicest thing he ever said to her.

The ship's crossing from Liverpool to Canada made Dudley remark that he was lucky he never went for the Navy, as he'd have died from vomiting before ever reaching land. Not one for journeys, Dud. After days of tiring travel, they came in on the train to the Saskatoon railway station, the platform filled mostly with men in bowler hats, grey and brown suits, smoking, loafing, stepping onto the train. On disembarking, they found themselves in the heart of the city, the streets filled five or six deep with taxicabs, automobiles and horse-drawn carts pulling all manner of people and produce down the sandy track-scored roads, all dodged by hundreds of citizens crossing the street, wearing flat caps and straw boaters. Drugstores, the Bank of Canada, Pool, Meals 50c, Wilson's Lunch Counter, Sporting Goods, Dentist and Arctic Fish were all advertised on signs and the sides of trucks. When she'd dreamt of Saskatoon, Saskatchewan, Canada, she'd imagined only the prairies, the miles of air travel and the sweeping acres for horses. It was a surprise to find themselves in a thriving, dusty city. But the countryside encroached here and there, with ox-drawn buckboards loaded with farming families a reminder of the rural wilderness surrounding Saskatoon, peopled by ranchers and stubble-jumpers (local slang, she was to learn to her amusement, for grain farmers).

The MacNeill family home at the end of 22nd Street West was a clapboard house coloured dove-grey, set in a plot surrounded by a low, weathered picket fence. Inside, everything was small and neat. An ordinary family before the war with their one son and again an ordinary one after, with their first- and only-born dead and gone. They looked old, the wife slate-haired, the husband snow-white. Tired eyes. That look, of loss, utter loss never to be recovered. Della knew it so well.

Dud showed such sweet compassion to them. He told them everything Matthew had said to him, how brave he was, that he died very quickly and painlessly, that Dud had arranged a burial for him with a wooden cross. It was half lies, what he told them, but they were necessary ones. Nothing to be gained by the truth in that situation, just like Puck's secret letters staying secret. Gertie had been right about that.

The MacNeills were so touched, so grateful, they treated the Willows like family and helped with everything. Where to find an airfield and look for contacts to buy Della's aeroplane: a Curtiss JN-4 Canuck, an old trainer sold cheaply as war surplus. Where to find work for Dud on a ranch and how to arrange for him to buy his own horse. They recommended local builders to make the Willows' home, in a scrubby patch of land on the outskirts of Saskatoon, small and humble, simple but a good start. They recommended a lawyer for Della's application to begin an airmail service across the prairies. Mr MacNeill provided Dud with seeds for his vegetable patch and helped him plant trees to grow as windbreaks. He also found Della a job as a mechanic at a town garage, the weight of his local recommendation swaying the sceptical owner to hire a woman.

For Della's airfield they bought a square of land a couple of miles up the road from where their house and acres were and built a hangar there. Dud said he didn't want his horse

frightened by the sound of the aircraft engine; Della suspected
it was really Dud who didn't want to hear the sound of aeroplanes. But that was all right with her – it was always her love
to fly, his to read about it. He was still jittery around aeroplanes, around any loud noise really; he wouldn't go in the
kitchen when the kettle was whistling. Sometimes he'd still
wake at night in a sweat, say he was breaking into pieces. The
shadow of the war lay long. Yet physically, Dud was improving.
His chest was much better, though the extremely harsh winters
weren't ever going to be easy, the temperature dropping to
as low as minus thirty their first year. This English couple
born and bred had never known a winter half as harsh, but
both had known cold – one in the trenches, the other in the
high sky. They managed. Della had to prime her aeroplane
by adding alcohol to the fuel, while she found that draining
her oil at the end of the day, then warming it before refilling
the tank, helped it to flow more freely. She figured she could
fit skis to her Canuck for winter flights the following year.
Mrs MacNeill brought them hot meals and pickled vegetables
in the chilly early months, then knitted blankets for them
when Della told them she was expecting. The baby was born
in September 1920. Weeks before, Della had felt sick with
nerves, fearful that the child would come early like Cleo,
wouldn't feed like her, or that the birth would be hard, away
from Mam, alone in this new country. But it wasn't so bad.
He came at just the right time and he thrived. They called
him Matthew Puck Willow. Matty for short.

Now there was another reason for broken sleep, but a good,
hopeful one. Actually, the boy's presence in their bedroom
had a calming effect on his father and as time went on there
were fewer and fewer nightmares. Mam and Cleo came to
visit when Matty was one, staying for a month; it was a wrench
when they had to go back. Cleo, at the grand age of eleven,
was so tall and ladylike she took Della's breath away, but she
hadn't lost any of her spark, and played raucous rough and

tumble games with Matty outside till bedtime. Della suggested Mam persuade Pop to up sticks and come and live out there with them. Mam looked torn, said she'd think about it, but as appealing as it was out here, Della knew it was her and Dud's life, and was alien to Mam and the rest of the Dobbses. They had made their life out here and it belonged to them.

As working parents, they shared their time with their little boy, Della tending him in between airmail runs and shifts at the garage, and Dud taking the baby to work in a Moses basket when he went to the ranch. The ranch's owner was Mr MacNeill's sister, another of the war-widowed bereaved mothers found all over in those years. Her son was Matthew's cousin and the lads had once trained the horses there, the ones Matthew had told Dud about in the trenches. In her forties, her boy passed on, she was more than happy to have a new baby to pet, then an infant to toddle around in her kitchen while Dud was outside. He worked with her Quarter Horses and Clydesdales, learning the peculiarities of each breed and reporting their qualities daily back to Della, who was delighted to see his joy in learning everything there was to know about these beautiful animals. Some of the other ranch hands were Dakota people and Dud befriended them easily, united as they were in their love for and knowledge of horses. There were some Dakota families in log cabins not far from the airfield too, wigwam-shaped piles of wood propped up beside each shack ready to burn all the bitter winter through. The Dakota mothers would carry their kids over to come and stare and potter about with Matty beside the hangar. Della took some of them up in her Canuck. Nobody spoke much. It was peaceful that way, being with the Dakota folk.

By the age of two, Matty was a seasoned flyer, as passenger (for the time being), his first flight characterised by screams of laughter between which he shouted one word over and over: 'Again, again!' Matty was a natural with horses too. He was always kind to them and soft-hearted with the other animals on the ranch, the ducks in the pond and the rabbits the owner kept for pets and food, talking to them incessantly, gossipy and fun just like his Auntie Cleo.

Della and Dud saved as much money as they could, planning to buy more horses so Dud could start his own horse-training business. He'd offer his services in horsemanship, a natural way with horses, no whips, no cruelty, nothing medieval. Della's airmail service began in the first spring after they'd arrived in Canada, from Saskatoon up to Prince Albert and down to Regina. She had plans to lengthen her route and for her humble airfield to become a licensed 'air harbour', with pleasure flights, expanding into an aero club for instruction, exhibitions and so forth; modelled on Hendon – why not? Even Claude had had to start with an empty field. Her Canuck, which the Canadians called Jenny, had two seats, dual controls and was an easy flyer. Ideal for training. It was light, climbed easily and had ailerons on all four wings, so its rolling was superior. She took to it immediately. She'd use Jenny to help teach post-war Canada to take to the air. She'd buy another when they could afford it. They called their business CC Aviation. The two Cs stood for Calcraft Candle.

It was never lonely, up in the air. Any troubles you had you left outside on the wing, and when you were up and circling, your troubles were lifted and blown away on the four winds. She'd never lost her joy of flight, the eagle's-eye view of the earth. After all, she never had to fly to kill or be killed; despite the risks, she only flew for the love of it, so it was not tainted in the way it was for Dud. It was still pure.

As the blood-red sun dipped below the horizon, she was heading south, to Saskatoon, to home, dusk darkening the sky a deep blue. Tomorrow, she'd be off again, further south to Regina, as the crow flies (it's preposterous, really, flying. It's just deflecting air). The palace of the winds, the air like the sea, wild and itself, and pilots had the privilege of sailing on it, playing with it, dancing with it. You strapped on your aeroplane, this clumsy thing of wood and linen, and you joined the things that flew in the sky, you became a bird. It was fear and it was freedom, all at once. She turned Jenny towards home, dipped down, saw the squat hangar of her dusty airfield waiting for her. Sometimes she didn't want to land, so homely was the sky for her. But for this evening she was cold and tired, and she longed for her other home, on solid ground, with her beloveds, exactly where she wanted to be that evening. She had two homes, Della, one on the ground and one in the air. They gave her perfect balance, like the wings of a bird.

AUTHOR'S NOTE

In my historical novels, I do my best to base everything I can on the facts of the time, while also allowing my stories to take a flight of fancy. In my previous novels, I've found that some readers have enjoyed hearing about the historical basis of my heroines' exploits, so to that end, here is some information about the background to this novel set in the early days of powered flight.

Kitty Hawk

Betty Perry, Della's great-aunt, comes home to Cleethorpes, having lived in Kitty Hawk. When analysing data about the inhabitants of this tiny place that was to become world famous because two brothers from Ohio happened to visit and fly their machines there, I discovered one immigrant from England who lived in Kitty Hawk at that time, a woman, about whom I could find no more details than that. But she intrigued me and gave me the narrative permission to place Auntie Betty there for a few years, married to her beloved Truman.

Cleethorpes in the Edwardian era and during WW1

All of the streets and other locations mentioned in the novel are real Cleethorpes places that existed during the period, and many are still around now – including the pier, which looks virtually identical. I took a liberty with the manager of the Dolly, or the Dolphin Hotel, who is my own invention but the Dolly was indeed there and its building still stands near the seafront today.

Female aviators of the Edwardian era

Every time I start researching about women in history, I always find the most extraordinary stories of women who circumvented the restrictions of their time and lived lives of adventure and exploration that defy expectations. Most of these women are almost completely lost to history and remain unsung. I've chosen to create my own main character for this novel, but her experiences and ambitions are typical of many an aviatrix I read about.

Firstly, the real-life aviatrixes who have a cameo appearance:

Hélène Dutrieu – this Belgian aviatrix known as the 'Girl Hawk' was the first woman in her country to earn her pilot's licence. She was a champion cyclist, stuntwoman and all-round speed freak before becoming an aviatrix. During the war, she became an ambulance driver and director of a military hospital.

Hilda Hewlett – as Dud reports, the first British woman to gain her pilot's licence, she also opened the first flying school in England. She became a highly successful aircraft manufacturer and businesswoman.

Melli Beese – an extraordinary woman, the first female German to get her licence, she was a pilot and aircraft designer with her husband, just as she is in this story. However, the Great War did for both of them and their story ends in tragedy. Imprisoned as an alien and as wife to an alien, both Melli and her husband grew ill and weak throughout the awful years of WWI-era Germany. Their business was also taken by the government, so that after the war they were penniless. They later separated and Melli killed herself. A terrible end for a brave, heroic young woman who was beaten by the system. But history bears witness to her glorious career and her role as a pioneer in women's aviation. (By the way, I couldn't find out if Melli was a fluent English speaker, but I needed her to speak English in order to help Della, so I hope the reader will forgive this potentially fictional skill to serve the narrative.)

Other aviatrixes of the period:

Lilian Bland – an Anglo-Irish journalist who designed and built her own aeroplane from scratch. It didn't fly far but it's the effort that counts. A pioneer of aviatrixes and female aircraft designers, she deserves her place in aviation history. Betty's plans to design and build their own aeroplane and fly it from Cleethorpes beach finds its inspiration in figures like Bland.

Katherine Stinson – an American aviatrix, who was known as the 'Flying Schoolgirl' (you see, it's not only Meggie Magpie who was given a daft epithet). She was a flying instructor and the first woman to perform a loop. Amongst other feats, such as being one of the first women to carry airmail, as well as night flights and skywriting, she toured China and Japan giving demonstrations of her aeroplane, an extraordinary accomplishment in any time, for woman or man.

Marie Marvingt – a French aviatrix who disguised herself as a man and fought on the front lines for a while until she was discovered. Then, while serving as a nurse in 1915, a tale is told that she treated a pilot patient who was upset because he was going to let down his crew on a mission that day. The story goes that she took his place and flew several missions over German-occupied territory. She was later awarded the Croix de Guerre.

There are other stories, some real, some perhaps apocryphal, of unofficial aviatrixes flying in France, Italy, Germany and Russia during WW1. Women pilots were refused in their bid to join the air forces of many countries, including Britain. We'll never know what effects there may have been on the lives of the men in the trenches below if those women had been allowed to fly for the RFC above them, but it could only have helped. What a waste. (It's worth noting that WWI has often been characterised as a period of emancipation for women, where many took over the roles of the men who had gone off to fight. What we sometimes forget is that after the war, pre-war chauvinism towards women and work returned and some of that hard-won progress was set back. A good example is to be found in the fact that women became train drivers during WWI and yet post-war, the first woman to become a train driver in this country again did not come along until the 1970s. (See Kate Adie's *Fighting on the Home Front: The Legacy of Women in World War One* for this nugget of information, including many more.)

Above, I've listed just a handful of the many pioneering women who learned to fly during the Edwardian and Great War era, most of whom are long forgotten now. Mention female pilots and if anyone has anything to say it's usually about Amelia Earhart or Amy Johnson, about whom Hollywood movies were made and countless books written. And those women certainly were fabulous figures in the history of flying females. However, they were flying in the wake of earlier heroines, many of whom died in their pursuit of flight, yet laid the foundation for women everywhere to think, If she can do it, so can I.

Please see the book on the history of the aviatrix, *Before Amelia: Women Pilots in the Early Days of Aviation* by Eileen F. Lebow, which was extremely helpful in understanding the challenges women faced in these difficult times.

Edwardian & WW1-era aeroplanes

I have the Shuttleworth Collection and everyone associated with it to thank for much of the factual detail about aeroplanes to be found in this novel. This extraordinary collection of aircraft from the earliest days of flight, situated at Old Warden in Bedfordshire, is well worth a visit, especially on one of their marvellous airshow days. The depth of knowledge and expertise housed in this place is phenomenal. Through this marvellous place I also made contact with vintage aircraft experts and pilots Robert Millinship and Roger 'Dodge' Bailey, who contributed hugely to the factual basis of all the flying sequences in this story (see Acknowledgements). And yes, pilots really didn't wear seatbelts in most early planes. Unbelievable but true!

Blackburn aeroplanes

Thanks to 'Dodge' Bailey for his expert help on Blackburns in particular. As both he and Rob Millinship told me, those who can fly the early planes are the best pilots, as modern planes are designed to almost fly themselves, whereas you have to fight to control the early planes as they're full of imbalance and instability. Dodge explained that the Blackburn was extraordinary for its day and in fact would pass the test of stability in all three axes now, whilst most planes up until WW2 would not have passed that test. The Blackburn would have back in 1912 – an extraordinary accomplishment for such an early plane and in my opinion Robert Blackburn should be far more famous and well-remembered than he is, for this achievement.

Some readers may question the likelihood of flying the Blackburn across the Channel in 1918, with enough fuel and oil to get there and back. To them and all doubters of extraordinary feats in any of my novels, I quote verbatim Dodge's marvellous pronouncement upon the topic, proving once and for all why a novelist like me needs experts like Dodge:

To answer your question I'm going to assume that the aircraft is fitted with the same engine as our Blackburn, i.e. 50 HP Gnome, and that the fuel and oil tanks have the same capacities, namely 12 gal fuel and 4.5 gal oil. Fuel weighs 7.2lb per gal and castor oil weighs 9.5lb per gal. The Specific Fuel Consumption for the Gnome is about 0.6lb/HP/hr and the Specific Oil Consumption is about 0.12lb/HP/hr, therefore the engine will consume fuel at about 4.2 gal per hour and oil at about 0.83 gal per hour. The tank capacities would allow for 2¾ hours' flying from the fuel but the oil tank should last nearly 6 hours. So this would allow the aircraft to fly safely for say 2 hours or about 100 miles in no wind. On landing there should be nearly 4 hours' worth of oil remaining. So, if the fuel tank is refilled, it should be possible to make another 2 hour flight without having to top up the oil tank. So full fuel (12 gal) would weigh 86lb and full oil would weigh about 43lb making 129lb altogether. Now 129lb is 9 stone – the weight of a light passenger. Therefore if no passenger was carried, 12 gal of fuel and 4.5 gal of oil could be carried in the passenger seat and used to top up the tanks.

Claude Grahame-White and other pilots

A major personality of early aviation, Claude Grahame-White is rightly revered for his place in the history of flying. So, this is what's true and what isn't about Claude Grahame-White in this book: he was very good-looking – just look at any photograph! And he was married to a wealthy socialite. He was instrumental in the creation and development of Hendon and the art of flying: just read his book *Learning to Fly* to hear his expert voice and demonstrate his love for flight.

But his dialogue, personality and of course Della's imaginings about him that are presented in this novel are pure fiction. In aviation history, one could say that Claude was not particularly an advocate of women pilots. His school at Hendon did offer training to a few women – and in that respect they differed from some other contemporaries who refused to teach women at all – but he did make pronouncements from time to time on women's natural unfitness for flying. In this respect though one must view him as a man of his time, with typical views of his era. He was such an interesting character, I really wanted Della to meet him – and when she did, and saw what a handsome devil he was, and found herself shoved up against him on the narrow seat of the Bristol Boxkite, she promptly fell for him, much to my disapproval. Well, what can you do with characters? They will up and do their own thing. So, I hope the reader will forgive me for allowing Claude to improve somewhat his rather shabby record towards women in aviation, my only excuse being that perhaps if he'd met Della Dobbs in real life and seen her fly as brilliantly as she did, he might well have changed his opinion slightly, just as he does in this novel. And whatever one might say about his attitudes towards women, there's no doubt that he was a true hero of early aviation and I have tremendous respect for him. I used his excellent book *Learning to Fly*, published in 1913, to gain insight into the man and his love for flying.

Other pilot cameos played in this novel include B.C. Hucks and Hubert Oxley, amongst others. I've based these representations on the few facts I could glean from contemporary accounts about their appearance and demeanour, but mostly they are from my own imagination.

Aviators' Certificates

Della's pilot's licence is gained on the 25th day of May 1913, on a Grahame-White biplane, at the Grahame-White School, Hendon, Aviator's Certificate 492. The real pilot to be given the certificate of that exact number was Lieut. Paul Augustine Broder (5th Worcestershire Regt.) on a Bristol biplane of the Bristol School at Brooklands. See the wonderful Grace's Guide online for details but I needed a date around that time and his fitted the bill, so I'm hoping he would forgive me for pilfering his for Della.

Electric lights on an aeroplane

As seen in Della's flight over Cleethorpes, electric lights really were used at a night flight airshow at Hendon during this era, in case you were wondering.

The Grimsby Chums

These soldiers were part of the ill-fated idea of local men joining up together, training together, shipping out together and ultimately dying together. The so-called 'pals' regiments, formed up and down the country in the early years of the war, condemned many villages and small towns to the most devastating kind of loss. The Chums were no exception and Puck's fate was tragically typical of this brave bunch of Grimsby lads.

Despatch riders

Della speeding her motorcycle around London during the war was based on the experiences of despatch riders such as Mairi Chisholm who worked for the Women's Emergency Corps. Mairi went much further, to become an ambulance driver in war-torn Belgium. As ever, my fictional characters' experiences pale beside the true heroism of real people in extraordinary times.

Puck's letters

Some readers may be surprised to read the honesty of Puck's letters in terms of conditions in the trenches and his feelings about what's happening to him. I direct you to the real letters themselves, published in a range of books about the period and many unpublished found in the Imperial War Museum, for examples of searing honesty that escaped the censor. Some soldiers kept quiet during the war itself and for the rest of their lives. Others did not, and some of those wrote in astonishing detail about the horror they'd witnessed as well as their disgust and misery for what they were experiencing in the trenches.

Please see the compilation of real WWI soldiers' correspondence, 'Letters from the Trenches', ed. Jacqueline Wadsworth, for an eye-opening range of words from the men themselves.

Dudley Willow

In many ways, Dud Willow is his own person. He stepped out of my plans and strolled along Cleethorpes beach fully formed. In other ways, Dud is based on some aspects of my lovely Papa, my grandfather who fought in the First World War and lived to have a son who was my father. My Papa was tall and willowy, was gentle and kind, had a quiet smile on his face whenever you saw him and was also a radio ham. Once, a couple of years before Papa died, I had to do some school homework on WWI and I telephoned him to ask about his experiences. He barely told me a thing and I remember hanging up feeling frustrated but also humbled by his voice, small and quiet on the telephone line, a man born in the nineteenth century, who spoke from another age. Years later, I found a fascinating box of photographs and documents relating to Papa's service, which set me off to discover more about his path through the Great War. Through archives and online forums, books and records, as well as the wealth of material in that beloved box, I found that Papa studied textiles in Bradford, trained at the Leeds OTC, left for Clipstone Camp, joined the 4th (R) King's Own Yorkshire Light Infantry, then the 8th KOYLI. There the similarities between Papa and Dudley end, as Papa didn't go on to become a pilot. Instead, he was lucky enough firstly to contract influenza and be shipped home in January 1917 and secondly to survive the deadly flu and spend the rest of the war at the Northern Command Depot. If he hadn't, of course, I'd most likely not be here writing this about him today.

Weelsby Old Hall

There was a convalescent hospital here during the war, where recovering soldiers wore the blue uniforms and escaped the trenches for a while. Nearby Weelsby Woods, where Della and Dud take their walks, is still there today and provides a woodland oasis in the centre of the busy town of Grimsby.

Royal Flying Corps

I based Dud's experiences on the records of 60 Squadron, in particular to give some details of what happened from September 1917 when Dud is there. However, I have fictionalised his comrades' names in order to give me freedom over

Dud's movements and sorties. I used other RFC published memoirs as well as visiting the Research Room at the Imperial War Museum. There I read a wide range of unpublished letters from RFC pilots sent during the war and other unpublished RFC documents, such as diaries written during the war and memoirs written after the war was over. Dud's letters are faithfully based on the letters of these men, most of whom died in the skies over France and Flanders.

Dropping spies over the lines

This is all true about RFC pilots doing spy drops and did happen regularly. Famous pilot Albert Ball did it many times and some of his spies refused to get out of the plane after he'd risked his life getting them there (see the excellent book on the RFC, *No Empty Chairs* by Ian Mackersey). As for RFC pilots on the run and getting home, see the extraordinary story of Claude Alward Ridley, on whose experience of landing across the lines and being helped by locals to evade capture the early part of Dud's experiences is based. Their paths diverge when Dud meets up with his saviour Della, but Ridley's real-life exploits went on through Europe, where he escaped back to England and freedom, entirely without speaking a word of French and helped by every local he asked. Hilda Hewlett – a real aviatrix and aircraft maker who appears as a character in the novel – had a pilot son who went missing in France and was mourned as missing in action, who then returned to England after having been rescued by a Dutch trawler, surprising and delighting all who'd thought they'd lost him. Truth, fiction and strangeness. It never ceases to amaze me.

Canada

Della's pioneering role in Canadian airmail is a bit early, as the first airmail service here didn't begin till a bit later in the 1920s, but if Della had been there, I suspect she'd have hurried things along in her trusty Jenny.

Flight today

In writing about an aviatrix, I intended to create the whole
story through research and imagination, as writers are wont
to do. Having met Rob Millinship early on in the research
process, who told me that I really ought to go flying if I was
going to write about it, I said Maybe . . . but never actually
intended to go through with it, terrified as I was at the thought.
I put it off and put it off for about eighteen months, until
one sunny perfect Good Friday I thought, Oh stuff it, and
went down to Leicester for my first flight in a light aircraft.
Della's first flight is entirely based on that experience and
how glad I am now that I finally did it. I thought I knew
about flight, because I'd read about it and interviewed pilots
and watched videos. But I didn't know about it, not really,
not from the inside out. Only doing the damned thing can
give you that. It was fear and freedom all at once and it was
bloody marvellous. Thank you again to Rob for that amazing
day and for giving Della's flights the texture of truth. I know
the book is immeasurably better for it.

In interviewing Diana Britten, a champion aerobatic aviatrix, I found that the position of women in aviation had in
some ways improved since Della's time, but I was surprised
to find that in other ways little progress had been made. There
are still relatively few women airline pilots. I was shocked to
read of an interview with an airline pilot from only a couple
of years ago who had passengers refuse to fly on her aircraft
when they discovered their pilot was a woman. Della would
be so disappointed to find that a hundred years of progress
had come to this. I can only hope that young women are not
put off by such stories and instead see them as a challenge
to overcome. Let us hope that as time goes on, more and
more women are encouraged to make the sky their home, as
Della did.

As Dud says, flight is preposterous. It just doesn't really
seem possible, when you think about it (especially bumble bees

and jumbo jets). Today we are still learning about flight and, in particular, how birds and insects do it so effortlessly. To date in 2017, it was only recently that researchers finally proved exactly why and how migratory birds fly in V formations. It's all to do with upwash and how each bird's position in a V maximises lift. Birds worked this out themselves, the clever things, whereas we had to think our way into the air, as Auntie Betty tells Della. I take my hat off to those early pioneers of flight, both women and men, many of whom diced with death to drive flight forwards, and many of whom died trying. As war overtook aviation, many pilots from different nations became guinea pigs in the rapid development of aircraft and paid for this with their lives. Throughout the history of aviation, from gliders to space shuttles, many women and men have died in our pursuit of this glorious dance with the wind. This story is a celebration of their bravery and spirit.

ACKNOWLEDGEMENTS

This is my third published historical novel and thus I've been engaged in the process of research for quite a few years now. I've learnt that you need books and libraries and the internet and visits to key locations, but more than anything, you need people. I'm still astounded by the generosity of strangers when researching and writing my books, as well as honoured by the same from friends and family. I'm also so grateful that some of these strangers have then become friends, through our mutual interest in what to me is a new topic and to them is often a life-long beloved subject in which they are an acknowledged expert. This novel has been no exception. I have many people to thank, who have helped me immeasurably along the way.

First and foremost, I have one person in particular to thank, without whom this book would be a shadow of what it has become, who completely engaged with the whole idea from the first moment of hearing about it! This person is ace pilot Robert Millinship. For talking to me over several hours on a cold, dark October afternoon at the Shuttleworth Collection, allowing me to climb up and sit in the Avro triplane, shivering and nervous as I was, to imagine Della's dawn lessons. For countless emails and phone calls, discussing the finer points of Edwardian flight. For reading the first draft and editing it with copious post-it notes. And most of all, for taking me flying, in the Cessna and the Pitts, for knowing I'd be frightened but it would soon turn to joy, for showing me the earth as birds see it.

The other person I'd like to single out is Papa. This is my

own grandfather, who went to fight in the First World War in 1916, who luckily contracted influenza which brought him home, and even more luckily did not die from it. My Papa – Arthur Leslie Chadwick – was a lovely, kind and gentle man who I think about often, though he died over thirty years ago. His journey to war inspired me in the writing of this book and helped me feel closer to him. Miss you, old chap.

Huge gratitude also goes to:

Everyone who helped me at the Shuttleworth Collection at Old Warden – Ciara Harper, Marketing and Communications Manager; Ken Hyde, Collection Volunteer; and Roger 'Dodge' Bailey, expert pilot for the Collection. Ciara for organising and Ken for his brilliant introduction to the machines and how they work. Particular thanks to Dodge for his expertise on Blackburns and horsemanship, as well as his detailed and generous help, which even extended to taking photographs of Blackburn parts from various angles and labelling them most helpfully!

The staff of the Imperial War Museum research room, where I read numerous letters and accounts from real RFC pilots and learnt the terrible cost of war for those men and their families. Their experiences were heart-breaking and described with such honesty and courage.

Andy Johnson, for his expertise on WWI airfields in Lincolnshire.

David Harrigan MBE, Outreach & Learning Officer, Aviation Heritage Lincolnshire, for informing me about Shuttleworth as well as lots of info on Lincolnshire aviation.

Jenny Ashcroft, novelist, for sending me pictures of Remy Siding, where Papa was taken to a Canadian Casualty Clearing Station in 1917.

Iona Grey, novelist, for sending excellent books on WWI aviation and women in WWI.

Russ Drewery, for an invaluable afternoon patiently explaining to me how kites and wings work, as well as allowing

Poppy and I to watch him kite surfing on Cleethorpes beach and see close up how the great kite takes to the air.

WWI online forums and their members: the Great War Forum contributors & Alan Greveson's WWI Forum, for helping find out information on Papa's movements.

The Grimsby library local history section for help on Edwardian Cleethorpes & the staff of the *Cleethorpes Chronicle*, including Samantha Blake and also local history expert Alan Dowling, for information on Cleethorpes dialect.

Mexborough and District Heritage Society, for information on the 1909/10 Doncaster Air Shows.

Diana Britten and her daughter Sophie Biggs. Diana is a champion aerobatic pilot and shared her thoughts in two long interviews on being a competitive pilot and also how it is to be a woman in a pursuit largely peopled by men. Her comments on learning to fly and the joy of flying in particular were hugely influential on the writing of this novel. Sophie gave me a fascinating insight into what it's like to live with someone who is mad about flying! Thanks also to dear Suzie Dooré, for remembering the connection and making the introduction, as well as commissioning this story in the first place.

Ian Kingsnorth, Trustee (retired) & Volunteer with Life Membership & Tracy Fern, Retail Sales and Visitor Co-ordinator, from the South Yorkshire Aviation Museum, for excellent help regarding the 1910 Doncaster Air Show and the Burton-upon-Trent aviation meeting, including the sharing of contemporary newspaper articles and photographs.

Dr Mark White PhD, FHEA, Senior Lecturer, Department of Engineering Dynamics at the University of Liverpool and Dr Philip Perfect, Modelling and Simulation Engineer, for kindly giving of their time and letting me loose on their beautiful flight simulator, where Rob Millinship taught me how to fly a Bristol Boxkite. Thanks, guys, for not laughing too loudly when I smashed up your Antoinette.

Philip Jarrett, aviation historian and author, for informative and useful help with WW1 training aircraft and other aircraft matters.

Jean Fullerton, author, for such helpful information on Edwardian midwives.

Dr Tim Bruning, Dr Himanshu Gupta, Nurse Paula Donald & Jim Airey, physiotherapist, for healthcare above and beyond the call of duty during the writing of this book. Also, much love and gratitude to Pauline Lancaster, Kerry Drewery, Adele Webster and Fran Jaines, as well as Marie & Kevin Porter, for help at that time with the best of childcare.

Allan Kendall and Kathy Kendall for exceptional help on the history of their home town Saskatoon, Saskatchewan and other information on Canadian aviation and horses.

Andrew King, pilot, for invaluable information on the JN-4 Canuck, how it flies and how to look after it in the harsh Saskatchewan winters.

Early readers of this novel, for their helpful comments and support: Simon Porter, Lynn Downing, Pauline Lancaster, Louisa Treger, Vanessa Lafaye, Teresa Rouse, Ann Schlee, Sue White and Kathy Kendall.

All my writer friends in the Prime Writers and the Historical Writers' Association, as well as my longest-serving writing friend, Kerry Drewery. You guys give me courage and keep me smiling every day.

My new friends and colleagues teaching English so brilliantly at the Grimsby Institute and to the amazing kids we teach – I salute you all! You keep me on my toes, inspire me and make me laugh.

Francine Toon, my editor at Hodder, for always being a champion of my books, including this one. And to everyone at Hodder, including Claudette Morris, Jenny Campbell, Susan Spratt and the amazing designers who keep on producing such stunning and beautiful book covers.

Also, a huge thank you to the brilliant copyedit and proofreading team at Hodder, who were eagle-eyed and invaluable as ever and to the publicity team for all their efforts.

Jane Conway-Gordon, for her support and belief, advice and help and always reading so extraordinarily quickly! Thank you, Jane, for everything, for all these years. Much love and gratitude to you.

Laura Macdougall, my agent at Tibor Jones, for brilliant editing and negotiating skills, for her vision and energy, and for coming to Cleethorpes and strolling on the beach talking about The West Wing.

To my own dear Mam and to Russell, for love, belief, strength and, oh, everything. Same goes to Dad and Anna, to my lovely brothers & their wives, my nephews and niece, my aunties and uncles, my cousins and second cousins for never-ending support and love.

Lastly, to Poppy, my pride and joy, my champion, my buddy, my inspiration, my cleverest pal, my dearest girl. What will you do with your beautiful life, my darling? Whatever you choose, I know your spirit will take to the skies and become a bird.

QUESTIONS FOR DISCUSSION

- Did *The Wild Air* make you think differently about women and aviation in World War I?

- How much have things changed today? If Della were a young woman now, how many challenges would she still face?

- Even though Della faced many obstacles in her own career, do you think it made her a better person?

- How would the course of Della's life be different if she hadn't met
  - Great Aunt Betty
  - Dudley?

- Did you have anyone in your life who encouraged you in the same way as Betty supported Della? Is there anyone you encourage?

- How did Della's feelings for Claude Grahame-White differ to her feelings for Dudley?

- Did your opinion of Puck, Cleo, Pop and Mam change over the course of the novel?

- Was Della right to track down Dud, even though it was dangerous and against the advice of the RFC?

- Do you think Canada is a good place for Della and Dudley to settle, more so than England?

REBECCA MASCULL

The Visitors

Imagine if you couldn't see
couldn't hear
couldn't speak . . .
Then one day somebody took your hand
and opened up the world to you.

Adeliza Golding is a deaf-blind girl, born in late Victorian England on her father's hop farm. Unable to interact with her loving family, she exists in a world of darkness and confusion; her only communication is with the ghosts she speaks to in her head, who she has christened the Visitors. One day she runs out into the fields and a young hop-picker, Lottie, grabs her hand and starts drawing shapes in it. Finally Liza can communicate.

Her friendship with her teacher and with Lottie's beloved brother Caleb leads her from the hop gardens and oyster beds of Kent to the dusty veldt of South Africa and the Boer War, and ultimately to the truth about the Visitors.

Out now

HODDER

REBECCA MASCULL

Song of the Sea Maid

*An orphan in a Home for the Destitute
dreams of being a scientist.
But this is the 18th Century . . .
and she is a little girl.*

As a child living on the streets of London, then in an orphanage, Dawnay Price grows up determined not to let her background stand in the way of her ambitions.

In an era when women rarely travel alone, especially for scientific study, Dawnay sets sail aboard *The Prospect* to the beautiful Iberian Peninsula. Amid rumours of mermaids in the sparkling waters, she makes some unexpected discoveries, including what it means to fall in love.

Having fought hard against convention, Dawnay is determined to put her career above all else. Yet as war approaches she finds herself divided by feelings she cannot control.

Told in Dawnay's words, this is an unforgettable story about what it takes to achieve your dreams, even when they seem impossible.

Out now

HODDER